the Last Open road

the Last open road

Burt "BS" Levy

THINK FAST INK
OAK PARK, ILLINOIS

1ST PRINTING: JULY, 1994
2ND PRINTING: OCTOBER, 1995
3RD PRINTING: MAY, 1998*
4TH PRINTING: FEBRUARY, 2001
5TH PRINTING: OCTOBER, 2002
6TH PRINTING: JUNE, 2006
7TH PRINTING: JULY, 2009
8TH PRINTING: SEPTEMBER, 2012
9TH PRINTING: AUGUST, 2015
10TH PRINTING: MAY, 2019
11TH PRINTING: JULY 2022

*ST. MARTINS' PRESS EDITION

OTHER TITLES BY BS LEVY
MONTEZUMA'S FERRARI 1999
A POTSIDE COMPANION 2001
THE FABULOUS TRASHWAGON 2002
TOLY'S GHOST 2006
THE 200MPH STEAMROLLER, BOOK I: RED REIGN 2010
THE 200MPH STEAMROLLER, BOOK II: THE ITALIAN JOB 2015
THE LAST OPEN ROAD RADIO PLAY (AUDIO) 2019
THE 200MPH STEAMROLLER, BOOK III: OUT OF THE MIST 2021

LIBRARY OF CONGRESS CATALOG-IN-PUBLICATION DATA:
LEVY, BURT S., 1945—
THE LAST OPEN ROAD
1. SPORTSCAR RACING IN THE 1950S 2. YOUNG MEN 3. TITLE
LIBRARY OF CONGRESS CATALOG CARD NUMBER 94-60833

ISBN: 978-0-9642107-2-1

FOR CAROL AND ADAM,
MY WONDERFUL FAMILY.

CONTENTS

Special thanks to my friends: Art Eastman, John Gardner, Bill Green, Bill Siegfriedt, Jim Sitz, David Whiteside; my brother Maurice, and the late Brooks Stevens for their invaluable assistance in researching this book.

the last open road

1

THE OLD MAN'S
SINCLAIR

MY NAME'S Buddy Palumbo, and I guess this stuff all started back
in the spring of '52, when I was working as head mechanic at Old Man
Finzio's Sinclair station in Passaic, not a year out of high school. Actually, I was more or less the *only* mechanic working at the Sinclair
back then, on account of Old Man Finzio wasn't exactly what you could
call a whiz around a set of tools. Which made you wonder why he
picked the garage business in the first place. But you couldn't just flat
out ask him, *"Hey, jackass, whyd'ja ever wanna go inta the garage business?"* because he'd spit right in your eye. Old Man Finzio was one of
those mean, scrawny old farts who walk like there's no oil in their joints
and kick stray dogs just for the fun of it. And he always managed to
have a three- or four-day growth of stubble on his chin. All the time.
Which made you wonder sometimes how he did it. I mean, you either
shave every couple days or it eventually grows out into a beard, right?
But not Old Man Finzio. No sir. It was one of those Eternal Mysteries,
like they talk about in church.

Now don't get me wrong, the Old Man was pretty sharp about
running his gas station, and no question he knew a thing or two about
automobiles. He just wasn't any good at *fixing* 'em. Didn't have the
hands for it. Or the patience. Oh, he could change a tire OK, or maybe
flush out a radiator, but he'd get stuck—and I mean *stuck!*—on jobs a
real mechanic could breeze right through without even thinking about
it. Especially if he hit a frozen-up bolt or a rounded-off nut hidden
away under an exhaust manifold or water pump pulley where you
couldn't hardly get at it. Or take a simple brake job. Often as not, he'd
get one of the drums wedged all catty-wumpus on the axle, and naturally the harder he tugged, beat, and levered on it, the worse it got.
Why, he'd squint and sneer and spit at that brake drum, cussing a blue
streak through the few teeth he had left, and pretty soon he'd be reaching for the cutting torch. Within minutes, he'd have the whole damn
business glowing bright cherry red and be wailing away like a country
blacksmith with the biggest damn sledgehammer in the shop. By the
time he was done, the brake drum, wheel studs, and mounting flange
would be junk, and sometimes he'd even get the wheel cylinders. So

you can see how important it was for the Old Man to have a decent mechanic working for him at the Sinclair.

Old Man Finzio's gas station was right down the street from my folks' house in Passaic, and I'd pass it every day on my way home from school. Usually, I'd stop by after classes and just kind of hang around for a few hours. Maybe even help out a little here and there. I don't really know why, but I always *liked* watching automobiles get fixed. It fascinated me how cars were made of all these strange-looking chunks of metal and snaky rubber tubes and endless strands of copper wire, all of it carefully pieced together like some enormous jigsaw puzzle. And if all those bits and pieces were bolted together just right, you could twist a key and it would come *alive* and turn into a living, breathing, ready-for-street-prowling steel animal. But the best part was when a car stopped working—when it *died*—a sharp mechanic could bring it back to life again. Good as new. Maybe even better. A guy could feel pretty damn swell about something like that.

This tough, crew-cut ex-Marine named Butch Bohunk was chief mechanic at the Sinclair back then, and for my money he was sharp as they come. Especially when it came to Fords. Butch had a beat-up old Ford himself (I think it was a '40, but you could hardly tell from the rust), and I swear he kept that heap running by just *thinking* about fixing it. Honest he did. I don't know if you've noticed, but automobile mechanics generally drive the sorriest-looking cars on the highway. Like the old story about the shoemaker's kids, you know? That's because mechanics understand precisely what's wrong with an automobile and consider it a matter of professional pride to see just how long they can keep it running on mechanical sympathy alone.

Fact is, Butch's Ford was so raggedy that Old Man Finzio made him park it out behind the building where the paying customers couldn't see it. I remember Butch took me for a ride across town one afternoon, and I swear the wheel was shaking so bad he could hardly hang on. "Gee whiz, Butch," I asked him, "what the hell's wrong with the steering?"

"Aw, I got me a busted shock and a bent rim on the left front, and it's just about finished off the damn tie-rod end." He fished a cigarette out of his pocket and calmly lit up—just to show me it was nothing to worry about, you know? Come to think of it, that cigarette lighter was about the only thing on the whole damn dashboard that worked.

Anyhow, we're flying down this side street in Newark with everything wobbling and shaking so bad you couldn't hardly focus, and I had to swallow a couple times before I finally got up the nerve to ask, "Jeez, Butch, isn't this sorta, you know, *dangerous?*"

"Naw," he grinned, taking himself a long, deep draw through a fresh Pall Mall, "not unless the whole damn wheel falls off."

General opinion around Passaic held that Butch was a pretty mean article, mostly on account of he'd get into bar fights and scrapes with the law every now and then when he drank, and recreational drinking was something he did on a pretty regular basis. But Butch always treated me right, no matter what anybody else thought about him. He was a burly, beat-up fireplug sort of guy, with tattoos all up and down his arms and a nasty scar down his forehead from the front of his Marine crew cut clear through the arch of his left eyebrow. Damn near took his eye out, whatever it was. Sometimes when he was working on a bolt he couldn't see or pouring oil into a crankcase, Butch'd get this strange, faraway look and tell me the story of how he got that scar. It was always something different (so I knew it was all bullshit, right?) but they were some pretty neat stories anyway—each one uglier and gorier than the last. Old Man Finzio said the *real* scoop was that Butch's wife, Marlene, came after him with a meat cleaver when he staggered in around sunup one ayem with his shirt buttoned wrong.

Marlene was a short, dumpy, white-trash girl from Tennessee with stringy red-orange hair, a beer belly that made her look pregnant all the time, and one hell of a nasty temper. Butch always called her "my mean Marlene," and was she *ever*. Fact is, I could never figure what made Butch want to marry her in the first place. Or stay married to her, for that matter. I mean, they didn't seem to *like* each other, you know? But then there's just no figuring guys when it comes to women. No sir. Not that Butch Bohunk was any damn Prince Charming. He drank and he cussed and he brawled, and when you get right down to it, most women don't want anything to do with mechanics in general.

Especially after they've taken a good long look at your hands.

Married or not, Butch was pretty much a loner, and that made sense because there were all sorts of people Butch just flat out didn't like. He didn't like rich people because they were rich, and he didn't like poor people because they were poor. And he didn't much care for bosses, managers, noncoms, lawyers, librarians, insurance salesmen, tax accountants, niggers, kikes, krauts, polaks, wops, japs, chinks, a-rabs, beaners, or college-professor types. In fact, about the only people he could tolerate at all were grunt-level working stiffs like himself. Unless they were union men. Butch didn't have much use for trade unions, either. All of which made him a pretty hard guy to get along with. Especially after he'd had a few.

Although you never would've thought of Butch as a religious type— not hardly!—he believed in a sort of redneck, blue-collar code of ethics that strictly divided *what a man did* from *what a man didn't do*. Not that it was ever written down anyplace on a set of stone tablets. It was just something a guy like Butch *knew*. Which was probably why he got in so many bar fights, because one of the key things a man *didn't* do was back down when somebody yanked his chain. Even if that somebody was six inches taller and sixty pounds heavier. Or smaller, but packing a meat cleaver.

Truth is, I learned most of what I know about fixing cars from Butch. He didn't so much sit me down and *teach* me as just let me watch and maybe help out now and then by grabbing him a wrench or maybe holding a bolt while he ratcheted off the nut on the other side. He'd been a hard-hat diver in the Marines—you know, the guys with the bulky rubberized-canvas diving suits and the big brass helmets?— and always bragged about how they sent him all over the world because he could weld a perfect bead underwater. Believe me, that's not an easy thing to do. And though he bitched about it constantly, you could tell Butch really loved life in the Marines. That's where he learned how to duck a sucker punch, throw a knife so's it'd stick in a wooden door, find the back way out of any bar, and cuss a blue streak in five or six different languages.

That's also where he learned mechanics, and believe me, Butch was one of the best. He had a knack for understanding exactly what was wrong with sick machines, and the skill to go in and fix whatever it was without thinking twice. It was quite a contrast to Old Man Finzio, who most usually made things worse instead of better. Sometimes the Old Man'd get himself worked up into a foamy-mouthed frenzy on a job, cursing and beating and heating it up cherry red with the torch, and eventually he'd have no choice but to shuffle over and ask Butch to bail him out. "Hey, Butch," he'd mutter through clenched teeth, "cud'ja maybe c'moverhere an' take alooka this?"

Butch always pretended like he didn't quite hear the first time, so the Old Man'd have to ask him again. Only louder this time. But Butch'd keep it up until the Old Man was beet red and bellowing right in his ear. Then he'd turn around real slow and say, "Gee whiz, old man, you ain't gotta yell. . . ."

It drove the Old Man *nuts*.

At any rate, I wound up working part-time at Old Man Finzio's Sinclair during senior year, pumping gas and changing tires and helping out here and there, and even though it wasn't steady, Butch'd always slip me a few bucks or make Old Man Finzio slip me a few for my trouble. By the time graduation rolled around, I was fixing most cars all by myself. Hard stuff, too, like clutch jobs and cylinder heads, not just tires and oil changes. Hell, I'd clear twenty-five bucks on a good

week. And I was learning a *lot* about auto mechanicing. Watching
Butch taught me how to puzzle things out and make proper repairs,
and watching the Old Man taught me, well, what *not* to do. The better
I got at fixing automobiles, the more I enjoyed working at Old Man
Finzio's gas station. It made me feel like I could, you know, *do* some-
thing. . . .

Of course, there was something else that kept me hanging around
the Sinclair. Her name was Julie Finzio, and she was the Old Man's
niece. Julie dropped by every few days to straighten up the office and
help out with the books on account of she had such nice handwriting.
She was just out of high school herself, but I never really knew her
because I went to Fillmore and she went to Immaculate Conception
with the rest of the good Catholic girls. Sure, I'd seen her around town
here and there, but I never paid too much attention. But then she sorta
filled out after sophomore year—I mean *really* filled out—and all of a
sudden she was OK to look at. Better than OK, even. In fact, she was
sort of pretty (in a baby-fat kind of way) with curly black hair, dark,
happy eyes, and this wicked red-lipstick smile she picked up off the
cover of a movie magazine. Not that I spent all that much time looking
at her face, since I was eighteen myself and kept getting distracted by
the mysterious new bulges squirming around inside her sweaters. And
Julie always knew *exactly* what I was looking at, and had the mouth to
let me know about it, too. "Hey, pop yer eyeballs back in yer head,
willya?" she'd snort. "Yer startin' to *drool.*" But then she'd give me a
big smile and maybe even lean over the counter a little so's I could get
an even better look.

That drove me crazy.

So did the way she'd wink at me out the corner of her eye or roll
the end of her pencil around with the tip of her tongue while she
worked on the books. And I loved the way her butt blossomed up like
a big, heart-shaped valentine every time she bent over to pick up something I'd, um, *accidentally* dropped on the floor. Not that Julie was a
slut or anything. She was just a nice, respectable, Immaculate Conception girl who liked to flirt and tease around until it drove you right up
the goddam wall. Of course, that was more or less the favorite sport of
the Italian Catholic girls around Passaic. Even the nice ones. They all
want to make sure the old equipment is working. No question Julie's
did, because she'd turn me all steamy-queasy inside every time I saw
her. I even had this inkling that she maybe really *liked* me. But I
couldn't be sure. You know how it is with girls. And of course Old
Man Finzio was always skulking around and giving me the hairy eyeball
anytime I started getting too chummy with Julie. The thing I could
never understand was how a mean, ornery old fart like him rated a

bubbly, hormone-pie of a niece like Julie. It just didn't seem natural, you know?

Julie had her heart set on being a fashion illustrator for the Sunday newspaper supplements, drawing all those high-fashion women with flowing gowns and swanlike necks that are always posed arched over backward like any kind of decent breeze would topple 'em clear over. I thought they looked pretty dumb, but Julie said they were real *artistic* and *dramatic*, and spent a tremendous amount of time doodling those artistic, high-fashion women in dramatic, topple-over poses inside the spiral-bound sketchbooks she carried around with her. She kept talking about going to art school, but there was no way on account of her dad got killed in the Philippines and her mom couldn't do any better than a job as a hairdresser and a cheap apartment on the second floor of somebody else's house. So Julie was stuck helping out in her uncle's gas station three days a week and working part-time at the Doggie Shake up on Fremont Avenue evenings and weekends. It was a shame, too, because Julie could draw really good—and not just those arched-over fashion models, either. Her sketchbooks were filled with prancing horses and creaky old farmhouses, flowerpots on windowsills and driftwood on the beach, and even some of the cars she saw around the Sinclair. Those were my favorites, of course, and I figured they were a hell of a lot more interesting than any of those topple-over women from the Sunday newspaper supplements.

Needless to say, my folks weren't too keen on having their one and only son turn into a grease monkey. Especially my dad. Heck, I had four older sisters, and he never complained when one of them took a job as a waitress at the grill over on Camden Street. Or when the youngest one, Mary Frances, decided she wanted to cut hair and paint nails for a living someplace in downtown Manhattan. Sure, my mom wasn't too happy about the apartment Mary Frances shared with three other girls near Greenwich Village. But they let her do it, you know? The way my dad figured, girls spent their formative years mostly just waiting around to get married so they could raise families and have kids of their own to worry over and yell at. My two oldest sisters were already married, and the third one, Sarah Jean, had been pretty close with this guy whose family ran a trucking company over in Jersey City. The word around town was that his dad and uncle actually did most of the important lifting, hollering, and decision making, and that this guy was just another of those overpaid son-in-the-business bozos who amount to a kind of permanent skin disease on the face of American commerce. My dad was pretty high on him because of the way he flashed money around, but I figured right away he was just stringing

Sarah Jean along for what he could get (and of course I was right, not that anybody will admit it, or even talk about it much anymore).

But I was a son, and somehow that was *different*. Especially since my dad was a big union shop steward over at this chemical plant in Newark, and naturally he wanted me to come to work there, too. He even had this notion I ought to save up and maybe go off to college someplace to study chemistry, while I figured I was damn lucky just to make it through high school algebra. Hell, it took me two tries. Besides, I was eighteen, and all I really wanted in life was to get out of school, fix cars at the Sinclair and goof around with Julie whenever I got the chance. But my old man wasn't having any part of it. "You're gonna work down at the chemical plant," he'd tell me, eyes hard as tombstones, "and *that's the way it's going to be!*"

That was kind of an old standard around our house.

My old man could be a real jerk when he put his mind to it. And he put his mind to it a lot. He'd spend all day bossing people around at work, 6:30 ayem to 4:30 P.M., five days a week, and then he'd come home and do a little light evening bullying on my mom and me. Just to keep in practice. My poor mom always got the brunt of it when my dad and I had a fight, and after I started hanging around the Sinclair, we had them on an increasingly regular basis. But it never seemed to bother her too much. My dad and me could be screaming at each other at the top of our lungs and she could just *sit* there, darning a sock or copying a recipe or thumbing through one of her pocket-sized bird-spotter guides as if nothing was happening at all.

See, my mom was a bird-watcher. She kept this old pair of Army surplus field glasses over by the kitchen window, and I swear she'd damn near wet her pants when one of her favorite sapsuckers flew through our yard. She'd stand at that window for hours at a stretch with those binoculars jammed into her eye sockets, making birdcalls through her teeth like she was holding a *conversation* with those damn birds. She'd coo at pigeons and twitter at chickadees and warble at warblers until it got to where I just couldn't bring anybody *over*, you know, because my mom would get so blessed weird about those stupid birds of hers.

Truth is, a lot of stuff seemed to sneak right past my mom. Or maybe she was smart enough to know it was better to stay stupid about things you couldn't do anything about. Like my old man's temper, for example. She was a tiny little thing with a laugh like chickens in a henhouse and eyes always lit up dumb and sparkly as a kid's on Christmas morning. Everybody thought she was the nicest, sweetest person on earth, and she was always volunteering for the school paper drive or selling tickets to the church variety show or baking a triple chocolate layer cake for somebody who was laid up with the stomach flu. You have anybody like that in your family? Sometimes they can be so stinking sweet and nice that you just can't *stand* it anymore.

But she was a dish of ice cream with a cherry on top compared to my dad. What with three sisters gone already and Sarah Jean being one of those quiet cooking-and-sewing types herself, it didn't leave much for my dad besides concentrating his considerable talent on bossing *me* around. He'd make me mow the lawn or wash his Mercury while he laid in the hammock out back, listening to the Yankee game and downing himself a fresh beer every inning. Afterwards, regular as clockwork, he'd tell me what a lousy job I'd done on the edging or how I'd left a Criminally Negligent number of water spots on the hood of his car. Then he'd launch into one of these long, rambling, parental-type lectures about *ambition* and *direction* and *career opportunities*, none of which had anything to do with Old Man Finzio's gas station as far as he could see. Of course, he didn't know how much ambition and direction I had focused on getting into Miss Julie Finzio's underpants. But I had to admit it wasn't exactly what he or anybody else would consider a career opportunity.

Anyhow, this chemical plant job paid union scale (which was a hell of a lot of money for a kid just out of high school), but I just flat couldn't stand it. The place was hot and dark and smelled something awful, and every day was the same stupid grind, over and over and over again. I never understood how those union guys could keep doing it—day after day, week after week, year after year—without going batty one morning and blowing their brains out. Every single day they'd swap the same wisecracking hellos, put on the same baggy coveralls, hard hats, and safety goggles, drink the same thermos of coffee, eat the same tin-box lunches, and spend eight solid hours loading and unloading drums of chemical shit that made your eyes burn and your nose run like a damn faucet. You'd work as slow as you could get away with (always a matter of fierce professional pride in any union shop), and every night you'd hear the same stale dick jokes in the shower, blow the same weird, yellow-green globs of snot out your nostrils, and head home for a few beers and dinner before going to bed—just so's you could get up in the morning and do it all over again....

You call that a life?

Plus it was no barrel of laughs working for my dad. Some guys'd maybe take it a little easy on their own kid. But not my old man. No sir. He didn't want anybody thinking I got this job just because he was my father (which, of course, is exactly why I did), so he made damn sure I worked twice as hard as anybody else.

It got to where I hated waking up in the morning.

But even while I was working at my old man's stupid chemical plant job, I'd drop by the Sinclair every now and again to shoot the breeze with Butch or maybe see Julie and goof around a little. Then I showed up one drizzly Saturday morning when the leaves were just starting to turn and noticed that Butch's old Ford was missing. For a crazy second, I thought maybe he had it up on the lift, fixing that bad tie-rod end. But Old Man Finzio was all alone inside the shop, torch ablaze and sledgehammer in hand, trying to beat a helpless Buick into submission. "Where's Butch?" I hollered over the banging.

Old Man Finzio looked at me with the queerest expression on his face. He laid down the hammer and turned the acetylene down until the cutting torch shut off with a hollow *pop*. "Ya don't know, d'ya?" the Old Man said softly.

"Know what?"

"Butch got hisself inna car accident with that Ford of his. A bad one. He's in the hospital down by Elizabeth."

"He *what?*"

And that's when the tow truck pulled in, dragging what was left of Butch's Ford. Why, you could hardly even recognize it was a car anymore, and looking at it turned me icy-white inside. The front end was pushed clear back to the firewall, the roof was buckled, and the tail shaft off the transmission was sticking right up through the middle of the front seat like one of those compound fractures where the bone comes through the skin. You could see where his hands busted two solid chunks out of the steering wheel, and there was shattered glass and streaks of dried blood all over the place. It made you sick just looking at it, and you knew that whoever was behind the wheel of that car ought to be dead.

The story going around was that Butch and Marlene got into a big god-awful argument and she wound up packing and heading back home to Tennessee. And good riddance, far as I was concerned. But later that night, right after the bars closed down, Butch took a notion to chase after her. The poor bastard didn't even make it to Perth Amboy before he flattened that old Ford of his against a concrete bridge abutment and damn near killed himself.

Naturally, I went to visit him in the hospital, and it was a real, honest-to-God horror show. I hate hospitals anyway. I hate the smell of disinfectant and the fluorescent lights that don't cast any shadows and the way the nurses' shoes squeak on the polished linoleum floors. And I most especially hate how everybody talks in these hushed funeral parlor whispers out in the hall. It gives me the creeps, you know? Anyhow, they had Butch all covered in plaster and gauze like one of those Egyptian mummies, what with his arms and legs dangling on pulleys and all kinds of tubes and needles running in and out of him. You could tell right away he was never going to be the same again, and it was tough understanding how a car accident could change your whole life in an instant—just like *that!*—as if an invisible hand reached down out of the sky and flicked you off like a damn light switch.

The thought of it made me go all dry and hollow.

But I knew I was there to visit Butch and try to make him feel a little better, so I swallowed hard, walked over by the bed, and tried my best to make a little small talk. To tell the truth, it was like talking into an empty closet. But I gave it my best shot, rambling on about Old Man Finzio and what a jerk my dad was and how much I hated his stupid chemical plant job over in Newark. It didn't seem to have much effect on Butch. About all he could do was just lay there, arms and legs dangling, staring up at the ceiling like he couldn't really see it. It made me feel dumb and clumsy trying to carry on a conversation by myself, but every time I'd stop, Butch'd give off a coarse little grunt—like the sound a car with a flat battery makes when you try to turn it over—just to let me know he was listening. Then I more or less ran out of stuff to say and just stood there watching what looked like bloody pee drain out of Butch through a clear plastic tube. But when I finally turned to leave, Butch gathered up every bit of strength he had and called me back over by his bedside. His voice came out so faint and hoarse that I had to lean my ear right up next to the gauze to make it out. *"The Plymouth . . . ,"* he rasped, fighting for every word, *"bad water pump . . . parts under bench . . . toolbox key . . . under trash drum . . . don't let Old Man . . . get near that car. . . ."* It took a moment to sink in, but then I nodded to let him know I understood. *"An' lissen,"* Butch choked, his whole body straining upward, *"you take care a'my fuckin' tools or I'll break yer goddam arms fr'ya. Y'hear me?"*

I stopped by the Sinclair early the next morning, and just like Butch said, I found his key hidden under the trash drum, Mr. Altobelli's Plymouth in the service bay, and a rebuilt water pump under his workbench, neatly wrapped in oiled paper. Now you have to understand that Butch never let *any*body mess with his tools. Oh, he'd let me borrow a socket or a wrench when I needed it, but just one at a time, on a strictly ask-and-return basis. Most often I worked with Old Man Finzio's tools, which were always scattered all over the place like the remains of a recently detonated fragmentation bomb. Hell, you could never find *any*thing. But Butch kept his tools neat, clean, and perfectly organized, and was careful to wipe them off and pack them away whenever he finished a job. Or even part of a job. Every topflight mechanic I ever met was the same way. So it was really an honor that somebody like Butch would trust me with his toolbox key.

Old Man Finzio didn't offer me a job that day. Not in so many words, anyway. But he allowed as how I could maybe help him out while Butch was laid up if I thought I could spare the time. So I played hooky from the chemical plant and spent my morning replacing the water pump on Mr. Altobelli's Plymouth. Then I repaired some lady's Ford with a bum U-joint, and it sure felt good to work on cars again. I decided right then and there I was going to stay on at the Sinclair. Hell, I'd had it up to *here* with that dumb-ass chemical plant. Sure, fixing cars didn't pay as good (in fact, it didn't pay anywheres *near* as good) but at least you got to work on your own, at your own pace, and every single job had its own special challenge. Best of all, there was always a golden little Appreciation Moment at the end when you finally got a car all buttoned back together and running like a fine Swiss watch.

As you can imagine, my old man was pretty burned about my decision to stiff his stupid chemical plant job and go to work at the Sinclair. Not to mention that it made him look pretty lame in front of all his union hall buddies. So we naturally had a big enormous fight about it. You know, the kind where you end up storming out of the house and slamming the front door so hard it shatters all the little glass windows on top.

I wandered the streets for hours that night, feeling pissed at my old man, sorry for my mom, worrying about Butch and wondering just what the hell I was going to do next. I wanted to call Julie, but it was late and I was afraid her mom might answer. Plus I didn't especially want her to hear my voice, on account of I was pretty choked up and might've even cried a little. Not a *real* cry, of course, but one of those restricted male versions where your face goes all taut and flushed and you can feel the old eye juice backing up in the ducts. But you don't let it leak out. After all, that's for girls and little crybaby sissyboys who've fallen down and skinned their knees. At the very least, you don't let anybody see you.

I remember it was awful chilly that night, and I'd been in such a mad, stinking rush to get out of the house that I forgot to grab my jacket, so now I was even shivering a little and hadn't the foggiest notion where to go or what to do next. I counted up the money in my jeans pockets to see if it was maybe enough to take me anywhere—anywhere at all, in fact—but it was just a bunch of loose change. And mostly pennies at that. I thought about walking the mile and a half to the bus station and spending the night there or maybe trying to break into the Sinclair so's I could sleep in the office next to the space heater, but neither of those sounded any good since I'd just have to limp home the next day with my tail between my legs and take another heaping dose of bullshit from my dad. A giant, economy-sized dose, for sure. And breaking into Old Man Finzio's gas station might easily get me fired, and the whole idea was that I wanted to work there as an automobile mechanic instead of wasting my time at that piece-of-shit chemical plant job.

And then I had a brilliant idea. My Aunt Rosamarina lived a couple blocks away on Buchanan, and she had this empty sort of loft apartment over her garage that would be *perfect* for a young guy just out of high school. She was a retired librarian, lived alone with about three dozen cats, and spent most of her time reading musty old books with small type and no pictures. She was one of those thin, sad-eyed old maids who get real nervous around other human beings. Why, even the simplest everyday encounters with the mailman or the kid who delivered her paper could get her all stuttering and trembling and shaking at the knees. I remember she used to come over by my folks' house for Christmas every year, and sometimes they'd arrange to have some "eligible male" on hand to talk to her or maybe even ask her out. But she'd just park herself in the corner—all by her lonesome—and not say a word. My mom would keep pouring her glasses of Asti Spumante to get her loosened up, but Aunt Rosamarina could suck up eight or ten of them without so much as cracking a Christmas smile or even tittering now and then like most of your elderly retired ladies do when they've gotten a bit too chummy with the punch bowl. To tell the truth, we all suspected my aunt might be putting in a little solo practice with the old liquor bottle back home.

But now, the fact that Aunt Rosamarina was never real chatty or comfortable around other people turned into a fabulous asset. It meant I could count on her to leave me alone if I moved into that loft apartment over her garage. It was *perfect!* Sure, she'd watch my every move through her favorite little crack in the draperies, but that didn't matter because she'd never actually *say* anything. Except maybe to her cats.

To tell the truth, the "apartment" over my aunt's garage wasn't really an apartment at all, but more like some pygmy-sized storage space under the rafters. A couple summers before, my dad and me put in a space heater and a couple rolls of tar-paper insulation and even a john and an eighteen-by-eighteen shower stall (which is the smallest size Sears sells, and has barely enough room inside for both a live human being and a decent-sized bar of soap). The idea was that my aunt could rent it out to some convenient recent widower or a quiet young divinity student and have herself a little extra income. My dad even put an ad in the paper for her when we were done, but when people showed up to take a look, she'd check them out through her little crack in the draperies and never even answer the door. So that apartment over my aunt's garage was just sitting there—*waiting* for me, you know?—like somehow it had all been planned out in advance.

I went over and sneaked in about three ayem, shinnying up the cherry tree and going in through the window, and next morning I knocked on my aunt's front door and made a deal to move myself in and pay her at the end of the month. Twenty bucks sounded a little steep, but I could afford it. After all, I had a job that paid . . . well, to tell the truth, I wasn't sure exactly what it paid. But I figured it'd be more than enough. As I remember, my aunt made the entire transaction without ever taking the chain lock off the door. Not once.

That apartment over Aunt Rosamarina's garage was everything a young guy on his own could ask for. Oh, maybe it was a little strange that the shower and sink were right in the middle of the floor, but that's because the roof was shaped like the inside of a pup tent and it was the only place you could stand up straight to shave or brush your teeth. Well, almost straight, anyway. And I had to remember not to wake up real quick (like if I had a nightmare about that chemical plant job) because the bed was over where the ceiling was only a foot or so off the floor, and you could split your head wide open if you sat up in a hurry.

But it was *mine*, and I couldn't believe how great it felt to be out on my own, enjoying the *dignity* and *privacy* of my own apartment. Why, I could drink a beer anytime I wanted to (so long as I could get one of the local rum-pots hanging around the liquor store to buy it for me, anyway) or even invite Julie over to share one with me if I had the notion. Not that I had the nerve to actually *ask* her, you understand, but you need the privacy of your own place to even think about doing that kind of thing. And speaking of that, I could think about being with Julie as much as I wanted, without worrying about somebody hearing me or waltzing in unexpectedly from the next room. You worry about that a lot when you grow up in a house with four older sisters. But now I was *free!* Independent! By God, in *my* apartment, I could do *whatever* I wanted, with *whoever* I wanted, and whenever the hell *I* wanted to do it.

After the first couple weeks, I was bored a lot.

Meanwhile, I kept filling in for Butch at Old Man Finzio's Sinclair through the winter months, and damn near froze my ass off doing it. We'd only put in a couple thin sheets of tar-paper insulation under the roof, and if I stoked the space heater up enough to take the frost off my mirror, the snow would start to melt and I'd get leaks. *Serious* leaks. They always seemed to be right over the bed, no matter where I moved

it (not that you could move *any*thing very far in the apartment over
Aunt Rosamarina's garage), and it sure didn't help that I worked in a
gas station every day. You ask anybody how cold it gets inside a con-
crete-and-brick garage during the wintertime (especially when you're
raising the damn overhead door all the time to bring in sick cars that
have been sitting for three days with snow up to the hubcaps and icicles
hanging off the grille). I swear, my body never thawed out until spring
that year.

Fortunately, things had smoothed out a little with my folks by then,
and my dad would even pass the meat or vegetables when I came over
for dinner on Sunday evenings. Of course, he wouldn't say much—just
grunt now and then and mutter under his breath—but that still represented a major improvement. My mom naturally wanted me to move
back home (what else?) but I'd counter with the old "how important it
was for a young man to assume responsibility" gambit. It was one of
my old man's favorites, but I sure wasn't above borrowing it when the
situation demanded. Besides, my aunt's house was only a couple blocks
away if the worst happened and the Commies launched an all-out mis-
sile attack on New York.

Old Butch was doing better, too. Or at least that's what the doctors
said. They'd moved him to the V.A. hospital near Iselin, and I went
down to visit him there a few times. It was a long trip by bus (no way
was my dad gonna lend me his Mercury to go see another grease monkey—not even in the hospital) so I didn't make it very often. But I'd
call every week, and Butch'd tell me how the doctors and nurses were
saying he was making progress, but that they were really all full of shit
and didn't know what they were talking about. And I had to agree,
since I couldn't see much change except that he could sit up and talk
a little better. Then again, I guess that *is* progress when you start out
like a busted bag of stew meat.

2

BIG ED'S JAGUAR

BIG ED Baumstein owned the first Jaguar sports car I ever saw. It was an XK120 roadster, creamy white with red leather upholstery, and my whole world stopped cold the first time he wheeled it into the station in the early spring of 1952. Big Ed was a rich Jewish guy from Teaneck who'd had three or four divorces and dealt in scrap industrial machinery. Actually, he was only half-Jewish, seeing as how his mother's side of the family was Italian. Calabraese, I think. Anyhow, Big Ed and his cousin Vincenzo (on his mother's side, natch) had this huge wrecking yard over by the Jersey shore, and although they never wore suits or ties except to weddings and funerals and stuff, they had plenty of money to throw around. Not that they made a big show of it or put on airs like those highly manicured jerks you see in the society pages.

Big Ed had been a regular at the Old Man's gas station because he liked the way Butch took care of his cars, and far back as anybody could remember, Big Ed always drove Cadillacs. In fact, he had two of them when I started at the Sinclair: an enormous black Sixty Special sedan for the fall and winter, plus an absolutely *gorgeous* white-on-white convertible that he only drove in the spring and summer and never took out of the garage if it was raining. They were hardly a year old, either one of them, but Big Ed was forever dropping them off for an oil change and lube job or a full Simonize wax or maybe to fix a little squeak or rattle. Big Ed didn't trust the mechanics at the Caddy dealership and he took a real shine to me when I tracked down a nasty grating noise behind the dash of the white convert. It was just the speedo cable, for gosh sakes. Needed a little grease. But he was thrilled when the noise vanished and I only let Old Man Finzio charge him a dollar. I mean, it was *nothing*, you know? Big Ed flashed me a wink and palmed me a five-buck tip. That was one hell of a big tip in 1952.

Big Ed could afford it. Sure, I'd heard the whispering about how his scrap business was somehow, umm, *connected*. Like how maybe a few ex–business associates of certain Influential People might have accidentally gotten mixed up with the blocks of crushed steel his workers sent back to the smelters for reprocessing. Perhaps even a key prosecution witness or two. But I never asked how Big Ed made the fivers he started slipping me every time I passed a wrench over one of his

Caddies. I figured that kind of curiosity was for the people who work downtown in the federal building. Besides, I *liked* Big Ed, because he loved his cars and wanted them to be perfect. You had to respect a guy who felt that way about automobiles.

As you probably figured, Big Ed Baumstein was a genuinely massive edition of a human being. He stood six-four and a yard wide, and could pretty much fill up your average doorway in all directions. Not that you'd figure him for that tall if you saw him standing out in the open, seeing as how he was shaped like an Anjou pear and favored bright, clashy clothes that broke up the landscape of his body. But standing right next to him, you'd all of a sudden realize that you were barely eye-level with his neck (or where his neck would've been if Big Ed had such a thing) and talking into his chest hairs. Not that you ever got to do much talking around Big Ed Baumstein. *Listening* was more like it.

I'll never forget the bright spring morning Big Ed wheeled his shiny new Jag up to the pumps for the very first time. Jee-*zus,* I'd never seen a car like that in my life. The bodywork arched and curled from one end to the other like some huge steel jungle cat, and the sound was perfect, too: a rich, buttery growl that just seemed to purr its way out the tailpipes. *Jaguarrrrrr!!!* Boy, they sure picked the right name for *that* automobile. "Whaddaya think?" Big Ed grinned, his dollar cigar sticking up like an exclamation point.

"Boy, it sure is *something!*" I said, running my eyes up and down the bodywork, trying to take in all the curves.

"Wanna go for a ride?"

"Jeez, I dunno," I told him. "Old Man Finzio'll have himself a conniption fit if I just take off...."

"Ahh, screw him," Big Ed snorted. "C'mon, climb aboard."

Needless to say, I decided to chance it. Only I couldn't find the door handle! Big Ed let out a huge laugh—*Haw-haw-ha-haw-haw-hawww*—and reached over to open it from the inside. That's how you open the door on an XK120 roadster. Right away I could see this car was different from the Fords, Chevys, and even Cadillacs I was used to. I also noticed Big Ed was wedged in just about solid between the seat back and the steering wheel. Big as it was (and that XK120 was goddam *big* for a two-seater automobile) it didn't really have much in the way of gut, chest, or shoulder room for a guy the size of Big Ed Baumstein.

To this day, I remember leaning back in that rich red leather upholstery for the very first time. It smelled like fine kid gloves, and felt just as soft against my skin. Warm, too, as if some elegant lady's hands were still inside them. Then Big Ed revved her up and dumped the clutch (he was never real arty with a stick shift) and we squealed away from the pumps in a haze of burning rubber. I caught a glimpse of Old Man Finzio out of the corner of my eye as we rocketed out onto Pine Street, and he just stood there and stared—dumbstruck, you know?—as if Big Ed's Jaguar was a naked blonde on roller skates. XK120s did that to *everybody*. They were so damn gorgeous it made your eyes ache just to look at them.

Big Ed drove out past the edge of town and gave it a quick blast in second and third. Jeez, was that car ever FAST! *"That's eighty!"* Big Ed hollered over the wind noise, *"and we're not even outta third yet!"* Right at that exact moment, with hair whipping in my eyes and the howl of that big twin-cam six filling my ears and the white lines on the highway coming at me like tracer bullets, right *then* I fell in love with Jaguars.

Old Man Finzio didn't say a word when we tooled back into the station a half hour later. Not one. He just eased his way over by the pumps—real nonchalant, you know—to get himself a closer look at Big Ed's new toy. I can't recall I'd ever seen so much white around the Old Man's eyeballs. "Say," I asked, "d'ya think we could maybe take a look under the hood?"

"Suuure," Big Ed grinned. But then we couldn't find the damn hood release. I swear we crawled all *over* that car before I finally located a suspicious-looking knob that the Jaguar factory people had thoughtfully hidden under the passenger side of the dashboard, clear back against the firewall. I popped it and walked around front, pausing to wipe my hands on my coveralls before daring to lift that crocodile-snout Jaguar hood. Underneath was the single most beautiful automotive powerplant I'd ever seen, what with two long, gleaming aluminum valve covers fastened down with neat little rows of chrome-plated acorn nuts and these strange, stately S.U. carburetors standing at attention off the side like a pair of medieval guards in shining armor. It was like a piece of sculpture, honest it was.

"Y'know," Big Ed mused while the Old Man and I drooled our way around the Jag's engine compartment, "I wonder if you guys could make it so's the seat moves back a little more. It's kinda *snug* in there, y'know? And maybe fix the turn signals, too. I can't seem t'get the damn things to work."

"I don't know . . . ," Old Man Finzio started in, kind of shaking his head.

But I broke right in: "Sure I can, Mr. Baumstein. I can fix it. No problem at all."

Big Ed gave me one of his patented five-dollar winks. "I bet you can, Buddy. I bet you can."

And sure enough I could.

After a couple false starts, anyway.

Big Ed's XK120 became a frequent visitor at the Old Man's Sinclair that spring and summer, since it always seemed to be needing a little attention. It was *fussy,* like some high-class woman who's used to silk clothes and servants and stuff. I even got Big Ed to buy me a special set of British Standard socket wrenches because nothing in Butch's tool-box fit properly except the sparkplug wrench. If you tried using them, they'd invariably slip off at an inopportune moment (like just when you're trying to torque that final quarter twist into a bolt head hidden down in the bottom of the engine compartment) and leave half the skin off your knuckles embedded in the radiator core like a smear of the suet my mom leaves out for her birds in the wintertime.

Those British Standard wrenches were expensive, too, and it took our regular tool guy more than a week to get them. Plus no way would Old Man Finzio lay out *his* money so I could work on Big Ed's Jag. But I didn't mind. In fact, I was real glad to have Big Ed's XK120 dropping by for service every few days, because working on it made me feel pretty damn special compared to the Nash Ambassadors, Henry Js, and even Cadillacs and Lincolns I was used to. Not to mention that the Jag was nothing short of a gold mine for a decent automobile me-chanic—and that's not even counting Big Ed's five-buck tips! Best of all, it intimidated the hell out of Old Man Finzio. Why, he couldn't even look in the Jag's engine bay without his eyelids starting to twitch and his jaw tightening up a few notches. Truth is, Old Man Finzio didn't understand or appreciate Jaguars one bit, and I did what I could to encourage the situation by sort of *talking* to that car whenever I had it in for service. Like my mom talks to her stupid birds, you know? I came up with this phony-baloney Lord-Earl-of-the-Sinclair British ac-cent, see, and every now and then I'd hold a dashpot dampener or voltage regulator up to my ear and pretend like it was answering me back. I guess it must've looked pretty loony, because soon I had Old Man Finzio creeping around the back of the shop on tiptoe every time I worked on Big Ed's XK120. In fact, sometimes he'd just give up and go hide in the can or hang around the gas pumps until he heard it fire up and roll out of the service bay.

That sure beat hell out of putting brake shoes on some tax account-ant's Plymouth.

But there were a lot of mechanical secrets to learn about Jaguars, and at the beginning, I didn't know any of 'em. Like I'll never forget the day Big Ed's Jag staggered into the station with the engine popping and banging and huge, sooty black clouds blowing out the tailpipe. He'd only owned it five or six weeks then, and did he ever look *pissed*. In fact, Big Ed's face was about the color of a fresh radish, and you could tell by the droop of his cigar that he was well past merely disappointed. *"This goddam limey piece of shit,"* he snarled, yanking the hood cable so hard it damn near came off in his hand. *"Take a look at it fr'me, willya?"*

To tell the truth, I hadn't the foggiest notion what was wrong. But I pulled the sparkplugs (always a reasonable place to start) and it didn't take a rocket scientist to see they were all seriously gas fouled. So I sandblasted 'em and screwed 'em back in, and then just kind of stared at those weird S.U. carburetors for twenty minutes or so, trying to figure out how they worked. Can't say as I'd ever seen anything remotely like S.U.s before. They had these elegant-looking aluminum towers on top, and I had no idea what they had to do with mixing air and gasoline into something an internal combustion engine might want to swallow. Finally, I gave up and punched the starter button—just to see what would happen, right?—and of course the Jag fired up instantly and settled down to an absolutely *perfect* 550-r.p.m. idle. It was a miracle!

Needless to say, my stock soared with Big Ed, and this time he slipped me a tenner. Honest to God he did. But my newfound stardom as a British car expert fizzled out less than twenty minutes later, when the Jag came stumbling back into the station again, its engine halting and bucking on maybe two live cylinders and even bigger, blacker-looking clouds belching out the back. There was a purple cast to Big Ed's face this time, and his cigar was dangling straight down his chin on account of he'd bitten clear through it. *"Wh-What the hell's wrong with this g-goddam thing!"* Big Ed sputtered, really on a boil.

So I checked it over again—same thing exactly—and to say I was mystified just about covers it. "I'm sorry, Mr. Baumstein," I told him, sounding extraordinarily lame, "but your Jaguar is really, aah, *different* from the other stuff I've worked on. It's gonna take me a little time to figure it out." Then I fished around in my pocket and handed him back his sawbuck.

To my everlasting surprise, Big Ed's face came down a few shades until it wasn't much more than a warm pink. "You'll figger it out though, won'cha, Buddy?" he growled, pushing the sawbuck back into my pocket.

"S-Sure, Mr. Baumstein," I nodded.

"Good fr'you!" he nodded, slapping me on the back hard enough so there was maybe a little hint of a warning in it. Like maybe I sure *better* figure it out.

So I looked into the engine compartment again, and all those strange, foreign-looking pieces stared right back at me. "Y'know, Mr. Baumstein," I told him, "at the very least I'm gonna need a shop manual. You got any idea where I might find one?"

"Tellya what, Buddy, I'll borrow y'the black Caddy tomorrow so's

ya can drive over t'Manhattan an' buy us one." It was springtime, so
Big Ed wasn't using his Sixty Special for much of anything. "And one
more thing . . . ," he continued, resting a hand the size of a calf's head
on my shoulder.

"What's that, Mr. Baumstein?"

"Call me Big Ed, willya?"

And that's how I wound up driving into Manhattan in Big Ed's
black Caddy sedan (which, by the way, had *real* thick glass in all the
windows) for my first-ever look at a foreign sports car dealership. Naturally, I'd asked Julie if she wanted to come along, since Big Ed's Sixty
Special had by far the widest, softest, most sumptuous front seat you
ever saw (I don't even need to mention what the back seat was like!)
and thinking about Julie and all that soft, cushy real estate was enough
to get my hormones working overtime. But she couldn't make it on
account of she had a date to go over to the beauty parlor with one of
her girlfriends to get their hair done and nails painted. How *that* ever
compared to visiting a Jaguar dealership in Manhattan was beyond me,
but I guess that's just one of the many important differences between
women and normal people.

Anyhow, the next day I followed the directions Big Ed scribbled
on the back of an old envelope for me, crossing the George Washington
into Manhattan and eventually finding the Jaguar agency on a lumpy
little side street near the river, mixed in with a bunch of factories and
warehouses and stuff. It was really just an ordinary cinderblock garage
that somebody'd dressed up with a fresh coat of whitewash and some
brown two-by-four trim to make it look like one of those two-door
English houses. There was a small wooden sign over the door done up
in that fancy Old English script you see on scotch labels and eye doctor
diplomas. It read:

Westbridge Motor Car Company, Ltd.
'Thoroughbred Motorcars for Discriminating Drivers'
Colin St. John, Proprietor

Just as I pulled up, this tall, natty-looking guy with a tweed cap
and a gold-topped cane stepped out the front door, took a long, down-
the-nose gander at me, and limped briskly over to one of the MGs. He
tossed his cane behind the seat, folded himself inside, pulled the choke
out, yanked smartly on the starter, and listened with his head cocked
to one side as the engine ground a few times and clattered to life. While
it warmed up, the gent gave himself a quick once-over in the little
pocket-sized mirror perched on top of the dashboard. He straightened

his tie, tweaked the ends of his mustache, realigned his cap, then wet
the tip of his finger and ran it delicately over both eyebrows. "Righto,"
he nodded at last, giving himself an appreciative wink. Then he reached
in the door pocket and pulled out the most enormous curlicue smoking
pipe you have ever seen. I swear, it looked big as a damn French horn,
and the guy spent the better part of five whole minutes getting it
packed, tamped, leveled off, and fired up just exactly the way he wanted.
Once the pipe was puffing away to his complete satisfaction, he folded
his tobacco pouch away, blipped the throttle once or twice, and tootled
off down the street, looking jaunty as all getout and trailing an aromatic
cloud of burning Cavendish in his wake.

He was *perfect,* you know?

Inside the Westbridge shop were more blessed British automobiles
than I'd ever seen in my life. There must've been five or six XK120s
and near a dozen MGs, and almost every damn one of them had its
hood wide open or was perched up on jack stands with the wheels off.
Or both. There were even cars I'd never heard of before. Like this
magnificent Jaguar Mk. VII sedan that looked like the Lincoln Mon-
ument on wheels. And right next to it was a pudgy little Morris Minor
that easily could've belonged to Elmer Fudd. Toward the back was this
torpedo-shaped Frazer-Nash two-seater done up in a deep string-bean
green. It had cycle fenders and racing numbers painted on the sides,
and it sure didn't look like any Nash automobile *I'd* ever seen. Of
course, I didn't know that Frazer-Nash was just one of many pint-sized
English sports car companies that nobody on this side of the planet ever
heard of, and that it didn't have one single thing do with Nash automobiles here in the States. Over in England, anybody with a gas welder,
a pile of steel, and a roof over his head can set himself up in the sports
car manufacturing business. All you have to do is hang out a shingle.

Anyhow, that Frazer-Nash was the first actual *racing* car I ever
stood right next to, and gee whiz, did it ever give me goose bumps. Oh,
it was a little beat up and scruffy-looking, what with genuine, hundred-
mile-an-hour stone chips and insect splatters on the nose and fenders.
There was just this little half-moon racing windscreen in front of the
driver and a serious-looking leather strap buckled across the hood to
keep it from flying open at top speed and a naked exhaust pipe running
right below the driver's elbow. *Wow!* No question about it, that Frazer-
Nash was a real war machine. I didn't see much of anybody around,
and I started thinking about maybe unbuckling that leather strap and
taking a peek under the hood. In fact, I'd just started unfastening it
when an unknown finger tapped me on the shoulder. "Need any 'elp
there, guv'nor?" said a voice right out of Piccadilly Circus.

I wheeled around to find this short, hollow-faced guy in a blue shop coat staring at me through a pair of sad, watery-gray eyes. "Mister St. John?" I asked, real formal-like. A name like Colin St. John does that to you.

"Naw, Barry Spline's the naime," he wheezed through a nose pointy enough to open oil cans. "Glad t'meetcher." He had one of those rare British accents that never once made you think about royalty. "Yer missed 'is bleedin' 'ighness. That was 'im sportin' off in the TD just now. Bloody supercharged, that one is. Quick as a blink."

"I saw."

"But not near s'quick as *this* little beauty," he grinned, patting the Frazer-Nash on its nose emblem. "She's just got back from Sebring. Florida, y'know. Won the big bloody twelve-hour there. Yer probably read about it in the papers."

"Sure," I lied, wondering what the hell he was talking about.

"Any'ow," he continued, extending a hand that obviously worked on cars for a living, "I'm the bloke gets most things done 'ere around the Westbridge shop. 'Ow can we be of service, eh?"

I explained as how I was looking for a Jaguar XK120 shop manual, and right away the smile melted off his face. "And just *why* would yer want a Jagyewahr shop manual, eh?" So I told him about the Sinclair and Big Ed's Jaguar and the fouled plugs and clouds of black smoke, and as I did, Barry Spline's lips spread out in a mean little sliver of a smile. "Starting carburetor," he snickered.

"What?"

"Thermostatic actuator fr'the starting carburetor. You'll find out."

"I will?"

Barry Spline nodded. "As a general practice, we don't h'encourage the h'untrained to h'attempt maintenance or repairs on Jagyewahr automobiles. Company policy, y'know. But seeing as 'ow you're way over in Jersey, and seeing as 'ow it's only one bloody car"—his eyes swept around the shop—"... and seeing as 'ow I've got more flippin' work than I know what to do with, I suppose we might be able to make an h'exception." He leaned in close and whispered, "Just don't let 'is bloody 'ighness know about it, eh?"

"Mum's the word."

"Right. Just step yerself over t'the parts counter and ring the bell. Our Spares Consultant will be only too 'appy to 'elp yer out."

So I went over to the parts counter and rang the little bell and who pops up on the other side but Barry Spline. Only now he's wearing a *white* shop coat. "'Ow can I 'elp yer, sir?" he says with a perfectly straight face.

"I want a shop manual for an XK120. You know that."

"Shop manual for an hex-kay-one-twenty," he says real slow, like he's mulling it over. "I'm h'afraid we're fresh h'out of stock at the moment."

"All right," I said. "When do you expect you might have one?"

Barry Spline the Spares Consultant rubbed his chin thoughtfully. "Most normally, we don't sell Jagyewahr shop manuals to the public. Matter of general company policy." Then he leaned over the counter and added in a near whisper, "You h'understand, of course. . . ."

"Oh, of course," I nodded, not exactly sure that I did. "But you said yourself it was just one car, and that it's way over in Jersey. . . ." I was starting to get a little annoyed, you know?

"Ah, well," he said with an elaborate sigh, "I suppose we *could* put one on order for yer, seeing as 'ow it is just one bloody car, and also 'ow it's way over in Jersey."

"Gee," I told him, trying not to grind my teeth, "that'd be *real* swell of you."

"Takes h'about six weeks . . . h'unless yer wanter pay air freight, that is."

"Air freight is fine."

"Payment in h'advance, of course."

"Oh, naturally."

So I handed over a large wad of Big Ed's folding money and, after making a few quick mental calculations, Barry Spline returned to me a quarter, a nickel, and a few pennies in change. Judging from the price, they must write those Jaguar shop manuals on parchment from the Dead Sea Scrolls. Then I asked for a receipt so I could prove I hadn't bought a gold watch or booked myself a private railcar to Atlantic City. Barry Spline seemed offended that I'd ask for such a thing, but then he shrugged one of those homegrown New Yorker shrugs— *what can you do?*—and dashed one off longhand on an ordinary white paper notepad he had sitting on the counter. "There you are, guv'nor," he cooed through the self-satisfied grin of a man who has really put the screws to a fellow human being. "That oughter do yer up right and proper. And willyer be needin' anything else terday?"

"Yeah," I growled, doing a slow burn, "can anybody tell me how to keep one of these damn Jaguar shitcans *running?*"

Barry Spline stiffened up a couple notches. "If yer 'ave a *specific* sort of problem, yer might take it up with the Shop Foreman."

"And just where do I find the Shop Foreman?"

"One moment, eh?" And Barry Spline the Spares Consultant (white coat) vanished, only to reappear a few seconds later as Barry Spline, the Shop Foreman (blue coat). "What seems ter be the trouble, guv'nor?"

It took me awhile to get the gist of things, which was that Barry Spline, Spares Consultant, and Barry Spline, Shop Foreman, had to be *paid* separately. See, you could buy any Jaguar part you wanted from Barry-in-white (as long as you were willing to pay a left nut for it—in advance, of course—and wait until the Twelfth of Never to get it), but then you still had to pay Barry-in-blue for whatever information, advice, or encouragement it took to get the damn thing properly installed. And we're not talking about tips like the fivers Big Ed palmed off, either. Barry-in-blue charged "consultation" fees whenever he could get away with it, and he'd even write you up one of his plain white paper "receipts" if you wanted one. At least if Colin St. John wasn't around to see him do it, anyway.

But once he'd relieved me of all the loose cash I had on my person, Barry lightened up considerably and actually took me on a tour of the Westbridge shop. One mechanic to another, you know. "Yer've gotter h'understand about sports cars," he explained, waving his hand through the air. "The people who buy them could all drive bleedin' Cadillacs if they wanted. Cars like that great bloody black sedan yer rolled up in." His eyes glazed over just thinking about Big Ed's Sixty Special. "Oh, those are some marvelous smooth cars, Cadillacs are"—you could tell Barry Spline admired Caddies—"but that's not what these flippin' people want. Oh, no! They claim t'*like* the 'ard ride and the 'eavy steering and enough bloody 'eat through the floorboards to roast bleedin' chestnuts. These people *h'enjoy* the engine racket and picking insects out of their 'air after every bleedin' run t'market. And believe me," he said, raising an important finger toward the rafters, "they absolutely *live* for the roadside breakdowns and h'expensive repairs." Barry Spline looked me squarely in the eye. "And do you know *why?*"

I shook my head.

"Because they're all bloody *masochists!*"

"They're what?"

"Masochists."

"What the hell are masochists?"

Barry Spline licked his lips and thought for a moment. "Before intercourse, 'ave yer ever been tied down to a bed with fine silk ropes and 'ad somebody go over yer private parts with an eggbeater?"

I couldn't say as I had.

"Neither 'ave I," he said wistfully. "But the point is that a masochist *h'enjoys* such things as pain, suffering, and humiliation."

I looked it up in my aunt's dictionary when I got home, and Barry Spline was telling the truth.

Honest he was.

———

Colin St. John came to these United States in early 1946, carrying a slight limp that was a souvenir of The Big One and deep, empty pockets he intended to fill with Yankee greenbacks. He was a tall, elegant-looking English gent with leather patches at his elbows and the aristocratic bearing of a stiff buggy whip. Colin always wore one of those snappy tweed caps "whilst motoring in an open car," and was forever puffing on this big curlicue Swiss pipe with little silver dangle chains and perforated tin breeze lids. I thought it was the coolest thing I'd ever seen. And the way he talked! Like a blessed duke or prime minister or something. Why, it made you feel like some kind of crude, boorish New Jersey Neanderthal just listening to him.

The disappearing act Colin pulled that first time I drove up to the Westbridge shop was part of a carefully orchestrated scheme he worked on every new prospect. By vanishing the moment you appeared, he set the idea in motion that he was a *very* busy fellow who really didn't need any additional business—thank you very much—but if you wanted, you could wait around for a chance opening to appear in his *frightfully* busy schedule (pronounced shedge-yewel).

You did have an appointment, didn't you?

I witnessed that performance many times over the next several months, on account of I was forever dropping by for a few odds and ends or some of Barry Spline's "consultation" to keep Big Ed's Jag running right. Or just running, if you want to get technical about it. Not that the XK120 was a *bad* car. Hell no. It was the most magnificent automobile I'd ever worked on in my life. But it needed to be stroked and petted now and then to keep it purring. And that's the only way Big Ed wanted any of his cars. It got to where Old Man Finzio didn't mind much either, since Big Ed was paying him a small fortune for my time (including those frequent trips into Manhattan) and that's not even counting the fivers Big Ed was palming me every time I passed a wrench over his Jag. Which was often.

I got to know Barry Spline and Colin St. John pretty well, and spent a lot of company time listening to Colin tell exciting World War II adventure stories in that fancy British accent of his. Once Colin saw I was spending some serious cash in the parts department, he'd flash me a behind-the-hand wink and draw me off to the side for a semi-private snort of scotch. Especially if it was around lunchtime or toward the end of the day. Colin kept a couple souvenir shot glasses from Niagara Falls and a bottle of Glen-Something-or-Other scotch hidden behind the service counter (where everybody and his brother knew exactly where it was) and it was a sign that you had indeed joined the Inner Circle when Colin St. John invited you to "share a swifty" with him. "Care for a swifty, sport?" he'd say, pouring a couple quick shots down Niagara Falls. Personally, I thought Colin's fancy scotch tasted an awful lot like mineral spirits, and suspected he might be topping up the bottle now and then with whatever was on sale at the liquor store down the street. So I put a little pencil mark on the label one day when Colin wasn't looking, and would bet you a double sawbuck he's got that same damn bottle today, still precisely two-thirds full of the cheapest rotgut Scotch, Irish, Rye, Canadian, or Old Kentucky sour mash whiskey he can lay his hands on.

He doesn't think Americans can tell the difference.

Like everyone else in England, Colin had a rough time of it during World War II. That's where he got his stiff-legged limp (which sometimes—I swear!—seemed to move from one leg to the other) along with the most astounding collection of eyewitness combat stories you ever heard. A couple snorts would get him rolling anytime: Up against Rommel in North Africa! Barely scraping out at Dunkirk! Taking on Goering's finest in a shot-up Spitfire! Cheating death with the bomb disposal lads! They were all *true*, too. Every single one of them. That's because Colin heard them all firsthand in the hospital ward where he spent the majority of 1943 after falling off the tailgate of a truck in a dark London alley while unloading a shipment of black-market creamed chipped beef. I guess it was touch and go for awhile and there was some question as to whether Colin would ever walk again (at least before the war ended, anyway), but a Luftwaffe bombardier brought about a miracle recovery one night when he accidentally dropped a thousand-pound incendiary smack on top of the hospital wing. Colin amazed the entire staff by being first man to the far side of the lawn, handily beating out an Army surgeon who'd been something of a track star at Cambridge.

After the war, Colin St. John journeyed to America to seek his fortune (or anybody else's that might be available—he wasn't real particular in that respect) and opened a little back-alley foreign car agency on the west side of Manhattan, just off the George Washington Bridge. Colin decided to call it Westbridge (get it?) and the moniker was just *perfect* for a lah-de-dah British sports car shop, on account of it sounded so upper crust, blue-blooded, and snooty. Jaguar customers expected that sort of thing.

Colin's foreign car business grew and prospered over the years in spite of high prices, shoddy service, and the business ethics of an Armenian rug merchant. That's because every single playboy, sugar daddy, and black sheep heir in the greater metropolitan New York area just *had* to have himself one of those sexy new Jaguars. Or at the very least an MG. As Colin explained repeatedly to every virgin sales prospect,

"A true *sport* requires a true *sports car*," and the rich, fashionable types around town were all ears.

Colin St. John sold just about everything that crossed the Atlantic at one time or another (including such gems of European automotive artistry as the Renault Dauphine, Hillman Husky, Humber Super Snipe, and the usual assortment of Fiats) but his main stock in trade was always Jaguars and MGs. Business was better than good, and Westbridge moved to larger quarters in 1951. Colin made himself a *lot* of money during the 1950s.

But success in the car business came naturally to Colin, since he "grew up in the motor trade" (as he called it) and knew all the ropes to pull, fancies to tickle, and angles to shoot. His father owned a garage near London that sold rough, high-mileage Rolls Royces and Bentleys to people who probably should've bought a new Ford instead, and Colin learned at his father's knee that the key feature in any automotive transaction was the split between how cheap you could buy and how high you could sell (after bumping out a few dents and covering it all with a quick-and-dirty respray, anyway). Barry Spline told me a great story about a would-be gentleman who bought a well-abused Bentley from Colin's dad, then tried to return it the same afternoon after hitting a pothole and knocking a chunk the size of a league ball out of the rocker panel. Underneath was nothing but a huge rust crater filled with wadded-up newspaper. As you can imagine, the guy was pretty upset. *"Look at THIS!!"* he screamed, waving his fists under Colin's father's nose, *"You told me this car was in absolutely PRISTINE condition!"*

"Oh, and I truly thought it *was*," Colin's dad told him, real sincere and disappointed-like. "The agent I bought it through has always been *tot*ally reliable in the past." He wrung his hands as though his entire faith in human decency had been savagely trampled. "Just *imag*ine," he continued softly, shaking his head, "the scoundrel swore it came from an estate sale. Told me the motorcar belonged to a third cousin of the duke of Windsor himself! Why, to think *any*one would have the brass to patch up a *Bentley* with putty and old newspapers...."

"Old?" the guy bellowed, grabbing Colin's dad by the necktie, *"why, this is YESTERDAY MORNING'S BLOODY FIRST EDITION!!"*

Of course, Colin's Manhattan dealership was entirely different from his father's used car garage in England, on account of the new car and used car businesses were, to use Colin's words, "as different as chalk and cheese." After a few shots of scotch, he'd explain at length how "every *used* car is unique—has its own character, its own perfume, its own *romance*—while every new automobile is essentially *ident*-i-cal to every other blasted one they push off the assembly line. The only real differences are color and trim."

"So?"

"So, indeed!" Colin would snort, tamping a fresh wad of Cavendish into his pipe. "The price of a *used* car is governed only by the glimmer in a chap's eye or the faintly detectable quickening of his pulse, whilst the profit on a *new* car is sadly subject to the eternal and inescapable laws of supply and demand."

Colin St. John understood those laws perfectly, and that's why he kept every shipment of new Jaguars stashed in a windowless meat truck garage on the other side of town. All except one, that is, which he would place on the little twelve-by-sixteen Oriental carpet in front of the fake maple partition that separated Colin's "showroom" from the rest of the Westbridge shop. That's how every single XK120 Colin had came to be "absolutely the last one in the country." And he wasn't above taking multiple deposits (or multiple futures on "the next one coming in") and using the money for general operating expenses. Plus there was *always* a story. A little romance. Like, "This par*ti*cular example was ordered for the Earl of Buxton. He summers in the Hamptons, don't you know. But the poor chap was killed in a hunting accident before he could take delivery. Happened just a fortnight ago. *Most* unfortunate business. On Safari in Africa with his new bride (don't think she was a day over eighteen—it was *quite* the scandal in the House of Lords) when the poor devil got himself trampled by a charging bull elephant. Bloody gun jammed. A shame, really. And the lads in Coventry worked *so* hard to match that precise shade of royal blue from the family crest."

Colin's upscale New York customers ate it up.

But the *real* money at Westbridge didn't come from selling cars. No sir. It came from the maintenance and repair business they generated once those Jags and MGs were out prowling the streets. That's because if there was one thing a Jaguar or MG needed with great regularity, it was to be fixed. Especially if it belonged to some country-club rube who grew up on a diet of substantial American cars like Packards and Lincolns and such, and even more especially if it spent a lot of time scuffling around Manhattan in bumper-to-bumper traffic. The more cars Colin sold, the more sick ones came stumbling and coughing and wobbling their way through the service entrance, desperately in need of attention. Tune-ups, lube jobs, valve adjustments, timing chains, clutches, generators, voltage regulators, gearbox synchros, cylinder heads—it was all money in the bank to Colin St. John. Easy money, too, since Colin wasn't above cutting corners, and fully appreciated the ignorance of stylish, high-line New Yorkers when it came to nuts-and-bolts mechanical stuff. Why, fastening up a simple loose wire could be good for the price of a brand-new starter motor (so long as you kept a can of shiny black spray paint stashed behind the service counter).

The hard part—*always*—was finding competent, reliable mechanics who could actually fix the damn cars. Let me explain to you how it is with automobile mechanics. I personally divvy them up into three distinct categories. First off, you've got your basic Shadetree Butchers. Old Man Finzio was a Butcher, even though he ran a gas station for a living. But most Butchers are home-garage amateurs who only bring their cars to a professional after they've already made a godawful mess out of whatever they were trying to fix in the first place. Butchers can be counted on to snap studs, shear bolts, strip threads, wedge bearing races in cockeyed, and turn every electrical problem into a stinking, smoldering glob of molten plastic and charred insulation. No self-respecting mechanic likes working around a Butcher, and cleaning up after one is even worse.

One giant step from the Butcher is the Parts Replacer. Parts Replacers know their way around an automobile all right, but they don't comprehend *at all* how car stuff really operates. To them, every mechanical component is like a sealed vault filled with some kind of rare magical pudding that makes it work. So they invariably start yanking off old parts and throwing new ones at a problem until it either goes away or the car's owner declares bankruptcy. God certainly must have loved Parts Replacers, because he made so many of them.

And then you've got the Fixers. The maestros. The Real McCoy. Fixers can diagnose a hiccup in your carburetor or a death rattle in your crankcase just like a medical doctor, and then go in so slick and clean that when they're done, you can't even tell the car's been worked on. Except that it runs better than ever. A Fixer can even *make* parts. "It's all done, Mr. Jones. The choke cable was sticking because it was going over-center, so I made a new bracket to bring it in at a better angle."

Those guys are hard to find. And even harder to keep.

And it was difficult to locate top-notch foreign-car mechanics who could meet the stringent Westbridge employment standards. To begin with, you had to be foreign. It didn't matter exactly what *kind* of foreign (except for maybe Eskimo) but it was absolutely essential to have an exotic, offshore look and some sort of impossible-to-understand foreign accent. Part of the image, don't you know? Plus not just anybody could learn how to fix cars the Westbridge Way. For example, not many mechanics know how to repair a car so it runs perfectly when it leaves the shop, yet assure that something totally unrelated will break, fail, burn out, or fall off within a maximum two weeks time. And a Westbridge employee had to uphold the time-honored tradition of returning every car with at least one greasy handprint on the upholstery or a smear of Permatex sealant matted into the carpeting. Most important of all, a job could never, *ever* be finished on time. Colin was a real stickler about that, since it was the cornerstone of the carefully-nurtured relationship between Westbridge Motor Car Company, Ltd., and its trendy, upscale clientele. Due to these rigorous standards (not to mention low pay and lousy working conditions) the Westbridge technical staff amounted to an endlessly-rotating parade of thickly accented grease monkeys that included, at one time or another, a Graham, a Raoul, a Vito, a Hans, one each Martine and Bjorn, two Hugos, a Philippe, and even a Juan. All in less than a year.

And then there was Sylvester. Sylvester Jones. He was a colored guy from Harlem who worked at Westbridge on and off from the very beginning. Although he didn't have much in the way of formal training, Sylvester was a natural-born handyman who'd lived out of a toolbox most all his life, and hard experience had left him with a keen practical sympathy for machinery. Even Uncle Sam's Army recognized Sylvester's talent, and they had him wrenching on everything from Jeeps to tanks to the broken jukebox in the officers' club bar during the war. But then the war ended, he got his discharge, and it didn't take long to discover that he was shit out of luck as far as finding any kind of civilian job with a title, future, or decent take-home wage attached. Sure, a lot of it was because he was colored, but you had to factor in that Sylvester Jones was a surly, argumentative sonofabitch with a little bit of a drinking problem. Not that Sylvester ever saw drinking as a problem. No sir. He considered it more of a hobby.

Then again, he had a lot of things to drink about. His wife was already on the chubby side when they got married before the war, and she put on another two or three pounds every month he was away in the service. So she was not exactly the kind of woman you dream about coming home to (unless your tastes run to the fat lady at the Barnum & Bailey Circus, that is). And the cute little twin babies Sylvester left behind had likewise turned into a sticky, bawling, foul-smelling pair of toddlers. Plus it wasn't long before his big fat wife had another set of twins on the way. "Sheee-*it!*" he'd shrug with a bewildered sense of pride, "Ah jus' shoots doubles ever' damn time. It mus' be in the genes here, see," and he'd nod toward the bulge under his zipper like it was a prize bowling trophy or something. But there wasn't much work around town for a handy colored guy with special jeans like Sylvester Jones—just cruddy factory jobs and stuff—so he kind of split up his time between drinking half-pints of sweet wine and fixing broken-down cars to sell on the cheap in Harlem. Sylvester made pretty good money doing that, but it wasn't steady and every now and then his lard-ass wife would get after him to find a job with a regular paycheck. In fact, it was on exactly such an expedition that Sylvester wandered past the old, back-alley Westbridge garage one Tuesday afternoon in 1949, just as Barry Spline was attempting to yank a stubborn transmission out the bottom side of a Mk. V Jaguar sedan. Barry worked pretty much alone in those days, and just between you and me, he was never real good at grunt work. Oh, he could tune an engine razor sharp or true a wire wheel so's it'd spin like an electric motor, but when it came to the heavy, knuckle-busting in-and-out jobs, he was better off letting somebody else do it. Which is exactly what must've run through his mind when that Jag tranny popped loose and landed on top of him, pinning him under the car. *"Help! Help! Help!"* he screamed into the cast-iron driveshaft flange that had come to rest across the bridge of his nose. Sylvester heard the commotion and came in to see what all the fuss was about, and in two shakes he had the car jacked up a foot higher, freed the shifter where it was snagged on the carpeting, unscrewed the speedo cable, and dragged Barry and the Jag's transmission out by the heels.

He was hired on the spot.

Of course, Barry could only offer Sylvester Jones a position as a car porter, on account of he was colored. That went without saying. Now car porters are the guys you see knocking around the back of car dealerships washing cars and cleaning floor mats and changing license plates—you know, nigger work—but it wasn't long before Barry Spline and even Colin St. John realized what a talented guy Sylvester was when it came to automobiles. He *understood* sick machinery, and could usually see right through all the blackened oil and busted metal to the root cause of every breakdown and failure. And *nothing* intimidated him. Not Jaguar valve adjustments or Bentley bottom ends or anything else on this earth that ran on four wheels and an internal combustion engine. "They's alla same upside down," he'd explain with a wolfish smile, "jes' like wimmen."

Although Sylvester Jones's official title remained "car porter" for as long as he worked at Westbridge, he was the best damn mechanic they ever had. And everybody who worked there knew it.

"I say, Sylvester, could you pop over and 'ave a look at the voltage regulator on the one-twenty in my stall?"

Sylvester'd be lying on a creeper under some Jag or MG, and he'd sputter when he talked because he always had the butt end of a Lucky Strike poking up out of the corner of his mouth. "Aw shit, man, jus' push the damn blade down. Same as on my old Plymouth parked in the lot out there. Sheee-*it!*"

And Graham or Raoul or Vito or Martine or whoever would wander back to the car they were working on and know exactly what to do next—even if they hadn't the slightest notion why.

To be perfectly honest, Sylvester Jones wasn't a particularly nice edition of a human being. He had a mean streak a mile wide and didn't

like anybody "messing with him." "Don't mess with me," he'd tell Graham or Raoul or even Colin St. John himself. And, if they knew what
was good for them, they wouldn't. In that respect he was a lot like
Butch (although Butch would've given me a solid punch in the nose for
suggesting he was similar to any sort of colored person).

Sylvester's dark moods came and went like the weather, and probably had something to do with his shitty job, his 360-pound wife, his
four kids, his occasional side girlfriends, a mean dice habit, and most
especially drinking the old sauce. Every so often, Sylvester'd get himself
a king-sized thirst and more or less disappear for a few hours. Or days.
Sometimes a week, even. But he always came back. And each time,
regular as clockwork, Colin St. John would fire him. I swear, Colin
must've fired Sylvester once or twice a month. *"You're bloody fired!"*
he'd holler, his cheeks going all ruddy pink. *"Do you understand?!"*

"Fine wit' me, man," Sylvester'd sneer right back. "Dat's jes' *fine*
wit' me. Sheee-*it!*" and he'd walk out the door. Then Colin would look
around at all the sick automobiles in his shop and wonder how the hell
he was going to get the damn things fixed without Sylvester Jones.

So when Sylvester shuffled in a few days later to pick up his tools
and paycheck—eyes all yellow and bloodshot, hands shaking just a little,
Lucky dangling from his lower lip—Colin would inevitably be ready
to grant him "one last chance. Just *one more.*" Sylvester'd nod and grunt
and blow his nose in his hand while Colin rambled on (like it made a
damn difference, you know?) and then they'd shake on it and Colin'd
head for the can to wash the snot off his hand while Sylvester went
back to fixing whatever needed to be fixed so he could earn enough
money to take care of his family, his dice game, his girlfriends, and
maybe disappear with a bottle again the next time he felt like it.

I learned most of what I know about fixing foreign sports cars from
Sylvester Jones. Not that he'd ever sit me down and *teach* me stuff, but
if I asked the right questions—like, fr'instance, why Big Ed's Jag was
fouling its plugs and blowing sooty black clouds out the tailpipe—he'd
first off growl and shake his head like I was some kind of prize-winning
moron, but then he'd show me what was wrong and how to fix it. Barry
Spline couldn't always do that. Not even for money. When Barry talked,
he wrapped everything up in that snooty brand of English they use in
the British shop manuals, and sometimes I got the impression he didn't
really know what he was talking about. But Sylvester could pick up
something—like the S.U. carburetor that was sitting on his workbench
the first day I met him—and explain how it worked in language an
ordinary knucklehead wrench-twister from Jersey could understand. He
stuck one lumpy finger into the throat of that S.U. and worked the
piston up and down so I could see how it made the needle move up

and down in the jet, giving more fuel as the engine inhaled more air. It was simple, really. Then Sylvester showed me the starting carburetor, which was nothing but a little solenoid doohickey on the rear float bowl that let extra fuel into the manifold to richen up the mixture when the engine was cold. *That's* what was making Big Ed's Jag foul its sparkplugs all the time. The damn solenoid wasn't shutting off like it should when the engine warmed up.

Like I said, it was *simple*.

3

JULIE

BIG ED was thrilled when I finally got the starting carburetor problem sorted out on his Jag, and for a reward he decided to lend me his
Caddy convert so I could take Julie out on the town. Can you believe
it? Like I explained, Julie and me had gotten pretty friendly around
the Sinclair, but we'd never had what you could actually call a date.
One reason is I never got up the nerve to ask her, but a lot of that was
because I didn't have a car to take her anyplace. Needless to say, my
old man was not about to lend me his Mercury, and you'd have to be
a real doofus to ask a girl to *walk* to the movies. Especially the drive-
in. Then this one Saturday afternoon—right out of the blue—Big Ed
tossed me the keys to the white Caddy and said, "Hey, why don'cha
take that Julie out someplace nice, huh?" and slipped me a couple saw-
bucks to take care of the expenses, too. You don't find many guys
who'd do a thing like that for their garage mechanic. "Have a swell
time, kid," Big Ed grinned as he climbed into the Jag (which was
purring like a well-fed kitten, if I do say so myself), but then he
grabbed a fistful of my shirtsleeve and added: "You put so much as
scratch on that Cadillac and I'll rip yer goddam head off an' use it for
a bowling ball."

He would, too.

I watched the Jag squeal away up Pine Street, leaving the smell of
burning rubber and six months' worth of clutch lining behind it, and
then I was standing all alone with two crisp ten-spots in the palm of
my hand and Big Ed's Caddy keys dangling from my fingertips like a
live baby water moccasin. Truth is, I think I might have been just a
little nervous. After all, inviting Julie out on a real live date was a lot
different than just goofing around with her at the station. I mean, what
if she turned me down? I swear I must've dialed her number and hung
up two dozen times before I finally got the nerve up to let it ring
through. And then I spent a long time hemming and hawing and beating around the bullshit before I gathered up the gonads to ask her point-
blank if she might sorta possibly be interested in a sit-down dinner and
then maybe a show or a cruise over by Palisades amusement park in
Big Ed's white Cadillac convertible. I made sure to mention that car
twenty or thirty times, and, to my everlasting surprise, Julie said *yes*. In

fact, she sounded real eager to go. "Oh yeah, that sounds *great,* Buddy," she just about gushed. "Pick me up around seven."

Oh *boy!*

"And, Buddy . . ."

"Yeah?"

"Wash your hands real good, okay?"

So I hustled like mad to finish the muffler job I had up on the lift (muffler jobs are the *dirtiest!*) and afterward took a good quarter inch off a bar of Lava soap trying to get all the rusty, gritty exhaust-pipe grunge off my hands. Then I spread an entire Sunday edition of the *New York Times* across the front seat of Big Ed's Caddy and headed over to my folks' house, since a date with Julie required a real family household–type bathroom with shampoo, clean towels, and underarm deodorant (not to mention clean socks, undershorts, and a freshly ironed shirt) and not one of those items was regularly on tap in the apartment over my Aunt Rosamarina's garage.

I felt pretty damn smug wheeling Big Ed's Caddy into the driveway by my old man's house, and I was actually a little disappointed that I didn't see his car in the garage. I was kind of hoping the rat bastard would be home, you know, just so's I could see the expression on his face. Nobody answered when I knocked, so I circled around back and found my mom at her usual station, leaning up against the kitchen window with her field glasses pressed against the glass. She was watching a squadron of her dirty brown twitterbirds flitting around the garbage cans (real exciting, huh?) and stuff like that got my mom so wrapped up she wouldn't even hear the phone ring. So I sneaked along the outside wall like Jimmy Cagney in one of those old black-and-white gangster movies and crouched myself down under the windowsill. When the timing seemed right, I just sort of popped up in front of her binoculars and went into an exotic little bird dance of my own, flapping my arms and scratching for worms and making noises like a duck caught in a hydraulic press.

It got a pretty good rise out of her, no lie.

Like always, my mom seemed real happy to see me, and of course nothing would do but that I try some of her famous Dutch apple pie (à la mode, natch) while she told me all about the nice young couple of Baltimore orioles who were building a nest *right in our own backyard!* To hear my mom tell it, this was the biggest news to hit our neighborhood since old Mr. Pasquinelli had a heart attack and died in his living room window. I think he was about eighty-five or ninety at the time, and the poor guy had been living all alone in this big stucco house on Monroe Street ever since his wife passed on. You'd see him there all the time, sitting in a big overstuffed chair in his living room window

with a blanket over his lap and a glass of iced tea at his side, watching
the grass grow and the kids playing and the neighborhood dogs peeing
on the fire hydrant. A whole week went by before anybody much noticed how he just *sat* there in the same exact position—morning, noon,
and night—without moving or changing his pajamas or getting up to
take a leak or *any*thing. Finally, the postman saw how the mail was
backing up in the chute and tiptoed around the bushes to see what was
up, and he couldn't help noticing how old Mr. Pasquinelli was all sort
of puffy and purplish and didn't even blink when he tapped on the
window glass. So the mailman called the cops, and next thing you know,
a bunch of medical-emergency types in white uniforms showed up and
carted poor old Mr. Pasquinelli away in an ambulance. Naturally, they
had the lights flashing and siren wailing (not that there was any particular hurry anymore) and since it happened on a Saturday afternoon
in the middle of August, all the neighborhood kids swarmed around
like that ambulance was a Good Humor ice-cream wagon or something.
Only the smell was more like bad hamburger meat than butterscotch
sundaes or toasted almond bars.

But we were talking about my mom's Dutch apple pie, weren't we?
Well, it was better than scrumptious, and my mom would've happily
kept feeding me fresh slices and filling me in on all the latest hot bird
gossip until my gut burst and my ears fell off. But I had to get ready
for my big date with Julie, so I excused myself in the middle of a story
about three sweet little wrens and a cantankerous blue jay and went
upstairs to shower, shave, and sneak some of my dad's Old Spice after-
shave out of the medicine cabinet. He never used the stuff anyway.
Besides, *I'm* the one who gave it to him for Christmas every year.

Speaking of my old man, I heard his Mercury pulling into the drive
just as I was buttoning the shirt my mom ironed for me, and I couldn't
wait to see the look on his face when he got a load of Big Ed's Caddy
parked in his driveway. But the weasel didn't so much as lift an eyebrow. "Who the hell left that kikey road barge in front of my garage?"
was all he wanted to know, looking around the kitchen like there was
maybe somebody besides my mom and me in the room. What a jerk.
But then he was still pretty burned about how I blew off his stupid
chemical plant job. You know how parents can nurse a grudge.

Anyhow, I left my folks' house in time to cruise over by the liquor
store on Fremont and wait for one of the wobbly regulars who'd pick
you up a little something in return for a small monetary consideration.
Being Saturday night, it didn't take long, and pretty soon I was tooling
my way over to Julie's mom's place with a smile on my face and a fresh
pint of Bacardi dark in the glove compartment. Along the way, I kept
thinking what it would be like to kiss Julie Finzio—right on the lips,

you know?—and this lady in a blue DeSoto caught me at a stoplight with my eyes half closed and my lips all puckered up, and I had to pretend I was whistling along with Bing Crosby singing "Count Your Blessings" on the radio.

Julie and her mom lived on the second floor of an old frame house over on Fourteenth that really could've used a little fixing up. Or at the very least a fresh coat of paint. But the guy they rented from was one of those two-bit, broken-English real estate tycoons who are mortgaged up to their assholes in two or three shitty buildings and clawing for every last nickel so they can someday get it up to four. Which made me feel like some kind of knight in shining armor when I pulled up front at the wheel of Big Ed's freshly waxed Cadillac. I beeped the horn, of course, just so's everybody on the block would take a gander out their windows, but then I walked up the steps and rang the bell, too. I mean, I didn't want Julie's mom to think I was one of those greaseball hoods who wait for a girl out in the car.

Luckily, Julie answered the door (thank goodness) and boy oh boy, did she look *great!* Her face was so fresh and bright it seemed to glow, and she was wearing this sleeveless yellow angora sweater that really, you know, *clung.* And believe me, Miss Julie Finzio had some really interesting stuff for a tight sweater to cling to! Her mom was hovering in the background (you know how girls' moms do), giving me the hairy eyeball like I'd just bitten the head off a live chicken. Julie's mom was a short, tough-looking Italian woman with penciled-in eyebrows and a big hairdo that was stiff and shiny as patent leather. "Yooda boy from my brudderenlaw's gas station?" she wanted to know.

"Yes, I—"

"What kinna future you ever gonna have inna lousy job like dat, hey? Workin' in alla'dat grease and filt'?"

"Oh, *Mom!*" Julie groaned, hustling us out to the car.

"You takecarra my girl Joolie, you hear?" Mrs. Finzio hollered after us. "She gotta be home by eleven."

Jee-*zus!* She sounded just like my old man, you know?

"Sorry about my mom," Julie said once we were safely on our way.

"Aw, that's okay," I told her. "My folks are the same way. Sometimes I think they have secret meetings just to find new and better ways to embarrass their kids."

Julie laughed and squeezed me on the arm. Boy, it sent a charge through my system like I'd stuck a couple straight pins in a wall socket.

Thanks to Big Ed, I had enough ready cash to take Julie just about anyplace in Jersey. New York, even. But all she wanted to do was cruise over by the Doggie Shake and show off a little in front of the other girls. And I had to admit, Julie and me looked pretty damn sharp in

Big Ed's Caddy convert, sitting there on all that creamy-soft leather with the top down and the breeze rustling our hair and Nat King Cole coming in so loud and clear you would've sworn he was in the back seat.

When I fallll in love, it will bee foreverrr...

About two blocks from the Doggie Shake, Julie almost caused us to have a serious accident. Without saying a word, she slid herself across that huge front seat so she was sitting right next to me. I mean *right* next to me. I felt the heat of her all up and down my body, my nostrils filled with the scent of her perfume, and next thing you know, I damn near drove us into the back end of a bus that was stopped to pick up passengers. *"Hey!"* Julie yelped, "be careful, willya?"

"S-Sure, Julie. You know me ..."

"Yeah," she snickered, "*suuure* I do. My uncle says Big Ed's gonna use your head for a bowling ball if you hurt this car."

"Aw, that's just what he *said*...."

"You think he really would?" Julie giggled.

"Well, Big Ed's never given me reason to believe he wouldn't do something he said he would, so let's just say I'd rather not find out."

"Sounds like a wise plan."

"Besides, I don't think my head would make too good a bowling ball."

"Yeah, you'd probably hook to the right. And your holes look a little too small for Big Ed's fingers."

"We could always use a reamer."

"A what?"

"You know, a reamer. Like you use on valve guides. To open up the holes."

"That's disgusting."

"And we could use an orbital sander to take down some of the high spots."

"Like your nose, for example?"

"Yeah, like my nose."

"No, I think I like your head better the way it is," Julie said through her best movie magazine smile. "It's a *nice* head."

"It is?"

"Yes, it is," she whispered in my ear. All by itself, Big Ed's Caddy picked up eight or ten miles per hour, and I knew there was no way I'd be able to climb out of that car and walk into a damn restaurant. Not for awhile, anyway. But we were in luck and found a curb-service slot, and you should've seen all the pointing and tittering going on inside the Doggie Shake when the other girls got a load of Julie and me in Big Ed's Cadillac. Sure, I was in love with his Jaguar, but there's a lot to be said for a white-on-white Caddy convert parked center stage in front of the local burger shop on a warm Saturday night. Especially with somebody as pretty as Miss Julie Finzio sitting there beside you— smiling like a prom queen—holding an olive burger with all the trimmings in one hand and a root beer with a quarter-pint of rum in it in the other. Everything seemed so damned *perfect*, you know? Which, I have come to learn from bitter personal experience, is almost always the way things feel just before they go straight to hell.

After the Doggie Shake, Julie and me cruised up the parkway to the Palisades amusement park, polishing off the last of the rum-laced root beer along the way. I had my arm around her shoulder and she let her head lean over so I could feel her hair against my cheek, and even though I'd filled Big Ed's Caddy clear up to the top out of my own pocket, I would've gladly kept driving like that until the very last drop drained through the fuel line. But all too soon we arrived and had to get out. That was a hard thing to do, if you catch my drift.

With Julie by my side and Big Ed's greenbacks burning a hole in my trousers, nothing would do but that we rode all four roller coasters—one right after the other—not to mention the Flying Turns and the Flash Gordon Sky Scooters, and stopped at every concession stand along the midway for caramel corn and peanut pralines and chocolate fudge and even a butterscotch ice-cream sundae shoveled in on top of the olive burgers, onion rings, and spiked root beer we'd already packed away. We were having a swell time, and I kept asking Julie if she wanted to maybe go on the Tunnel of Love boat ride with me. I figured I might get a kiss off her back there in the darkness where nobody could see. But Julie wasn't having any part of it on account of one of her girlfriends told her she'd seen a rat in there once. Heck, it was probably just a mouse, you know? But there was no changing her mind, so I switched tactics and steered us over by the Ferris wheel. I thought perhaps I could do some good when it stopped up at the very top, high over the midway. Just the two of us, all by our lonesome up there in the nighttime sky.

It didn't quite work out that way.

Now you've probably been to an amusement park yourself and noticed how stately and graceful a Ferris wheel looks from a distance. In fact, you'd swear they were powered by the world's smoothest-ever fluid drive. But climb aboard one of those suckers and you discover that they clank and creak and scrape and shudder every time they move. And the damn things have to start and stop every twenty seconds to load and unload passengers. So it takes absolutely for*ever* to go all the way around. Which leaves a person entirely too much time to look down at the ground—*waaaay* down at the ground—and likewise glance around at all the rust-infected rivets, guy wires, clevis pins, and turn-buckles that hold your average Ferris wheel together. Confidence in-spiring they are not. In fact, if you have any sort of mechanical aptitude whatsoever, they can get you very nervous indeed. To make matters worse, there was a stiff breeze blowing in off the Hudson that night, making the gondolas sway back and forth, baack and forth, baaack and forth. . . .

About fifty feet up, Julie's face suddenly turned the same shade of green the Hudson River gets in summertime. "Hey, Julie," I asked her, "you feelin' okay?"

She opened her mouth to answer, but all that came out was this sickly sort of groan. Followed shortly thereafter by approximately five dollars' worth of olive burgers, onion rings, rum-laced root beer, and assorted candy snacks. Fortunately, she managed to blow most of it over the rail. Unfortunately, it landed on the gondola just below. Jee-*zus*, you should've heard all the yelling and screaming. Those people were *very* unhappy. Pretty vocal about it, too.

After she was finished, Julie's face changed color again (this time to a chalky off-white) and she sagged back the seat, not looking well at all. "Hey, Julie?" I whispered gently (while making sure her head stayed pointed in the opposite direction), "you feelin' all right?"

She half-nodded, wiping off her chin.

"Do you think you can walk?"

She looked at me with this blank expression.

"How'bout *run?* Huh, Julie? You think you can *run?*"

Julie didn't understand, but the instant we hit bottom, I grabbed her arm and took off lickety-split down the midway—fast as I could go!—dragging her behind like a coaster wagon with a busted wheel. We sure didn't want to be around when that next gondola car hit ground level. Not hardly.

Poor Julie got sick again out in the parking lot (before we sat down in the Caddy, thank goodness!) and, needless to say, that first date with Miss Julie Finzio didn't quite turn out the way I'd planned. In fact, I even took a pass on a good-night kiss. You would have, too.

I remember Julie made herself pretty scarce around the Sinclair for a few weeks after that. Embarrassed, you know? And I can't say as I blamed her. For sure it was a long, long time before I could kid her about that night and get a laugh instead of dagger eyes. Not that it stopped me from doing it. But Julie was a good sport—she could *take* it—and that's one of the reasons I got so excited when she said she'd think about going out with me again. Even if I didn't have Big Ed's

Caddy to tool us around. *Wow!* Of course, I never knew if it was because Julie really *liked* me or just because there wasn't much of anybody else around for her to date. But, whatever the reason, Julie and me started going out to the movies and stuff pretty regular on Friday and Saturday nights.

As you can imagine, Old Man Finzio wasn't real keen about me dating his niece, and he made it clear he'd knock one of Big Ed's Caddies off the jack stands while I was working under it if "anything happened." And nothing did. But that wasn't for lack of trying on my part. On the other hand, the Old Man *would* borrow us his scruffy Dodge tow truck every now and then when I couldn't get my hands on Big Ed's off-season Caddy. But I had to beg and plead and crawl on my belly like a reptile anytime we wanted to use it, and the Old Man made me fill the damn thing with gas, too (out of my own pocket, natch), and you can bet your ass the needle was stuck on empty anytime he felt like letting us use it.

Saturday-night dates with Julie usually started off with a movie show or maybe a round of miniature golf, and afterward we'd head over to Weedermen's for Cokes or malteds and a couple orders of fries. Julie didn't especially want the girls at the Doggie Shake to see us in her uncle's beat-up tow truck. But every now and again, when I'd fixed his Jag up extra nice, Big Ed would lend me one of the Caddies so Julie and me could hit the Doggie Shake in *style*. Maybe even take in a movie at the drive-in. No way would she consider anything like that in Old Man Finzio's truck.

In fact, that's where we kissed for the very first time. At the drive-in. I remember we were in Big Ed's black Sixty Special sedan (the one with the extra-thick window glass) watching some dim-bulb Bible movie with Victor Mature in it. I had my arm around Julie and she was sort of nuzzling into my neck, and that of course made the action in the front seat of Big Ed's Cadillac a lot more interesting than watching Victor Mature parade his biceps around in a used beach towel. During one real boring scene, I leaned over into Julie's hair and my lips sort of grazed her left eyebrow—hell, I wasn't aiming or anything, you know?—and just like that her face rolled up into mine and we were *kissing!* Boy, she was one hell of a good kisser (in fact, I kind of wondered where she'd picked it up) and that's about all we did for the next two hours. Of course, she wouldn't open up her mouth to French on account of she was a good Immaculate Conception girl, but to tell the truth, I wasn't sure I knew how to do that anyway. When we came up for air this one time, there were headlights flashing and horns honking all around us. The damn picture had been over for ten minutes! It was kind of embarrassing, really.

After that, making out in a parked car became sort of a regular part of our dates (and, not surprisingly, it was the part I looked forward to the most). In fact, it got to where I was daydreaming about making out with Julie all the time. And I mean *all* the time. It never failed to get me all hot and bothered—just *thinking* about her, you know?—but I'd also get this dry-mouth, queasy feeling whenever I'd dream up something really vivid and sexy about Julie. Then I'd feel all ashamed and guilty about it afterward. I believe it's a sure sign your brain is suffering from some sort of serious pulp disorder when you start feeling guilty about your blessed daydreams.

Most of our dates usually wound up with Julie and me parked out back behind the Sinclair, kissing and groping and wrestling around in the two-by-four cab of the Old Man's tow truck. It wasn't the most accommodating place for that sort of thing—not hardly!—what with the floor shift sticking up right in the middle and the steering wheel so close you couldn't really get two healthy human torsos wedged in behind it (and no way would Julie ever let us get more than 15 degrees off vertical plumb). But at least it was dark and quiet back there behind the Sinclair and nobody could see us from the highway. That was real important, on account of Julie didn't want any flack from her mom or uncle about being, you know, one of those *easy* girls. Plus I sure as hell didn't fancy the thought of one of Big Ed's Caddies falling on my skull. Or his Jaguar either, for that matter.

A couple times I asked Julie if she maybe wanted to come over to the apartment over my Aunt Rosamarina's garage, but no way would she even consider it. Personally, I couldn't see the difference between making out in the Old Man's tow truck and making out in my apartment (except that my apartment would've been much more comfortable) but Julie had a kind of Major Distinction about it. Girls *always* have Major Distinctions when it comes to making out. For example, they have these Invisible Boundaries laid out across their bodies—like the Great Wall of China, you know?—so that touching one spot passes for Acceptable Behavior, while a half inch farther south amounts to Criminal Trespass. You figure it out. But I had to admit Julie's make-out boundaries were a lot closer to pay dirt than any of the other girls I'd known. Then again, the girls I'd known didn't exactly represent a cross section of national opinion. Either one of them.

Anyhow, Julie and me would park out behind the Sinclair and start kissing and stuff—boy, could she ever *kiss!*—and pretty soon she'd have me worked up into a genuine, grade-A hormone frenzy. It took all of about thirty seconds on an average Saturday night. Then she'd just sort of hold me there—right on the brink of explosion!—for the next forty or fifty minutes like she was going for some kind of new world record.

But whenever I'd get really, *really* desperate (like when I'd start peeling the chrome trim off the dashboard with my fingernails), she'd all of a sudden back off and make that whimpering little "please stop" noise all the girls knew how to make. And then she'd sit up, straighten her skirt, brush out her hair, and say something like, "Gee, Buddy, it's getting *awfully* late," as if nothing was going on at all! Can you believe it? Oh, I'd beg and plead and drool all over my shirt, but once Julie decided it was time to go, there was no changing her mind. So I'd drive her back to her mom's apartment, grinding my teeth into powder the whole seven blocks, and when we finally pulled up in front she'd always give me one last, long, wet, deep, lingering, Hollywood-style kiss, after which she'd lean up and whisper, *"I had a wonderful time, Buddy,"* directly in my ear and maybe even run her tongue lightly down the lobe for punctuation. Just to drive me nuts. I don't know where the hell she learned that trick, but it was about equal to pouring a bucket of molten-hot lava in my lap! By the time I got back to the apartment over my aunt's garage, I damn near needed a cold chisel to get my shorts off.

4

MANUAL LABOR

FORTUNATELY, I found something besides Julie Finzio to keep my mind occupied during that spring of 1952. Which was a good thing, since otherwise I might've worn out some of my more precious body parts. Big Ed's copy of the official *Jaguar Service Manual* arrived—airmail, no less—all the way from Coventry, England, bound in dark maroon leather (or maybe leatherette, but so good you couldn't tell) with a snarling Jaguar's head and fancy gold lettering embossed on the front like a damn encyclopedia. It was thick as an encyclopedia, too (and not one of those skinny volumes like "I" or "V," either), and I started taking it home every night and reading it like a detective story or something. Then I'd bring it back and leave it in the john at work, so's I could thumb through it whenever I had a little time to myself.

To tell the truth, that *Jaguar Service Manual* was harder to figure than any school textbook I'd ever come across, on account of the English speak a different brand of English than we use here in Jersey. F'instance, a "hood" in Passaic, New Jersey, is a "bonnet" over in England. And a "hood" over there is what we call a "convertible top" here in the States. And that's just the tip of the damn iceberg, as they say both places. I learned that an open-end wrench was really a "spanner" and that a Jaguar's "petrol gauge," "screenwiper switch," and "revolution counter" were mounted on a "centre facia" rather than an ordinary Jersey-style dashboard. A muffler was a "silencer" (at least that one made sense), while a piston was fastened to its connecting rod with a "gudgeon pin." What we call a "generator" in American English was a "dynamo" in English English, and British cars were generally "positive earthed" instead of negative ground like normal automobiles. It was as if Jaguars were some kind of mysterious private club with split-finger handshakes and secret insider passwords.

But the biggest kick was the way that Jaguar manual described routine repair procedures. Such as:

Fit a new felt washer into each recess in the striking rod holes at the rear of the cover. Thread the plate over one or other of the outside rods and slide the rod into the cover, not forgetting to fit the change-speed fork before the rod enters the front hole in the cover, until it occupies the neutral position.

This can be checked by looking through the grub screw hole on top of the cover and aligning the neutral groove in the rod under the hole. Enter the other outside rod in a like manner through the plate in the change-speed fork, into the neutral position. Place an interlock ball in the groove in each rod using the centre hole to gain access to the rods which are already in position.

Whaaa? Or try this one:

The torsion bars, which are 52" (127cm.) long, are positioned along the inner vertical faces of the chassis frame side members. Both ends of the torsion bar have raised splines, a reaction lever with companion splines and clamp bolt being attached to the rear end while a splined muff is fitted to the front end. The reaction lever is forked and the forks are supported on a trunion positioned by an adjusting barrel nut and bolt, the bolt being attached to the chassis frame.

Sure thing. But even if some of it read like Sanskrit, other passages in that Jaguar manual were downright elegant:

Attention to the following points of maintenance will be amply repaid by satisfactory operation of the engine and will materially add to the life of the unit.

Pure poetry, right? Made you feel like putting on a jacket and tie before you ever touched a wrench to one. Or maybe a judge's robe and powdered wig might be more appropriate, since a Jaguar mechanic had to:

Check the top face of the cylinder block for truth.

But my overall personal favorite was:

Offer up the camshaft sprocket to the flange.

It sounded like some kind of pagan sacrifice, you know?

Of course, Big Ed's Jag didn't really need any heavy-duty fixing since it was damn near brand-new, but I enjoyed reading that stuff anyway and figured it might come in handy some day. Anytime I got stuck on an unfamiliar word or weird-ass explanation, I'd dream up an excuse to go over to Westbridge and have a talk with Sylvester. I'd usually come by around noon, so I could treat him to lunch (which was a half-pint of sweet wine every day but Friday, when he generally switched to rock 'n' rye to kick off his weekend) and it never failed to amaze me how Sylvester could turn all those highbrow paragraphs into a few simple grunts, shrugs, and finger-circles in the air that an ordinary knuckle-buster from Passaic could understand.

The Westbridge shop was always busy in springtime, since that's when all the Jaguars and MGs came out of hibernation and started running around with their tops down and gas pedals mashed to the floorboards. That inevitably resulted in an epidemic of burnt clutches, shredded gearboxes, broken engines, pretzelized suspension pieces, and assorted electrical malfunctions requiring immediate (and expensive!) service attention. In fact, Colin's shop got so swamped that Barry Spline even offered *me* a job. Honest. I was real flattered (especially seeing as how I didn't have much in the way of a foreign accent) but I had to turn him down. I mean, who wanted to take the damn bus in and out of Manhattan every day? Not to mention that there were some undeniable advantages to my situation at the Old Man's Sinclair. Like I was pretty much my own boss in Passaic (as long as I got the work done, anyway) but I could see how the deal at Westbridge was more like my old man's chemical plant job. You had to punch a damn time clock—even for lunch!—and take a lot of guff off Barry Spline and Colin himself whenever they felt like dishing it out (which looked to be a pretty regular occurrence, best as I could tell). Plus I was still working out of Butch's toolbox, and it didn't seem right to haul it off to another state, even if it *was* just across the bridge in Manhattan. But the most important thing was they didn't have a Miss Julie Finzio hanging around the shop at Westbridge, and that was a major consideration as far as I was concerned.

So I begged off. But I did it in a proper, forthright, and gentlemanly fashion. In other words, I lied right through my teeth, telling some bullshit story about my poor old sickly maiden aunt and how it just wouldn't *do* for me to be way over in Manhattan in case she needed anything. It was a load of crap, since all I did around Aunt Rosamarina's house was haul the garbage cans out to the curb when the smell of used kitty litter got strong enough to make your eyes water and your ears ring. But I knew it was important to decline Barry's offer in such a way that he'd be sure and keep me in mind if things ever changed. After all, you never want to burn your Westbridges.

Turns out I made the right move, because who should roll into the Sinclair a few days later but my old mechanical mentor Butch Bohunk. And I do mean roll. The poor bastard was laid up in a wheelchair with none other than Mean Marlene doing the pushing. She was wearing her usual "I'd rather be *any*place else" scowl and a pair of bright turquoise slacks about four sizes too small for her. Gee whiz, they made her ass look like two party balloons full of butterscotch pudding. Lord only knows how she got them on and off. But fat and nasty as she was, Marlene still looked a hell of a lot better than Butch. One of his legs

was in plaster clear up to the hip—sticking out like a concrete post!—
and he was wearing big, dark sunglasses to cover up the purplish scar
tissue spiderwebbed all over his face. I guess that's what happens when
your head goes through a windshield. *"Hey, Butch,"* I hollered, *"long
time no see. How'ya doin'?"* Not that I really meant it, since moron could
tell that old Butch wasn't doing very good at all.

"Aw, I'm doin' real fuckin' great," he grunted, extending a hand
with most of the fingers missing. It was just a thumb and a bunch of
crooked stumps, and felt like a lump of Easter ham when I shook it.

"So," I said, still staring at his hand, "howz things?"

"Couldn't be better, Buddy, couldn't be better," he allowed, working up half a smile. "But I don't guess I'll be playing no concert piano
anymore."

"I guess not."

"Hey, what the hell. I can still pick my nose, wipe my ass, and beat
my meat. What more could a guy ask?"

"Not a thing, Butch. Not a thing."

"You got that right."

"And how're *you* doin'?" I asked Marlene, trying to be polite.

"Somethin' wrong with yer eyes, honey?" she answered in her high,
hillbilly twang. "Anybody kin see I'm havin' me the time of my en-tire
life here, wheelin' *this* fat asshole around town like a blessed shopping
cart." I guess Marlene wore out her welcome back home in Tennessee
(not hard to imagine) and decided to come back once she found out
Butch was laid up in a wheelchair and couldn't fight back if she took
a notion to pop him one. Which I'm sure she did from time to time.
Not to mention that Butch was getting some pretty decent disability
benefits through the Veteran's Administration, and no question that
made him a lot more desirable as far as Mean Marlene was concerned.

Anyhow, we shot the shit for awhile—just small talk about car
stuff and old times, you know—and behind the dark glasses I could
see Butch's eyes sweeping around the shop, checking out his tools and
the car projects in progress. Since he showed up right out of the blue,
I didn't have a chance to clean or tidy up (which is probably exactly
what he had in mind) but I'd been doing things the way he taught me
and the service bays didn't look too bad at all. At least if you didn't
count the new smudge on the ceiling from when Old Man Finzio tried
to braze a filler neck on a Buick radiator without taking it out of the
car first and set the carburetor on fire. Outside of that, the shop was
pretty well squared away (if I do say so myself) except for the few
specific sockets, extensions, and box-end wrenches I needed for the Pontiac head gasket I was working on. Butch allowed me a nice little half-

nod of approval. "So," he wanted to know, "how're things goin' fer you, Buddy?"

"Real good, Butch. Real good."

"I hear you been workin' on a coupla those Jagwarz."

"Just one, Butch. Big Ed Baumstein bought himself one of those XK120 roadsters. White with red leather. Wait'll you see it."

"That fat hebe. You an' the Old Man'll rake in a pisspot fulla money offa him. Them fuckin' Jagwarz needs work alla time."

"They sure do," I nodded, "But gee whiz, Butch, when they're *runnin'* . . . "

"Yeah," he sighed, "I 'spect they're pretty slick, all right."

"'Course, Old Man Finzio can't *stand* 'em."

"Figures."

"Yeah."

"Hey, that reminds me. I heard you been dickin' his niece." Boy, I turned *bright* red. I mean, Marlene was standing *right there*, you know? But she didn't so much as bat an eye. In fact, she hardly even seemed to notice. "So," Butch repeated, "You been puttin' the old pork t'Julie or not?"

"Jeez, Butch," I gulped, "It's not like *that*. . . ."

"Oh, *sure*, honey," Marlene snorted, giving off a dirty little knife-blade of a laugh. I guess she was listening after all.

We shot the breeze a little after that, but then we sort of ran out of things to say and it got real quiet—like it always does when you're around hurt or sick people who aren't likely to get much better—and the only sound was the cars and trucks rumbling past on the highway. I remember wishing one of them would pull in for gas or to ask directions or something.

"Say," Butch said at last, "where's that old fart Finzio, anyway?"

"Aw, he's out chasin' parts or something."

"Good. I can't stand that sonofabitch."

"Aw, he ain't so bad."

"*Sure* he is," Butch grinned. "He's gotta be the worst goddam tight-ass, mean-streaked, camel-faced sonofabitch you ever met!"

"You know," I said, mulling it over like I was giving it careful consideration, "you're probably right!" We got a good laugh off that.

"Well," Butch said, wiping his eye with the back of his bum hand, "you be sure and tell the old prick I stopped by."

"Sure will, Butch."

He turned his wheelchair to go, but Mean Marlene stopped him with a sharp cuff to the back of the head. "*Ask* him," she hissed in his ear, "like yew promised."

"Aw, Marlene, he don't know—"

"Ah said ASK him!"

Butch squirmed around like he wanted to crawl off under a car and die, but Marlene had her mind made up and jammed him another good shot in the ear to get him going. You could see all the air drain out of him, and he had to clear his throat a couple times before he spoke. "Uh, lissen, Buddy," he mumbled into his lap, "would'ja do me a little favor when the Old Man comes back?"

"Sure, Butch. Anything you want. Just name it."

His voice went down so quiet I had to bend down next to him to make it out. "Would'ja mind askin' the Old Man if he can maybe use a lil' help around the station here? Part-time, even. I can still do lotsa stuff. . . ."

"Sure you can," I told him.

"Yeah," he sighed in barely a whisper, "sure I can."

There wasn't much of anything to say after that, and I caught myself listening to the cars out on the highway again. Like the sound of the ocean in a seashell, you know? But then Butch shook it off and flashed me a shadow of the rugged old smile he used to whip out now and then around the Sinclair. "Well," he said, "me an' Marlene gotta be gettin' along. We got stuff t'do. . . ."

"A'course you do, Butch."

"You takin' good care a'my tools, boy?"

"Sure am, Butch. You know that."

"You damn well better had."

Marlene started rolling him toward the street, but all of a sudden I got a bright idea. "Say, Butch," I yelled after him, "maybe I oughta be *paying* you something for those tools."

Butch grabbed the wheels and spun that wheelchair around, angry as hell. *"What th'FUCK makes you think I'd wanna sell my goddam tools?"*

"N-Nothing, Butch," I stammered. "I mean, that's not what I meant. Not at all, Butch. No sir."

"Well, that's sure what th'fuck it *sounded* like."

"Geez, Butch, I just thought, you know, like maybe I oughta be *payin'* you, I dunno, some kinda *rent* or something."

"Rent?"

"Sure," I said. "After all, I been using your tools for quite awhile now. Maybe I oughta be payin' rent for 'em, doncha think? I mean, it's only fair. . . ."

Butch thought it over, rubbing his chin with his bad hand. "Naw," he said finally, shaking his head, "I don't think I'd feel real happy about that. You just take care a'them tools until I'm ready t'use 'em again."

"Honest, Butch, I can afford it. I'm doin' *real* good here at the station."

"I 'spect you are, Buddy. I 'spect you are. But I'm doin' okay, too. I got some money comin' in from the disability insurance and stuff. Fact is, I got more now than I ever had when I was workin'. Can't get out t'the damn tavern anymore an' spend it. Ask Marlene."

"Sure thing, honey," she cooed, real sarcastic. "Ol' Butch here is one *hell* of a provider these days. . . ."

"Ah, button yer lip, y'old bag."

"Or else *what*, jerkoff? Yew planning t'button it *for* me?"

Butch arched up like he was gonna take a swipe at her, but Marlene simply stepped out of range and there was nothing Butch could do but paw the air where she'd been. Finally, he slumped back in his wheelchair, shook his head, and slowly pushed those armor-plate sunglasses up over his forehead. "Lissen, Buddy," he said, staring me square in the eyes, "it ain't just about money, see."

"It isn't?"

"Hell no, it ain't. A man's gotta *work*, Buddy. He's gotta get out of th'damn house an' *do* something. Life ain't worth two shits just sittin' around with yer dick in yer lap." And with that, Butch spun around so Marlene could grab the handles and wheel him off down the street.

In a heartbeat they were gone.

I told Old Man Finzio about Butch's visit when he got back, to the station, but I had to be honest about the shape he was in. I mean, there was no point lying about it. So naturally the Old Man wasn't real keen on hiring him. And to tell the truth, I couldn't blame him. Sure, I felt bad about it, but it was just one more lousy deal in life that I couldn't do a single goddam thing about. It seems like the older you get, the more of that shit you run into.

We had a sort of warm spell toward the middle of May, and right on cue Big Ed's XK120 started overheating whenever he got stuck in traffic. It wasn't one of your steaming, gurgling, car-disabling boil-overs, but rather one of those irritating deals where the temp needle creeps up into the worry zone and the engine starts skipping a little because fuel is percolating someplace in the pump, lines, or float bowls. As you can imagine, that aggravated the hell out of Big Ed—hey, he wanted his cars *perfect*—so he brought the Jag over one evening for me to check it out. But of course it was cooler then and so naturally the engine ran like a charm and never missed a beat. Happens every time.

"Aw, this g-goddam thing," Big Ed sputtered. "If Cadillac built cars like this, they'd be outta goddam business."

"I'm sorry," I shrugged, "but I can't find anything wrong, Mr. Baumstein. She seems t'be runnin' fine."

"Oh, suuurre," he grumbled. "*Now* th' damn thing runs fine. Purrs like a goddam kitten. Lissen, Buddy, *you* drive the sonofabitch over t'Westbridge tomorrow. Across the bridge during rush hour. *You'll* see," and Big Ed handed me the keys to his brand-new Jaguar. Just like that.

Naturally, Big Ed needed a lift home, and believe it or not, he let *me* drive. Probably wanted to see if I could handle it, you know? As you can imagine, I took it *very* easy, squeezing the gas and brakes so gently you could've set a line of beer mugs down the hood and not lost a drop. Even so, that XK120 was the most exciting piece of machinery I'd ever had my hands on, and I couldn't wait to drop him off so I could maybe stretch its legs a little.

Big Ed's house in Teaneck was set back at the end of a long, woodsy drive that just about deserved its own street sign, and I swear I'd never seen a place like that in my life. It looked more like a country club or a small municipal library than the private home of an ordinary two-armed, two-legged, shot-and-a-beer human being. Why, it was two stories high and damn near half a block long, and there were big marble columns and one of those rounded turret deals with a pincushion top like you see on Russian Orthodox churches. In fact, there were fancy architectural doo-dads *all over* Big Ed's place, including carved stone gargoyles on the corners of the roof and a pair of mean-looking concrete lions flanking the main entrance. Across the driveway was this big oval fountain with green ceramic carp spouting water at one end and a little bronze boy pissing off a rock at the other. To be perfectly honest, I thought Big Ed's house was just a tad, you know, *overdone* for a private home. But it was sure as hell impressive, and I guess that was the whole idea.

Of course, a guy like Big Ed needed a special place for his auto-mobiles, and around the side was a five-car garage—all brick, natch—with Big Ed's two Caddies on one side, an empty slot for his Jag in the middle, one of the maroon-and-gold GMC half-tons from his scrap yard up against the wall, and his wife's butterscotch-yellow Chrysler con-vertible in the stall beside it. It was one of those "Town and Country" jobs with the real wood trim, and even though it was two years old (same as Big Ed's marriage to the current Mrs. Baumstein) you couldn't tell it from new. Big Ed wanted to buy her one of those hot new '52 Packard ragtops, but the reigning Mrs. Big Ed wouldn't hear of it because she was so fond of the solid maple trim on her Chrysler. I kind of liked it myself, and could never figure why Chrysler decided to shitcan the woodwork for the '51 model year. When you get right down to it, Chryslers were fat, lardy-looking cars that needed all the dress-up help they could get.

Nobody at the Sinclair had ever met Big Ed's wife, and I have to admit I was more than a little curious as to just what kind of woman a guy like Big Ed Baumstein might marry. Not to mention vise versa. But I begged off when Big Ed invited me in for a bite to eat. After all, I was still dressed in my greasy mechanic's coveralls and Big Ed's house didn't look like the kind of place where a guy with a full day's garage work spread all over him could plop down in a swivel-backed chair, prop his feet up on an empty soda case, and scarf down a quick bottle of Coke and a hamburger sandwich. Not hardly. Besides, I had *better* things to do. It was a beautiful spring evening and I had the keys to Big Ed's Jaguar XK120 burning a hole in my pocket. Who needed to eat?

I took it easy on the way back to my apartment—just getting the feel of it, you know—and spent a few minutes in my aunt's driveway disconnecting the Jag's speedo cable (it's easy on an XK120, you just reach behind the dash and unscrew the fitting) so I could go for a little spin without anybody being the wiser. Then I went inside to shower, shave, and put on the freshest shirt and pair of pants I could find. I mean, you don't go cruising in a gleaming ivory-white Jaguar roadster looking like a blue-collar working stiff who adjusts valves and greases kingpins for a living, do you? Even if that's exactly what you are.

After I got myself all spiffed up, I went down to the corner grocery store and rang Julie up to see if she'd maybe like to join me for a little late-night Jaguar prowl on the Parkway. But her mom answered (what else?) and no way would she even consider it. In fact, she flat refused to put Julie on the line and gave me a major-league earful about calling so late. You know how that goes with girls' moms. So there was nothing to do but take Big Ed's Jaguar for a spin all by my lonesome. Which was okay, too, but not near as nice as sharing it with Julie. Especially since it was such a perfect spring night, what with the smell of new green things and just enough chill in the air so's a person could really appreciate the soft waves of heat rolling up off the Jag's transmission tunnel. The Manhattan skyline was shimmering over the Hudson like the string of lights on a cruise ship, and I just drove up and down the Jersey shore for hours, enjoying the gutty purr out the Jag's tailpipe, the rich smell of that English leather upholstery, and the taut, *right there* feel through the steering wheel and suspension. Every once in a while I'd double-clutch her down to second and lay into the gas, just to feel that big twin-cam six uncoil. Boy, it had more urge than any car I'd driven in my life! Why, I didn't make it back to my apartment until the sky was getting light. But who cared? Jaguar roadsters were just *made* for nights like that.

Naturally, I was groggy as hell when my alarm went off at 6:45 the next morning, and I had half a mind to shut it off, pull the covers up over my head, and go right back to sleep. But I'd promised Big Ed that I'd drive his Jaguar into Manhattan, and by God, that's exactly what I planned to do. Just as soon as I could find the damn keys. And my socks. And my toothbrush. And my cleanest remaining pair of undershorts. Truth is, I was stumbling around my apartment like a broken-down Bowery wino that particular ayem, and probably set a new world's record for bumping my head on the rafter beams. But an ice-cold shower and a couple cups of reheated, day-old coffee (*ugh!*) blew out enough cobwebs so's I could make it down the stairs, hop into Big Ed's Jaguar, and take off for the city.

Traffic was packed like a tin of sardines on the George Washington Bridge that morning, and it didn't take but fifteen minutes of bumper-to-bumper creeping before the needle on the Jag's temp gauge started climbing toward the peg. Yup, overheating all right. No two ways about it. In fact, by the time I pulled up in front of Westbridge, Big Ed's Jag was gurgling like a turkey with its throat cut and little wisps of steam were curling out from under the hood. Barry Spline heard the hissing in his driveway and wandered out to see what was up.

"Yer drove the bloody thing over 'ere during *rush hour?*" he gasped, watching Big Ed's Jag pee hot coolant all over his sidewalk.

"She's been overheating," I told him, "and Big Ed wanted me t'drive her over here and check it out."

Barry Spline sighed and slowly shook his head—the way mechanics do when you've proved beyond doubt that you have no mechanical sympathy whatsoever. "Jagyewahr one-twenties over'eat in traffic as a matter of routine bloody operation, Buddy," Barry explained. "Think of it as the car's way of telling yer it rather prefers the open road."

"But that's *crazy!*"

"Maybe so, mate, but a bloke's gotter be *sensitive* t'such things if 'e ever expects ter get along with a bleedin' Jagyewahr."

Well, I personally figured there ought to be some way to keep any damn car from overheating—maybe a bigger radiator core or a smaller fan pulley or a different thermostat or *something*—but Barry wouldn't even discuss it. He told me to have Big Ed run it with the heater on full blast—in the goddam *summertime!*—or, better yet, avoid routine commuting in an XK120 entirely. Boy, Big Ed's face was going to turn the color of a beefsteak tomato when he heard *that* little tidbit of professional Jaguar service advice. I asked Barry if we couldn't maybe try this or that to fix the problem, but he wasn't the least bit interested in any sort of mechanical improvements that didn't come direct from the

Jaguar factory in Coventry. "If there was a better bleedin' way ter do it," he sniffed, "I'm certain the lads at Jagyewahr would've sussed it out by now themselves." Over the years, I've observed a lot of that head-in-the-sand crap in new car dealership service departments. In fact, it's more or less universal.

While waiting for Big Ed's Jag to cool down, I noticed a real flurry of activity going on in the shop. There must've been two dozen cars packed in cheek by jowl and no less than five (or maybe even *six*) coverall-clad mechanics climbing all over them. And they were *hustling,* too, which seemed completely out of character considering the shop's normal pace of operation. MGs and Jaguars were getting oil changes, sparkplugs, grease jobs, brake shoes, and freshly balanced tires every-where you looked. I noticed Westbridge's latest foreign mechanic (the second of the two Hugos) bent over that torpedo-shaped Frazer-Nash, trying his best to balance the carburetors. That was no easy task, on account of the Frazer-Nash had no less than three Solex carburetors, and Sylvester had already advised me that even one Solex could give even a good mechanic fits. To make matters worse, the Frazer-Nash didn't have much in the way of mufflers, so Hugo II had to jam his ear right down into the carburetor throats to hear them hiss, and lis-tening to the exact pitch and volume of that hiss is the essence of ac-curate carburetor balancing. Now Sylvester had showed me that first day at Westbridge how a wise mechanic could use a length of rubber hose to keep his head a meaningful distance away while attempting to balance carburetors, but I guess Hugo II made a big point of never asking Sylvester *any*thing, and for sure Sylvester Jones was not about to offer advice where it wasn't wanted. Anyhow, the engine was ap-parently still a little cold (or maybe running a trifle rich) because all of a sudden it backfired—*KA-BANG!*—and damn near blew Hugo Two's right-side eardrum out his left-side ear.

"Oh, this one's a real bleedin' *genius,*" Barry muttered as we watched Hugo the Deuce reeling around the shop like he'd taken a solid right from Rocky Marciano. "Why, the idiot damn near *killed* Sylvester yesterday. Backed a bloody great Mark Seven inter the TC Sylvester was under. Almost knocked h'it clear off the jack stands!" He shook his head disgustedly. "Took out *both* bloody 'eadlamps on the TC and put a god-awful crease in the Jagyewahr's fender. 'E won't be here past week's end, that one won't. Mark my words."

"Why the heck don'cha just *fire* him?" I wondered out loud.

"Bloody can't," Barry shrugged. "Too much flippin' work t'finish by Friday."

That sounded a little odd, since getting cars back to customers on time had never been a real priority around the Westbridge Motor Car Company, Ltd. Not hardly. "What's the big rush?" I wanted to know.

Barry looked at me like I'd just arrived from outer space. "Bridgehampton," he said simply, like that one word should mean something to me.

"Bridgehampton?"

"Why, the S.C.M.A. races at Bridgehampton," Colin St. John chimed in from behind my back.

"The *what?*"

"The S.C.M.A.," Colin explained while oh-so-casually filling his pipe, "puts on a bit of a speed event at Bridgehampton every spring. Real wheel-to-wheel stuff, you know. Many of our best customers compete. It's *quite* the place to be."

"You mean actual *racing?!*"

"Righto, sport."

Boy, I could feel the old pulse picking up. "Jeez, that sounds *neat!* Say, where the heck is Bridgehampton, anyway?"

Colin pulled a stick match out of his jacket and struck it off the edge of the service counter. "Out on Long Island," he said thoughtfully, sucking through his pipe, "near the very tip."

"They got some kind of racetrack out there?"

"We race on the country roads around town, actually. You know, uphill, downhill, left, right, sweeping bends, tight hairpins. . . ."

"Jeez, don't the locals get kind of, you know, *upset?*"

"Certainly not. In fact, it's something of a major occasion for them." Colin leaned back against the doorway and folded his arms across his chest like a college professor. "The S.C.M.A. chaps have a sort of, um, *arrangement* with the local Lions Club organization. Charity and all that. Here," he said, pointing to a poster tacked to the fake maple partition between the Westbridge showroom and service department, "see for yourself." Sure enough, right in the middle were two wheel-to-wheel Jaguar 120s—charging right *at* you!—with hundred-mile-an-hour speed lines streaking off the fenders and huge dust clouds trailing off behind. Wow! In large type up at the top it said:

ROAD RACES
*** *Bridgehampton, Long Island* ***
SATURDAY, MAY 24

Underneath the drawing, in much smaller type, it read: *"Presented by the S.C.M.A. and the Bridgehampton Lions Club."* And at the very bottom, in the smallest type of all: *"By invitation."*

"Say, what the heck does S.C.M.A. stand for, anyway?"

"Why, Sports Car Motoring Association, of course," Colin said like you had to be from under a rock not to know. But I didn't care. I was too busy imagining what a herd of Jaguars might look like barreling flat-out toward a hairpin turn at a hundred-plus miles an hour.

Barry Spline nudged my elbow. "Wanter see the winning car?"

"The winning car?"

"Righto," Colin nodded.

"Hey, wait a minute," I protested. "How can you know it's the winning car if the race doesn't even happen till this weekend?"

"I'll lay yer a bloody fiver on it, mate," Barry grinned. "C'mon back and 'ave a look fer yerself." With that, Barry led me into the rearmost corner of the shop, and there, hunkered in the shadows, was the biggest, meanest, *toughest*-looking sportscar I had ever seen in my life. It was slippery jet-black with red wire wheels and roughly the same size and shape as the atom bomb they dropped on Nagasaki. It looked just as dangerous, too.

"Jee-*zus*, Barry," I gasped, "what the hell *is* it?"

"An Allard J2X, Buddy. Brand-new model fresh in from England last week."

My God, what a *beast!* The grille was nothing but a monstrous chromium sneer and there were scoops and vents and louvers chopped all over to let the heat breathe out (or cool air in, I couldn't figure out which). Plus you couldn't miss how they had the hood fastened down with no less than five butterfly clips and a pair of leather straps hefty enough to harness a prize bull. Whatever sort of motor was in there, they weren't taking any chances on it breaking out.

"Gee whiz, Barry," I asked in a dry-mouthed whisper, "what the heck kind of motor's *in* that thing?"

"See fer yerself, mate," Barry grinned, and set about unbuckling the straps. When he finally lifted the hood, my eyeballs damn near popped out of my skull. Stuffed inside that black monster was an enormous, hulking, made-right-here-in-America Cadillac V-8. Just like the one in Big Ed's Sixty Special sedan.

"B-B-But you said this was an *English* car...."

"English as the Queen, it 'tis."

"But this is a goddam *Cadillac* engine."

"Sure as bloody hell is," Barry grinned. "Sylvester and I just finished buttoning 'er in this morning."

"Sylvester and you?"

"Right," Barry nodded. "See, the chaps at Allard generally ship their cars across without engines. That way owners can put in whatever bloody pleases them. Some use Fords and some use Mercurys, but they're all great cracking American V-8s. Lots of bloody displacement. Bags of torque. Cheap to run. And reliable as a bloody ten-pound sledge."

I let out a low whistle.

"The owner wanted one of those new Cadillac 331s in this one. Bloody good choice." You could see this wasn't any garden-variety Caddy V-8, either, what with twin carburetors on a Detroit Speed Equipment manifold and a bright blue Scintilla Vertex magneto sticking up off the back of the block.

"What kind of horsepower d'ya think it makes?"

"Well, we've gotter bored and stroked to damn near six liters, so I'd reckon somewheres around 265," he shot me a wink, "give or take a few."

"Jeez, Barry," I wondered, "is it faster than a Jaguar?"

"Bloody hell *yes!* Why, just *look* at the bloody thing. There's not an ounce of fat on it! Not one. And do the bleedin' math. Six thumping liters to a tiddly three-point-four? No bloody contest."

Somehow, the idea of anything as blunt and ugly as an Allard outrunning Big Ed's sleek, double-overhead-camshaft Jaguar didn't sound right. Especially with a homegrown Detroit sedan engine under the hood.

Just then Sylvester shuffled over carrying a piece of throttle linkage. "This been one hell of a fuckin' deal," he growled, shaking his head. He positioned it between the carburetors and eyeballed it carefully. "Sheee-*it!*" he groaned, "I ain't got it right *yet!*" and went back to his workbench to shorten it up some more.

"We've been working on this bleedin' job three days solid," Barry said softly, "and it's been some bloody rough going for old Sylvester there. Why, yer should've *seen* the bleedin' thing when it rolled through the door. Nothing but a bloody chassis and body with a great empty 'ole in the middle."

You had to be impressed with something like that. I mean, it's one thing to take a car on a little test-drive and diagnose what's wrong, then tear a car apart, replace the bad pieces, and screw it back together so it works properly again. No sweat. But building from scratch is something else entirely. You have to be a real maestro to get away with that sort of thing. Every single part has to be measured and figured and worried over and cussed at a kazillion bazillion times before you get it right. If you ever do. And most guys don't.

You could see there was still a bunch of plumbing and wiring yet to be done, and I wondered out loud if they'd get it all buttoned up in time for the race that weekend. "Yer can bank money on it, mate," Barry assured me, patting one of the Caddy's valve covers. "Why, old

Sylvester's near got it licked already, and we've two bloody days in hand. Mark my words, Buddy. Yer lookin' at this year's winner at the bleedin' Bridgehampton road races." He sounded pretty definite damn about it.

I walked around to the driver's side and stared into the cockpit. "Say, Barry, d'you think I could maybe *sit* in it? Just for a minute?"

"Sure thing, mate. Climb aboard."

So I opened the flimsy aluminum door that was about the size of a cigar-box lid and eased myself inside. Geez, what a view! The dash cowling was shaped like the top of Jane Russell's swimsuit, and there was a little half-moon plexiglass windscreen mounted on top of each hump. Speedboat fashion, you know? The instrument panel was all done up in shiny, engine-turned aluminum, and you couldn't miss how the tachometer was right smack in front of the driver's nose while the speedo was way over on the other side where it couldn't do much except scare the bejesus out of passengers. What a swell idea! You would've thought the steering wheel and shifter came off a damn school bus or farm tractor or something, and it obviously took a lot of muscle and moxie to wheel a brute like this around. Which got me wondering precisely what sort of human being was planning to set himself down behind that little plexiglass windscreen come Saturday morning and mash that new throttle linkage all the way to the stops. "Say," I asked Barry, "who's gonna be driving this monster, anyway?"

"Tommy Edwards."

"Who's he?" I'd never heard of the guy before.

Colin St. John looked at me like I was a bad smell. "Tommy Edwards," he answered down his nose, "is *only* the premier Allard driver in the entire United States of America. Perhaps even the world."

"He's won the bloody Bridgehampton race two years on the trot now," Barry added. "And last year at Watkins Glen, as well."

I nodded like I knew what the hell Colin and Barry were talking about. "So," I said, "where'd this Tommy Edwards guy come from?"

"Well, he's English, of course," Colin said like it should be obvious, "but I believe he makes his home in White Plains these days. Don't know exactly what the fellow does for a living—if anything—but no question he's one *hell* of a decent racing driver. In fact, he drives for the factory team at Le Mans every year."

"Le Mans?"

"Over in France, don't you know? Biggest bloody motor race in the world."

"It *is?*"

"Without a doubt, young man. Without a doubt. Why, it's a full twenty-four hours long—night and day, day and night—*flat-out* and balls-to-the-wall against the greatest teams, fastest cars, and most skillful drivers in the world."

"Wow!" I said, my mouth hanging wide open. "And this Tommy Edwards guy has raced there?"

"Indeed he has. In fact, Tommy most usually shares a car with Sydney Allard himself. Why, they damn near won the bloody thing outright two years ago. Would've, too, but the transmission packed up and the poor devils had to run the last eleven hours in top gear. Rotten luck, that. But they came through to finish second in spite of it. Bloody gallant effort."

"That's *always* the bleedin' problem with Allards," Barry grumbled. "Can't find a bloody gearbox stout enough ter 'andle all the bleedin' torque. The monsters tear up whatever yer put in 'em."

"True enough," Colin agreed.

"They're 'ard on brakes, too," Barry added. "An Allard driver either learns to baby 'is brakes or 'e bloody well learns t'do without."

I swallowed hard, mulling over the potential consequences of 265 thundering horsepower and no brakes. "Jeez," I mumbled, "this Tommy Edwards guy must be pretty good."

"He's quite a bit better than *pretty* good," Colin sniffed, looking at his nails.

I laid awake the whole night trying to imagine what that twenty-four-hour Le Mans race might be like. I could see race cars hammering down a pitch-black midnight straightaway—the fast ones topping 150!—their headlamps burning furious holes into the night. And there *I* was, standing on the pit wall, watching *my* Allard bellowing out of the darkness and slithering to a halt right in front of me. Tommy Edwards (who looked exactly like Errol Flynn in the movie *Dawn Patrol*) jumped out, swiped a blackened hand across his brow, and informed me that first and second gears were gone. *Gone!* I leaped underneath while the rest of the crew gassed her up, but it was obvious the trouble was inside the box, so there wasn't anything I could do. Not in the middle of the race, anyway.

I watched my pit crew finish up—they were good lads, every one of them—and then my second driver (a dead ringer for David Niven in the same movie) climbed aboard. "Take care," I told him. "You've nothing left but top."

"Well then, we'll just have to make do," he grinned through one of those devil-may-care David Niven smiles.

"Right then. Off you go."

"Cheerio," David Niven shouted over the engine's growl and pulled away, slipping the clutch something awful. You could hear the busted gears gnashing around inside that poor transmission.

I climbed up on the pit counter and put my arm around Errol Flynn's shoulders. "It looks a bit dodgy at the moment," I told him in my best Earl-of-Passaic accent, "but I reckon she just might hold together long enough to win this bloody race." He smiled and thanked me, the hint of a tear glistening in the corner of his eye.

Of course the gearbox held together (what else?), and afterward everything went into one of those swirling Hollywood dissolves that ended with me up on top of a bunting-draped podium with a grimy Errol Flynn and an even grimier David Niven flanked to either side. The three of us were smiling and laughing and waving to the crowd, and it took an entire regiment of uniformed gendarmes with gold braid on their caps to hold the people back. Corks popped off a hundred bottles of the finest champagne, and Errol, David, and I toasted ourselves repeatedly. Meanwhile, beautiful French girls in cocked berets and slit leather skirts swarmed around us, begging for attention. They were all virgins (of course!) but the more adventurous ones would look you right square in the eye, wink, and smile. . . .

You must admit, I've got a pretty lively imagination when it comes to stuff like that!

5

BEATEN WITH
A CLUB

NEXT DAY Big Ed came in to pick up his Jaguar and I told him what I'd heard about those races out at Bridgehampton. Right away that big Cuban stogie started rolling from one side of his mouth to the other. Clear out of the blue, he asked if I'd like to join him on a little Jaguar excursion across Long Island for a personal look-see. *Would I!* He even said I could ask Julie along, which sounded better yet. Especially considering the amount of room you had in an XK120 once you had somebody the size of Big Ed Baumstein wedged behind the wheel. The notion of me and Julie riding out to the tip of Long Island and back with our laps mashed together had an undeniable appeal.

But one of Julie's cousins or neighbors or something was getting married that day, so no way would she consider it. In fact, Julie wanted *me* to dress up in a dumb suit and tie and tag along. Can you believe it? I mean, who the hell cared about some stupid old wedding in Jersey City—two people you don't even *know*, for Chrissakes!—when an actual hundred-plus-mile-per-hour, wheel-to-wheel sports car race was happening out at Bridgehampton the very same day. Get serious! But Julie had her heart set (you know how women are when it comes to weddings) and she got pretty upset when I told her I wasn't about to miss that race. She even cried a little. But it wasn't a *real* cry—just one of those pouty whimpers girls pull out of their bag of tricks when they realize you're not gonna do what they want you to do. The whole idea is to make you feel guilty, see, so that *next* time you'll cave in and take 'em wherever it is they want to go.

It's like an investment.

Big Ed wanted me ready by 5:30 ayem that Saturday morning, but I was up much earlier on account of I couldn't sleep too well. Excited, I guess. And maybe even a little guilty about Julie and her stupid damn wedding. Ever notice how women can eat and eat and *eat* at you—even when you know in your heart that you're doing exactly what you want to do? It's the damnedest thing.

Anyhow, it was still pitch-dark and there was no way I could fall back to sleep, so I just laid there, staring at the glow-in-the-dark numerals on my alarm clock and wondering why the hands barely seemed to move at all. I finally gave up about quarter past four, made myself a pot of coffee, and decided to put in a little housekeeping time, picking up the odd shirts, socks, and undershorts that were forever scattering themselves around my apartment. Sometimes I wondered where the hell they came from, you know? Especially the orphan half pairs of socks.

Needless to say, I was out front waiting a good half hour before Big Ed was due, and gee whiz, was it ever *quiet* out there. The sky was just turning that serious purplish-gray it gets right before sunup, and the only sounds were a few trucks rumbling along the highway a half mile away and some of my mom's insomniac birds fluttering around in the treetops. It made me think about her, you know, and how she looked standing there at the kitchen window with those dumb-ass Army surplus binoculars pressed against the glass, making goofy chickadee twitters with her lips all pursed together like she'd been sucking on a lemon. And for a second it was like I was really *there,* for sure, because I thought I smelled bacon frying and muffins baking and waffle batter rising up golden-brown in the griddle. You move away from home for the Saturday nights, but you can sure miss your mom's kitchen on a Saturday morning.

Then I heard the unmistakable growl of Big Ed's Jaguar tooling down the highway, and I could follow it with my ears as he turned off on Taft, cruised up the hill to Cherry—left on Cherry—and on down to Buchanan, where my aunt lives. Boy, it really got my blood pumping when Big Ed glided that XK120 up to the curb, all freshly waxed and glowing in the early light like polished ivory. He flashed me two halves of a smile with his fat Cuban stogie stuck in the middle, handed over a thermos of coffee, and off we went—without a word!—like we were on some mysterious secret mission that both of us understood.

We headed east out of Passaic under a mother-of-pearl sky, drinking coffee against the chill and watching the sun come up clear and fine behind the Manhattan skyline. It was a perfect late-spring morning, but I was glad I brought my jacket on account of Big Ed had the top down (natch) and there was plenty of cold wind spilling over and around the XK120's fighter-style windshield. On the other hand, the crisp air and light traffic sure agreed with the Jag's engine and she was running cool, sweet, and strong. Which of course meant Big Ed had a huge smile plastered across his kisser—stogie angled up at about 45 degrees—and I remember he was wearing this bright yellow cap with a gold Jaguar emblem embroidered on top. He got it out of some mail-order catalog from California. Believe me, they've got every kind of car shit you can imagine out in California. As we continued east, we started seeing more and more Jaguars and MGs and such heading our way, all piled high with picnic baskets and folded lawn chairs and other assorted racing paraphernalia. It was like there was some enormous foreign car magnet out on the tip of Long Island, pulling every damn two-seat roadster on the eastern seaboard towards Bridgehampton.

If you closed your eyes, you could almost feel the suction.

But the coolest thing was how those sporty-car people would wave and smile and flash their headlights and tootle their horns at us—like we were dear old close personal chums or something!—just because we were driving a damn Jaguar. That's all it took . . . we *belonged!* Naturally, we waved and smiled and tootled right back, and if it happened to be another XK120 (or if there was an especially pretty girl on board) Big Ed'd give a blast off the Maserati air horns he had me install behind the Jag's radiator. They came from that same mail-order outfit out in California, and I'm not exaggerating when I tell you the sound would lift you clear off the seat if it caught you by surprise. It was like a damn crash-dive alarm on a submarine!

Personally, I thought all this arm waving and horn honking and headlight flashing was really *neat*. I mean, Buick and Oldsmobile owners didn't do that sort of thing. Not hardly. And if (God forbid) your Jag was pulled over to the side with a flat tire or a duff fuel pump or a cloud of steam rising from the hood, another Jaguar driver would stop to help you out—even if he was on his way to his own kidney operation! Hell, a Buick owner could be lying in the middle of the road with his large intestine wrapped around his earlobes and nobody'd give the poor bastard so much as a courtesy head-swivel.

Anyhow, Big Ed and me made it out to the village of Bridgehampton a little before ten, and the whole damn town was absolutely up for grabs. There were banners flying and bands playing and people all over the place—*thousands* of them!—and cars searching for parking places everywhere you looked. Not all of them sports cars, either. Fact is, most of the cars clogging the streets of Bridgehampton that Saturday morning were ordinary Fords and Dodges and Chevys and Mercurys that the rank-and-file rubberneckers drove out to watch the races. They were parked bumper-to-bumper up and down the side streets and overflowed onto private driveways and front lawns where local fast-buck artists were charging a quarter or more for the privilege.

Of course, Big Ed figured his XK120 entitled us to something more than Ordinary Drool Spectator status, so he gunned right past the guys with the S.C.M.A. armbands who were halfheartedly directing traffic toward some empty fields about a mile outside of town. The armband people would take a gander at the Jaguar, see Big Ed grinning and waving his cigar around like we were somebody important, and finally leap aside when they realized he was not about to stop. Not hardly. A few of them were apparently a bit upset (at least judging by the names they called us and the way they shook their fists in the air) but at least none of them chased after us. It was slow going, though—like trying to drive down a carnival midway—and I had to keep one eye glued to the Jag's temp gauge. The needle would creep up past 200 every time we got bogged down a particularly dense herd of pedestrians, and then I'd give Big Ed a nudge in the ribs and he'd reach under the dash and punch the button for those Maserati air horns. Jeez, people scattered like we'd opened fire with a Thompson submachine gun!

We came to this big roped-off parking area just as the Jag hit full broil, and you could see it was Race Central on account of it was filled with more damn foreign sports cars than you ever saw in your life. At the entrance was this huge yellow-and-white tent full of laughing, jabbering, glad-to-see-you-how've-you-been S.C.M.A. sportycar types getting themselves signed up and organized for the day's activities. So naturally Big Ed pulled up smack-dab in front, right between a red XK120 drophead and this pea soup–green Mk. VII sedan. We weren't there ten seconds before this skinny little twerp with thinning hair and basset-hound eyes came barreling out of the tent full tilt, flapping his arms like he was trying to take off. "Wait! *Wait! WAIT!*" he wailed. "These spaces are re*served!*"

"Who sez?" Big Ed wanted to know.

"*I* do," the skinny guy shot back, leaning in over our windshield and staring Big Ed squarely in the kisser. "You simply *cannot* park here. It's im*poss*ible!"

"Oh, yeah? Why not?" You could see Big Ed didn't like this guy's tone one bit. Neither did I, come to think of it.

"Because these spaces are reserved for *official* cars." The guy had one of those nasally, upper-crust New England voices with sort of a permanent sniff to it. It was the kind of voice you'd just as soon have shut up, if you know what I mean.

Big Ed peeled his eyes around at the other two Jags. "Saaay, how d'ya know *this* ain't an official car, huh?"

"Nice try," the guy sneered, "but I know *all* the officials and *all* the official cars. Besides, you haven't got a sticker!"

"A sticker?"

"Yes, a sticker. An *official* sticker." He pointed a lump-jointed finger at the red Jag's windshield. Sure enough, down there in the lower lefthand corner was a silver-and-red wire wheel decal with SPORTS CAR MOTORING ASSOCIATION written across it in dark blue letters.

"Oh, really?" Big Ed snorted, not sounding particularly convinced. Then he opened his door and started to climb out.

"WAIT!" the skinny guy shrieked, his voice going up five or six octaves, *"Where do you think you're GOING?!"*

"Me?" Big Ed said calmly, closing the Jag's door behind him, "I'm goin' inta this tent here and see about gettin' me one a'those parking stickers." And with that, Big Ed walked right past the skinny guy like he was a fence post or something.

As you can imagine, this left me in a pretty awkward position, sitting there on the passenger side of Big Ed's Jaguar while this enraged parking-lot monitor glared at me full blast through his saggy little basset-hound eyes. I swear, he had his arms folded so tight across his chest that it must've damn near cut off the circulation. It didn't look like he was planning to stop anytime soon, so I eased myself out the other side of Big Ed's XK120 and more or less melted off into the crowd, eyeballing the scuff marks on my shoes along the way.

Things didn't look too interesting inside the tent—just a bunch of high-class sportycar people drinking coffee and smoking cigarettes and shooting the breeze while they waited in line at the registration tables— so I drifted off to reconnoiter the area and maybe snoop around the cars a little. The vast majority were the MGs and Jaguars I'd come to know from Westbridge, but there were others, too. Like that Frazer-Nash thing that won the big twelve-hour race in Florida. And maybe five or six of those brutal Allards from England that carried big all-American Ford, Mercury, and Cadillac V-8s under their bulging hoods. I recognized the shiny new black one with the red wire wheels that I'd seen Sylvester and Barry Spline buttoning together, and I sort of wondered how they were doing with it. You know how it goes when you throw something together in a last-minute panic. Right next to the Cad-Allard were these two delicate-looking French Bugattis with elegant horseshoe-shaped radiators and machined alloy wheels. They were sleek as sailboat hulls, even though I heard somebody say they were built way back in the thirties. Across from them was this incredible Alfa Romeo 2900 from Italy, which was also from before the war but still a hell of a lot more exciting than any of the new cars, you saw rolling off the assembly lines in Detroit. They had the hood up, and underneath was the most magnificent supercharged straight 8 I had ever seen, all done up in machined brass fittings and finned aluminum castings. Wow! Farther on were a litter of these runty-looking Porsches from Germany, all squatted down over their tires like puppy dogs taking a dump. They didn't look like much compared to the Jags and Allards (or even that old Alfa) but their owners seemed awful damn proud of them anyway. No kidding. And what a sound when all those different cars with all their different engines fired up and drove around the paddock. Each one had its own special voice and its own private song. It was like *music*, you know? For a guy who loved automobiles, the paddock at Bridgehampton was like a forty-acre dessert cart.

The only hard part was figuring where to look next.

Besides all the wonderful cars, there were real live big-screen celebrities meandering all over the place. Like who should I see standing next to a white SS100 Jaguar—not two feet away from me!—but that Dave Garroway guy from *The Today Show*. No lie! And I saw Jackie Cooper (I'm *sure* it was him!) yakking with a few of the armband people in the registration tent. And Robert Montgomery—you know, the movie actor?—was on hand to drive the brand-new Nash Healey pace car for all the races. Boy oh boy, I'd never been around so many famous, lah-de-dah people or snazzy, expensive automobiles in my entire life. Why, you could damn near *smell* the money. In fact, if you want the truth of it, it made me feel a little out of place. But those celebrity types blended right in with the S.C.M.A. club regulars. It was like they were all poured from the same mold, you know, all tanned and groomed and dressed to the nines in the kind of perfectly pressed "casual" clothes you see in glossy magazine ads featuring yacht parties and country-club golf outings and that sort of thing.

Poor Julie would've gone *nuts*!

Everywhere I looked around that Bridgehampton paddock, I saw people hustling like mad to get their stuff unloaded and their cars ready for the races. They were rummaging in toolboxes and stacking cases of oil and pulling off spare tires and folding down windshields (or even undoing a few bolts and taking them right off!) and laying out racing numbers with liquid shoe polish or rolls of white tape. You couldn't miss the buzz of urgency crackling in the air.

I noticed this intense-looking older guy squatted down in front of a white XK120 like Big Ed's, putting layer after layer of adhesive tape over the headlights. I kind of wondered what it was for, so I cleared my throat a couple times and asked.

"Hey, uh, 'scuse me, mister, but what the heck's all that tape for?"

The guy wheeled around and looked me up and down with flinty little eyes that had maybe a hint of mental disturbance in them. "It's for a *shunt*," he snapped—like it was obvious, you know?—and went right back to his taping.

"A *what*?"

But it was like he didn't hear me. He just kept layering on adhesive tape until the Jag's headlamps looked like lead characters from one of those old black-and-white Mummy movies. You could see the guy wasn't particularly handy, since not one single strip of tape went down straight or laid the least bit flat. But he compensated with sheer volume, and didn't stop until he had tape globbed on a half-inch thick over both lenses. Then he stepped back and eyeballed his handiwork like it was the roof of the damn Sistine Chapel. "*Purrrr-*fect!" he purred, rolling his *r*'s like a tomcat. "Just *purrrr*-fect." He swiveled around and flashed me this strange, misshapen smile with a gold tooth glittering in the middle of it. "It's for a shunt," he said proudly, puffing out his chest.

"A what?"

"A shunt. A spin. An off. A—heh heh—*misadventure* amongst the hay bales."

"You mean an accident?"

The guy nodded gravely, eyebrows pumping up and down. "It can happen, young man. Believe me it can. Should the worst occur—heh heh—we *must* keep shattered glass off the racing line. It could—heh—puncture a tire and cause *untold* mayhem." He waved his hand through the air so I might understand just exactly how untold the mayhem might get. Then he leaned in real close and snaked his arm around my shoulder. "This your first time, sonny?" he whispered, like we were parachuting behind enemy lines or something.

"Uh, yeah. It is. I came up with Bi—I mean, Ed Baumstein. He's got a white XK120 just like yours."

The guy's eyebrows just about popped off his forehead. "*Just like mine, you say? JUST LIKE MINE?!!* Do you realize what you're *saying*, young man?!"

I allowed as how I didn't, and without warning the guy launched into a fifteen-minute dissertation on the differences between an *ordinary* Jaguar XK120 roadster and an XK120M Special Equipment edition. Then we got to phase two: the important differences between an *ordinary* XK120M Special Equipment edition and this *particular* XK120M Special Equipment edition, which was a certified *ex-works* racing car. The very one, in fact, that Creighton Pendleton the Third drove to six S.C.M.A. production-class victories in 1951! I made a point of looking real impressed, even though I hadn't a clue what *M* stood for or what was so damn special about Special Equipment or who the hell Creighton Pendleton the Third was. Far as I could see, the only difference between this guy's Jag and Big Ed's was it had knockoff wire wheels and no fender skirts. Personally, I thought it looked kind of naked without the skirt panels over the rear wheels. But I didn't say anything. I mean, who wanted to encourage this guy?

Turns out I'd chanced upon the infamous Skippy Welcher, sole heir to the Welcher Waxout ear swab fortune. His real name was Reginald, but he got the nickname "Skippy" from the way his conversation regularly skipped from one topic to another. Often in midsentence. Skippy's family had piles and *piles* of money, and The Skipper was justly proud of the fact that he'd never worked a day in his life to earn any of it. Skippy Welcher was known as an "investment principal" in Manhattan, a "sportsman" in Connecticut, a "yachtsman" in Palm Beach, and a "pigeon" in Atlantic City, but the truth is he was nothing but a stinking-rich, ne'er-do-well nutcase who'd been born into more goddam money than he knew what to do with.

It made you want to puke, honest it did.

Turns out Skippy Welcher was one of the original founding members of the S.C.M.A. and made a big point of attending every single race, club meeting, and social event on the S.C.M.A. calendar. Then again, he didn't have much else to do, did he? This fine attendance record made him a real key fixture around the sport, even if nobody on the S.C.M.A. membership roster could stand to listen to him for more than two minutes at a stretch or look him in the eye while they were doing it. Believe me, people did a lot of staring off in the opposite direction whenever they found themselves around Skippy Welcher. He wasn't much of a race driver, either, in spite of being ignorantly confident behind the wheel and brave to the point of foolhardiness. The Skipper drove his cars with all the style and sensitivity of an ax murderer on a rampage, and most always found ways to break them, blow them up, or run them into the local scenery. Which is precisely why he loved the S.C.M.A., since nobody could deny him his inalienable right to be there, no matter how brutal, stupid, or ham-fisted he was behind the wheel. After all, he had all the necessary S.C.M.A. credentials: He was rich, he owned a bunch of neat cars, he showed up for all the club's events, and he hadn't killed anybody yet.

While I was standing there gawking, this chipmunk-faced geek with Coke-bottle glasses, orthopedic shoes, and baggy olive-green coveralls with M. F. embroidered above the pocket wandered over carrying a small red toolbox and a little piece of tan sisal floor mat rolled up under his arm. Turns out it was Milton Fitting, The Skipper's own personal race mechanic. He looked like a sort of grown-up version of Howdy Doody, and likewise moved as though his arms and legs were dangling from invisible guy wires. Skippy regularly referred to Milton Fitting as "my attendant" and "my squire" all the time (like The Skipper was Sir Lancelot of the Round Table or something) and I didn't much care for that at all. But it didn't seem to bother Milton. In fact, not much of *anything* seemed to upset that character, and you had to figure it was because he was off in his own little world most of the time. Somewhere slightly northeast of Neptune, if you catch my drift.

It didn't take long to reach the conclusion that Milton Fitting and Skippy Welcher were both nuttier than fruitcakes. But that's what made them such a perfect pair. Skippy Welcher needed a full-time wrench on account of he was forever bending, breaking, or blowing up his ex–works, ex-Creighton Pendleton XK120M, and likewise not too many car shops would carry a drool like Milton Fitting on the payroll. Oh, he could fix stuff all right, but he was without a doubt the *slowest* automobile mechanic I have ever seen. Bar none. Even the simplest jobs took him for*ever,* and I honestly believe he worked slower than the night-shift union stiffs at my dad's chemical plant in Newark. And those guys barely move at all.

I tried striking up a conversation with Milton—you know, one mechanic to another—but it was more or less like talking to a bowl of raspberry Jell-O. Like I asked him what carb needles he was using (just to show him I knew all about S.U.s), but all he did was gurgle and wheeze a little and stare back at me through a pair of glasses that made his eyeballs look like fried eggs. Never said a word. The Skipper made up for it, though. In fact, you couldn't shut the bastard up. Why, Skippy Welcher could peel off into fresh topics without so much as pausing to take a breath.

Which is why I was still standing there a half hour later, listening to a highly convoluted dissertation on the relative merits of vegetable-based versus mineral-based lubricants for dual-overhead-camshaft racing engines (like the one in his Jaguar, for example) and I might as well have been a cardboard cutout propped up with a stick. The Skipper really got himself worked into a lather whenever he got rolling on one of his favorite subjects, what with every muscle on his face popping and twitching like pea soup coming to a boil and sweat beads snapping off in all directions. And there was just no stopping the sonofabitch once he got up a head of steam. I was worried that Big Ed might be missing me, but there was simply no way to disengage yourself from Skippy Welcher once he thought he had your attention. It was like having your bumpers locked with a shit wagon. So, about halfway through The Skipper's *personal* recommendations concerning proper waxing and polishing techniques for authentic English paint finishes, I said, "Nice t'meetcha. Seeya. Bye," and simply walked away. When I looked back, Skippy was still hard at it, yakking away into the empty atmosphere as fast as he could make the words come out.

I found Big Ed back in the registration tent, huddled over a card table with that same skinny twerp who tried to shoo us out of the "official" parking spaces. His name was Charlie Priddle, and sure enough, *he* turned out to be the S.C.M.A.'s Membership Chairman. Oh, swell. In fact, Charlie Priddle was on every damn committee the S.C.M.A. had. And believe me, they had *plenty*. Now, you have to understand that Charlie never once drove in a car race—not *ever*—but for some inexplicable reason, he considered S.C.M.A. club activities the most important thing in his life. And no, I didn't understand it either.

Turns out Charles Winthrop Martingale Priddle came from some old, old, *old* Old Money up in Connecticut somewhere, and he owned maybe five or six of the latest, most expensive sports cars you could buy. Not one of which he could drive worth a lick. But Charlie bragged about his fancy European automobiles all the time, not to mention about how much better the *racing* was "on the Continent" and how much better the *food* was "on the Continent" and how his family originally came *over* "from the Continent" on the damn *Mayflower*. First-class, to hear him tell it.

Anyhow, Big Ed was trying to find out how he could join the S.C.M.A., and, without actually saying it in so many words, Charlie Priddle was making it clear he didn't much care for families who arrived in this country by way of Ellis Island or believed in any off-brand, non-Protestant religions or actually had to *work* for a living. Which was three strikes against Big Ed right off the bat. Not to mention that, in the short period of time they'd known each other, Charlie Priddle had developed a deep personal dislike for Big Ed that had nothing to do with his occupation, religion, or family background. So Charlie was giving Big Ed the runaround. And he was pretty damn good at it, too.

"Say, whazzit take to join this goddam club, anyway?" Big Ed was asking for maybe the sixteenth time, leaning forward so the business end of his cigar was maybe a half inch from Charlie Priddle's eyelid.

"Well, let's see," Charlie sniffed, looking Big Ed up and down like he was 300 pounds of horse manure. "First, you must of course own an example of one of the *recognized* marques. . . ."

"Whatsa *mark*?" Big Ed wanted to know.

"A marque is—hmm, what would *you* call it?" Charlie Priddle rolled his eyeballs like he was fishing for a word somebody as dumb and coarse as Big Ed Baumstein might understand. "A marque," he said at last, "is what a person such as yourself might refer to as the 'brand name' of an automobile."

"Oh, yeah?" Big Ed nodded. "Well, y'saw my Jag 120 parked out front."

"Ah, yes. Indeed I did. But you *also* have to be ap*prov*ed by the S.C.M.A. *mem*bership committee."

"So tell me," Big Ed asked without skipping a beat, "just how does a guy get himself approved by this here membership committee?"

"Oooh, they have to *vote* on it, of course."

"So how do I get voted on?"

"Oooh, I'm afraid they won't vote on *you*."

"Why not?"

"Because I'm quite *cer*tain your name won't come up."

"Whyzzat?"

"Because your name won't be sub*mit*ted."

"Submitted?"

"Of course. Every *new* club member must be *spon*sored by an ex-*ist*ing member. Can't you see? That's the only way *any* name can come before the members of our membership committee."

"Lookee here," Big Ed growled, biting into his cigar, "why don'cha just do us both a favor and put my name up t'yer damn committee, huh? Whaddaya say?"

"Oooh, I'm afraid I couldn't do *that.*"

"Why not?"

"Because I don't *know* you. And, more importantly, Mister Bomb-Steeen, I'm not quite sure you'd fit in. Besides," Charlie continued, delicately stroking his chin, "shouldn't you be off in one of your, uh, *sin*-a-gogs today?"

Boy, you could really feel the heat starting to rise off Big Ed.

But Charlie Priddle wasn't finished. He rolled his face upward with all the righteous sincerity he could muster in those basset-hound eyes of his. "You do *practice* your faith, don't you, Mister Bomb-Steeen?"

Big Ed's nostrils flared like a bull ready to charge, but he somehow held himself in check (Lord only knows how!) and when he finally spoke, the words came out so soft and carefully measured it was down-right scary. "I don't *need* t'practice, see. I do it fine already." Then he leaned in so close you about needed a feeler gauge to check the distance between Big Ed's nose and what remained of Charlie Priddle's hairline. "Now I'm gonna ask you one more time, Bub: *Will you put my friggin' name up t'yer friggin' membership committee or not?!*"

Charlie took a deep breath and eased his chair back out of Big Ed's shadow. "I'm afraid that's im*poss*ible," he sighed without looking up. "You see, I'm *chair*man of the committee. It wouldn't work out, don't you see?"

"No, I don't."

"Good. I'm glad you understand."

"But I DON'T understand!" Big Ed bellowed, slamming his fist down so hard it made the table legs buckle.

That startled the hell out of Charlie Priddle (not to mention every-body else in the tent) but I gotta hand it to the little pipsqueak. He didn't spook easy. In fact, he rose up out of his chair, squared his skinny shoulders, leaned right into the glow of Big Ed's cigar, and explained the way things worked in the S.C.M.A. real loud and slow—like you do when somebody doesn't understand English very well. "Look here, Mr. Bomb-Steeen," he said with a threatening tremble in his voice, "I have a lot of *very* important things to do today, and talking to you is definitely *not* one of them. So let me give you a little advice. There will be a tow truck outside this tent within the next three minutes, and I suggest you either move your automobile *immediately* or be prepared to

make separate arrangements with the Bridgehampton Police Department later on this afternoon. It's entirely *your* choice, Mr. Bomb-Steeen.
And now, if you will ex*cuse* me . . . ," and with that, Charlie Priddle sat
back down, buried his skinny Anglican nose in a stack of entry forms,
and started ignoring Big Ed. He was a true world-class talent when it
came to ignoring people.

6

THE BUG BITES

EVEN OUR run-in with that asshole Charlie Priddle couldn't put a damper on the swell day Big Ed and me had out at Bridgehampton. Oh, he was plenty pissed about having to move his car from our cozy spot in front of the tent to some local farm geezer's stinking weed patch damn near a mile and a half away. Especially when the guy charged us fifty cents to park there, just on account of we were driving a Jaguar. On our way back, Big Ed's fat Cuban stogie was about doing figure eights from one side of his mouth to the other, and you could almost hear the wheels turning under his bright yellow Jaguar cap. It was a question of class—yeah, *that* was it! Big Ed understood all about class, and was savvy enough to know he didn't have any. At least not the kind those tight-ass, nose-in-the-air S.C.M.A. bastards cared about. So what? He was *proud* of his family and religion (even if he didn't pay much attention to either on a regular, day-to-day basis) and how he and his cousin had built up that scrap machinery business—from *nothing!*— so he could afford any damn car he wanted. Or any car *club*, for that matter. He sure didn't enjoy getting the high-hat routine from a snotty WASP creep like Charlie Priddle. Not one bit. And Big Ed wasn't the kind of guy to take it lying down, either.

I tried to get Big Ed's mind off the situation by telling him I'd seen Dave Garroway and Jackie Cooper and Robert Montgomery, but I could tell he wasn't really listening. So I steered us over by Skippy Welcher and his ex-everything XK120M, just to give Big Ed a close-up personal glimpse of the kind of top-quality membership standards they had in the S.C.M.A. As you can imagine, Big Ed's eyes lit up like a pair of Marchal driving lamps when he saw The Skipper's Jag. "Say," he grinned, "I gotta XK120 just like this one."

Naturally, that got Skippy's face popping and twitching like there were weevils under the skin, and in less than a heartbeat he was off into that same rambling speech I got earlier about the many important differences between an *ordinary* XK120 and *his* goddam car—blah, blah, blah. It didn't take Skippy more than thirty seconds to start getting on Big Ed's nerves—especially since he had a habit of putting his face right up into yours and then talking loud enough so you could hear the sonofabitch two blocks away. You'd get wet, too, on account of The

Skipper always blew a little spit once he got up a head of steam. Not to mention that any discussion with Skippy Welcher was bound to be full of strange tangents, hairpin turns, mental bank shots, and twirling about-faces. I remember he was smack-dab in the middle of explaining why you should never, *ever*, use anything but genuine, high-altitude mountain air to fill racing tires ("Air's thinner and cooler up there—heh—with fewer impurities. That's why I have my squire Milton—heh—that's him over there with the tire gauge—heh—haul our compressor and tanks up to Bear Mountain every couple of weeks to get some for us. Y'gotta be over three thousand feet to get the really *good* stuff, of course. Makes an *enormous* difference on the track....") when he made one of his trademark conversational U-turns, put his hands up on Big Ed's shoulders like they were old long-lost Army buddies, and blurted out of his absolute sincerest misshapen gold-tooth smile, "You know, Mr. Blackstone—"

"Ah, that's *Baumstein,*" Big Ed corrected him.

But it was like The Skipper didn't hear him at all. "Yes, sir, Mr. Bockstein, I can't tell you how *thrilled* and *dee-lighted* I am to meet another Jaguar *aficionado.*" Then again, I bet old Skippy was always "thrilled" and "dee-lighted" whenever he got a run at a fresh pair of ears. By that time Big Ed had gotten himself a good, deep gander into The Skipper's eyes and realized that you could no way see bottom, so he and I made screwy finger and eyeball signals back and forth while The Skipper rambled on about all the races his car had won (none with him at the wheel, far as I could tell), how to clean wire wheels with your toothbrush, and the size of the larger bug splats he'd picked off his Jag's windshield after a good high-speed run.

Twenty minutes later The Skipper was still at it, explaining techniques for proper braking point selection ("Y'gotta find yourself a shut-off marker, see. Preferably in a—heh heh—*tight* sweater"), when this enormous black-over-silver Rolls Royce Phantom IV limo slinked into the paddock with a tarp-covered race car strapped to a trailer behind it. The sight of it stopped Skippy dead in mid-sentence (honest it did!) and you could see heads swiveling like gun turrets and hear tools thudding to the ground all over the paddock. I looked at Big Ed and he looked back at me as that mysterious Rolls limo glided past, ghostly silent except for the soft crunch of gravel under its tires and a faint, mouselike squeak off the trailer springs. Behind the wheel was an honest-to-gosh Park Avenue chauffeur, all done up in brass buttons and a peaked cap, but you couldn't tell who was in back because they had pleated wool curtains drawn over the rear windows. The Massachusetts license plate read CP3, and it was mounted above the only trailer hitch I have *ever* seen mounted on a Rolls Royce automobile.

The race car strapped on the trailer was even more intriguing. They had it all covered up with a fancy tan chamois tarp (which was even *tailored*, with special seams and darts and stuff to show off the car's shape) but you could see it had a lean, *muscular* sort of build to it, making the fabric stretch over the fender arches like those tight cashmere sweaters the Hollywood starlets wear. Even covered with a tarp, you knew this was no ordinary sports car. Not hardly. I sized it up as a good bit sleeker and lower to the ground than any Jag or Allard, and whatever it was, that tarp-covered race car was gathering itself one hell of a crowd as it toured slowly around the paddock. "Jeez, what the hell is *that?*" Big Ed wanted to know.

"Oh," The Skipper said grandly, "that must be Creighton Pendleton's new four-point-one Ferrari. Used to drive a two-point-six, but she didn't—heh heh—have enough of the old *steam* down the straightaways. See, y'gotta have that *BIG* horsepower for those long straightaways—heh—*always* gotta have the ponies." Then Skippy leaned in like he was letting us in on some big atomic secret or something. "You watch. Creighton'll blow everybody's doors off with that baby. Suck their headlights out. Make 'em eat dust. Run away and hide..."

But Big Ed and me were *gone,* off to join the crowd following that Rolls Phantom around the Bridgehampton paddock. Why, it was like some rich stiff's funeral procession, what with everybody shuffling along behind that shroud-covered race car on careful little steps and talking in those hushed funeral parlor whispers where your lips hardly move.

The Rolls/trailer rig made two stately parade laps around the paddock before pulling up next to a spanking white International Travelall with CARLO SEBASTIAN IMPORTS and a little Italian tricolor painted on the doors. Which instantly flew open and two swarthy, tough-looking southern Italian (or maybe Sicilian) types in matching white coveralls leaped out and sprinted toward the trailer. They had barrel chests and huge, hairy forearms, and they pounced on that mystery race car like hyenas on a fresh kill, shouting and arguing and cussing the living hell out of each other along the way: *"Ey, Stugatz, at's notta way!"*

"Waddaya mean, at's notta way?"

"You gonna droppada whole fuckin' ting onna groun'!"

"Ba fangu, Stroontz! You tinkin' widdayou dick again!"

"Yeah? I'm-a bedder tink widda my dick den talk outta my fuckin' asshole!"

"Yeah? Well why donnayou getta you ear down a liddle close, ey? I'm-a no tink you can hear me so good."

"Oh, yeah?"

"At's a'whaddeye said."

It kept up like that nonstop, and a couple times I thought it was going to actually break out in a fistfight. But it never did. And did those guys ever know what they were doing! In less time than it takes to tell, they had that trailer chocked, angled, ramps down and ready to unload. Another guy in white coveralls appeared carrying a special flannel-lined canvas bag for the car cover. Unlike the other two, he was thin, pale, and gangly, with thick wire-rim glasses and a perfectly matched set of enormous, flamingo-pink ears. He had a real whopper of a nose, too, but it was more one of your vulture-beak Hebraic models than the rounded, Roman Empire variety sported by the other two.

By this time, a crowd twelve- or fourteen-deep had gathered in all directions, and for exactly that reason the two tough-looking dagos changed tempo (just to get the proper dramatic effect, you know?) and very slowly—almost painfully—one of them lifted the rear corner of that chamois tarp and gingerly began rolling it back. You could almost feel a breeze off the mass intake of breath as the fabric gently peeled away: Underneath was the leanest, meanest, reddest, most dangerous-looking chunk of metal I had ever seen in my life. It was the color of arterial bleeding and shapely as a young woman's body, what with smooth, graceful fender lines and huge finned alloy brake drums—big as ash-can lids!—peering out from behind the wire wheels. When the tarp came off the front, I found myself staring into the wide-open jaws of a vicious killer shark! I tried elbowing my way around to get a better angle, and I swear the headlights on that car seemed to follow me like eyes. Why, you could damn near feel a *pulse* off that thing if you leaned in close against the fenders.

Above the grille was a small enameled badge featuring a wild black stallion reared up against a brilliant yellow background and the word "FERRARI" spelled out below in serious block letters. *FERRARI!!!* The name was like fire on your tongue.

With help from the other two, the mechanic with the big ears folded up the special chamois car cover (doing it four times lengthwise and then in neat little triangles, like a troop flag) and then more or less stepped off to the side while the two burly-looking guys eased the car down off its trailer like it was a damn concert grand piano, working the winch one or two clicks at a time and checking underneath every six inches or so to make sure the tires were still properly aligned on the ramps. The pale guy with the big ears just stood over by the panel truck, shifting his weight from one foot to the other and chewing nervously on his fingernails. My guess was they didn't trust him with much except tarp-folding duty, and it was easy to see why. He was one of those tight, jittery types who seem to drop things all the time and stumble over their own feet a lot.

About then one of the Sicilian mechanics popped the hood for an instant to give everybody in the peanut gallery a quick glimpse of the magnificent all-alloy Ferrari V-12 nestled underneath. What a motor! It had three Weber carburetors lined up down the center of the vee— each with its own louvered air cleaner—and the valve covers were done up in that crinkly black satin finish you usually find on expensive tele- scopes and binoculars and such. I was hoping they'd leave the hood open so I could move in for a closer look (or better yet, fire it up!) but it was just a tease for the crowd and the other mechanic closed the lid as soon as he'd checked the oil and water. After that, the vulture-beak guy brought them over a couple cold sodas and the three of them just kind of leaned back against the fenders (but *carefully,* since it was all hand-shaped aluminum alloy) and lit up a round of cigarettes. Real nonchalant, you know, as if nobody was watching them at all.

You could tell they really enjoyed the limelight.

Pretty soon we heard a bunch of little four-cylinders revving like a swarm of six-pound bumblebees on the other side of the paddock, and I sure as hell wanted to get over by trackside and see what was up. Big Ed had the fever, too, and in a heartbeat he was elbowing his way through the crowd, heading for the noise, plowing us a path that would've done credit to the Notre Dame offensive line. We finally broke through up against a wobbly stretch of snow fencing, about fifty yards downstream from the start/finish line. To tell the truth, it was nothing more than an ordinary small-town village street dressed up with a cou- ple K.L.G. spark-plug signs, some Shell Oil pennants, and a big banner strung across between a tree and a light pole that read:

S.C.M.A. BRIDGEHAMPTON SPORTS CAR RACES
Sponsored by the Lions Club of Bridgehampton

About then we heard the angry swarm of bumblebees again, and a whole jostling freight train of MGs, Porsches, and stuff I couldn't rec- ognize came roaring around the last corner and pouring down the straightaway. They blew past us at a giddy 65 or 70 miles per hour— engines twisted clear to the redline!—and in a flash they were gone and everything went quiet again. Big Ed looked at me and I looked back at him, and I swear both of us were blinking like we had short circuits in our eyelids.

Wow!

Big Ed bought us a souvenir program (which was all of four pages and cost him half a buck!) and inside was a map of the so-called Brid- gehampton Grand Prix Road Racing Circuit. Why, it was nothing more than four ordinary country roads stitched together in a squiggly sort of rectangle, and it didn't take long to figure out that the *real* action had to be out on the corners. So Big Ed bulled us a path down toward the first turn. It was really just a regular, everyday crossroad intersection where the racers made a sharp, 90-degree right off Ocean Road onto Sagaponack. The S.C.M.A. had fixed things up for the occasion by positioning three or four armband people with a bunch of colored flags on the inside and a few stacks of hay bales on the outside to keep overeager drivers out of the local scenery. Cars came barreling toward us—the faster ones doing damn near 90!—and somewhere along the line, each driver had to make a Major Personal Decision about removing his foot from the gas pedal and laying into the brakes. As you can imagine, the general idea was to stay on the loud pedal until the last possible instant, but you could see there were a *lot* of different opinions as to exactly where and when that might be. Plus they had to drop down a gear or two, and it obviously took a bit of skill to get that handled while you were pushing down for all you were worth on the brakes. Some of those guys were lurching and weaving all over the place as they desperately attempted to operate three pedals with two feet. But the really slick ones could "heel-and-toe," so they could goose the throttle for each downshift while simultaneously keeping hard, steady pressure on the brakes. It was sheer magic when a guy got it exactly right, hauling his car down straight and true while blipping the motor to match the revs for each lower gear. Hell, you could sort out the legit hotshoes just by the sound!

And you should've seen all the different driving styles! Some guys steered around that corner on tiptoe, like they were afraid it was gonna bite them. Some fought their way around in a jagged, sawtooth assortment of feints and darts. A few others would just grit their teeth, yank the wheel, and hang on for dear life. But you could pick out the fast guys easy. Why, they skated through that turn in a single, graceful swoop, greasing their way around like oil on ice.

It got even better when two cars charged toward us side by side, battling for position. See, the racing line turned pretty much single file through the corner (at least if you didn't want to ricochet off somebody's fender or go charging off through the hay bales, anyway) so a sort of *funneling* process had to take place. Very simply, it boiled down to who was gonna be last guy on the brakes. Like a big game of "chicken," you know? Only better.

That first session was for cars under 1500cc (which works out to about 90 Cubes American if you do the math) and the great majority were MG TCs and TDs. But they were in against those tubby little Porsches from Germany, and far as I could tell, the Porsches had them *covered*. Sure, they looked like ripe tin fruit and sounded worse than a fart in a bathtub, but those things were *fast*. In fact, this one guy in a stripped-down, bare aluminum Porsche roadster had the legs on everybody. The owner/driver was a guy named Hoffman, and I overheard as how he was some kind of major bigwig European sports car importer in Manhattan. No question he'd imported himself one hell of a fast automobile with that tin-silver Porsche. The thing I didn't understand (at the time, anyway) was how one Porsche or MG or whatever could be so much *quicker* than another Porsche or MG or whatever. I mean, they were basically the same, right?)

In a pig's eye.

Why, a sharp mechanic could even *hear* the difference! Some of those Porsches and MGs sounded a whole lot healthier than the rest. All lean meat, you know? And that intrigued me, the idea that you could *build* yourself a better Porsche or MG or whatever than the next guy. Take that tin-silver Porsche, for example. You could see how it was stripped to the bare bones (they didn't even *paint* it, for gosh sakes, which I suppose makes sense if you've ever hefted a can of paint) and its engine note was a whole lot crisper than any of the other German piglets. That Hoffman guy looked to be a pretty decent driver, too, even though he'd lock the brakes now and then or maybe drop a wheel in the dirt every few laps. Then again, he was pushing pretty hard.

After the small-bore practice, the armband people strolled out to perform their well rehearsed Inspection of The Pavement ritual (like what they were doing was real scientific and important, you know?) and then the *big* cars came out to play. Jee-*zus*, what a spectacle! We heard them thundering out of the paddock from damn near a mile away, and it was the kind of sound you never, *ever* forget; the Jag sixes blaring like the brass section from hell and the gut-rumble of the Allard V-8s throbbing right up through the ground we were standing on. And then came a voice above all the others: a perfectly meshed howl that was more teeth and claws than iron and steel. Of course it was Creighton Pendleton's new Ferrari V-12, snarling up through the gears like something escaped from a cage.

And that Creighton Pendleton character could *drive*. He started at the very back (on purpose, most likely) and carved his way up through the field like there was nothing to it, passing car after car until he'd gotten around damn near everybody. Looked smooth as silk doing it, too, leaned back all calm and relaxed behind the wheel with his head cocked ever so slightly to one side. Why, the sonofabitch made it look *easy*. Far as I could tell, the only car anywhere near as quick was that new Cad-Allard from Westbridge with Tommy Edwards at the wheel. But he didn't look smooth at all. Not hardly. In fact, you didn't have to be much of an expert to see that he was fighting that beast every inch of the way. He'd haul it down for the corners with the brakes snatching every which way, grab himself a handful of lock, and heel it *hard* into the turn. And the car would fight him *back,* bucking and snorting and pawing the air with its inside-front wheel. *Wow!* But once Tommy got it pointed straight again, he'd put the spurs to the hot-rodded Caddy under the hood and that monster would damn near *take off,* snaking side to side from the wheelspin and bellowing like a bull elephant. He'd be over the next rise before you could so much as blink! To tell the truth, driving the absolute limit in a Cad-Allard didn't exactly look like ha-ha fun. But it was sure as hell spectacular to watch, no two ways about it.

After practice Big Ed bought us each a couple hot dogs and we wandered our way back through the paddock to nose around the race cars. Everywhere you looked, people were crammed under fenderwells or armpit-deep in engine compartments, hustling to get things ready (or just back together!) in time for the afternoon races. As I told you before, a lot of these so-called "pit crews" were nothing but wives and cousins and next-door neighbors and old school chums, so not too many of them were particularly keen when it came to actual hands-on, nuts-and-bolts mechanical stuff. Not hardly! In fact, it was difficult for a legitimate *professional* grease monkey to keep a straight face. Sure wish I'd had the Band-Aid, iodine, and burn ointment concession at Bridgehampton that day!

I noticed Barry Spline and this guy in an Army jacket thrashing away like madmen on that black Cad-Allard from Westbridge, so naturally I waltzed over to see what was up. They were in dead trouble all right, what with the brakes torn apart and pieces scattered all over the ground. Looked like the linings had more or less disintegrated right off the shoes (lousy riveting job was my guess) and Barry and the Army jacket guy were humping like crazy to get new ones installed in time for the afternoon race. Boy, you could sure feel the urgency of A Big Job and No Time Left sizzling in the air.

I asked the guy in the Army jacket if I could maybe help out (you could see right off he wasn't much with a set of tools) but he just snarled at me like a chained German shepherd and waved me away. Nasty, too, on account of he was having one devil of a time with the return springs. So I stuck my hands in anyway and showed him how an *experienced* foreign car mechanic could hook them up in a jiffy (without putting holes in both thumbs!) and in two shakes he was up and out of the way so I could get the job done properly. "How yer doin', mate?" Barry Spline called over from the other side of the car.

"Real good," I grunted as I wrestled one of the Allard's huge aluminum brake drums back into place.

"Bloody glad yer could make it, Buddy. Right on time, too. Think yer can get that side screwed down by yerself?"

"Piece of cake, Barry. Piece of cake."

"There's a good lad."

So Barry and I got the front brakes buttoned up, reset the click adjusters on the rears, and finished up with plenty of time for the Army jacket guy to sit behind the wheel so's we could bleed a couple quick squirts through the hydraulics. We had him pump the pedal a couple times to build up pressure and then lean on it hard while we opened the bleed screws in perfect unison with our thumbs pressed over the holes so no air could leak back into the system. It's messy that way (and no good at all if you've gotta live with the floor where you're working) but it's sure as hell quick. Then we topped up the brake fluid, ditto the oil and water, checked the tire pressures, gave the knockoffs one final make-sure slap with the hammer, and finished up in what must have amounted to an all-time world's record for an Allard J2X brake job, if only somebody'd had a watch on it.

Hey, what do you expect from a couple *professionals?*

While we were bleeding the brakes, I had a chance to check out Mr. Army Jacket in the driver's seat. It was an R.A.F. jacket, actually, and the guy inside it was a broad-shouldered Englishman with ruddy cheeks, a pencil-thin mustache, and eyes like a fighter pilot. Which, it turned out, is precisely what Tommy Edwards was during the war years, personally downing eight German fighters (and going down twice himself "the bloody 'ard way," according to Barry Spline). Sure, he didn't look much like Errol Flynn or David Niven, what with thinning salt-and-pepper hair slicked back across the top of his head and the beginnings of a middle-aged paunch rolling over the top of his trousers, but you could tell from the moment you looked in his eyes that Tommy Edwards had whatever kind of moxie it took to drive a racing car. Even a musclebound brute like that Allard.

After we were done with the final flight check, Tommy clambered out and walked right up to me. "Hey, thanks an awful bunch, sport," he said with a smart British clip to his voice. "I'm afraid I might have been a bit rude to you when you first popped over...."

"Aw, that's okay," I told him.

"No, really. No bloody excuse for that type of behavior. Not at all."

"'E's useter worse, Tommy," Barry grinned. "Yer can bank on it."

"Well, we couldn't have bloody well done it without you," the Royal Air Force jacket continued, extending a freshly manicured hand with little halos of grease under all the fingernails. "Can't tell you how much we appreciate it." Boy, he had a grip like a damn bench vise!

"Aw, it wuz nothin'."

"For *you*, perhaps," Tommy Edwards laughed, "but I'm all bloody thumbs when it comes to mechanical things. Ask Barry."

"It's God's truth," Barry agreed, wiping his brow with the back of his hand and leaving a spectacular grease smear all the way across his forehead.

Tommy looked at the black smudge over Barry's eyebrows and shot me a wink so quick I hardly saw it. "Well," he sighed, tossing a weather-beaten green racing helmet into the passenger side, "I'd best be getting off. Want to be on grid when Mr. Pendleton arrives so I can put the needle in a bit."

"Think yer can put him off his game?"

"Oh, I doubt it, actually. He's a pretty cool customer behind the wheel. Then again, it's always fun trying. . . ."

"Well, 'ave yerself a good run. And try ter bring the bloody car back in one piece, eh?"

"That is *always* my intention, Mr. Spline," Tommy nodded with a little two-finger salute. Then he turned to me. "Thanks again for lending a hand, sport. Ever so much. Never could have done it without you. No bloody way a'tall."

"Hey, no problem," I told him again, the color coming up in my cheeks.

"You be sure and pop by for a cold one after the shooting stops, uh . . . bloody hell, I don't even know your name."

"'Is name's Buddy Palumbo."

"Well, Mr. Buddy Palumbo, thanks again for saving the day. As I said, I'm not very much good at mechanics. . . ."

"Yer can bloody well say that again!" Barry snickered.

"Very well, Mr. Spline, I believe I shall." And with that, Tommy Edwards took a deep breath, raised his jaw skyward, and bellowed, *"I'M NOT MUCH BLOODY GOOD AT AUTO MECHANICS. NOT MUCH BLOODY GOOD AT ALL!"* Jeez, it made people all around us drop what they were doing and stare. "There," Tommy said with a sharp military heel-click, "*that* ought to put a proper cap on it, I should think. I trust you're satisfied, Mr. Spline?"

"Suits me," Barry agreed from beneath his magnificent grease smear, "'owbout you, Buddy?"

"Well," I said, trying to get just the right hint of swagger in, "I *guess* so."

"Very well," Tommy nodded, "that should do it. Oh, and Mr. Palumbo?"

"Yes?"

"Do see if you can find Mr. Spline here a bloody mirror and a handkerchief, won't you?"

As you can tell, we were getting a pretty good charge off the feeling of a job well done and finished in the nick of time. Believe me, there's nothing like it. In fact, as I watched Tommy fire up that hot-rod Caddy—Jee-*zus*, it made the damn *ground* shake!—and roar away, I realized my hands were trembling and my mouth tasted like I'd been chewing on a roll of medical gauze. That's how *pumped* you can get when a race is on the line and you've only got thirty minutes to finish a job that books two hours-plus in the flat rate manual.

With Tommy safely on his way to the grid, Barry and me decided to head over by trackside to watch what was left of the small-bore contest. Along the way, I asked why he didn't bring Sylvester Jones along to help out with the wrenching. "Oh, we couldn't do *that*," Barry said, raising his eyebrows like it should have been obvious. "Why, Sylvester'd be a bit of a bloody, er, *problem* 'ere at Bridgehampton. After all, we don't exactly wanter *advertise* that we've got a bleedin' Jungle Bunny workin' on people's Jagyewhars, do we?" Looking around, I could sort of understand what Barry was talking about. I mean, you didn't see anybody like Sylvester Jones in the paddock at Bridgehampton. Not hardly. Or many like Big Ed either, come to think of it.

Anyhow, we muscled our way down to turn one, and sure enough that Hoffman guy in the tin-silver Porsche was way out front. Second place, damn near forty seconds back, was a nifty little Italian job called an OSCA. It was bright red (what else?) and quite a bit prettier than the Porsche. Made a nicer noise, too. But it wasn't near as quick (at least not with that particular driver behind the wheel) and so that hopped-up, stripped-down Porsche was simply running away. Not much of a contest, if you want to know the truth of it.

But things were hardly dull, since we had a whole passel of TCs and TDs scrapping for the MG-class honors farther back, and those guys were really going at it. In fact, there was one certified lunatic in an old green '47 TC who single-handedly kept the crowd on its feet by braking so late and hauling into the corners so incredibly deep that everybody figured he was going to wind up in the hay bales. But he never did. And was he ever exciting to watch! Lap after lap, he'd wait until he was almost *in* the damn corner before laying on the brakes, then snatch her down a gear, toss the car sideways, and *drift* his way through in a wild, shuddering slide, barely kissing the dirt at the exit every time. Wow! Not that it did him much good, since the motor was loading up real bad through the middle of the corner (float level or needle-and-seat, most likely) so it stumbled and ran rat all the way down the straightaway.

What can you do?

Big Ed's program said the driver was a guy named Calvin Car-

rington from Palm Beach, Florida, and believe me, he was braver than
Dick Tracy. But, like I said, his car wasn't much good, and no question
he was driving a little *past* the ragged edge of control in a desperate
effort to make it up. Which is probably why he went missing about
halfway through the event. "Yer can't carry a bloody car on yer back,
mate," Barry sighed. "No driver on earth's so bleedin' great 'e can make
the bloody metal do more than it's willing."

There was an important lesson in that.

And speaking of lessons, the guy in the tin-silver Porsche had the
race all sewed up, but didn't have the smarts to just back off and cruise
to an easy win. No sir. Why, he was shifting at the redline, braking at
the last possible instant, dropping a wheel off the pavement here and
there . . . and then he simply didn't come around. There was just this
big, empty silence where the Porsche should have been, followed about
forty seconds back by that pretty little OSCA, tooling along all by its
lonesome, leading the damn race! The Porsche was nowhere to be seen.
Then came another long silence and the quickest of the MGs zipped
past, still battling each other tooth and nail, and behind them (at long
last) the tin-silver Porsche reappeared with its left-front fender all crumpled to shit. I couldn't believe it! Seemed like it was still running okay,
since it managed to pick off most of the MGs before the checker fell,
but that slick little OSCA was long gone. Boy, I bet that Porsche driver
felt stupid. I mean, he had the race in the bag. And so I learned the
next of my invaluable motorsports lessons: *it's not who goes fastest at first,
but who FINISHES first at the end!*

There was a lot of cleanup work to be done between races, including deceased-car removal for Calvin Carrington's ratty but spectacular
'47 TC, which had lost a front wheel and clobbered the hay bales out
on the backside of the course. Big Ed bought Barry and me a couple
nickel sodas (at a quarter *each!*) from some pop vendor who was working on his early retirement plan at Bridgehampton that weekend, and
then we strolled over to check the grid for the big-car feature. I was
proud to see Tommy Edwards's Allard on the front row (I mean, he
was *my* driver now, right?) but right next to him was that Creighton
Pendleton character in his blood-red Ferrari. "That's sure one hell of
an automobile," I observed with a low whistle.

"Yer bloody well right about that, mate," Barry nodded. "All-alloy
Vee-twelve. Over'ead cams. Triple Webers down the middle. The 'ole
bleedin' lot. She'll be a man-sized load for our boy Tommy t'manage.
No doubt about it." Then Barry leaned in a little closer and added,
"'E's a stuck-up bastard, that Creighton Pendleton is, but the bloke can
bloody well *drive* . . . ."

"Saaay," Big Ed wanted to know, "how much does one a'them Ferrari things *cost,* anyway?"

Barry Spline rolled his eyes. "Damn near three times a Jagyewahr one-twenty." *Three times!* "And that's *if* yer can get yer 'ands on one."

Even Big Ed had to be impressed with that.

Lined up behind Creighton Pendleton's Ferrari and "our" Cad-Allard were a few more Allards with assorted Cadillac, Ford, and Mercury engines, followed by a whole squadron of Jaguar XK120s mixed up with a couple of those cycle-fendered Frazer-Nash things and some oddball stuff I didn't recognize. Our friend Skippy Welcher and his ex-everything XK120M were situated back toward the end of the grid (occupying the outside slot on the second-to-last row, in fact) and it did my heart good to see the old asshole doing so poorly. I'd never been around the start of a big-bore sports car race, and it I must admit was pretty damn exciting. First everything was quiet, with just a few desperate, last-minute *whaps* of brass-head hammers on knockoffs to punctuate the hushed chatter of the S.C.M.A. officials and some off-the-cuff wisecracking between drivers gridded side by side. Then one of the armband people circled his arm in the air and all those mighty engines exploded to life—Jee-*zus*, it sounded like a damn artillery barrage!— and then that Robert Montgomery guy in the brand-new Nash Healey convertible led the pack around on a parade lap. You could tell he had a thing or two to learn about racing engines, because he took it so slow that a lot of those cars were steaming hot and snorting back through the carburetors by the time they lined up again at the start/finish line. And there they sat, glistening in the sun, twenty-six of the newest, fastest, most exciting sports cars in the world. Waiting . . .

Right on cue, this important-looking stiff in a sort of Great White Hunter outfit (no kidding!) marched up between the rows of cars with a large green flag rolled up under his arm. He did a smart about-face when he reached the front of the pack, keeping the flag hidden behind his back, and engines revved like crazy as twenty-six left feet poised hair-trigger to sidestep their clutches at a split-second's notice. But the Great White Hunter guy just stood there, glaring back at them, waiting to see if anybody was going to flinch. Engines raced even higher, and just as I was preparing to dodge a meteor shower of connecting rod fragments, the Great White Hunter whipped out the green and waved it like his arm was on fire. Clutches popped, engines screamed, and tires shrieked in protest as the field exploded toward corner one in a haze of burning rubber and castor-oil fumes. I thought Tommy's Allard got the jump off the line, but then I saw Creighton Pendleton's Ferrari nip inside as the pack disappeared from sight. "Hey!" I hollered. "Let's go watch down by the corner." Big Ed nodded and began bulling us a path toward turn one, and we were about halfway there when the pack blasted by again, with Creighton Pendleton's Ferrari on the point and "our" Allard right on his decklid. And you wouldn't *believe* the blessed noise, what with the hot-rod Caddy's angry gut-rumble all twisted up around the wild animal howl of that twelve-cylinder Ferrari, both of them W.F.O. (Wide Fucking Open!) and straining for more. Why, it was enough to crust your jeans, honest it was!

Next lap, the Allard was in front—*just*—with the Ferrari right up his tailpipes and crowding to get by. You could see Tommy was having to battle that brute every step of the way, and no question the Ferrari looked every bit as fast (or maybe even faster) and a *lot* less work to drive. It braked without slewing all over the road and went through the corners in neat, nicely balanced drifts instead of bucking and snaking every which way like a rodeo bull. In fact, you got the notion that Creighton Pendleton was just playing cat and mouse with Tommy Edwards. But every time he sneaked into the lead, Tommy'd put on a wild-ass charge and somehow manage to get him back again. I swear, they must've swapped positions a dozen times—maybe more!—and the crowd was whooping and hollering every time they came by like it was the final minute of an Army-Navy football game.

What a *race!*

But a hundred miles at Bridgehampton is a long, *long* way, and by two-thirds distance Tommy was trouble with the brakes again. You could see he was having to back off earlier and earlier for the corners, and it was only a matter of time before Creighton Pendleton pulled alongside, gave him a little "I told you so" finger wave, and motored off into the distance. There wasn't a damn thing Tommy could do about it. But he hung on and finished second (*with no brakes left at all!*) and you had to give him credit. Not many drivers know how to ease off and keep their cool when things get really desperate and first place is on the line.

Why, some guys can't even keep their wits about them muddling along at the back of the pack! Take Skippy Welcher, for example. He was soldiering on in his customary position near the tail of the field when Creighton Pendleton came up to lap him toward the end of the race. I guess the sight of that red Ferrari looming up in his mirrors got The Skipper a little excited. Or perhaps he thought it was time to show the world that *he* could go through a corner just as fast as the leader. Which, of course, he couldn't. Or maybe Skippy simply forgot where one of his precious braking markers was. Whatever the reason, The Skipper came charging into turn one *waaay* too hot, realized he was in over his head, and slammed down full force on the brakes (instantly locking all four, so now he couldn't steer, either). The Jag slewed left-right-left and snap-spun into the hay bales—*KA-WHUMPHFF!*—showering straw and dust all over the place. Creighton Pendleton had to make a Phenomenal Avoidance so as not to collect The Skipper broadside, and instantly we had armband people chasing around in all directions, blowing whistles and waving yellow flags and tossing chunks of busted hay bale off the racing line. To tell the truth, there wasn't much in the way of serious damage—just an ugly ding in the Jag's rear fender and a busted taillight lens—but the crowd went absolutely bug-nuts, cheering and hooting and clapping as Skippy reversed out of the hay, flashed his misshapen gold-tooth smile, waved to his imagined legions of fans, and fishtailed away, scattering straw and terrified S.C.M.A. corner workers in his wake. What a moron.

Creighton Pendleton went on to win the race easily, with Tommy's brakeless Allard a distant second, and afterward he paraded around on a victory lap accompanied by, without question, *the single most gorgeous female creature I had ever seen in my life!* Her hair was the iridescent chestnut of a Kentucky Derby winner, and I swear you could catch the sparkle off her smile from the far side of the fences. The two of them made quite a pair, laughing and smiling and waving to the crowd—checkered flag snapping in the breeze—looking like some sort of bill-board advertisement for a life the rest of us poor slobs could only dream about. When they disappeared over the next rise, everything went terribly quiet, like after the circus closes down.

Neither me or Big Ed felt much like leaving, so we headed over by the start/finish line to check out the trophy presentation. To tell the truth, it was a pretty dull affair, since the S.C.M.A. had trophies to hand out down through sixth place in a bewildering assortment of classes, not to mention all sorts of special awards for Sportsmanship and Hard Luck and Best-Looking Car and Furthest Distance Traveled (which went to some masochist who drove his TD all the way from Nebraska!) and Lord Only Knows what else. The important thing was for every single S.C.M.A. driver to get some sort of pewter cup or dangly trinket to hang on the old mantelpiece back home. And if you somehow didn't manage to *win* anything, a bent or broken race car was almost as good. Just so long as you had something to brag about in the bar after the racing was over.

Unless you were Cal Carrington, that is. That poor kid looked absolutely shell-shocked, walking around and around his busted-up TC with his head in his hands, trying like hell to figure out what he was going to tell his father. You could see from his clothes that Cal Car-

rington came from some pretty serious money, but it didn't take Sherlock Holmes to figure out he'd put that ragtag MG together out of
embezzled college money and gone racing on the sly. And now it was
in pretty sad shape, what with the fenders bashed in and the steering
gear skewed hard left on the right side and hard right on the left (sort
of pigeon-toed, you know?), not to mention that the brake drum was
ground through to the shoes on the side where the wheel came off. No
question that TC looked pretty damn grim.

And so did Cal Carrington. He was a lanky, good-looking kid with
sun-blond hair, Bass Weejun loafers, and eyes as blue as the Pacific
Ocean on a picture postcard from Hawaii. He didn't look a day older
than me, so he must've had himself a top-notch line of bullshit (along
with an exemplary set of phony I.D.s) to get the S.C.M.A. regulars to
let him race. Of course, Cal *was* from a good family, and that always
counted for a lot with the S.C.M.A.

I walked around that old TC a few times, and it didn't take more
than a single tour to reach the conclusion that Cal Carrington didn't
know jack shit about automobile mechanics. Why, he was worse than
Old Man Finzio! Like the reason that tire parted company with his car
and put him into the hay bales was because the rim had come completely
unlaced from the hub. That has a habit of happening when you don't
bother to check the spoke tension on wire wheels every now and again.
But this was front-page news to Cal when I explained it to him. "Gee
whiz," he said, "I sure wish I'd known about that. Why, my old man's
gonna *kill* me when he sees this."

Considering the way Cal drove that old heap before the wheel came
off, I felt like maybe doing a little something to help him out. He was
one of those helplessly handsome all-American-boy types you just can't
help liking, even though it'd drive you nuts how Cal never seemed to
have any cash in his pockets—not *ever!*—even though he came from a
wealthy family. And it'd also make you crazy how Cal never seemed
to get dirty when he worked on cars. Even scruffy old shitboxes like
that ratty TC. It was like grease just wouldn't *stick* to him! Plus he was
one of those infuriating natural athelete gazelle types who could jump
over any obstacle on a dead run or one-hand a set of keys whenever
you tossed them over.

I swear, sometimes it made you want to tie his shoelaces together.

Anyhow, I noticed a New Jersey tag on the back of the busted TC
and a little light popped on in my head. "Say," I asked, "you come up
from Jersey?"

Cal nodded.

"But the program says you're from Palm Beach."

"Aw, that's just my uncle's winter place. I put it down on the entry form so they won't send any newsletters or race results or anything to my folks' house. Why, they'd ground me for*ever* if they ever got wind I was racing."

"Don't you worry your uncle might say something?"

"Nah, not really. He's dead."

"Then who lives there?"

"Oh, just the servants, mostly. I guess we go down now and then in the wintertime, and so does my mom's sister."

"And they never see the mail?"

"Nah. I got a deal with the gardener. He burns everything addressed to me."

"You have to pay him off?"

"Not necessary. I saw him with my older sister once. He's happy to help out. Besides, he likes me."

I'd only known Cal for five minutes, but I could see why. He was just that kind of guy. "So," I asked him, "whereabouts you live back in Jersey?"

"Cedar Grove. Why?"

"Why, that's *perfect!*"

"It is?"

"*Sure* it is! I work at a Sinclair station over in Passaic. I'm a mechanic, see. In fact, I'm the *head* mechanic around our place...."

"You *are?*"

"Sure am," I nodded, showing off my knuckles as proof. "And if you can get this heap towed over there, I'll be glad to help you fix it up to go racing again." You say stupid stuff like that when you've just gotten your first taste of racing and it's still buzzing around in your head like a hornet in a glass jar. You'll notice I didn't consider for one solitary second what Old Man Finzio might think of the idea.

"Gee, that'd be *great!*" Cal whooped. But then his eyes narrowed and he looked at me kind of sideways. "Now, you gotta understand, I don't have a lot of, um, *ready cash* on hand for parts or anything...."

Big Ed cleared his throat. "Well, I could maybe see my way clear to lending ya a few dibs. Just t'help out, see. Yer *good* fer it, aint'cha?"

Cal looked down at his shiny Bass loafers. "Yeah. Sure I am... *eventually.*"

Big Ed pulled out a wad of cash thick as a ham sandwich and peeled a couple crisp greenbacks off the top. "You be sure I get this back, bub, or else..."

"...or else he'll use your head for a bowling ball!"

"That's *right!*" Big Ed growled, slipping me a wink.

"Wow! *Thanks!*" Cal gushed, stuffing the bills in his pocket. "Now all I gotta figure is what to tell my father. Geez, if he ever finds out I been *racing* . . ."

Fortunately for Cal, he was pitching to my greatest strength: making up believable stories about broken automobiles. "Oh, just tell him, um, tell him the car broke down near Passaic and, um, and you hadda leave it off to be fixed. Tell him, um, tell him the *clutch* went out."

"But I just had a clutch put in. Just last month."

"Okay, no problem. How 'bout a starter motor."

"Just had one of those, too."

"Say, you don't get your work done at Westbridge, do you?"

"How'd you know?"

"Just a lucky guess."

Then Cal went off to hunt up a tow truck and me and Big Ed wandered over by Tommy Edwards's Allard to congratulate him on a super race, even if it only got him second at the checker. After all, he still beat all the other Allards. Tommy was sitting on the ground with his shoulders propped up against a tire, drinking beer out of his shiny new second-place mug. You could see the race with Creighton Pendleton's Ferrari had taken a lot of the starch out of him. But he brightened up the moment he saw us. "Hey, sport," he called out, waving his free hand weakly through the air, "how about a tall, cool one."

As you can imagine, Big Ed and me were happy to oblige.

"Thanks again for all the help," Tommy said. "That was one hell of a decent job you did on the brakes."

"But they went out again," I reminded him.

"Of *course* they went out again," Tommy grinned. "Allards *always* run a bit shy of brakes toward the end of a race. Especially on a circuit with fiddly, tight little corners like this one. Bloody characteristic of the breed. But they lasted a bit longer than usual today, so nicely done."

While we were standing there, this short, dimply brunette wandered up carrying a wrinkled stub roll of toilet paper and a distinctly unpleasant look on her face. It was Tommy's wife, Ronnie, and you could see she was less than impressed with the powder room facilities at Bridgehampton. "This is undoubtedly the last roll of toilet tissue on Long Island," she announced, "and by God, I'm hanging on to it." Tommy's wife had big front teeth and a pushed-up little pug nose that made her look kind of cute (if you like mice, anyway) but she came off a tad too neatly pressed and domestic for my tastes. Anyhow, Tommy introduced us all around and asked Ronnie to rustle us up a couple cold beers. She said, "Sure," but it came out in such a way that it could've easily been mistaken for, *"Drop dead, asshole."*

Turns out Ronnie Edwards came from some well-to-do banking

family in Westchester County, and she met Tommy while working as
a U.S.O. volunteer in London during the war. It must have been very
romantic, what with him a devil-may-care fighter pilot who might not
survive his next mission and her working with all the famous bandlead-
ers and movie celebrities who came over on tour. My guess is they only
saw each other once or twice a week, and probably most of that time
was spent in the sack. But then the war ended and they came over
stateside to join her family (not to mention her family's money) and
that's when things started going straight to hell. Without the R.A.F.
and the U.S.O. and the drama and uncertainties of war to keep things
interesting, their marriage quickly disintegrated into an uneasy truce
between two people who didn't so much *hate* each other as not have
much in common. Ronnie liked charity balls and garden parties and
theater openings and such, while Tommy Edwards liked Ronnie's family's money and how it allowed him the free time and wherewithal to
go racing. She struck me as one of those well-bred finishing-school types
who work hard at being gracious and pleasant even when it's obvious
there are maybe eight or nine thousand other places they'd rather be
on a particular Saturday afternoon.

Anyhow, Ronnie brought us a couple beers and we helped them
load up, and I guess we must've congratulated Tommy a dozen times
apiece for the fine job he did in the race. "Oh, it wasn't much of
anything," he shrugged. "After all, we didn't manage a win, now did
we?"

"Maybe not," I argued, "but geez, you ran outta brakes. Besides,
this thing looks like a real damn *handful* compared to that Ferrari you
were up against."

"Oh, it's not so bad as it looks," Tommy grinned, patting the Allard
gently on its nose. "These old girls are just a mite *stubborn* about slowing
down and turning every now and again. One gets used to it. And the
buggers *do* go like bloody stink down the straightaways, don't they?"

"Yeah, they do," I agreed. "But they're sure all over the place in
the corners."

"You know, a chap once said if I ever saw what it looks like from
the outside, I'd never get *in* the bloody thing again."

We had a good laugh over that, and I must admit I felt pretty
damn special, hanging around and shooting the breeze with an ex–
fighter pilot/automobile racer the likes of Tommy Edwards.

Right out of the blue, Big Ed asked if he could sit in Tommy's
Allard. "By all means," Tommy told him. So Big Ed scrunched himself
inside—*ugh, scrape, grunt*—and I swear Big Ed couldn't do much more
than *breathe* once he got himself crammed behind the wheel. And shallow, at that. But you should've seen the light flickering up in his eyes

as Big Ed glared out at the world through that little speedboat-style racing windscreen. Why, you could almost hear the old gears turning again under Big Ed's yellow Jaguar cap, and his fat Cuban stogie was damn near twirling between his teeth.

After Tommy and Ronnie took off, Big Ed and me made our way over to the big victory celebration around Creighton Pendleton's first-place Ferrari. It looked just magnificent, glistening in the late-afternoon sun with heat waves still shimmering off it and the smell of crisp metal and roasted brake linings hanging in the air. Race people were milling all around it, laughing and joking and guzzling beers, and right in the middle of everything was Creighton himself: a tall, dark, cologne-ad type wearing powder blue Dunlop coveralls with CREIGHTON PENDEL-TON III embroidered above the breast pocket in silvery thread. Boy, did he ever look the part! He had perfect teeth and a Bermuda tan and wore his jet-black hair slicked back from his forehead like Rudy Valentino. A gaggle of well-wishers were pumping his hand and slapping him on the back—one right after the other—but he just stood there, nonchalant as can be, nodding and shrugging and every now and again flashing this knowing smile he kept on tap for special occasions. You could tell he got a lot of mileage out of that smile. Then the girl who rode with him on the victory lap—without a doubt the smoothest, sleekest, most thoroughbred specimen of a young woman I had ever seen—stepped out of the crowd, draped her arms around his neck, closed her eyes, and drew him down into a long, deep, lingering kiss with a whole lot of tongue in it.

Wow!

7

AUNT ROSAMARINA'S
RACE SHOP

IMAGINE MY surprise when I showed up at the Sinclair Monday morning and found Old Man Finzio in the process of throwing Cal Carrington's busted-up MG off the property. I guess Cal managed to get it hauled in late Sunday evening and then just sort of *left* it there—right in front of the overhead door!—without so much as a note or a phone number or *any*thing. Naturally it wouldn't roll, what with the steering gear all bent to shit and the right-front brake drum scraping on the pavement, so the Old Man was hitching it up to his tow truck so he could drag it off to an alley someplace and ditch it. "Hey, Mr. Finzio," I yelled over, "where ya goin' with that *customer's automobile?*" See, we never worked on "people's cars" at the Sinclair. Oh, no. They were always "customers' automobiles."

"This heap?" the Old Man grunted. "I thought mebbe I'd haul it over by the boneyard and see if they'd gimme ennything fer it."

"You can't do *that*," I told him. "Why, that's a *race* car."

"A race car? This piece of shit? *Haw!* You gotta be joking."

"No, honest. It just had a little, er, a little *racing accident,* that's all."

Old Man Finzio dug yet another mashed-up Camel out of his pocket and gave Cal's MG a thorough eyeballing. "Looks t'me like it's had itself a whole damn *assortment* of accidents. And none of 'em was particular little, either.... Say, who owns this shitbox, anyways?"

"It belongs to, aah, *Mister* Carrington," I told him, "from over in Cedar Grove. Big Ed and me met him at Bridgehampton this weekend. Gee whiz, you shoulda seen him *drive* this thing. Until the wheel came off, anyway...."

"Hmm. I s'pect that slowed him down a mite, didn't it?"

"Yeah. That and the hay bales. Anyhow, I told him to haul it over here so's we could fix it up for him."

"*Fix* it?!" the Old Man snorted. "And just where in the hell didja plan t'*start*?" He took a hard drag on his cigarette. "Lissen t'me, sonny, the only thing *this* car needs is a decent burial." The Old Man thought that was pretty funny and started to laugh, but like always it turned into a monumental coughing fit (imagine a truckload of wet coal rattling down a rusty tin chute) and sometimes it got so bad you'd swear he was about to flop over dead right in front of you. Which is probably why Old Man Finzio worked so hard at not being amused.

There was no question we had to do *something* with Cal's MG—we couldn't very well leave it blocking the entrance to the service bay—so we hitched it up and dragged it back behind the building, where the Old Man and me had to wrestle that heap around like a pair of dock-workers with a floor jack under the right front, and it didn't help any that the concrete turned to gravel right there so the damn thing kept trying to fall off on Old Man Finzio's toes. Needless to say, we were both worked into a pretty good lather by the time we got Cal's ratty TC snug up against the outside wall, and it didn't take any special genius to see that the Old Man was developing a very deep personal dislike for this particular MG. Not only had it been abandoned in front of his place of business, but it had since managed to scrape his knuckles, bang his knees, repeatedly attempted to crush his toes, and got him to wheezing and coughing so bad he sounded like the local Jaycees' spook house on Halloween. Like always, the Old Man simply lit himself up another fresh Camel to take care of it.

Three whole days passed before Cal Carrington bothered to drop in and talk to Old Man Finzio about his car. He just tooled in out of the blue in his mom's new two-tone Packard, and immediately set a rookie world's record for pissing the Old Man off. I didn't have a watch on it, but I'd guess he got the job handled in thirty seconds flat. Cal just didn't see anything *wrong* with dumping his busted MG smack-dab in front of the service door, not calling for three days, and then expecting Old Man Finzio to drop whatever he was doing and devote his undivided attention to Cal's broken TC. I guess you could say Cal was maybe a little bit spoiled. Maybe more than a little, even.

"Now see here, sonnyboy," the Old Man hissed, running his eyes over Cal's mom's new Packard, "we *work* fer a living around this here service station. We got things t'*do*, unnerstand?"

"Yeah, sure," Cal said, not understanding one little bit. "All I wanna know is when my MG'll be ready."

"Ready fer *what*? A decent burial?" The Old Man started to snigger again, and I was afraid he might go into one of his laughing/coughing/choking/gasping-for-air jags. But fortunately the joke wasn't so funny the second time around. "Now lissen here, sonnyboy," he said, taking a long, thoughtful drag on his cigarette, "if y'want, I can have my *associate* here"—the Old Man nodded in my direction—"write'cha up a *estimate* on that automobile of yers."

"An *estimate*?" Cal gulped, flashing me one of those wide-eyed Judas looks.

"That's right, sonnyboy, a *estimate*," the Old Man nodded, blowing a cloud of smoke in Cal's face. "An' I want you should check it over *reeeal* careful. Make sure it looks *right* t'ya, see. Sure wouldn't want fer there t'be no *misunderstandings* later...."

"Oh, of course not," Cal mumbled, swaying back on his heels.

"An' then y'could mebbe give us, say, a little *deposit* on the parts?"

"A d-deposit?" Cal stammered.

"That's right, a deposit. You just check over that estimate real careful, then fork over a little earnest-money deposit t'cover the parts. *That's* when we'll get started on fixing yer car." The Old Man took a deep drag off his cigarette, savored it, and slowly exhaled. "You unnerstand?"

"Uh, well, er, exactly how *much* of a deposit are you thinking of?" Cal wanted to know.

Old Man Finzio looked Cal up and down, checking out his Ivy League clothes and Bass Weejun loafers. Then his eyes shifted to the new, two-tone Packard parked out by the pumps. "Oh, I dunno," the Old Man mused, rubbing the four-day growth of stubble on his chin, "how does, oh, say, a hunnert dollars sound."

"*A hundred dollars?!*" Cal yelped. "Geez, mister, I, uh, never, um, that is, I never carry that much cash *on* me."

"But you could *git* it, right?"

"Oh, uh, s-sure I could. No problem. It's just that, well..." Cal's eyes slipped down to the cuffs of the Old Man's coveralls—"...that my, uh, *assets* aren't real, aah, *liquid* right now...."

Well, Old Man Finzio may have been just a grizzled old grease monkey from Passaic, but he sure as hell understood flat broke when he heard it. In *any* language. The Old Man raised up a tobacco-stained finger and waggled it under Cal's nose. "Now lissen here, sonnyboy. We ain't runnin' no charity benefit fer runny-nose rich kids around *my* service station. No siree. Way I figger it, y'owe me a dollar fifty fer storage already. An' that's not even *countin'* haulin' that wreck of yers around back. Normally, I charge two bucks just t'hitch up."

You could tell Cal wasn't used to getting pushed around like that— especially by dirty-fingernail types like Old Man Finzio—and no question he was starting to get a little hot under the collar. Which of course was the worst thing he could do. "Now look here, mister," Cal growled with a steely new edge to his voice, "I don't think you *understand*...."

"*Like HELL I don't!*" the Old Man snapped, jumping out from behind the counter and jamming his chin squarely up into Cal's face, "It's *you* who don't unnerstand things, sonnyboy. Y'got till noon Sattiday t'come up with *at least* fifty bucks, or I'm draggin' that so-called automobile of yers t'the junkyard an' sellin' it fer scrap t'cover the storage an' towing charges."

Cal's eyes flew open. "B-But you can't *do* that."

"You just *watch* me, sonnyboy," the Old Man sneered, calmly putting a fresh match to the remaining half-inch stub of his latest Camel.

And that, in a roundabout way, is how Cal Carrington's busted TC wound up just downstairs from my apartment in my Aunt Rosamarina's garage (at least *after* I lent Cal one of Big Ed's five-buck tips so's he could pay off Old Man Finzio's towing ransom). Now don't get me wrong, Calvin Wescott Carrington was a nice guy in a lot of ways, and I'd have to say we got to be really good friends. But to *know* Cal was to be *owed* by Cal, even though he came from more damn money than people like you and me ever see in a lifetime. As he told Old Man Finzio, his "assets" weren't always "liquid," and believe me, that's the way they stayed for as long as I knew him. And on those rare occasions when Cal *did* happen to be carrying a little folding money (which happened every now and again on a totally irregular, flash-flood kind of basis), he'd invariably blow it on anything and everything that struck his fancy until it was all used up—like he was in some frantic, balls-out race to see just how quickly he could get himself flat broke again. Then he'd be back to his usual old "not liquid" self for as long as it took him to glom on to another pocketload of the old Carrington family cashola. But there was a huge fundamental difference between Cal Carrington and all the other deadbeats I knew in that Cal always *felt* rich and *thought* rich, even when he had nothing but lint in his pockets. Maybe that's on account of it was 100 percent cashmere lint.

Anyhow, I wound up arranging bail for Cal's MG and even managed to borrow the Old Man's tow truck for my date with Julie that Friday evening so's I could haul it. I was supposed to pick Julie up at 7:30, and naturally I had it all timed down to the last split second. I'd figured fifteen minutes to hitch up, ten minutes (tops!) for the tow, and a generous twenty-five minutes to get the MG into my aunt's garage, which, according to my calculations, would've got me up to Julie's front door with an easy forty-five or fifty seconds to spare. Except that I ran into a few, aah, Unforeseen Obstacles along the way (which is *always* what seems to happen whenever race cars and garages are involved). Like, fr'instance, the Old Man had shoved Mr. Beadle's Oldsmobile 66 into the slot beside Cal's TC, and wouldn't you know it had a busted spring because old Grandma Beadle (who had to be at least a hundred years old and couldn't see as far as the damn hood ornament) ran it over a set of railroad tracks where there wasn't an actual crossing. So now I had *two* three-legged, ground-gouging automobiles to shove around before I could hitch up the TC. Plus Cal came along to help, and that meant I was spending a lot of time getting cars back up in the air after he'd put his shoulder to it and popped them clear off the jack. He was only trying to help, of course, but brute muscle just doesn't account for much unless you know where and how to apply it, and my buddy Cal was a textbook example of how an inexperienced person— no matter how strong, eager, or willing—could be counted on to get it all wrong and make thing worse instead of easier. As Butch often told me, the mark of a True Mechanic was knowing exactly where and how much of a hit you could give something to bust it loose without breaking it. And my new friend Cal had no idea.

Then we got to my aunt's house (I was barely a half hour late at that point) only to find there wasn't room for MG in my aunt's garage. In fact, there wasn't room for much of *anything* in there, on account of she had it piled wall-to-wall with rusty garden tools and old yard furniture and sections of picket fencing that were apparently too beat up to use yet too good to throw away, not to mention fifty or so cardboard boxes filled with moldy, cat turd–decorated books and magazines. I swear, my Aunt Rosamarina must've had every damn issue of *Life*, *Look*, *Collier's*, and *National Geographic* ever published, along with every coloring book, study text, project folio, and class notebook she'd ever laid a finger on from kindergarten clear through college, all of it covered with a gritty layer of dust and these sad little brown spitballs of spider eggs. I glanced through a few of them, and to tell the truth, it felt kind of creepy, what with the pages all yellow-orange around the edges and smelling like last year's leaves after the snow melts. But the weirdest part was seeing how they didn't have cars or airplanes or anything back when my aunt went to grammar school. Why, I would've been flat out of a job! It made me feel kind of strange inside, you know?

What with nosing around those old magazines and one thing and another, it was damn near ten before Cal and me got his crippled-up MG squared away in my aunt's garage. But we did it, and that old TC was resting peacefully (if a bit off-plumb) on three flat-spotted tires and a wooden pop crate, surrounded by teetering stacks of yard furniture, garden tools, picket fencing, and book boxes, with just enough space left for a slender human being to walk all the way around it without banging his shins more than twice.

"Mission accomplished!" Cal grinned, and we shook on it.

"How 'bout a beer?"

"You got any?"

"Does a chicken have lips?"

"Absolutely!" Cal grinned even broader.

So we headed up to my apartment for the celebratory beer that absolutely *must* accompany the completion of every race car project, regardless of how late you may be for any real-life appointment, engagement, or commitment. Like a date with Julie, for example. As we climbed the stairs, I noticed Aunt Rosamarina peering out from behind her flower-print curtains like a cornered ferret (albeit wearing bifocals) and I wondered if she was planning to do or say anything about the chunk of abused English iron we'd just left in her garage. But she never came out, so I figured we were home free. That was a good thing, seeing as how it looked like Cal's old TC might be convalescing for quite a spell.

I was cleaned up and on my way over to Julie's by 10:35, and, as you can imagine, I couldn't *wait* to tell her about Cal Carrington and the MG in my aunt's garage and the races out at Bridgehampton. But for some inexplicable reason, Julie seemed more interested in precisely why I was three hours late. Of course, she would soon discover that was about spot-on average for a Race Garage evening, but I recall she was plenty pissed off at the time (not to mention still a little miffed about that wedding in Jersey City). In fact, I remember doing the whole drive over to Weedermen's with my head pulled down inside my collar (tortoise fashion, right?) so as not to get frostbite of the ears.

But after I bought us a couple double-scoop hot fudge sundaes and casually mentioned Robert Montgomery and Jackie Cooper and Dave Garroway a couple dozen times, Julie started to come around. You know how women are about movie stars—like some of the glitter maybe rubs off when you actually get to see one in person. You'd think they were baseball players or something, you know?

Anyhow, Julie's eyes got all bright and sparkly when I told her about all the in-the-flesh celebrities and fancy-pants rich people I'd seen hanging around at Bridgehampton. And right away I started thinking what a swell deal it would be if I could get Julie to come up to the races with me. It's always nicer when you have somebody, you know, *special* to share the excitement. Especially somebody as easy on the eyes and soft to the touch as Julie Finzio. Besides, according to the S.C.M.A. schedule Cal had tacked to the wall of my aunt's garage, a lot of those races were two-day weekend events, and the idea of getting Julie away someplace where she didn't have to be home by eleven o'clock (or home at all!) had an appeal all its own. In fact, the possibilities alone were enough to put my entire glandular system on red alert. The problem was Julie's mom (what else?), who'd been around the block a few times herself and didn't much fancy any long road trips or overnight lodging arrangements that included her daughter and any male person over the age of six. But every once in awhile, I'd allow myself a little daydream about it, and they inevitably ended with Julie and me waking up to-gether. In the same room. In the same bed. With nothing on but the sheets. Then I'd generally have to go lock myself in the john to think about it some more. . . .

So I kept hammering the old hard sell at Julie every chance I got, talking about sportycar racing pretty much nonstop every time she dropped by to tidy up the office or help Old Man Finzio with the books. I talked about it on our way to the movies on Friday nights, too, and usually picked up wherever I'd left off at Weedermen's or the Doggie Shake over Cokes and a couple orders of fries. Truth is, I was yakking about it all the time. Except when we were parked out behind the Sinclair, that is. I mean, a guy's gotta keep his priorities straight.

I knew I was making progress the day Julie casually allowed as how the races might be a good place to do some sketching. *"Yeah!"* I told her. "They got some *great* subject matter at those races." That's what artistic types look for, see, is subject matter. "In fact," I told her, "there's no question that racing is absolutely *lousy* with prime, grade-A subject matter."

"It is?"

"Absolutely!"

Julie didn't look entirely convinced, and that was easy to understand if you ever leafed through her sketchpads. Truth is, I didn't think too much of the stuff Julie picked to draw, since most of it was flowerpots and driftwood and whole production-number garden parties of slender, stylish, arched-over-backward young women in flowing gowns and piled-up hairdos that about required external scaffolding. Dullsville, you know? I thought a couple MGs and Jag 120s (or better yet, Tommy Edwards's Allard mixing it up with Creighton Pendleton's 4.1 Ferrari!) would put some real *zing* in Julie's artwork. Besides, I was tongue-hanging-out *dying* to have Julie come to the races with me, and if "subject matter" would get the job done, hell, I was all for it.

Meanwhile, Cal Carrington was dropping by the garage behind my aunt's house every couple days to help out with his MG (or maybe leave off some fresh parts from Westbridge if he was in one of his flash-flood "liquid" stages) but it was slow going on account of everywhere I looked on that rattletrap TC, the more stuff I saw that needed attention. Why, every single wheel spoke was either bent, busted, or in serious need of tightening. And the tires were shot—even the spare!—what with the rubber worn down to nothing and the cords showing through on the edges (not hard to understand at all if you'd ever seen Cal drive). I figured we needed two complete wheel rims, four tires, a fistful of inner and outer spokes, a new hub, a new brake drum, and a set of tie-rod ends. And when I finally managed to worry that ground-up brake drum off the right front (following two solid hours of hammering, prying, levering, and cursing in the best Old Man Finzio tradition), I discovered linings down to the rivets, brake fluid weeping all over, and wheel bearings that smelled like burnt toast. The bushings were shot, the shocks all needed rebuilding, there was play in the steering—and we hadn't even *started* with the engine or driveline yet (not that you could miss how the carbs leaked like lawn sprinklers and that either the gauge was flat busted or that poor old motor didn't have much in the way of oil pressure). To put it bluntly, I couldn't find *anything* on Cal's MG that wasn't in desperate need of repair, with possible exceptions awarded to the gas tank, shift knob, hood latches, and rearview mirror. And I wasn't real sure about the hood latches.

To make matters worse, my Aunt Rosamarina's garage was a shitass *lousy* place to work. There was hardly any room, the lighting stunk (as did the used kitty litter in the garbage cans just outside), and I had no lift, hoist, compressor, bench vise, torch, hydraulic press, or even a decent floor jack to work with. In fact, the only tools I had were the assortment of Stone Age implements that come in what the MG factory laughingly refers to as a "tool kit," along with the ones I carefully selected out of Butch's toolbox late each afternoon and sneaked home in a folded-up grocery bag. And that's not even mentioning the teetering piles of books, magazines, picket fencing, yard tools, and old furniture that came crashing down on my head once or twice a night—regular as clockwork—as if the whole place had been booby-trapped by the North Korean Army.

But I kept after it, five or six nights a week, all afternoon and evening on Saturday, and of course all day Sunday, too, doing my level best with the cave-dweller equipment and facilities on hand and the piece-at-a-time hardware Cal brought me every few days from Westbridge. I was even sneaking stuff into the Sinclair so's I could work on Cal's TC while Old Man Finzio was out chasing parts or picking up dead cars. Of course, Cal would help out wherever he could at my aunt's place (he wasn't exactly welcome around the Old Man's gas station) and I must admit, he turned out to be reasonably handy once he had a little shop time in. Like I've explained before, Cal's problem was he just didn't *know* anything.

But that could change.

For example, Cal dropped by on Memorial Day, and the two of us sort of "borrowed" my aunt's old upright radio so's we could listen to the Indy 500 while we worked on the MG and swilled down an occasional cold beer. Troy Ruttman won the 500 that year in 3 hours, 52 minutes, and 41.88 seconds, and I swear it took that entire time for Cal to do the front brake and wheel bearings on one blessed side of the car. But then he turned around and got the other side handled in less than a half hour. All he needed was *experience*. Like anybody else who's ever dug his mitts into a toolbox, Cal had to pay his rightful dues in ruined parts, blood blisters, split fingernails, busted knuckles, and localized second-degree burns before he could call himself any kind of automobile mechanic.

But he'd come right, I'd see to it. Or at least I'd try. Once he got the hang of all the basic stuff (like not using pliers on bolt heads and never grabbing for the nearest screwdriver when what you really want is a chisel, punch, or prybar), Cal's biggest problem was that he was so damned *impatient*. He wanted that TC *done*. And I mean *right now* (if not sooner!) so he could toss his helmet in back and go racing again. That made him a bit of an angle-shooter in order to get jobs done quicker. He'd tacked this copy of the S.C.M.A. schedule to the wall of my aunt's garage, and all he could *think* about was the Giant's Despair Hillclimb and Brynfan Tyddyn Road Races (whatever the hell *they* were) coming up July 25th and 26th in Wilkes-Barre, Pennsylvania. As far as Cal was concerned, the whole blessed world would come to an end if he didn't make that event. Why, it was bigger than Judgment Day!

Now and then I'd let Cal's crazy enthusiasm get the better of me and I'd start ignoring everything in my life except that piece-of-shit MG and the stupid race and hillclimb we were trying to make in Pennsylvania. In fact, the only thing that saved me from a terminal case of falling-down, foaming-at-the-mouth racing mania was that I worked on cars all day at the Sinclair, and believe me, after eight or nine hours fixing Hudsons and Henry Js for Old Man Finzio, the last thing I wanted to see was another sick automobile. Especially a desperate case like Cal's raggedy TC. Plus every now and then I'd get this crazy notion that I was entitled to a life of my own. I wanted time to go out with Julie. Take in a show. Share a couple cheeseburgers at Weedermen's or the Doggie Shake. Park behind the Sinclair and neck for an hour or so. But that gets impossible when you're thrashing away on busted automobiles from seven ayem to three the next morning. And on those rare occasions when you *do* manage to steal a few hours to behave like a normal human being, you find yourself stumbling around like one of those dead-eyed zombies from an old Bela Lugosi movie.

Needless to say, Julie was not real pleased with the situation, and it all came to a head when I actually *dozed off* while we were parked out behind the Sinclair one night. *"Hey!"* she hollered, giving me a solid shot to the ear. "Sorry I'm keepin' you *up,* Palumbo!"

"Huh . . . oh . . . uh, sorry, Julie, I was just, uh . . ."

"Lissen, bozo," she growled, jumping to the far side of the seat, "you ain't gotta feel sorry fr'*me*. Not in this lifetime. I mean, if it's I *bore* you . . ."

"Aw, Jul—"

"... I mean, if I'm keepin you *awake*...."

"Aw, Julie, you know—"

"Yeah? *What* do I know? *Huh?* You *tell* me!"

"Aw, you know I—"

"Lissen here, Mister Buddy Palumbo, if you really *want*, I can fix it so I stay home and do my frickin' *nails* on Saturday nights. Makes no difference to me."

From there it only got worse.

But back at my Aunt Rosamarina's garage, Cal Carrington was after me like a hound on the scent, pushing for us to work *quicker,* work *later,* work *longer,* work *more nights a week,* even though we didn't have near all the necessary pieces to finish his damn car. No question Cal had gone absolutely blind *crazy* with the idea of making that S.C.M.A. event the fourth weekend in July, and there was just no reasoning with him. To tell the truth, I didn't think we had a chance. Time was running short and there was still a tremendous amount to do (heck, I hadn't even pulled the valve cover yet!), not to mention Cal kept running out of money every other week like a damn state legislature. But Cal's mind was made up, so he kept prodding me along and scrounging for parts wherever and however he could, and I suspected that he was rifling every stray purse, pocketbook, and pair of pants back home at Castle Carrington in order to feed his dirty little habit. This was really my first close personal look at the racing disease, and I can't honestly say I appreciated its seriousness at the time. But I learned . . .

Who should tool up to the pumps the first of July but Butch Bohunk and Mean Marlene in a rusty old Ford sedan with a sheet of plywood over the back window and a web of plumber's strap holding up the left-hand headlamp. But Butch was real proud of that heap on account of he had less than a ten-spot in it and said he did every bit of the mechanical work himself. "Take a look at this little beauty," he beamed, unhooking the coat hanger wire that held the passenger-side door shut. "I got her down in Tennessee fer five bucks. *Five bucks!* The engine was froze up s'bad she wouldn't turn a lick. Not even with a three-foot plumber's wrench on the pulley! Some jackass musta run her friggin' bone-dry on oil. *Haw!* Picked up another shortblock—outta the same damn boneyard!—and we was on the road in less'n a week. An' I did every goddam nut an' bolt myself!"

I had a little trouble believing that, what with Butch still all busted up like he was. Oh, he was getting around a lot better—even using crutches now and then—but Marlene still had to wheel him around like a tea cart if they wanted to make any time at all from point A to point B. And for sure Butch's hand wasn't about to grow any new fingers. That's when I caught a glimpse of Marlene's nails, and right away I knew who'd been helping on that old Ford. Now you have to understand that Butch's wife had always been real particular about her nails (you know how some women are) and generally sported a set of lipstick-red war claws that any cocktail waitress would've been proud to own. She knew how to *use* those things, too, clicking them against a windowpane to show she was bored, shaking them under your nose to get your attention, drumming them impatiently on a tabletop, or creating fresh scar tissue. But not anymore. Mean Marlene had the hands of an auto mechanic now, right down to bruises on the knuckles and a split nail on her right thumb. And she didn't look particularly happy about it, either. Then again, you'd have a hard time recalling when Mean Marlene looked particularly happy about *anything*.

Anyhow, Butch had to grab the doorframe with both hands to lever himself up out of the car, and then it was all he could do to just sort of hang there while Marlene brought his crutches around. "Hell," he gasped, trying to ignore it, "ol' Marlene an' me drove this sonofabitch all the way back from Tennessee an' she never skipped a friggin' beat. Not *one*. Oh, I may be a little tore up yet, but I still ain't lost my touch around Fords."

"'Course not, Butch. You was always the best when it came to Fords."

"Sure as hell was. And still *am*, y'little jerkoff. Don't you forget it!" He added a limp elbow dig. "An' this job was no goddam picnic, neither. You oughta see what Marlene's brother calls a 'tool set.' *Haw!* Guess it's ok if y'wanna mend a fence or lynch a nigger, but it was sure as hell crude fr'engine work."

That's when it dawned on me. "Say," I gulped, my voice going all lame on me, "you're probably gonna want yr'tools back now, arn'cha?"

"Aw, don't worry about it," Butch shrugged. "I'll let'cha know when I need 'em. Besides, I ain't exactly got anything, y'know, *lined up* right at the moment. S'you just keep 'em right here until the time comes I need 'em. Hell, maybe that old buzzard Finzio'll let me drop by an' use 'em if I got a side job or something."

"*Sure* he would," I agreed, not at all sure it was true. "You know how Old Man Finzio likes you. . . ."

"Yeah," Butch nodded, pumping out a weak laugh, "about as much as blood blisters an' cheap wine hangovers."

"Well, he always liked the way you fixed cars, anyway."

That got Butch to looking down at his hands—the right one like a huge thumb that'd been smacked with a five-pound sledge—and he slowly shook his head. "Truth is, I don't figger I'm quite ready t'start twisting wrenches again. Not fr'a living, anyways. I just can't get around good enough. . . ."

"Hell, Butch, you're doin' *great,*" I told him, "just great."

"Sure I am. Why, I'll be dancing the friggin' jitterbug in a couple more weeks, won't I?" He stared out at the cars rolling by on Pine Street. "Fact is," he added in a half whisper, "I about need a friggin' nursemaid just t'change a God Damn set of spark plugs. It makes me wanna *puke,* y'know?"

"Yeah," Marlene snorted, "an' listenin' t'ya bellyache about it makes everybody *else* wanna puke, too!"

Butch spun around like he was gonna belt her, but of course it would've sent him sprawling across the pavement if he took anything like a decent swing. So there was nothing he could do but just stand there and take it. And then, almost like slow motion, Butch's face softened up into a big, helpless grin and he started to laugh. And then I saw Marlene was laughing, too, and for the life of me I couldn't figure it out. I mean, those two scrapped like alley cats—all the time!—but it was obvious Mean Marlene did something pretty special for Butch, too. Even if she made him pay for it along the way.

Anyhow, Big Ed's XK120 was in for a grease and oil that day, and seeing as how it was a swell July afternoon and furthermore seeing as how the Old Man was across town picking up a dead Studebaker, I figured it wouldn't hurt anything if I took Butch and Marlene out for a little spin. Just a professional test-drive with an Established Mechanical Expert, you understand, not some sort of frivolous, irresponsible joyride in a customer's neat car. Right. So I turned the radio way up, popped the phone off the hook, locked the john door with the water tap running (like I was in there, you know?), and the three of us piled into Big Ed's Jaguar. It was a tight fit seeing as how Mean Marlene is *way* big in the butt and we had to be careful about Butch's legs, but once he gave me the thumbs-up, I fired up that sweet-running six and we were on our way. I cruised her nice and gentle to the edge of town, just enjoying the buttery growl out the Jag's tailpipe and the way everybody looked and pointed as we oozed down the street. That happened whenever you drove an XK120, and it never failed to make you feel pretty special. Why, even Mean Marlene was smiling.

Once clear of the city limits, I blipped her down a couple gears and gave the Jag a bootful in second and halfway out in third. To tell the truth, she felt a little sluggish with three people on board (not too surprising when one of them had a butt the size of a prize hog) but Butch got a huge kick out of it anyway. Marlene didn't look nearly so impressed. In fact, she was clutching the door so tight I was afraid she'd leave dents and yelling so loud and shrill for me to slow down that you could hear her over the wind and exhaust noise and *everything*. She had herself one hell of a vocabulary, Marlene did.

Back at the station Butch thanked me while Marlene yelled at me some more and then he leaned in close and whispered, "Now lemme show *you* something, Buddy." Without another word, Butch hobbled over and popped the trunklid of his Ford. Jee-*zus*! Crammed inside were more damn fireworks than you ever saw in your life. There were boxes upon boxes of skyrockets and Roman candles and showering pinwheels and blockbusters and Lord only knows what else! Why, that old Ford wasn't much more than a self-propelled incendiary bomb.

"Gee whiz, Butch, where'dja get all this?"

"Brought it up from Tennessee, Buddy. Hell, this stuff's cheaper'n pigeon crap down there."

"Jee-*zus*, Butch. Wasn't that kind of, you know, *dangerous?*"

"Aw, nothin' to worry over. See what I done here?" Sure enough, Butch had hung an old bus mirror off the door pillar so he could look back and see if anything was seriously on fire. That Butch thought of everything. Naturally, I had no choice but to buy a whole shitload of fireworks off him as a matter of professional courtesy (plus you never know when that sort of stuff is going to come in handy, do you?) and I even tried to overpay a little. But no way would Butch let me. "Lissen here, Buddy," he growled. "The only charity this Marine will ever need is a .45 with one bullet in the chamber. You unnerstand me, boy?"

"S-Sure, Butch."

"You damn well better had."

After I had my new collection of fireworks safely stashed under the tool bench, I bought Butch a soda and told him all about the sports car races out at Bridgehampton. I made sure to mention Tommy Edwards's brutal Cad-Allard and Creighton Pendleton's incredible Ferrari and Skippy Welcher's ex-everything XK120M and even Cal Carrington's broken-down MG TC that was sitting up on pop crates in my aunt's garage. You could see it brought a fresh gleam up in his eyes. "Haw! That sounds like a lotta fun," Butch mused, rubbing his chin with his bad hand. "I'd sure as hell like t'get in on something like that."

"Hey, no problem," I told him, "no problem at all."

"Oh, *great!*" Marlene snorted through her usual sourpuss sneer. "Just what I'd always hoped and prayed for. Car shit on the frickin' *weekends*, too."

Back at my Aunt Rosamarina's garage, Cal's MG project had pretty much ground to a halt. I had the steering and brakes squared away, but Cal hadn't rounded up enough ready cash for tires or the radiator yet, and we still hadn't so much as laid a finger on the engine. Which meant things were looking seriously unlikely for that S.C.M.A. weekend in Pennsylvania. To tell the truth, I didn't think we could make it, and now and then even Cal was starting to lose heart. No question we hit our all-time low on the Fourth of July, when Cal showed up at my aunt's garage with nothing but a grim expression and a brown paper sack that was way too small for any of the hardware we needed. "So," I asked him, "did'ja do any good on the tires?"

Cal shook his head.

"Too bad."

"Yeah. Seems like it's harder and harder to find any loose money around the old homestead. I think they may be getting wise to me."

"It's about time."

"Maybe so," Cal allowed. "Maybe so. But it wasn't a total loss."

"Oh?"

I saw an evil smile flickering up in the corners of Cal's mouth. "I did manage to find *this*." He reached into the sack and slowly withdrew an unopened fifth of fifteen-year-old Pinch whiskey. I'd never seen one before except in magazine ads, what with the bottle all sucked in like a football with half the air out of it. No question this was some pretty expensive hooch.

"Geez, Cal, where'dja get it?"

"I *pinched* it."

"You pinched your old man's Pinch?"

"It was the least I could do," Cal nodded, gently breaking the seal and taking a pull. Then he passed it over and I took a snort. The stuff had a pretty serious kick to it. And that's how we spent the rest of the afternoon, standing around Cal's TC with his dad's fancy bottle of whiskey, just shooting the breeze about cars and racing and life in general. On toward dark we heard the Fourth of July crackle of fireworks and the whistle-and-pop of bottle rockets starting up all over the neighborhood, and of course that and the whiskey gave me a splendid idea. "Say, Cal," I mentioned casually, "I bought some pretty decent fireworks off Butch the other day. . . ."

His eyes narrowed like an alley cat's. "You *did?*"

"Uh-huh. He brought 'em up from Tennessee in that old Ford of his." I took another pull off the whiskey. "I got all kinds. . . ."

Cal leaned over with one eye closed, Long John Silver style. "Arrr, and just where might they be, Jim boy?"

"Upstairs. Under the bed."

Cal decided to switch movies. "Um, Kemosabe," he scowled, folding his arms unsteadily across his chest like a cigar-store Indian, "fireworks go heap good with firewater."

Sure they do.

I'd have to say that we were pretty careful there at first (especially considering all the whiskey!), setting them off one at a time and watching the old flash-and-bang from a reasonably secure distance. But that got dull after awhile (that's *always* the problem with fireworks, isn't it?) so Cal rummaged around in my aunt's garage and found us an old wicker sewing box. We loaded it up with a whole damn brick of firecrackers, and you should've seen the way that sucker hopped and jumped and sputtered all over the place when Cal torched it off. "Wow, that was *great!*" Cal whooped as the remains of my Aunt Rosamarina's sewing box fluttered to a halt. "What else you got in there?"

"Looks like maybe a dozen skyrockets. Big ones, too."

"Super! Let's do 'em *all at once!*"

Now you're probably thinking we'd imbibed maybe a bit too much whiskey to be messing with fireworks. And you'd be right, on account of that's when Cal and me damn near burned down my aunt's garage. See, we set the busted wheel hub from Cal's MG out in the drive and loaded every blessed skyrocket we had into the hole in the center. Like a vase of flowers, you know? Cal rigged up a common fuse out of a ball of yarn my aunt's cats played with, but it was damp and dirty and wouldn't stay lit. So my resourceful buddy Cal sashayed back inside and dipped that ball of yarn in the MG's gas tank. . . .

As you can imagine, that yarn went up in a sheet of flame the instant Cal put a match to it, and in a heartbeat we had all the fuses fizzing at once. The first one blasted off exactly as planned—*FOOOOOOSSSSH!*—carving a handsome orange-red comet across the sky. But the shock was enough to make our jury-rigged rocket launcher wobble, teeter up on edge, and finally (in glorious slow motion) topple clear over. OH *SHIT!* I looked at Cal and he looked at me, and an instant later we were diving for cover as skyrockets went streaking across my aunt's yard in all directions. Two of them scored direct hits into the garage—*FOOOOSSH! FOOOOOSSH!*—where they impacted on more varieties of flammable material than you could list in an hour.

"*JESUSCHRISTALMIGHTY!*" Cal screamed.

"*HOLY SHIT!!*" I agreed, and the two of us charged in after them. We grabbed whatever we could find to beat at the flames (accidentally including a pan of mineral spirits—*KA-WHUMPF!*) and the whole shebang would've gone up for sure if my aunt hadn't come barreling out of her house dragging a huge brass fire extinguisher behind her. Fortunately she'd been watching through her favorite slit in the curtains (natch) and was by nature one of those perpetually terrified Civil Defense types who prepare in advance for every sort of household emergency imaginable. Which is how she came to have an industrial disaster—

size fire bottle right under her basement stairs. She knew how to use it, too, charging that fire like Duke Wayne himself and brandishing that big brass extinguisher like a battle-ax. By the time it ran dry, she'd gotten everything down to pretty much hissing and smoldering, and then Cal and me hooked up the garden hose and went on a little tour of her yard, putting out some relatively minor skyrocket damage to the lawn furniture and rose garden. I was sure my aunt was going to let us have it once all the fires were out, but she didn't say a word. Not one. She just *stood* there, alternately blinking and gulping for air like a goldfish on a living room carpet. And then she headed back into her house, dragging the empty fire bottle behind her. But she stopped at the screen door. "You know, boys," she said without turning around, "I really wish you'd be a little more *careful.*" And with that, my aunt disappeared into her kitchen and poured herself a water glass full of sherry.

"Jeez, that was *close!*"

"Yeah, it sure was," Cal agreed, shaking his head. But you couldn't miss the wicked little smirk flickering up around the corners of his eyes.

Cal and me came back the next morning to survey the damage, and to tell the truth, it was pretty damn depressing. "Gee whiz," I told him, "maybe we shoulda just let the damn thing *burn.* I mean, we're *never* gonna get it back together in time for that race in Pennsylvania."

"*Sure* we will," Cal said, trying to make it sound true.

"But we don't even have *tires,* Cal. And the radiator's gotta be recored...."

"No problem," he said. "No problem at all. I'll get the damn money somehow. You wait and see."

"But what about the *rest* of it," I groaned. "What about the damn *engine?* It runs like shit. And the gauge hardly shows any oil pressure at all."

"Maybe it's the gauge?"

I shook my head. "No way we're that lucky. And look at the damn bodywork. *I* can't straighten out those fenders...."

Cal eased himself down on a scorched pop crate, looking as glum as I'd ever seen him. But it wasn't ten seconds before his eyes popped open like mousetraps. "I *got* it!" he yelped. "We'll run *modified!*"

"We'll *what?*"

"Why, we'll turn this thing into a *real* race car. You'll see."

By way of explanation, the S.C.M.A. had one class for "stock" MGs (which seldom really were) and another for hopped-up, stripped-down examples, which were referred to as "modifieds." Cal figured it would be easier to rip more stuff *off* his TC than to try putting it back the way the folks at the MG factory originally intended. And he was probably right. Only problem was that Cal's TC never ran particularly strong against the other so-called stock MGs, and most of those modified cars were a *bunch* faster. They were stripped to the bare bones and had hot-rodded engines with high-compression pistons and high-lift camshafts and Lord only knew what else. Hell, some of those cars even had superchargers on them. "That's a *terrible* idea," I told Cal.

So of course we did it. After all, we had a race to make.

And that's why Cal and me spent all day pulling every damn thing that would come loose off that helpless old TC. We took off the bumpers. And the windshield. And the top. And both sides of the hood. I yanked out all the carpeting and door-panel trim. Cal went underneath with a hacksaw and cut off the muffler. By the middle of the afternoon, it had turned into sort of a crazed feeding frenzy, what with both of us clawing and ripping and tearing at that poor car like hyenas on a fresh carcass. It didn't help that we were still a little loopy from that bottle of Pinch and the garage fire the previous evening, so by nightfall we were stumbling around my aunt's garage like the Three Stooges, bumping into things and hitting ourselves in the head with car parts and making goofy Moe-Larry-Curly noises like *"Wooob-wub-wub-woob"* and *"Nyuck nyuck nyuck"* and that sort of thing. My old friend the Earl of Passaic even dropped in for a visit. "I say, Mr. Carrington," the earl asked, "won't you be a bit, shall we say, *shy on horsepower* compared to the other machinery in the modified division?"

"So *what,* your Dorkship," Cal grunted, tugging on a rear fender that still had one bolt attached. "We're gonna be *light!* You'll see. . . ."

Fact is, Cal's basic theory was pretty sound. Generally speaking, if you have to choose between *more power* and *less weight,* you go with lightness every time. Big horsepower may make a car faster in a straight line, but less weight makes it faster *everywhere*. Unfortunately for Cal, the drivers with the superchargers and six hundred–dollar engines in their "modified" MGs were also down to the bare bones on weight. In fact, some of them had expensive light-alloy body panels and even custom-made aluminum valve covers and shift knobs to make them lighter yet. Of course, we didn't know about that stuff at the time.

Anyhow, by midnight Cal's MG looked like it'd been picked over by vultures. The fenders were gone, ditto the sides of the hood, the top was history, the windshield, lights, and bumpers were gone, the muffler was leaning against the wall, the heater (or what passes for a heater on an MG) was in a corner, and that's not even mentioning the passenger-side seat cushion, the carpets, the inside door panels, the ashtray, and the horn. Truth is, we'd pulled everything off that car you could without resorting to a buzz saw, cutting torch, or explosive charges. And I gotta admit, it looked pretty neat that way, all lean and serious and stripped for action. It also looked a little, aah, *illegal* for general highway duty, and I started wondering just how the hell Cal was planning to get this—this *thing*—to that race weekend in Wilkes-Barre, Pee-Ay. Or anyplace else, for that matter. Not to mention exactly how Cal was going to explain the skeletal remains of his TC back home at Castle Carrington.

"Oh, I'll just tell my folks it was wrecked or stolen or fell off a cliff or something," he said, waving his hand through the air like it was no big deal. "At least I will when they get back from Europe, anyway."

Cal went suddenly flush on me the Wednesday before the race, showing up at my aunt's garage with a new set of Dunlops stuffed in the trunk of his mom's Packard and several cardboard boxes full of TC parts, including an upper and lower gasket set for the engine. Naturally, I decided to throw in a last-minute valve job, and of course we found all the exhaust valves burned—two of them badly—and a couple busted valve springs to boot. So Cal had to make an emergency run over to Westbridge first thing Thursday morning while I called in sick at the Sinclair, pinching my fingers around my nose so the Old Man would think I had pneumonia or something. Not that he believed me for one solitary second.

Cal didn't get back till two in the afternoon, and I busied myself mounting tires and shimming the relief spring to sort of kid the engine into thinking it had some oil pressure. Besides the valves we needed, Cal bought new points, plugs, carb rebuild kits with richer needles, and even a high-voltage Lucas Sports Coil. I told you what happens when Cal gets a little money in his pocket.

Working fast as I could, it still took six hours to get the head reassembled, the carbs rebuilt, and all the ignition stuff installed (which is probably some kind of new world record) while Cal took the wheels out for balancing, picked up the radiator over in Clifton, changed the oil, and generally did what he could so the TC might perhaps pass for street legal should anyone happen to ask. Like a police officer, for example. A little past nine, Cal asked for the keys to the Sinclair, and Lord help me, I handed 'em over. I didn't even want to *know*. He returned a half hour later with some flexible exhaust pipe and what appeared to be the fender-mount spotlight off Old Man Finzio's tow truck. For sure the Old Man wasn't going to be too pleased about that.

By then it was time to fire up my quick-and-dirty MG rebuild. I had Cal crank the starter while I flattened my palms over the S.U.s to choke them, but the damn thing cranked and cranked and wouldn't fire, and I spent thirty minutes checking the fuel pump, ignition wires, and Lord only knows what else before I realized I'd left the damn rotor out of the distributor! That sort of thing happens with predictable reg-ularity when you've been wrenching away for seventeen hours straight and should've been out the door and gone long before. It's an occupational hazard. But once I got the rotor back in where it belonged, the engine lit off on the very first rotation. And jeez, did it ever make a *racket,* boxed there inside my aunt's tiny garage with no mufflers or air cleaners to cut down the noise. It seemed to be surging and gurgling a bit, even after it was warm, so I spent the next hour showing Cal everything Sylvester and the *Jaguar Service Manual* had taught me about setting S.U.s. Or what I could remember, anyway. Anyhow, I'm proud to say that MG sounded pretty damn magnificent when I got done, idling with a nice rich lope and really snapping to attention when you cracked the throttles. Unfortunately, some of my aunt's neighbors turned out to have a tin ear when it came to crisply tuned racing engines. Especially after midnight.

Needless to say, it was into the wee hours when we finally tiptoed out of Passaic, kind of idling along in fourth to keep the noise down through the rusted-out Buick muffler Cal had found in the trash behind the Sinclair and halfheartedly wired to the MG's exhaust. The spotlight he'd gleeped off the Old Man's tow truck was strapped on right in front of the radiator—Cyclops fashion—with the feed wire going down the side, over the driver's door, behind the seat cushion, and directly to the battery terminal with no switch or fuse of any kind. In the back, Cal made do with a couple bicycle reflectors from Woolworth's five-and-dime. You'd have to say Cal was less than an expert in the automotive electrical field. Much less.

Without top or windshield, things were decidedly breezy in Cal's TC, and the wind whipped our faces until tears were streaming around our cheeks and puddling up in our ear canals. So Cal reached behind the seat and produced a couple underwater diving masks he'd picked up at Woolworth's along with the bicycle reflectors. They were bright yellow and properly sized for your average twelve-year-old, and no question made us look goofy as hell when we put them on. But they came in handy when we hit rain in the mountains outside Allamuchy. In fact, Cal probably should've picked us up a couple plastic snorkels while he was at it.

Believe me, that was one *scary* ride, what with the winding mountain roads and heavy rain and those stupid swim masks fogging up all the time and the damn spotlight in front of the radiator vibrating so bad that the beam bounced all over the road (and the trees, and the sky, and everywhere else). Not to mention that I was sitting on entirely the wrong side of the car. Especially when trucks came hurtling out of the blackness and damn near chewed off my elbow with their lug nuts. Right-hand drive may work fine over in England, but it sure leaves the passenger hung out to dry here in the states.

Plus my buddy Cal only knew one way to drive—*flat out*—no matter if it was daylight or dark, open highway or twisty blacktop, bone-dry or glare ice, perfect visibility or so you couldn't see your blessed hand in front of your face. But I must admit, the kid was *good*. Better than good, even. Why, we'd be skittering down a rain-slicked mountain with our headlamp beam shattering off a sheer rock face on one side and nothing but an empty black void on the other, and I'd look over at Cal with eyes big as coffee saucers and see him leaned back all calm and composed behind the wheel, nonchalantly chewing gum beneath that ridiculous Woolworth's swim mask as he braked, blipped her down a gear, and powered us through the bends in absolutely perfect four-wheel drifts. Cal Carrington was some kind of driver, no two ways about it. But he still wasn't worth dog shit when it came to mechanics, as we discovered once again when his jury-rigged headlamp shorted out in the Pocono Mountains, and even the great Cal Carrington had to pull over when he couldn't see the road anymore. At least the rain had eased off and you could even make out a faint half-moon through the clouds over toward the horizon. It was kind of pretty, actually. Not that we much appreciated it, since Cal and me were cold and wet as a pair of dead mackerels. And *real* tired. Naturally, we didn't have any spare electrical wire with us (although we were in excellent shape regarding the coat hanger and baling varieties).

There wasn't another car on the highway (what do you expect at four o'clock in the morning?) and about all we had in the way of illumination was a book of matches that were too soggy to light and a dinky pen flashlight with half-dead batteries. So we were pretty much stranded, you know? Up the road a bit Cal found a steep gravel drive-way disappearing up into the forest. "Hey, Buddy," he whispered, like somebody might be listening, "let's try up here!"

Well, there was a No Trespassing sign the size of a small billboard nailed up where you couldn't possibly miss it—not even at night—and I've always been a trifle funny about wandering up strange private drives in unknown backwoods areas at odd hours like four in the morning. I mean, I know lots of people right here in Passaic who aren't the least bit bashful about their constitutional right to keep and bear fire-arms. But Cal just shrugged it off. "Hey, what the hell, huh? You planning to just sit here by the side of the damn road until the sun comes up?" And with that, he fired up the TC and wheeled it up the driveway. Cal Carrington had himself a set of real brass balls, no two ways about it.

Naturally, he made me walk ahead with that worthless pen flash-light, trying my best to keep us on the gravel while Cal juddered the TC along behind me, playing the clutch, gas, and brake pedals like a

damn church organist. I couldn't see much of anything, so I was trip-
ping over rocks and tree roots and getting snagged by branches that'd
grown clear across the driveway since anybody'd been there. About a
mile up we came to the nicest little ski cabin you ever saw, but it was
buttoned up tighter than a drum with storm shutters padlocked over
the windows and the front door bolted solid. My buddy Cal didn't think
twice before taking the jack handle out of his TC and twisting the hasp
off one of the shutters. Then he used it to break a windowpane so he
could reach in, undo the latch, and slither his way inside.

I just stood there, frozen to the spot. "Well, Palumbo," Cal sneered
from the other side of the glass, "you planning to stay Out There all
night?" You couldn't miss the challenge in his voice, so I took a couple
deep breaths, swallowed once or twice, and crawled in after him. To
tell the truth, I was beginning to suspect that Cal Carrington might be
one of those bad-influence types your parents are always warning you
about. In fact, I was pretty sure of it.

The cabin was real dark and musty inside, but Cal managed to find
us some firewood piled by the door and a box of stick matches and
even a couple moldy old comforters and a can of coffee. So Cal and me
sort of set up camp—like Boy Scouts, right?—building ourselves a fire
and hanging our wet clothes up to dry and boiling ourselves a pot of
water for coffee. Cal wrapped himself in one of the comforters and
dozed right off to sleep, but I was too damn scared to do anything but
sit there in front of the fire with my eyes bugged out like Eddie Cantor,
listening to every owl hoot, bird chirp, and twig snap like it was the
hammer clicking back on a Colt .45. I rustled Cal awake a little before
seven, and would you believe it, he insisted on taking one of the
comforters with us and even leaving a note behind that went like this:

*Sorry we had to break in to your lovely cabin, but our car died out in a
terrible rainstorm while my prize cocker spaniel was in labor in the backseat.
I'm afraid she delivered on one of your comforters, and I will send it back
as soon as I have it properly cleaned. Naturally, I am happy to pay all
damages, along with a modest consideration for the use of the hall. Would
also offer one of the pups, but unfortunately they were half Labrador retriever, so we had to drown them in your toilet.*

Then he signed it with a flourish: *Creighton Pendleton III.*

8

GIANT'S DESPAIR

CAL AND I enjoyed a lovely ride down into the Susquehanna River valley the next morning, what with a warm July sun beaming through feathery clouds and Cal's old TC running better than ever, if I do say so myself. "You know," Cal grinned as we cruised down the last hillside into Wilkes-Barre, "this thing feels like a *whole new car.*" I remember glancing at the oil pressure gauge (which was straining to reach 25 p.s.i.) and allowing him one-third of an agreeable nod. "Why, I bet this is the best damn MG I've ever driven," he continued, patting the screw holes where the dash mirror would've been if we hadn't ripped it off to make that old heap a few ounces lighter. "Don't be surprised if I win the race *and* the hill climb with this little beauty. She's *ready,* I can tell." You must admit, my friend Cal didn't have any noticeable deficiencies in the optimism or confidence departments.

I, on the other hand, was going through one of those Grim Reality Inventories that come over you like stomach flu when you've been up all night, gotten thoroughly cold, wet, frightened, and exhausted, and moreover ache all over from being bounced around on the bare floor-boards of a stripped-down MG being driven by some crazy rich kid who thinks he can't die in an automobile wreck like ordinary people. And that's not even mentioning that I hadn't exactly, ahh, *made arrangements* with Old Man Finzio about skipping work again. Truth is, I didn't think the Old Man would consider an S.C.M.A. hill climb someplace in Pennsylvania as an acceptable reason for ditching work. In fact, I was sure of it. So when we stopped at a diner for some bacon and eggs, I took a pocketful of change over by the pay phone and called the station to try and smooth things over. I even held my nose, as if I could maybe fool the Old Man into thinking I still had the terrible head cold he never believed I had in the first place. But he must've heard the change drop or picked up all the static on the line, because right away he said, "Saaay, Palumbo, where the hell *are* you?"

"Uh, well, I'm kinda . . ."

"You're off at th' frickin' *car races* with that runnynose rich kid, aint'cha?"

Gee whiz, it was like the old fart had a crystal ball or something, you know?

"Well, geez, Mr. Finzio, I sorta..."

Click!

So much for that.

To cheer myself up, I single-handedly consumed an entire Triple Play Breakfast Special, which consisted of three large eggs, three strips of bacon, three pancakes swimming in maple syrup, a huge mound of hash browns, three slices of buttered toast, and a half dozen double-mugs of 90-weight coffee. Usually a feast like that will go a long way toward making me feel better, but it didn't help much and I still felt pretty miserable (only *stuffed* and miserable) as we waddled back to the car. That's when Cal reached into his pocket and tossed the keys over. "Here," he said, nonchalantly snaking a brand-new pair of aviator sunglasses over his eyes, *"you* drive." And just like that, the world was once again a wonderful place to be.

"Saaay," I asked my reflection in the mirrored lenses, "where'dja get those?" No question they were a tad more stylish than our Woolworth's swim masks.

"Inside," Cal shrugged. "I gleeped 'em off the counter by the cash register when the guy wasn't looking." Then he reached in his pocket and pulled out yet another pair. "Here's a set for you."

I looked at the sunglasses in his hand and back at my reflection in the chrome-plated lenses over his eyes. "You know," I told him, sounding exactly like my old man, "you're gonna get us in some *serious* trouble one day."

"That's what I'm here for!" Cal laughed, like it all made perfect sense.

I'd never driven a right-hand drive/left-hand shift car before, so naturally I had a few problems—like jamming the lever in third instead of first and stalling it at every other stop sign. "Hey, don't worry about it," Cal advised. "Just try to get used to how it feels. After all," he added, an inscrutable twinkle flickering around the edges of his new aviator sunglasses, "you may be *needing* it later."

We had some sketchy directions scribbled on the back of an old envelope, and did our best to follow them in a series of spiraling, misshapen, meandering, loops, crossing and recrossing the Susquehanna River while we searched in vain for that S.C.M.A. hillclimb. At least it gave me a little seat time in the MG, and except for the left-hand shift, a snappish clutch, sitting on the wrong side of the car, and steering so quick I occasionally darted into the path of oncoming traffic, it seemed I was getting the hang of it. Far as I was concerned, Cal's TC felt skittish as hell, but no question it could flick around corners quicker than anything I'd ever driven. And you could really get the feel of the road, too. Every bump, crack, and pebble, in fact.

As we passed through one particular intersection for the fifth or sixth time, we noticed a white XK120 coming from the opposite direction. Or make that an XK120*M*, since it was none other than Skippy Welcher and his faithful squire Milton Fitting, and for perhaps the only time in my life, I was happy to see them. "Say," I hollered, "you got any idea where this hill climb thing is?"

"Follow me!" Skippy whooped, waving his cap in the air like he was Teddy Roosevelt on San Juan Hill. Why, you half-expected the Jag to rear up on its back tires as he sidestepped the clutch and squealed away. What a dipshit. But at least he knew where he was going, which was more than you could say for us. We followed The Skipper's Jag back across the bridge and zigzagged a few blocks until we suddenly found ourselves in the midst of a whole herd of Jaguars and MGs and such, parked snoot-to-boot down a little side street that headed steeply uphill just past the last building in town. We had arrived.

The S.C.M.A. armband types had a registration table set up in front of a real estate office at the far end of the street, and Cal surprised the living shit out of me when he signed us up as drivers *both*. Can you believe it? Of course, I didn't have any I.D. to prove I was twenty-one (which I wasn't) or that I belonged to the S.C.M.A. (which I didn't), but Cal put a sly finger to his lips and calmly introduced me as his twenty-one-year-old cousin Bartholomew from East Point (wherever the hell *that* was) and explained as how I belonged to the highly regarded (not to mention highly imaginary) East Point Sports Car Club, and that I'd most unfortunately misplaced my wallet on our way over from Long Island. Boy, was he ever slick at that sort of thing. Never batted an eye. Not that he could've got that sort of B.S. past a seasoned registration pro like Charlie Priddle. Not hardly. But we lucked into a sweet old lady from Vermont who actually used to collect tree sap with one of Cal's aunts every February to make maple syrup, and she signed us up without a hitch. It always comes down to who you know and who knows you, doesn't it?

"Gee whiz, Cal," I grumbled as we made our way back to the TC, "why'dja wanna do *that* for?"

"Do what for?"

"You know. Sign me up to drive."

"Why not?" Cal grinned, waving a carefree hand through the air. "You *worked* on the car, didn't you? More than I did, in fact. Hell, I never could've made it without you. So why the heck *shouldn't* you drive?" Then he sealed it by giving me one of those quick little shots in the arm like guys do. "You just wait and see," he continued. "If things go right, we'll run quick enough to finish first *and second* in our class. You'll see."

"I dunno," I said, staring at the oil pressure gauge and wondering if this was really such a good idea. "What if it *breaks?*"

"Well," he shrugged, "then it probably would have broken anyway, wouldn't it? Besides, this little beauty is *not* about to let us down. Not with all the hard work we've put in. She didn't come all this way just to fall apart on us."

I wasn't so sure. "And what if I, uh, you know, uh, *hit* something? I mean, what if I *wreck* your car?"

Cal flashed me his absolute best rich-kid smile and said simply: *"Don't."*

Hill climbing was new to me, and it was a lot different from the road races out at Bridgehampton. Here the cars ran one at a time against the clock instead of wheel-to-wheel against each other, and that alone made hill climbing a lot less risky than racing. Not to mention that the steep grade, short straights, and tight corners made hill climbs mostly first and second gear, with just a few quick dabs into third for the most skillful and aggressive drivers. Which meant there was a lot less opportunity to damage your car, your body, and your precious self-esteem. Or, as Cal put it: "It's easy to be a hero in second gear."

All of which made hill climbing highly attractive to S.C.M.A. clubbies who would never dream of racing door handle to door handle with other cars. Why, even that tightass Charlie Priddle ran hillclimbs. And did amazingly well, since he always fronted up some strange, morphidite automobile that inevitably turned out to be the only car in its class. As you probably guessed, Charlie was on the classification committee. In fact, I think he was chairman. In any case, that pretty much guaranteed Charlie a first-place mug at every single event, no matter how slowly he puttered up the damn hill. Hell, even Skippy Welcher had more class than that.

This particular event, Charlie brought his 1922 Rolls Royce Silver Ghost to run in the "Over 2-Liter Vintage Touring Class." I swear, that thing looked like a damn parade float compared to the MGs and such everybody else was running. And Charlie drove it like one, too, trundling up the hill on the idle jets while he pretended to saw back and forth on the wheel and mugged for all the corner workers like Joe E. Brown. He took slowest time of the day by over a minute, but with nobody else in his class, that was enough to earn him yet another handsome first-place mug for the old marble mantelpiece back home.

What a dork.

The worst thing about hill climbing was that you had to wait in line for two hours or more for every little ninety-second burst up the hill, and then trundle back to the end of the line so's you could start your waiting all over again. Plus you couldn't see much of the action once the cars disappeared around the first curve and headed up the mountain. Not that I much cared, since I was really too damn tired to climb up and join the rubberneckers on the hill. Besides, it was a gorgeous summer day and real pretty country, too. Especially right there by the starting line, where none other than Creighton Pendleton's fabulous girlfriend was waving the green flag to turn the cars loose. She was wearing a crisp white shirt with the collar flared up and maybe three buttons undone, not to mention one hell of a pair of white shorts. In fact, I was glad Julie wasn't there to see how I was looking at her. Or where, for that matter. "Say," I asked Cal, pointing to where his eyes were already focused, "who *is* that?"

"Oh, that's Sally Enderle," he said, sliding his sunglasses down his nose for a better look. "She's a peach, isn't she."

"Boy, *I'll* say."

And no question she knew it, too, because every time a car rolled up to the line, she'd flash that toothpaste-ad smile of hers, ask the driver if he was ready, and wave the green flag with a tiny little shadow of a leap that made her leg muscles draw up like hot elastic. You'd hear the tires chirp and an angry snarl off the exhaust and look up from Sally's rear end just in time to see yet another Jag or MG or whatever vanish into the trees, engine straining against the incline. Then you could watch Sally a little more while the noise churned its way up the mountainside, fading like an echo.

Skippy Welcher's XK120M was in line a few spaces ahead of us, and he naturally got it all wrong when Sally waved the flag, dumping the clutch before he got the revs up and damn near killing the engine. Then The Skipper wailed that poor old Jaguar up to maybe six (or even seven?) grand before slam-shifting into second with a horrifying clash of gear teeth. I looked at Sally Enderle and she kind of rolled her eyes—*oh, brother!*—and I smiled back and rotated my palms up—*what can you do?*—and she laughed me a laugh with sleigh bells hung all over it. Boy, did *that* ever get the old electricity pumping!

Pretty soon it was time to roll Cal's TC up to the line. "Listen," he said casually, "since I've done this before, why don't *you* take first crack at the hill?"

"M-Me?"

"Why not?"

"Well, er, ahh. . . ." Truth is, I could think of *lots* of reasons. Like, fr'instance, my only experience with Cal's TC (or *any* right-hand drive automobile, for that matter) came between my Triple Play Breakfast Special and the hill climb that very morning. Not to mention that I'd never been in any sort of bona fide Contest of Speed before (unless you count a few casual stoplight drags in the Old Man's tow truck and one time with my dad's Mercury back when he was letting me drive it). Plus I hadn't the foggiest notion which way the damn road went once it twisted out of sight around the first turn. And then there was the little matter of the stunningly gorgeous Miss Sally Enderle standing up there at the starting line in her magnificent white shorts. I sure as hell didn't want to do anything stupid in front of *her*. No sir. But with all those doubts swirling in my head, I still knew I couldn't say no. That's because I knew the lamest, most embarrassing thing of all would be to back down.

My hands were shaking as I fumbled to get the side flaps of Cal's old polo helmet over the ear wires of my fancy new sunglasses, and Cal tried to calm me down by telling me to "just take it easy" and that I should remember to "*flow* the car through the bends" (which sounded rather difficult, seeing as how I couldn't hardly flow pee through my bladder at that point), but behind it all you couldn't miss the nasty little smirk of a challenge. Typical. Cal Carrington was as good a friend as I ever had, but he'd push you and prod you right to the limit—and *beyond!*—just to see how you'd handle it. Truth is, Cal got me to do things I never, *ever* would've done by myself. Things a guy could feel a little proud and cocky about afterward. Like going up that hill for the very first time.

The taste of fear was like dirty pennies in my mouth as I inched Cal's MG up to the line, and I was glad my knees were hidden under the dashboard where nobody could see them shaking. But I gritted my teeth, nodded *"ready"* in the general direction of Sally Enderle, and gave it everything I had. And boy oh boy, was it ever *hectic!* First you accelerated through first and second to a nasty right-left combination called "The Devil's Elbow," followed by a steep grade up through a tunnel of trees to a sweeping set of esses that some guys (like Cal, for instance) bragged they could take in third, followed by a final banzai charge to the finish line. I guess it sounds pretty simple now, but that's not what it felt like at the time. Not hardly! Trees and fence posts and telephone poles whipped past in a frothy blur on both sides, and every damn hump, twist, bend, and crest in the road seemed to *JUMP OUT!* at me like those spring-loaded spooks on the Ghost Train ride at Palisades Park. I swear, that was the longest one minute, thirty-eight-point-three seconds I'd ever experienced in my life! And I must've done it all on a single breath, since I found myself gasping for air after I crossed the finish line. My hands ached from hanging on so tight and I could hardly get my feet to work the pedals and slow down once I'd cleared the top. But by God I *made* it! And without spinning, crashing, or over-revving the engine. Not even once.

I have to admit, I was pretty damn proud of myself.

At least until my buddy Cal went up an hour later and knocked more than ten whole seconds off my time. And the sonofabitch claimed he was going *slow,* on account of he was just trying to learn the stinking course!

While we waited for our next run, Cal struck up a conversation with the owner of a shiny black MG TD lined up a few spaces in front of us. The car was absolutely showroom new, right down to squeaky-clean red leather that hardly looked like it'd been sat in and chrome hubcaps that glistened like wet mirrors in the sunlight. Standing next to the TD was this pale, somber-faced guy with hollow cheeks, sunken eyes, and a scant few strands of hair plastered down east-west across the top of his head as if to fool people into thinking he wasn't really bald. That never works. His name was Carson Flegley, and it turned out he'd just bought his TD from Colin St. John a few days before and that Giant's Despair was his first-ever S.C.M.A. event. So it came as no surprise that he was pretty well rattled (which *I* could certainly appreciate!) and his car wasn't helping any since it was running like shit up the hill. Oh, she'd start and idle and highway cruise just fine, but trying to power full throttle up that steep incline made her stutter and gag something awful. Naturally, my friend Cal figured he was now an Accomplished Master when it came to S.U. carburetors (I mean, he'd spent the better part of an hour watching me set the ones on his engine, right?) so it wasn't five minutes before he had his head wedged under the hood of Carson Flegley's new TD, fiddling indiscriminately with all the various float level, jet height, throttle position, and needle depth settings that make S.U.s work. At least when they feel like it, anyway. You could see Cal was making a real mess of it, but I let him go for twenty minutes or so before casually leaning in and asking, "Uh, Cal, did I ever explain Butch Bohunk's First Rule of Engine Tuning to you?"

He looked up at me over the bridge of his aviator sunglasses and shrugged. "Can't say as I recall. What's it about?"

I cleared my throat and did my best to deliver it the way Butch would have, right down to spitting on the pavement when I was done for proper emphasis: *"Y'all make sure you got yer damn sparks in order before y'start fuckin' around with th'God Damn carburetion."*

"Oh?" Cal said, reaching for the TD's distributor with both hands. It wasn't long before he had that poor MG screwed up so bad it wouldn't even run. He'd have Carson Flegley tug on the starter knob and she'd just grind and fart, grind and fart, and every now and again blast a two-foot sheet of flame back through the carburetors. Carson's face looked like milk going sour, and I got to thinking it was time to maybe reach in and lend a hand.

But you can bet your ass I waited for Cal to *ask*.

With Cal safely out of the way, I step-by-step put all the settings back where they belonged and only then went searching for the *real* trouble. And it didn't take long to find the renegade tuft of insulation that was jamming the advance mechanism in the distributor. Ah-*ha!* On top of that, the point gap was down to six thousandths and the dashpots on both S.U.s were bone-dry. No question the mechanics at Westbridge had performed a truly piss-poor predelivery inspection. Anyhow, I decided to do this Carson Flegley fellow a favor and put it all right for him. I mean, there wasn't much of anything else to do, was there? When I was done, that sucker fired up on the first pull and settled down to an absolutely perfect 800-r.p.m. idle. "There," I said, wiping an imaginary drip of oil off the rear carburetor dashpot, "*that* oughta do it." And it sure as hell did! On its very next run, that TD pulled clean and strong all the way to the top, and Carson Flegley came down off that hill happy as a guy who'd just gotten his ashes hauled by Rita Hayworth. He even sort of smiled. "Hey," he said, sticking out a pale, bony hand, "thanks a *lot*."

"Hey, no problem," I told him.

"Here," he said, reaching for his pocket, "let me give you a little something. . . ."

"Not a chance," Cal broke in. "You just put that away. Glad we could be of service. Isn't that right, Buddy?"

"Uh, s-sure," I grumbled as Carson's wallet disappeared back into his pants.

"Gee whiz," he sighed, "I sure wish I could find somebody like you to work on my MG *all* the time."

That's when I noticed the Jersey plate on his TD. "Might not be a problem," I told him. "You come from anywheres near Passaic?"

"Sure *do!*" Carson grinned, his head bobbing up and down. "My family runs a funeral parlor over in East Orange. I'm there most every day. Passaic's only a few minutes away."

To tell the honest truth, undertakers have always sort of given me the willies, mostly on account of I can't help thinking what it is they exactly *do* with the stiffs. Or if they wear gloves while they do it. But in Carson Flegley's case I had to put my personal feelings on manual override and make an exception, not only because he seemed to be a pretty nice guy and liked low-slung British two-seaters, but also because he had the makings of a grade-A service customer over at Old Man Finzio's gas station. Especially if he kept running his MG in events like this hill climb, which are absolutely guaranteed to wear out English mechanical parts even faster than normal street abuse. I figured a few more solid, cash-money service customers might just change Old Man

Finzio's attitude about sports cars. Or at least keep him from firing me, anyway. "You just bring the little rascal over to Finzio's Sinclair in Passaic whenever she needs a little attention," I told Carson Flegley. "I'll keep her runnin' right."

Once I got done field-tuning Carson's MG, the three of us hung around by the starting line, drinking lukewarm bottles of root beer and watching Sally Enderle flirt with all the drivers. Every time a new car rolled up to the line, she'd find some excuse to lean in and check her lipstick in the fender mirror or maybe kick up a heel like there was something stuck to the bottom of her shoe or bend clear over as if she saw some worrisome split on one of the tire sidewalls. But whatever she did, Sally Enderle made damn sure every red-blooded adult male on that hill was paying close attention. I know I was. "Saaay," I wondered out loud, "I thought she was supposed to be Creighton Pendleton's girlfriend?"

"Yeah, I guess so," Cal nodded, taking a swig off his root beer. "When he's *around,* anyway...."

"You mean, not *always?*"

Cal shrugged. "I hear Creighton's over in England this week, checking out some superspecial new Jaguar race car. I don't imagine Sally Enderle's the type to just hang around by the phone, waiting for some guy to call."

"No, I guess not."

And that's about when Sally decided it was getting a bit too warm over by the starting line, so she asked the next driver to wait just a second, parked the green flag between two perfect knees, and tied her shirttails together in front of her, exposing a magnificent expanse of sleek, tanned female midriff. "Oh, Lordy," I moaned, "that's got to be the most beautiful creature I have *ever* seen."

"Yeah," Cal agreed. "She thinks so, too."

We each got another run in later that afternoon, and although I went six seconds quicker than before (and—*ahem*—measurably faster than Carson Flegley and his new TD) Cal beat us both. By a *bunch.* In fact, his time of 1:26.8 was the second-fastest MG run of all, just a few tenths behind some well-known local hotshoe with a Shorrock supercharger on his TD. The rank-and-file S.C.M.A. regulars were mighty impressed with that, and a lot of them started casually wandering by every now and again to see if they could pick up on some of the closely guarded speed secrets we'd developed behind the tightly closed doors of my Aunt Rosamarina's garage.

It was actually kind of funny.

Naturally, I was happy for Cal, but I must admit it was gnawing at me a little how the sonofabitch could be *seven whole seconds* quicker than me up a ninety-second hill. In the same damn car! And that's how poisonous thoughts like *Why should he be so much FASTER than me?* and *We both put our pants on one leg at a time* and worst of all *By God, I'm gonna SHOW 'em!* started rattling around in my head and making me just a little desperate. More than a little, even.

So my jaw was set hard as prestressed concrete when I climbed behind the wheel for my third and final run up the hill. I was hell-bent on knocking *at least* five seconds off my time (maybe more!) and I wasn't too particular about how I got it done. I wasn't scared of that damn hill anymore. Not one bit. Nor was I particularly worried about crashing Cal's raggedy MG. No, I'd fallen victim to the single greatest fear a driver can have when he hops into a racing car: *the fear of not going FAST enough.* Which meant my eyes were narrowed down to gun slits as I rolled up to that sneering asphalt waterfall for my final run. Sally Enderle raised the green flag and flashed me her trademark thousand-kilowatt smile. "Y'all ready, darlin'?"

I looked right into her luminous green eyes, jammed the shifter into first, tightened my death grip on the wheel (in fact, it's amazing the rim didn't shatter), gunned the engine—*WWAAAHHHHHH!*—and nodded. And that's about when the number four connecting rod broke in half and flung itself (along with assorted valve pieces, piston bits, and crankcase fragments) clear through the side of the block—*WWAAAAHHHHHHHIIII-KLANKKK!*—and I suddenly found myself enveloped in a foul-smelling cloud of steam and oil smoke as the green flag fluttered down and everybody—Sally Enderle included—burst out laughing like a pack of hyenas. *Haw-haw-ha-haw-haw-haw!* A raw hole melted open in the pit of my stomach. "Hey there, sport," Sally Enderle giggled, damn near gagging on it, "that's one pretty fast MG you got there...."

Haw-haw-ha-haw-haw-haw!

I felt my face burning like a short in a battery cable, and I remember wishing I could shrink down to the size of a field mouse so's I could crawl through the hole in the TC's oil pan and be alone in there with all the other busted junk. Then Cal came stomping through the smoke and coolant mist with his fists clenched so tight it made all the blood drain out of his knuckles. But after standing there for a minute or two, alternately glaring at me and staring in utter disbelief at the pool of oil and motor fragments beneath the TC's engine compartment, it was like some sort of magic safety valve opened. Cal reached out and gently put his hand on my shoulder. "Hey, no problem," he said through the thinnest of smiles. "Why, it could've happened to *any-body*...."

And in my heart, I knew he was right.

After all, I hadn't *murdered* Cal's old TC. Not at all. The damn thing had simply decided *to commit suicide* while I was in the driver's seat. I mean, we weren't even *moving,* for gosh sakes. And we knew up front the oil pressure was down, didn't we? But somehow none of that offered much comfort. I watched Cal walk solemnly around to the front of the TC, slowly remove his stolen aviator sunglasses, and proceed to haul off and kick that damn MG squarely in the radiator core. Hard as he could. *"You worthless, two-faced pile of shit!"* he bellowed, giving it a couple more shots. *"We sweated fucking BLOOD over you!"*

But the MG just sat there, contemptuously drooling oil off its undercarriage. And then—all by itself!—the radiator sprung a leak right where Cal kicked it and peed a thin stream of steaming-hot engine coolant all over his Bass Weejun loafers.

No doubt about it, that car had a sense of humor.

And an ugly one, at that.

But one of the nice things about sportycar people is how they rally around a fellow racer who's hit a patch of trouble. Especially if there's a wreck involved or a mechanical disaster serious enough to be hopeless (which of course means nobody will actually have to *do* anything except maybe stand around shrugging their shoulders and murmuring condolences). As you can imagine, our new friend Carson Flegley turned out to be rather adept at that sort of thing (in spite of this being his first-ever S.C.M.A. event) but then, I guess you'd have to rank Carson as something of a ringer in the condolence business. For sure he had that look of sadness, hope, and deep, *deep* understanding that guys in his line of work have to turn on and off like a faucet a dozen times a day down pat. "Gee, that's a shame," he said with great yet understated emotion. "Is there anything I can *do?*"

"Tell you what," Cal said without skipping a beat, "I'd sure as heck like another crack at that hill. . . ."

Carson looked at Cal, then at the hill, then at his shiny new TD, and back at Cal again. "Er . . . uh . . . ah . . . ," he stammered, swallowing a half dozen times while Cal flashed his absolute best rich-kid smile directly into Carson's face. "S-Sure. W-Why not," he said in a crumbling voice. "H-Help yourself. . . ." And, just like *that,* he handed over the keys to his brand-spanking-new MG. Can you believe it?

"Hey, *thanks!*" Cal grinned, pumping Carson's arm till it damn near came loose at the shoulder. Then he took off with the keys before Carson could think twice about it—just in case Carson came out from under the ether and had himself a change of heart. That left Carson and me to push the TD forward as each car took off on its final, balls-out charge up the hill and we rolled another dozen feet closer to where Sally Enderle was standing in her fabulous white tennis shorts.

Cal didn't come back for damn near forty-five minutes, and you could see Carson was getting a little nervous as we inched closer and closer to the starting line and Cal (not to mention the keys to Carson's MG) was nowhere to be seen. But Cal didn't reappear until he had eyeballed every hump, bump, bevel in the road and pavement heave on that hill. He also watched how all the fast guys were taking the corners, and tried to figure how he might do it even a little better. Far as I could tell, Cal was about the only driver who did that all day.

We'd rolled Carson's TD all the way up to second in line by the time Cal came sprinting down the hill (at the last instant, natch) and gracefully hopped behind the wheel. "Well," he said, fastening his helmet strap, "I guess it's *showtime.*" Before Carson could say a word, Cal fired up the engine and nodded to Sally Enderle. "Okay, gorgeous," he said, patting the TD's dashboard, "let's *do* it!"

And did he ever.

Cal had the revs just right and sidestepped the clutch the instant Sally so much as *twitched,* and that black MG shot away with a smooth, solid screech off the right-rear tire. He snicked it into second precisely at the redline and arced out of sight with his foot buried in the floorboards, and you could hear that little four-banger wailing Wide Fucking Open all the way up the hill. He even took those fast esses at the top without lifting—in *third!*—and when his time came down, it was the fastest damn MG run of the day. *1:25 flat!* And in a bone stock, right-off-the-showroom-floor TD that he'd never so much as *sat* in before!

It was quite a performance, no two ways about it.

There was the usual blowout trophy party afterward, and naturally Charlie Priddle made a big show of collecting the first place mug he'd won by being the only car entered in the "Over 2-Liter Vintage Touring Class." Why, you'd have thought the asshole won the damn twenty-four hours of Le Mans the way he strutted up to the podium to get his lousy tin cup. And that after he made such a show of barely creeping up the hill—not even *trying* to go fast—and then acting like he could've gone as quick as anybody (maybe even quicker) if he'd only felt like bringing his supercharged Maserati single-seater instead of that monstrous old Rolls. That pissed Cal off to no end. "He's nothing but a damn poacher," Cal snarled into his beer. "What he does takes away from all the guys who really get out there and *try.*"

Even I could appreciate that, and the sooner Charlie Priddle was off the podium, the better I liked it. Fortunately, Charlie and some of his old money buddies had a dinner engagement at some fancy restaurant in town, and they took off in his enormous old Rolls as soon as he'd collected his hardware. Meanwhile, all the MG guys were crowding in around Cal and Carson and me, toasting us and congratulating us

like Cal was the great all-American quarterback who'd just won the
big homecoming game and we were, well, the guys who got to carry
his shoulder pads and helmet. But it was nice being the center of attention, and the MG crowd kept us well-supplied with Dixie cups of
cold beer (one right after the other, in fact) throughout the entire ceremony. The funny part was that the S.C.M.A. still had Carson Flegley
listed as the driver of the black TD, and that's how an exceedingly
happy undertaker from East Orange wound up swilling beer out of a
shiny first-place mug at his very first S.C.M.A. speed event. Cal told
him to keep it, too, which was a mighty nice gesture. But Cal never
cared much about the medallions and mantelware they handed out after
the racing was over. Just about the driving itself.

    After entirely too many rounds at the trophy party, some of the
local MG types helped us find a garage where we could stash Cal's
blown-up TC, and then a whole bunch of us went out to eat dinner at
some Chinese restaurant on the other side of the river. But, what with
the party at the starting line and dragging Cal's TC over to that garage
and getting lost once or twice and having to organize and reorganize
our meandering MG parade every ten blocks or so to pick up stragglers
and listen to the local MG guys argue over whether we were heading
in the right direction, the Chinese place was closed by the time we got
there. So we all got drunk as hooty owls instead. The local MG types
helped with that, too, since Cal and me were underage (although Cal
had some first-rate fake I.D.s) so they'd sort of sneak us into places in
the middle of a whole stampeding herd of them. I wore my nifty new
aviator sunglasses (which meant I was bumping into a lot of things,
seeing as how it was nighttime and none of the places we went were
particularly well lit) and somebody handed me a weatherbeaten old wool
fedora to put over my head so I would maybe look a little older. It was
the kind of hat Old Man Finzio might wear to church (if, in fact, he
ever went to church) and the MG people kept telling me to keep it
down low over my forehead so nobody could tell how old I was. I
figured I looked like one of those hot New York jazz musicians, you
know? Maybe a saxophone player (albeit with strangely raw knuckles
for a musician). Truth is, I don't remember if we ever actually ate a
meal that night (or, in fact, much of anything else) but I do recollect
the following morning in vivid and hideous detail.

    I shuddered awake to the shriek of tiny, high-revving racing engines
wailing past at full throttle, and discovered myself folded into the back
of somebody's light blue DeSoto four-door with Cal's stolen comforter
halfheartedly wrapped around my shoulders and a Sears Craftsman
toolbox for a pillow. It was not what you could call a particularly comfortable place to sleep (or even pass out) and I had absolutely no idea

where I was, how I got there, or why I was wearing a shoe with no sock on one foot and a sock but no shoe on the other. Not that I really much cared, since my body ached like I'd been worked over by the Gambino family and nothing in all of recorded human history hurt so much as my head. In fact, I remember reaching up with my fingertips to see if there was an actual crack in it someplace. Why, if I could've just laid my hands on that missing shoe, I'd have thrown it hard as I could at those damn race cars screaming past less than twenty yards away. With superhuman effort I hoisted myself upright, swung the door open, and gracefully fell out on the ground. "I declare," Cal snickered, looking down at me over the tips of his shoes, "it *lives!*"

"Real funny," I groaned, not the least bit amused. Oh, I'd had a few minor-league hangovers in my time, but never anything so wicked as this. Not hardly. One of the MG people offered me a couple aspirin and another fixed me up with a mug of hot coffee, but I was still feeling pretty rocky as I hunted for my new aviator sunglasses to cut down on the glare. "Say," I asked nobody in particular, "where the hell are we, anyway?"

"Why, Brynfan Tyddyn, of course."

"Brynfan Tyddyn?" I puzzled, turning the words over in my head. Just saying it was like trying to talk with your mouth full. Turns out Brynfan Tyddyn meant "Big Farm by the Hill" or "Big Hill by the Barn" or "Big Barn by the Farm" or something in this strange language used by the people who ran around England in animal skins before vowels were discovered, and it was the name of this enormous, woodsy country estate that belonged to an actual Pennsylvania state senator. The guy was *incredibly* rich (the kind you can only get by being born into it) and, like a lot of other wealthy, upper-crust individuals with plenty of free time to fill, he loved playing around with expensive European sports cars. And his estate at Brynfan Tyddyn was a swell place to do it, seeing as how it was big as a damn state park and had all these winding blacktop driveways and access roads snaking through groves of fruit trees and rolling across meadows full of dandelions and wildflowers and fat, industrious honeybees. It was pretty as all getout, and I suppose I should've felt privileged just to be there (I mean, garage mechanics don't generally get invited to many social functions involving country estates *or* state senators) but my head was pounding and my stomach was doing one of those ocean-swell corkscrew rolls, and all I all I really wanted was to be back in the apartment over my aunt's garage, gobbling handfuls of aspirin with Bromo-Seltzer chasers and not straying too far from the commode. Naturally, my buddy Cal suggested maybe a little "hair of the dog" might help, and assured me that all his old-money friends took themselves a little nip in the morning

after a rough night out. For medicinal purposes only, you understand. "Helps jumpstart the old batteries," he said. And Cal just happened to have a half-empty pint of bourbon handy. Seeing as how there was no way I could feel any worse, I held my nose, clenched my teeth, and took a slug. And then another. And then one more. And, believe it or not, I started to feel a little better. Although it started occurring to me that hanging around with this fashionable imported sports car crowd was turning me into a fine old specimen of a street-corner rum-pot.

I stuck around the MG bivouac for the next couple hours, drinking coffee laced with an occasional shot of bourbon and trying to get my eyes to focus again. But even with the edges all fuzzy, Brynfan Tyddyn was one of the most beautiful, elegant places I'd ever been, what with the forests and meadows and this huge, ivy-covered brick mansion right in the middle. It was also a swell place to hold a car race, even though it looked a bit *dangerous* with the pavement barely a lane and a half wide and trees growing right up to the edge in several key spots. A driver sure couldn't make many mistakes at Brynfan Tyddyn. Not unless he wanted to collect himself a brick driveway pillar or a stout tree trunk. Which is why the S.C.M.A. wouldn't allow big cars like Jags or Allards to race there. It was actually kind of nice, since the smallbore guys always raced in the shadows of the big iron and never got their fair share of the glory. Not to mention that my head wasn't at all ready for the blare of Jaguar sixes or the ground-throbbing rumble of Allard V-8s that particular ayem. Not hardly.

We had a tasty picnic lunch courtesy of the MG guys (which went down ok but didn't sit too well later on), and afterward Cal and me went wandering around to admire the estate and watch the races. As you can imagine, Cal was pacing up and down like a caged leopard the whole afternoon, muttering under his breath about what a damn shame it was that the car blew up and how he could drive goddam *rings* around the rest of those guys. It just wasn't *fair,* you know? Not being able to race was eating Cal up pretty bad, no two ways about it. But we had a good time anyway, and not being stuck under a car gave me a chance to learn a little something about the S.C.M.A. racing classes. First off we saw a heat for the little modifieds—Cal called them "tiddlers"—in which this strange, pygmy-sized Italian device called a Bandini (which looked like a kid's pedal toy and probably weighed about the same) streaked off to a commanding lead, only to drop out a few laps from the checker when the battery cable fell off. The Bandini's retirement left things to a much prettier Italian roadster called a Siata, which looked like a miniature edition of Creighton Pendleton's 4.1 Ferrari but sounded more like a sewing machine in heat.

Next up was a race for these little cigar-shaped English open-wheelers powered by 500cc Norton and J. A. Prestwich motorcycle engines and built to such ridiculously tiny proportions that they made the tiddlers from the first race look enormous by comparison. I guess those things were all the rage in England and a few American enthusiasts had brought them back to race here in the States. They looked like big tin water bugs, and you couldn't use them on the street since they didn't have lights or fenders or, in fact, much of anything except an engine, a gas tank, and a hole in the middle for the driver. Personally, I didn't see the attraction. I mean, they had no *stature* to them. Not like a Jag XK or a Ferrari. Plus the damn things popped and banged like firecrackers in a tin can and smelled something awful from the doped-up, alcohol-base fuel they were running. But I had to admit they were quick—especially around a tight, narrow, twisty little circuit like Brynfan Tyddyn—and one of them actually cut the fastest lap anybody ran all day. The problem was you couldn't *see* the speed. But you could tell the owners thought those little British single-seaters were pretty damn special. In fact, they were even kind of smug about it, waltzing around the paddock using uptown words like "monoposto" and "Gran Pree" all the time. But there were only four of the little boogers on hand (a Kieft and three Coopers, not that you could really tell them apart) and some guy named Dick Irish pretty much ran away and hid from the other three, so it really wasn't too exciting.

The last race more than made up for the other two, since we had ourselves a real wheel-to-wheel barn burner between this transplanted Englishman named John Gordon Benett in a stripped-down, Nordec-supercharged MG TD (which Cal told me was about the quickest damn MG in the country, bar none) and a *very* special Porsche roadster in the hands of some guy named Phil Walters. I'd never heard of either one, but Cal said they were both top-notch drivers and proved it by keeping his mouth shut through the entire race. And what a race! Those two charged around like they were tied together—lap after lap!—the Porsche skating around with its ass end hung out to dry and the front wheels ruddering into the skid, and the MG wailing along barely *inches* behind, sniffing and pawing for a way to get by. But the Porsche just had a little too much for the MG, and Walters took a squeaker of a win with John Gordon Benett's supercharged TD right up his tailpipe all the way to the checker.

"Boy," I said afterward, "those guys really know how to *drive!*"

"They should," Cal explained. "They're *professionals.*"

That kind of surprised me, since I knew the S.C.M.A. was pretty damn vocal about being strictly amateur and not allowing prize money or sponsor names on the sides of the cars like you saw at the Indianapolis 500. I sort of assumed that hired-gun professional drivers fell into the same category, you know? But some guys just have to *win* (even if all they're winning is a tin cup) and there was nothing in the books to prevent a car owner from putting a "quick friend" behind the wheel.

I mean, it was all just for fun, right?

Still, it's always a thrill to see great cars in the hands of great drivers, and especially when two of them wind up head-to-head in equal machinery and you're lucky enough to be perched on the fences. Only trouble is, it makes all the duffers, wannabes, and pretenders out there look pretty damn lame by comparison.

After the races, Cal and me wandered over to congratulate the drivers. They were standing around between the two cars, wrapped in the scent of brake linings and hot oil vapor, laughing and shooting the breeze with this short, solid little guy with sad eyes, a granite jaw, and black hair swirling up off his forehead like flames off a campfire. Naturally, Cal waltzed right up like we were old school chums and grabbed Phil Walters's hand. "Hey, that was one *hell* of a race," Cal said, working Phil's arm up and down like a pump handle.

"Thanks. Old John sure tried to make it tough on me though, didn't he?"

"*I'll* say."

"Made me run her right to the limit."

"We saw."

"Why, every time I looked in the mirror, it was full of this damn MG. I just couldn't get *rid* of the bastard."

"Oh, we did our best to keep it interesting," the English MG driver grinned, "but I'm afraid the Porsche was just a mite too quick for us today."

"Yeah, Mr. Walters," I tossed in, "that Porsche of yours is *fast!*"

"Oh, thanks," he said, "but it's not my car."

"It's not?" He shook his head. "Then who does it belong to?"

"Actually," the little guy with the sad eyes said, almost like he was apologizing, "it's mine."

"Well then, congratulations to you, too. That was one hell of a race."

"Oh, don't congratulate *me,*" he said in the softest, politest voice you ever heard. "I'm afraid John Gordon would have whipped us pretty soundly if *I'd* been at the wheel."

"Buddy," Cal said grandly, "meet Briggs Cunningham."

The name rang a little bit of a bell, but I couldn't really place it at the time. "Well," I said, shaking his hand, "that's an awful nice Porsche you got there anyways, Mr. Cunningham."

"Oh, this is just a toy we play around with. I have a couple big cars, too."

"Big cars?"

He nodded. "You'll see them sooner or later if you keep coming to the races. We bring them out here in the States every once in a while. Will you be at Elkhart Lake?"

"Elkhart Lake?" Heck, I'd never even heard of Elkhart Lake, and I was sort of embarrassed when I had to ask him where it was.

"It's up in Wisconsin," Briggs Cunningham explained. "About an hour north of Milwaukee. Great place. You shouldn't miss it. Wonderful spot. Absolutely wonderful."

"It's the week after Grand Island," Cal tossed in.

"Grand Island?" I said.

"Up by Niagara Falls," Cal nodded. "The last weekend in August. You guys planning to make that one?"

"No, we'll still be over in Europe," Briggs Cunningham said like it was nothing at all, "racing in France."

And slowly it began to dawn on me that there were people in this sport who could take off whenever they felt like it and go traipsing all over the whole damn country —all over the whole damn *world,* even!— just to go race their fancy sports cars. It made you wonder just what the hell they did for a living (if anything!), and why the heck *I* couldn't have been a member of the Lucky Sperm Club like them. It just didn't seem fair. On the other hand, simply getting to hang around all their snazzy cars and swell parties was a hell of a lot better than anything I had going back home. I wanted more out of life than wrenching on rusted-out Plymouths at the Old Man's Sinclair and listening to my dad lecture me about the wonderful union benefits of his chemical plant job in Newark. Maybe I even wanted something more than getting into Julie Finzio's pants.

Anyhow, we chewed the fat back and forth about racing and the relative merits of Porsches versus supercharged MGs until the sun was easing down behind the senator's mansion, and my silver-tongued friend Cal Carrington managed to work himself a deal to have his derelict TC hauled all the way back to Jersey in Briggs Cunningham's trailer. That was one hell of a nice gesture on Briggs's part, since it meant somebody from his crew (of which there were at least a half dozen) had to *drive* that stripped-down Porsche back to New York.

Naturally Cal stayed behind to help out with the TC, so I hitched a ride back to Passaic with Carson Flegley in his black TD. As you can imagine, it was nice having all the rudimentary amenities like a top and a windshield and a few inches of actual upholstery under my butt (which was incidentally on the correct *American* side in Carson's car), not to mention a heater under the dash for that trip through the mountains. But it still wasn't a particularly pleasant trip, on account of all the pick-me-up bourbon and beer had long since worn off and I generally felt like I'd eaten a dead rat, fallen down a fire escape, and been left in a damp alley to die. Plus it took us absolutely for*ever* to get home with Carson Flegley at the wheel. Now don't get me wrong, I was plenty happy that he didn't try to carve through the mountains in world-record time like my friend Cal, but he was so worried about getting a damn stone chip or a mud splash on his new TD that he'd pull over to the side anytime another car or truck got anywhere close to us. Plus he'd picked up this notion that you had to vary your speed and never exceed 50 miles per hour when breaking in a new MG. I tried to explain the difference between *engine* speed and *road* speed to him, and also how those flat-out runs up Giant's Despair made nonsense out of any normal break-in schedule. But Carson couldn't see it on account of he didn't understand gearing and never topped 40 going up the hill. He was *determined* to stick to the break-in procedure Barry Spline had carefully outlined for him when he took delivery of his car. Even if it made no sense at all. I mean, who was he going to believe? Some punk gas station mechanic or a guy who came from an actual MG dealership and wore a classy blue shop coat and moreover spoke with a genuine, 100 percent–authentic British accent?

And who could blame him?

So it was one long, *looong* ride back to the apartment over my Aunt Rosamarina's garage, and it seemed even longer on account of Carson wasn't all that much of a conversationalist. Then again, I didn't encourage him. After all, who wants to hear an undertaker talk shop?

9

THE GLAMOROUS LIFE OF
A RACING WRENCH

BELIEVE IT or not, I managed to get myself relieved of duty at the Sinclair come Monday morning. It started when I rolled in about two hours late, still bleary from the all-night ride back from Pennsylvania. As soon as I stumbled through the door, I found myself on the receiving end of a rasping, hacking, nose-to-nose lecture from Old Man Finzio about the difference between A Goddam Garage Business and A Goddam Nursery School. "We ain't a bunch of nose-in-the-air rich assholes 'round *here,*" he snarled, shaking a bony finger under my nose. "Not like them high-hats *you* been runnin' around with. Nossir. 'Round here folks gotta *work* t'earn a goddam livin'. An' they sure as hell can't *work* if they don't bother t' goddam *show up* in the mornin', can they?" The Old Man was pretty worked up, and it sounded a lot like one of my dad's famous post–ball game speeches. Only nastier. And no question Old Man Finzio's breath smelled worse. Especially at close range.

But I stood there and took it, nodding my head at appropriate intervals like I was listening, even though my antennae were apparently down that particular ayem and most of it was coming in as pure static. I do recall some stuff about the evils of foreign automobiles and the idleness and greed of rich people (especially the kind who drove those foreign automobiles) and how those third generation wealthy assholes were corrupting his beloved Republican Party from within. Which naturally led into the usual stuff about the lack of morals and proper work habits among my age group and me, Buddy Palumbo, in particular. I'm sure the Old Man could've gone on all morning, but he broke down in one of his trademark coughing jags about halfway through, so I missed out on the big *"and that's why this whole damn country's going straight to hell!"* payoff that inevitably comes at the end.

I think Old Man Finzio would've likely let it go at that if I hadn't spent the rest of that morning turning everything I touched into a certified class-A disaster. First I broke the coffeepot. Then I snapped three studs trying to get the damn exhaust manifold off some jewelry salesman's Dodge Wayfarer that was in for a valve job. Next I couldn't find the damn cutting torch (and I had it right in my *hand,* you know?) after which I set it down for a moment—in full operational mode—on the hood of Dr. Rossi's brand-new Lincoln Capri, which was in for its very first oil change. The flame seared a splendid, thumb-sized scorch about six inches back from the hood ornament where you couldn't miss it unless you had a damn laundry bag over your head.

But I think the Old Man still might have let it slide (hey, we all have bad days, right?) if only Julie hadn't showed up an hour later to pencil some numbers in the books. As you'll recall, I hadn't been seeing too much of her on account of all the time I'd been putting in on Cal's worthless TC, and to tell the truth, I hadn't been real good about calling her, either. So I could really feel the old frost when she walked by my workbench and smelled trouble right away when she motioned for me to meet her out behind the shop a few minutes later. No question she had something besides the usual "long-time-no-see" chitchat on her mind. Sure enough, we hadn't so much as rounded the corner when Julie started in on me full blast. *"Why should I NEED this garbage?"* she screamed, fire spitting out both eyeballs.

"But, Ju—"

"You think I got nothin' *better* to do? Is that what you think? *Huh? IS IT?!!"*

"A'course not, Julie, I—"

"Think you can just call me up any old time you feel like a little kissy-face at the drive-in? *Huh?* Is *that* the way it is?"

"Aw, Ju—"

"And then let me rot by the stinkin' phone for weeks on end while you go screw around with those frickin' racecars!"

"But, Julie—*honey*—Cal and me had an awful lot to do. It gets like that some—"

"Yeah, *sure* it does! You was so frickin' busy y'couldn't find *FIVE GODDAM MINUTES* t'pick up the frickin' phone and see if I was maybe still alive."

"But, *baby*—"

"Don't 'baby' *me*, Mister Buddy Palumbo. You make me *sick*. And I mean *SICK!* Why should I *need* this garbage. *Huh?* You tell me. *WHY?!"*

No question I wanted to stay on good terms with Julie, and not just because we did stuff out behind the station on Saturday nights (or used to, anyway). Heck, she was about the only female I'd ever been really close to. So I felt pretty damn scummy about ignoring her the way I had, and for that reason just stood there and took it like a man, nodding and shrugging and staring at my shoes while she paced back and forth in front of me like a damn drill sergeant and let me have it with both barrels.

But I was patient and kept my mouth shut and pretty soon I could see she was running out of steam and even starting to cry a little bit, and although I've never claimed to be any kind of expert when it comes to dealing with the female of the species, I *do* know that's your only chance to turn one of these deals around. "Aw, baby," I said softly, kind of easing my way toward her, "I'm *real* sorry. Honest I am. It's just that racing's so, I don't know, so damn *addicting*. Why, it's the most exciting thing I've ever done in my life. Really it is. Sometimes I just get sort of, you know, *involved....* "

"Yeah, I know you do," she sniffed. "But too involved to even pick up the phone?"

"Aw, listen, Julie..."—I cautiously reached out and wrapped my fingers around her elbows—"...someday you gotta come to the races *with* me. Then you'd see for yourself. Honest you would." I pulled lightly on her arms and felt her glide gently into me. We'd have a *super* time there together. Really we would."

"We would?"

"*Suuure* we would," I whispered, nuzzling into her hair. "You'd *love* it."

"Humph. Just like I love hangin' around gas station garages on Friday and Saturday nights, I suppose?"

"Aw, honey, it's not like that at all. Sure, sometimes you gotta pay the price. But believe you me, it's *worth* it. Why, you should *see* all the fancy cars and rich, classy people we hang around with at the races. Real live *celebrities,* even."

"Oh yeah?" Julie said, perking up just a little. "Like who?"

"Oh, well, ah, let's see." I was racking my brain for names that might impress her. "I've seen that Dave Garroway guy a couple times already...."

"He's the one with the chimpanzee on television, isn't he?" she said, not looking particularly stunned.

That's when I realized *movie stars* were what I really needed. "Well," I told her, "how about *Tyrone Power?*"

"*Tyrone Power?*" Julie's eyebrows slid up a notch or two. *"He* goes to the car races?"

"*Suuure* he does. And *Jackie Cooper,* too. He races a Jaguar just like Big Ed's...."

"He *does?*"

"Uh-huh. Why, he even wrote about it in a magazine called *Road & Track.*"

"He *did?*"

"Yup, he sure did. So did Clark Gable."

"CLARK GABLE??!!" Her eyes popped like mousetraps. *"The* Clark Gable?"

"Um hum," I nodded.

She looked at me kind of sideways. "Say, this isn't just another load of the old Palumbo bullshit, is it?"

"Of *course* not," I gasped, insulted that she would even *think* such a thing.

"Even the part about Clark Gable?"

"Absolutely. He goes to the races all the time when he's not all wrapped up shooting a picture."

"You're sure?"

"It's God's truth. I swear." And it *was* true. Or at least that's what I'd heard from a couple of the MG guys at Giant's Despair. Of course, I'd never actually *seen* Tyrone Power or Jackie Cooper or Clark Gable at the races, but that was simply because they did all their sports car stuff out in California. But Julie didn't need to know that, did she? "And listen," I added, watching the celebrity sparks flickering in her eyes, "you should see the *places* we go. Why, just yesterday we were at this huge country estate that belongs to a real live Pennsylvania state senator."

"You *were?*"

"Um-hmm. And you should've *seen* it, Julie. There were forests and gardens and a big brick mansion right in the middle. Why, we even *slept* there."

"You're *kidding.*"

"No, I'm not. And I can't wait to take *you* with me." As you can see, I decided not to mention that my "accommodations" at Senator Wood's estate amounted to a moldy stolen comforter, the lid of a Sears Craftsman toolbox, and the back seat of an old four-door DeSoto.

"Sounds pretty dreamy," she admitted, her eyes dancing.

"Gee whiz, Julie," I continued, pulling her in close, "I can't help imagining how much nicer it'd be to have somebody, you know, *special* to share it with...."

"You mean like *me?*" Julie whispered, rolling her head into my shoulder.

"Sure like you, Julie. Like you and nobody else. Why, you'd be about the prettiest girl there."

I felt her stiffen like a dead mackerel. "What do you mean, *about?*" Whoops.

"So tell me," she asked in a dangerously singsong voice, "they got a *lot* of pretty girls at those races?"

"Oh ... well ... ahh," I mumbled as visions of Sally Enderle's incredible white shorts popped in my head like flashbulbs. "Certainly none as pretty as *you*. ..."

"Honest?" She was twirling a few strands of hair around her finger like a female spider spinning its web.

"Oh, no question about it, Julie. No question at all."

"That's nice," she finally whispered, leaning in close so I could feel her various female parts pressing in against me.

"It sure is," I whispered back, nuzzling her cheek.

"Isn't it?" she purred with her lips right up to my ear so the words sent heat waves pulsing through my system. I wrapped my arms around her and Julie put hers around me and when we started to kiss, she surprised the hell out of me by opening her mouth a little bit and more or less inviting my tongue inside. *WOW!*

And that, of course, is precisely when Old Man Finzio came stomping around the side of the building to see what his niece and star employee were up to. Seeing Julie and me all tied up in a love knot stopped the Old Man dead in his tracks, and his jaw had to work itself up and down a few times before he could produce any kind of recognizable noise. Imagine the sound of a rusty nail being pulled out of an old oak plank. But a split-second later he was bellowing away at the top of his lungs. *"YOU!!"* he shouted at Julie. *"You get the hell INSIDE!"* Julie jumped off me and scurried around the corner like a mouse running for its hole. *"And as for YOU, Palumbo,"* the Old Man hollered with a dangerous waver in his voice, *"you pack up yer shit up and get the hell outta my gas station. And I mean NOW!!"*

"Aw, geez, Mr. Finzio, if you'd jus—"

"SHUDDUP!" he screamed, running his eyes up and down me like a rake. *"I'll be damned if I'm gonna let my little niece play God's Gift t'every damn hard-on west of the Hudson River. No SIR! 'Specially not with one a'my God Damn EM-PLOY-EES! And for damn sure not on my goddam company time. YOU HEAR ME, PALUMBO?"*

Sure I heard him. Hell, everybody in Passaic heard him.

"Now you got just ten minutes t'clear yer shit outta my shop!" he snarled, the loose turkey skin above his collar turning tropical sunset colors. *"You unnerstand me, boy? TEN MINUTES!!!"* And with that he spun on his heels and stalked back into the building.

All I could do was just stand there, reeling and blinking and praying deep down inside that I'd wake up and discover it was only a bad dream. But of course it wasn't, even though it didn't seem *real*. Like I was watching myself in a movie or something, you know? But there was no getting away from the reality of the situation when I tiptoed back into the service bay and found the Old Man hard at work on *my* Dodge valve job. Naturally, I wanted to talk to him—to maybe *reason* with him—but I was all choked up and hollow-feeling and afraid my voice might crack like a little kindergarten kid with a skinned knee. And I could see the Old Man wasn't in any mood to listen, seeing as how wherever I went, he'd make sure to keep his back turned so I was looking squarely at his spine. Julie was nowhere to be seen, either, and finally there was just nothing to do but pack up Butch's tools and go. I carefully wiped off each wrench, socket, and screwdriver, packed them neatly away, and closed the lid. "Okay if I leave these here?" I heard myself ask.

"You bet'cher ass you'll leave them tools here," the Old Man growled without turning around. *"Them is Butch Bohunk's tools, not YERS!"*

Then he jammed his head back under the hood of that Dodge and pretended like I wasn't there. So I locked Butch's toolbox, heaved it under the bench, covered it with a fender blanket, and slipped the key into my pocket. No way would Butch want Old Man Finzio messing around with his tools. After that, there wasn't much to do but hang up my coveralls on the nail over by the space heater and walk on back to my apartment. Gee whiz, it wasn't even noon.

When I got there I flopped down on the bed and tried to sleep, but of course I couldn't. My body and mind were beat-out exhausted from the weekend, but all my nerve ends were jangling like fire alarms and the best I could do was just lay there with my eyes slammed shut while all these *things* swirled around in my brain like scenery whipping past a car window. It must've been past midnight when I finally dozed off, and I more or less slept clear through Tuesday. Or at least I stayed in bed all day. I mean, what did I have to get up for? Truth is, I'd never experienced the humiliation of getting fired before, and it made me feel angry, depressed, confused, guilty, and totally worthless. All at the same time. And that's not even mentioning how I might eventually wind up broke, hungry, and homeless. All told, I had maybe sixteen dollars wadded up in a sock in my top drawer and maybe another buck or two in loose change scattered around the apartment. Period. Not much to show for a guy who was supposedly earning himself a full-time, adult-type living, was it?

On the brighter side, my Aunt Rosamarina wasn't the type to throw me in the street just because I was down on my luck, and I could always cadge a meal or two in my mom's kitchen, especially if I broke down and told my folks I'd got *fired* (although telling them sounded even worse than starving to death, but then I wasn't real hungry yet, either).

But time passed (as it does), and by Wednesday morning I was feeling almost human again. I even had this crazy notion I could maybe go over by the Sinclair and patch things up with Old Man Finzio. So I washed and shaved, put on the closest thing to a clean shirt I had, and headed over to see if the Old Man had softened up any. But when I got there he was just pulling a Help Wanted sign out of the window and some burly-looking stranger in a string T-shirt was heaving a big red toolbox out of an unfamiliar Chevrolet station wagon and hauling it inside.

Well, so much for that.

I went back to my apartment and sulked for awhile before gingerly peeling two dollar bills off the skinny roll in my sock and heading over to Westbridge to see if Barry Spline had any openings. Believe me, it was tough getting into New York without the Old Man's tow truck or one of Big Ed's Caddies, and I spent the better part of two hours on assorted buses and subway trains, each one smelling slightly worse than the last as I got closer to Westbridge's dirty little corner of Manhattan. I ultimately had to hoof it the last five blocks from the nearest bus stop, and it was past noon by the time I finally arrived. Naturally, Barry and Colin St. John were out to lunch, and the only people inside were Hans, Bjorn, and Vito, none of whom spoke any English unless they wanted something off you. So I went looking for Sylvester, and found him slouched against the brickwork in the alley behind the shop, thoughtfully drinking his lunch. I figured Sylvester would be an excellent person to talk to, seeing as how he was a seasoned expert on the subject of getting fired. *"Sheee-it!"* Sylvester grumbled, taking a long pull off his bottle. "What th'fuck *you* got t'worry about."

"Well," I said, trying to make it sound desperate, "I got *fired.*"

"So?"

"So I don't have a *job* anymore."

"So?"

"So I'm *outta work,* Sylvester."

"So what? You still *single,* right?"

"Sure."

"You ain't got no *kids,* right?"

"A'course not."

"You ain't missed a meal yet, has you?"

"No. Not really."

"You still got a lil' money in yo' pocket?"

"Yeah. Some."

"How 'bout yo' rent? Is yo' rent paid?"

"Through August, anyway. But my aunt'd probably let it slide awhile if she knew I was tapped. . . ."

"Sheeeee-it!" Sylvester cackled, slapping one of his big, calloused hands on my knee. "You ain't *outta work,* son. Hell *no!* You is on fucking *vacation!"*

You must admit, Sylvester had a unique way of looking at things.

Barry Spline was back behind the parts counter when Sylvester and me returned from lunch, and he seemed pretty interested when I told him I might be looking for employment. "Only trouble," Barry sort of whispered behind his hand, "is we got a bloody full crew right h'at the moment. Don't see how we could use h'another set of 'ands just now. Yer understand, of course."

"Uh, sure."

"But we'll be sure t'keep yer in mind h'if things change. . . ."

"Gee, th-thanks," I said, my insides going pale.

Then Barry looked me up and down with this unusually thoughtful expression on his face. "Then again," he mused, stroking the end of his nose, "we could *maybe* put yer on as a race mechanic."

My mouth popped wide open. *"You COULD?"*

Barry nodded. "We can most always find a spot for a decent race mechanic."

"Gee whiz," I gushed. "That'd be *great!*"

"I had a feelin' yer'd like it," Barry grinned.

But then I caught the glimmer of something sneaky in the corner of his eye. "Say," I asked, trying to sound real mature and professional about it, "what exactly does a race mechanic *do,* anyway?"

"Why, whatever bleedin' *needs* t'be done. 'Round here, we recognize race mechanicin' as a bloody highly skilled form of h'employment. Indeed we do. Most of yer garden-variety grease monkeys can't do the bleedin' job a'tall. Not a'tall."

"Hmm," I said, pretending to mull it over. I mean, I didn't want Barry to think he was dealing with some wet-behind-the-ears high school pushover who didn't know the score. I knew better than to just snap at it like some yahoo who just fell off a turnip truck, so I made sure to roll the idea around in my head for three or four whole seconds before telling him I'd take it. And I wasn't the least bit shy about staring him squarely in the eye when I finally got up the nerve to ask, "Ahh, say, Barry, d'ya think you could maybe tell me what this job, er, you know, how much it pays?"

"How's that?"

"This race mechanic job, Barry. Whazzit *pay?*"

"Oh, well," Barry shrugged, waving his fingers through the air like he was scattering stardust, "most usually our racing mechanics start out at ten dollars a day—that's a *full* day, mind you—and five dollars the half-day. Complete race weekends are twenty-five dollars each. That's expenses included, of course."

"Oh, of course," I nodded. But I wasn't real sure I knew what he meant. So I asked, "You mean I get *extra* money to cover expenses on race weekends?"

Barry looked at me like I'd just attempted to lop off his foot. "Certainly not!" he snapped. "A race mechanic's expense money is always considered to be *h'included* in the twenty-five-dollar weekend fee."

"Oh."

"But it never costs much to stay at the races. And there's always plenty of free food and drink about."

That I already knew.

"And you'll be doing most of yer bleedin' work 'ere in the shop, so I wouldn't worry much about it."

"And how many days would I be working, exactly?"

"Two, maybe three days a week. Sometimes more. You 'ave to understand, race mechanicin' is a bloody part-time position on a strictly as-needed basis."

"Uh-huh," I said, rolling the numbers around in my head like loose marbles. Far as I could tell, the sum total I'd be earning as a race mechanic figured to be roughly half of what I'd been making full-time at the Old Man's gas station (at least if you didn't count Big Ed's five-buck tips and the cost of daily public transportation into Manhattan), but on the other hand, it represented an opportunity to work on MGs and Jaguars and Allards all the time instead of the broken-down Fords, Plymouths, and Chevrolets I got at the Sinclair. Not to mention actually getting *paid* (albeit not much) to go to the races. "Well, Barry," I told him, trying to sound real casual about it, "that sounds pretty darn interesting. When exactly would I start?"

"Oh, I suppose we'd be needing yer t'come in afternoons and evenings each and every race week. Let's 'ave us a look at the schedule" (pronounced shedge-yewel, of course). He rummaged around in the drawer of Colin's desk until he found a dog-eared copy of the S.C.M.A. calendar. "Ah, 'ere it is. We've got ourselves a race at Grand Island— that's up by Niagara Falls, y'see—come the end of August. Then h'nother one at Elkhart Lake the following weekend. That's in Wisconsin. Mark my words, that'll be one damn *busy* five days in between. I reckon yer'll 'ave t'start comin' in, oh, say, the week before Grand Island. Our racing mechanics most usually start in right after lunch, and should always be prepared t'stay late as necessary t'get the bleedin' work done...."

"Oh, naturally," I said, my toes quietly doing jumping jacks inside my shoes. "So tell me, Barry, which cars will I be working on?"

"Why, whichever ones need attention, of course."

"Oh, of course, of course."

"Why, on some of the more 'ectic race weekends, yer'll probably have t'baby-sit the whole bloody lot."

I could hardly wait. But I had one more question. "Tell me something, Barry. Which car will I *ride* in? Up to the races, I mean." I was kind of hoping to get in with Tommy Edwards in that wicked Cad-Allard. Why, maybe he'd even let me *drive* it once or twice....

Barry looked at me like I had concrete setting up between my ears. "Actually, our race mechanics don't generally get to ride *anywhere* with the paying customers. That's what bloody wives and girlfriends are for."

"Oh," I said. "But then how the heck am I gonna get to Grand Island?"

"Why, that's h'entirely up to *you!*" Barry exclaimed like it was some kind of exciting Special Bonus you got with a position as a Westbridge Race Mechanic. "See, yer've got to h'understand. There's a lot of *freedom* and *h'independent thought* h'involved in a situation like this. Not just any bloke can do it."

I could see why. "Ah ... um ... well ... y'see, Barry, the truth of it is, I'm not real sure I can find a way up there."

Barry rubbed his chin and stared off into space like he was planning the invasion of Normandy. "Weeell," he mused, "I reckon yer *might* catch a lift with me in the parts truck ... *if* yer pay shares on the bleedin' petrol, that is."

I hadn't even started working there, and I was already beginning to understand the high turnover of wrenching personnel at Westbridge. Then something else occurred to me. "Y'know, Barry," I said, "August 30th is almost a whole month from now. What am I supposed to do in the meantime?"

"Well, if it was *me*," he advised through a cheery smile, "I believe I'd start looking for a *real* job."

Big Ed Baumstein called my aunt's house a few days later, and he was pretty bent out of shape about me not being around the Old Man's Sinclair to take care of his Jag and Caddies anymore. "Whaddam I gonna do now?" he groused, chewing his stogie into the receiver. "My damn Jaguar won't start an' I'll be damned if I'll let that butcher Finzio anywheres near it. Why'dja quit, anyway?"

"*Quit?* I got *fired*. Who the hell told you I quit?"

"Old Man Finzio."

"Figures." Then I told Big Ed about my newly acquired part-time race mechanic job at Westbridge.

"Jee-*zus,* Buddy, why you wanna work for that shyster sonofabitch Colin St. John for? Why, he'd steal the pennies off a dead man's eyes."

"Maybe so," I allowed, "but I get to be around sports cars all the time. I guess I'm kind of addicted, y'know?"

"Humph," Big Ed grunted at the other end of the line.

"In fact," I oh-so-casually continued, "we got a race coming up at

Grand Island at the end of August. Maybe you oughta think about coming up yourself."

"Hell, that's all the way across the whole friggin' state," he snorted. "And besides, the damn thing ain't even running right now."

"Aw, I can fix it. No problem. And I hear they got a really great entry lined up. Ought to be a real swell time." As you can see, I had visions of riding up to Grand Island in Big Ed's XK120 rather than bouncing along in the parts truck with prizewinning British Tightwad Barry Spline. Not to mention picking up shares on gas.

But Big Ed wasn't real receptive on account of he was having one hell of a time getting his name put up for membership in the S.C.M.A., and he'd be damned if he was gonna drive all the way across the state just to hang on the fences with the rank-and-file rubberneckers. After all, he owned a damn Jaguar 120 and by God, he wanted to *participate*. And who could blame him? Truth is, I didn't reckon Big Ed would ever be much of a racing driver, even if he got the chance. I mean, he wasn't exactly real arty with a stick shift or calm and smooth behind the wheel. Not hardly. But Big Ed figured he could at least drive as good as Skippy Welcher, and I had to admit there was a better than even chance he could be right.

The problem was getting *in*.

Big Ed had telephoned, written letters, bought drinks, and even asked a few of the S.C.M.A. heavyweights to fancy lunches and dinners. In Manhattan, no less. But none of them ever made it on account of they were always "booked up" or "too busy," no matter how many weeks in advance Big Ed called to invite them. You could tell it was pissing him off no end. And why shouldn't it? He sure didn't appreciate getting the Official Brush-Off routine from a bunch of ivy-covered, old-money Protestants just because he had a Jewish last name and traded scrap machinery for a living. Hell, his cash was as green as anybody's, wasn't it? And he was a *lousy* Jew. You could ask *any*body. He never went to temple or fasted on the big hebe holidays or wore one of those black silk beanies or *anything*. Not to mention that three of his wives (including the reigning Mrs. B.) were *shiksas*. But somehow the S.C.M.A. membership committee was real damn particular about what church you went to. Even if you never went to church.

Anyhow, I told Big Ed I'd be happy to check out his dead Jaguar, and it wasn't twenty minutes later he pulled up front in the black Caddy sedan. That seemed odd, since it was exactly the sort of sunny summer day when you'd expect Big Ed to tool up in his white Caddy convert if for any reason his Jag was on the fritz. So I asked Big Ed about it, and a black scowl rolled down his face like the corrugated steel curtains that come down over the store windows at closing time in Sylvester

Jones's neighborhood. "Oh, I guess you could say I had a little, er, *problem* with one a'my em-ploy-ees over at the new yard we took over in Monmouth County."

"What happened?"

"Well, I had t'fire the guy, see, because he was showing up drunk alla time."

"And?"

"Aw, he got all pissed off. Hell, it wasn't nine in the morning and he'd already had himself a snootful."

"So?"

"So the bastid rammed one a'my trucks—*my own damn trucks!*—into that poor caddy convert at damn near forty miles an hour. Smashed the living shit out of it."

"Geez, that's a real shame."

"That's *nothing!* Then the asshole pulled the friggin' lever and dumped the whole goddam load on top of it." Big Ed's voice went down to a mumble. "It was fresh off the farm route, too."

"Really?" I said, trying not to laugh. I mean, I just couldn't help it.

"Oh *sure,"* Big Ed snarled, "laugh it up. Real goddam funny...." But you could see his eyes were starting to sparkle a little, too, and pretty soon we were both laughing so hard he had to pull over because he couldn't see to drive.

"Gee whiz," I told him when we could finally talk again, "that's really too bad. Whaddaya gonna *do?*"

"Well, one thing I'm damn sure *not* gonna do is go driving around in a pile of pig shit and chicken heads. I mean, you'd *never* get rid of a smell like that."

"So whad'ja do?"

"Aw, we just kinda pushed that Caddy around the yard with a couple Caterpillar earthmovers. Like we was playin' field hockey with it, y'know? Didn't want to take a chance that the insurance company might not total it. Not the way it smelled." He flipped me one of his patented Big Ed winks. But then a melancholy mist drifted over his eyes. "It's a damn shame though," he sighed. "I mean, I really *loved* that car. Almost as much as my Jag...."

"You can always get yourself another one," I told him. "Heck, the new ones'll be coming out in a couple months, and I hear there's gonna be a brand-new convertible model from Cadillac."

"Yeah, I heard about it from my salesman at the agency," Big Ed allowed, peeling the cellophane off a fresh dollar cigar. "He says they're gonna call it 'the Eldorado.' "

"That's the one. I heard you'll even be able to get it with air-conditioning."

"Yeah," he sighed. "I s'pose I can always buy me one a'them. But there was something, I dunno, something *special* about that white car...." His eyes went all soft-focus on him. "The leather always felt, I dunno, sort of *warm* when you touched it. An' Jesus Christ, it had the strongest, sweetest-running engine of any Cadillac I ever owned."

"Yeah, it sure did," I agreed, feeling my own eyes mist up as I remembered the night Big Ed let Julie and me borrow it to cruise over by Palisades Park.

"Gee," Big Ed whispered, his voice cracking a little around the edges, "was it ever *fast* and *smooth* for a big, heavy car."

"Yeah, it sure was. And gorgeous, too."

"Uh-huh," Big Ed nodded. "Anybody tells you all cars are the same just doesn't know shit from shinola about automobiles." You could say what you want about Big Ed Baumstein, but no question he understood how things are with cars.

Turns out Big Ed's Jag wouldn't start because the fuel pump crapped out (hardly front-page news where S.U. electric fuel pumps are concerned!) but getting it fixed was something else again since Big Ed didn't have much in the way of tools at his monstrous house back in Teaneck. In fact, all I could find was a claw hammer, a pair of pliers and some screwdrivers that looked like they'd been used mostly to stir paint and pry up nails. Then again, Big Ed didn't spend much time at home (and virtually none puttering around with your typical home-owner/handyman-type projects) so all the various Mrs. Big Eds were in the habit of calling local tradesmen when anything around the Baumstein household required attention. "Jeez, Ed," I told him, "I could really use a socket set to get that thing out of there. Or at least a couple open-end wrenches...."

"This won't help?" He passed me a monkey wrench that looked like it went down on the Titanic.

"No, I don't believe it will. See, you really need a proper tool set to get a job handled the right way. I mean, you wouldn't want me ripping your Jag apart with a claw hammer and a set of garden shears, would you?"

Big Ed mulled it over. "You're *sure* that fuel pump is the trouble?"

"No question about it."

"Well, why don't we run in to Westbridge and pick us up another one, huh?"

"Oh, I could probably fix this one if I can just get it apart."

"Nah, let's get us a *new* one, Buddy. We can always fix the old one up later and keep it for a spare." And just that quickly, Big Ed had put his finger on the reason why so many sports car owners have garages packed to the rafters with so-called spare parts that are rarely (if ever) in fully operational condition.

We rode over to Westbridge in the black Caddy to pick up Big Ed's new fuel pump, and on the way back he casually stopped at a Sears store and bought a complete set of Craftsman tools. And I mean *complete!* I'd never been shopping with anybody like Big Ed before. He strolled up and down the aisles, pointing every which way at tool cabinets and socket sets and box-end combination wrenches and double-jointed flex knucklers and Phillips and flat-blade screwdrivers in eight different sizes and Lord only knows what else. "Y'need one a'*these?*" he'd ask, pointing at a set of channel locks or a rubber mallet or a rotary bench grinder.

"Yeah," I'd nod, "it might come in handy some day." And just that quick, Big Ed would own it. He even had to have a bunch of stuff delivered, on account of we couldn't fit it in the trunk of the black Caddy. And a Cadillac Sixty Special has one whale of a huge trunk, ask anyone. Fact is, I got Big Ed's Jag running in less time than it took us to unload the damn tools, and it ran like a champ all the way back to Passaic.

So I was kind of surprised when Big Ed rang me up the next afternoon and asked if I wanted to take another trip into Manhattan. I feared the worst (could I already be picking up the Westbridge method of sports car repair?) but was relieved to see him tool up in his XK120 with a big smile wrapped around his stogie. "Naw, she's purrin' like a kitten t'day. I got something *else* in mind. . . ."

"Yeah? Like what?"

"You'll see," he said, and you couldn't miss how his grin spread out another inch or two toward his ears.

We crossed over the George Washington Bridge and headed down toward the shipping docks, twisting through a tangle of narrow, uneven streets lined with firebrick warehouse buildings and double-parked delivery trucks and huge stacks of crates and cardboard boxes bringing every kind of stuff you can imagine in and out of Manhattan. Finally, we located what we were looking for: a nondescript cinderblock garage with no sign in front—not even a street address!—and a heavy steel fire door that was locked tighter than a bank vault. Big Ed knocked a couple times, but there was no answer. So he knocked again, only this time a little louder. Still nothing. So he hauled off and beat on it so hard it sent off vibrations like a cast-iron church bell. That got some muffled shuffling and cursing going on inside, and finally the door opened a crack and a large, familiar Italian nose stuck itself out and sniffed us. "Aay, whaddaya want?" the nose asked. I was sure I'd heard that voice before, but I couldn't quite place it.

"I'm lookin' for Carlo Sebastian," Big Ed told the nose.

"Yeah? An' who is it wants to know?"

"Ed Baumstein."

"Who?"

"Ed Baumstein. From over in Jersey. I'm a friend of Jimmy Lazzarro and Tony Cicci. I wanna see Carlo Sebastian."

"What about?"

I could see the color starting to creep up Big Ed's neck. "About a *car,* that's what! Now lemme in before I rip this friggin' door right off its goddam hinges."

The nose looked us up and down again. "Justa minute, ay?" it said as the door closed again, followed by more shuffling and mumbling and light, quick footsteps with maybe a set of steel taps on the heels. Then the door swung open, revealing a dark, perfectly chisled little wop with an elegant mane of silvery-white hair, flashing eyes, and a smile that reflected light like a gold dessert plate. At least when he wanted it to anyway. He was wearing a white silk shirt under a butterscotch leather vest, and had an extralarge shop coat draped over his shoulders like an opera cape. Real dramatic, you know?

"How may I help you?" he asked in a voice that resonated with Continental class and style, like the guys who sell women's perfume on the radio. I thought I'd maybe seen him someplace before, and for sure the other guy was one of the three mechanics attending to Creighton Pendleton's Ferrari at Bridgehampton.

"You Carlo Sebastian?" Big Ed asked. The guy nodded and ushered us in. It was dark in there, what with just a naked 40-watt bulb over the doorway and a couple trouble lights glowing in back where I could hear a ratchet wrench click-click-clicking and the unmistakable scrape of a creeper rolling across a concrete floor. I could make out five or six cars scattered in the shadows, and it took awhile before my eyes got accustomed to the light and I realized *they were all Ferraris! Every one of them!* My mouth went all dry on me, and I swear I could hear my heart pounding inside my chest.

Carlo Sebastian grandly introduced himself as "the ex*clu*sive Ferrari *fac*tory representative to the United States and *all* of North America." Which meant he probably got his hands on maybe a dozen cars a year. Not much by Ford and Chevy standards, but these weren't exactly Fords or Chevys. Not hardly. Why, you could buy yourself a couple each Fords and Chevys for the price of a new Ferrari. *If* you could get one, that is. There was a lot of pomp and strut to this Carlos Sebastian character, but you had to love him because he radiated excitement and could turn up that smile of his like a damn klieg light whenever he wanted to. "My shop is modest," he said, sweeping his hands around

like you might have missed how modest it was. "Ah, but my *cars*..."—
he softly kissed the tips of his fingers—"... there is nothing else like
them in the world. Not *any*where...."

"We know th—" Big Ed started in, but Carlo Sebastian stopped
him short.

"Come! Let me *show* you!" he said with a flourish, flipping a wall
switch that fizzed on a dim row of fluorescent lights. *"Look!"* he cried,
leaping between the cars. "See the kind of automobiles true *genius* can
produce!"

My God, you should've seen those cars! There were three coupes
and two roadsters gleaming in the half-light like a pack of sleek car-
nivores under a jungle moon. Each one had that unmistakable enamel
medallion on the nose with the rampant black stallion reared up against
a bright yellow background, but beyond that, it seemed no two were
exactly alike. Carlo Sebastian was nice enough to take us on a whirlwind
tour, explaining all about the cars, the great races they'd won, and all
the brave, skillful heroes who'd driven them to victory. As he spoke,
his hands sculptured pictures in the air and his shop coat trailed behind
him, swirling up little fanfare plumes of dust. That Carlo Sebastian was
one hell of a showman, no two ways about it.

The cars were enough to make you wet your pants, anyway.

"This," he said, pointing to one of the coupes, "is a 212 Export by
Vignale [pronounced Vihn-*yah*-laye] and that roadster is a *Barchetta*
[Bar-*ket*-ta] from Superleggera [Soo-per-ledge-*err*-a] Touring [just like
in English]." Naturally, I had no idea what he was talking about, but
I was as impressed as all getout anyway. Turns out the Ferrari factory
only builds the chassis and running gear and then ships the whole shebang off to one of these specialist panel-beating shops called *Carrozzeria.*
I think Italy must be absolutely lousy with them, on account of I heard
Carlo Sebastian mention Ferrari bodywork by Vignale, Touring, Ghia,
Bertone, Pinin Farina, Boano, Drogo, Scaglietti, and Zagato, and I suspect some of them aren't much more than little two-by-four, back-alley,
father-and-son bump shops. But that's where every single one of those
breathtaking Ferrari shapes comes from. One at a time. And that's why
each and every Ferrari is a little *different* from each and every other
Ferrari—like a signed piece of sculpture or something, you know? But
no matter who did the coachwork, every Ferrari manages to have that
special Ferrari *look,* and, as Carlo Sebastian took pains to explain, there's
simply nothing else like it in the whole damn world.

But the bodywork is just window dressing compared to what goes
on under the hoods and beneath the fenderwells where the *real* Ferrari
magic lives. Take the engines, for example. Ferrari V-12s are simply

the most elegant, symmetrical, awesomely beautiful automotive power plants you'll ever see. The idea is simple: for any given displacement, a large number of small cylinders can rev higher, run smoother, and produce more horsepower than a lesser number of large cylinders. But it's the way Ferrari engines are *built* that really sets them apart. They have overhead camshafts and hemispherical combustion chambers like a Jaguar, but they're all done up in fine cast aluminum trimmed in this high-class crinkly enamel finish. They've got *two* distributors—one for each cylinder bank!—that incidentally point straight forward to keep the hood as low as possible, and fancy Weber carburetors down the center of the vee (sometimes *three* of 'em!) that probably mix fuel and air together better than anything on the planet. Why, even the damn *air cleaners* look like dining table centerpieces! Two liters not fast enough for you? Then how about 2.3? Or 2.6? Or 3.3? Or 4.1? Or 4.4? Or even *more!* Why, Ferrari tools up whole new engines faster than GM cranks out fresh color schemes and new model year interior trim.

But Big Ed Baumstein wasn't interested in crinkle-finish cam covers or Weber carburetors or even Carlo Sebastian's fabulous Ferrari stories. What Big Ed wanted was to get his hands on a Ferrari of his own. *Any* Ferrari. That would show those tight-ass jerks on the S.C.M.A. membership committee that he meant business. Which is why Big Ed kept edging toward the heap of low, hot curves slumbering under a flannel cover against the far wall. "So what's that one?" he asked like he didn't really care.

"Aaahhhh," Carlo Sebastian sighed, his smile brightening up twenty or thirty kilowatts. "That, my friend, is *sculptured fire!*" He swept the cover back like a matador making a pass and underneath was the most dangerous-looking automobile I'd ever laid eyes on: a full-tilt 4.1-liter Ferrari racing car, done up in brilliant bright yellow with big white number circles on the hood and doors.

"Jee-*zus,*" Big Ed said softly, and Carlo Sebastian nodded.

"How fast'll it go?" I asked like a damn schoolkid.

"Fast enough, my friend, fast enough."

Right away Big Ed wanted that car—wanted it *bad!*—and it occurred to him that underneath all the buttery phrases and Continental veneer, Carlo Sebastian was just another smooth-talking automobile salesman. And if there was one type of person Big Ed knew how to handle, it was car salesmen. "Saaay, lissen," he said, running his hands down into his pants pockets, "how much would it take—*cash money*—to drive this thing outta here?"

Carlo looked at Big Ed like he didn't comprehend. "To drive it *where?*"

"You know, *outta* here. I'm talkin' *right now! CAAAAASH money!*"
As you can see, Big Ed hit every single car salesman hot button known
to man.

Carlo Sebastian sighed and shook his head like he was terribly,
terribly disappointed. "Oh, my dear friend," he said sadly, "this car is
not for *sale*." He swept his hand around the shop again. "None of my
Ferraris are ever for *sale.*..."

"They're *not?*"

"Oh, no! These automobiles are already *sold*. Ferraris are *always*
already sold...."

"They are?"

"*Certainly*. If you wish to buy a Ferrari, my friend"—Carlo held
up a manicured index finger—"you must be prepared to *wait*. As you
most assuredly know, nothing of value is ever easily attained." For just
an instant I thought about Julie and hoped Carlo knew what he was
talking about.

Big Ed and Carlo jawed back and forth for a while, and the gist
of it was that you could put down a deposit (a *substantial* deposit!) and
Carlo Sebastian would be happy to order a car for you. A "production"
model, mind you, not an ex-works racing car. Then it might take as
much as a year for the car to arrive (and sometimes even longer!) and
there was never any guarantee that what you ordered would actually
show up, seeing as how the factory was constantly changing, modifying,
replacing, and discontinuing model lines, not to mention that Enzo Ferrari always built what he bloody well wanted regardless of what his
customers had on order. After all, what did *they* know?

And that was just the production cars. Ex-works *racing* examples
were even more difficult to obtain. Why, *everyone* wanted a Ferrari
racing car, did they not? The Ferrari race shop produced only a scant
handful of competition cars every season, and they were *always* spoken
for when the factory team was done with them. Always....

"Get a Ferrari racing car? *Hah!* It is simply not possible, my friend.
Not possible at all." Carlo reached his tiny little arm as far as it would
go around Big Ed's massive shoulders. "You must understand," he continued in a fatherly tone, "it is not simply a question of money and time
and patience...."

"It isn't?"

"Certainly not, Mr. Baumstein. For example, *this* car is on its way
to a fine gentleman named Ernesto Julio. You are perhaps familiar with
the name?"

Big Ed nodded. Hell, anybody who's ever been in a damn liquor
store knows Ernesto Julio. Why, he did for the California wine business
what Henry Ford did for the automobile manufacturing business in

Detroit. Exactly, in fact. But I never heard that he raced sports cars. "Say, I didn't know he raced cars," I said.

"Oh, he *doesn't,*" Carlo Sebastian explained. "Not himself, anyway. Ernesto Julio is a great *aficionado,* a great *sportsman,* a true *patrone. . . .* "

"A *what?*"

"A *patrone,* my friend. He buys the very *latest* machinery—the very *best!*—and searches out only the most promising young talents—the *gifted* ones—to drive for him. That is why we sell him our most powerful and advanced machines, because . . . ," he looked Big Ed right in the eye—". . . because *my* reputation, *Ferrari's* reputation, is built on one thing: *winning.* We must ensure our cars have the best possible opportunity to do what they are bred for: *to win!* That is why they are entrusted only to those who have proven, shall we say, *capable. . . .* "

Big Ed didn't like that at all, and you could see the color starting to come up on his face again. Which meant that this was probably a good time to mosey off and take myself a tour of Carlo's shop. I hate scenes, and Big Ed had a real knack for creating them. So I followed the sound of that clicking ratchet wrench into the back of the shop, and located the source when I tripped over a pair of legs sticking out from under a 212 coupe with bodywork by Touring. I leaned in and looked down past the gracefully curved oil filler and the delicate branches of the exhaust header to where a pair of dark, beady black eyes and a familiar Italian nose were staring back up at me. "Hi," I said, "wat'cha doin' down there?"

"Whassit lookalike I'm a-doin', ey? Poundin' a-my fuckin' pud?" And that, by and large, was my formal introduction to Alfredo Muscatelli, one of the infamous wrench-spinning Muscatelli brothers from the old neighborhood in Brooklyn. There were three all told—Alfredo, Giuseppe, and Sidney—and they all worked for Carlo Sebastian. As you probably guessed, Sidney was more or less a half brother, and therein lies an interesting story. I first heard about it from one of Big Ed's truck drivers, about how Alfredo and Giuseppe's dad was highly respected around the old neighborhood for the stout and reliable explosive devices he could whip up out of a few sticks of dynamite and an ordinary Woolworth's five-and-dime alarm clock. The work wasn't steady, but it paid well, and Alfredo and Giuseppe's dad made quite a tidy living during the Prohibition years. But it all went wrong one black day in 1926, when the elder Muscatelli fell victim to some terribly shoddy workmanship on the part of whoever put in the low bid on alarm clocks to the Woolworth's chain that year. And so Alfredo and Giuseppe's father went to his eternal reward (along with a half block of choice Brooklyn real estate), leaving his poor wife and two little bambinos to fend for themselves. Needless to say, he didn't leave much in the way of life insurance, as it was rather hard to come by in his line of work. But Alfredo and Giuseppe's mother was recommended to a clever young Jewish lawyer named Sid Moskowitz with the intent of perhaps suing the Woolworth's people for leaving her in such a fix. The lawyer ultimately advised against it, but there was a silver lining in that he took a real shine to the widow Muscatelli. Especially after he found out about the safe-deposit boxes scattered all over New York and New Jersey under the names of obscure characters from Verdi operas. Soon afterward he and the widow Muscatelli were married in a civil ceremony, and little Sid Jr. followed right on schedule some seven months later. But during the widow's eighth month, slippery old Sid met an elevator operator with exceptional lungs named Loreli Pomerantz, and the two of them mysteriously disappeared just a few days after little Sid Jr. was born. Along with most of the safe-deposit box goodies. It was the talk of the stairwells and back porches of the old neighborhood for weeks, and the general consensus was that *something should-a be done!* Sure enough, Sid Moskowitz turned up a few months later in Havana, Cuba. All over Havana, in fact, seeing as how the starter solenoid on his brand-new Packard somehow shorted out against a half-dozen sticks of blasting powder. Rumor has it they put a few Packard parts in the coffin (just to give it a little heft, you understand) since most of Sid Sr. wound up as pigeon food in and around the greater Havana area. It was almost as if Alfredo and Giuseppe's dad had personally reached down from the heavens (or up from Someplace Else) and done the job himself. You gotta hand it to the Sicilians when it comes to revenge.

Anyhow, young Alfredo and Giuseppe inherited clever fingers and the gift of mechanical intuition from their father, and eventually went into the garage business in the old neighborhood. They were tough, hardworking guys with strong hands, gravelly voices, the right kind of connections (thanks to their father, God rest his soul), and hot loins for anything in a tight skirt, and soon earned an enviable reputation for souping up getaway cars and taking stray bullet holes out of sheet metal. Business was good, and pretty soon the Muscatelli brothers branched out into retail work, fixing the occasional carburetor or brake master cylinder for people without thick window glass, violin cases, or long criminal records.

To Alfredo and Giuseppe's everlasting credit, they took little Sid Jr. into the business with them, even though he couldn't so much as change oil without slicing off a knuckle or spilling the contents of the drain pan all over the floor. But Sid Jr. was quick with numbers and good with the customers and kept the best-organized parts inventory in all of Brooklyn, none of which were exactly strong points with his swarthy, barrel-chested half brothers. Sid Jr. was a spindly, happy-faced little geek with thinning hair, fading freckles, and a goofy, near-permanent smile. Also unlike the other two, everybody who met Sid Jr. seemed to like him.

Anyhow, the three of them got a reputation for fixing mechanical things so they *stayed* fixed and keeping their mouths shut about who brought what into their shop, and their business prospered. Especially during the depression and war years, when people had to hang on to older machinery instead of buying new and were always on the lookout for replacement tires, batteries, and extra gas ration coupons of no-questions-asked origin. But a crackdown by some cowboy assistant D.A. with dreams of becoming a councilman or judge or something brought unwanted attention to their thriving little business and ultimately caused many of their best customers to take their work elsewhere rather than run the gauntlet of unmarked police cars that inevitably parked at both ends of the alley. Plus they were getting hassled by the I.R.S. (theirs was strictly a cash business and the books amounted to no more than a couple old washtubs full of scribbled notes and receipts—mostly in Italian—that had somehow accidentally had a couple loads of laundry done in them. Heavy on the bleach). These were devastating developments, and just about the time the three Muscatelli brothers needed a place to run, Carlo Sebastian rang them up to ask if they'd like to work at his new Ferrari shop in Manhattan. To sweeten the pot, there was a free trip to the Ferrari factory in Italy for all three (at least until the heat blew over, anyway) if they signed on.

So Alfredo, Giuseppe, and Sid Jr. went to the factory for "training" in early 1951, and even got to join the Ferrari racing team for the Mille Miglia, which Ferrari won that year. That was one hell of a race, running flat-out from Brescia to Rome and back—*a thousand miles!*—on ordinary, everyday Italian roads. It took iron men with nerves of steel to drive a race like that, and Alfredo and Giuseppe always considered Stateside racing pretty tame by comparison. In fact, Alfredo's normal response to the S.C.M.A. brand of motor sport was to make a face like Benito Mussolini and sneer: *"Hah!* You call-a *dis* racing? *I* tell you racing: A tousan' miles, up anna down troo'da mountains, troo'da rain, troo'da fog so fuckin' tick you could-a no find-a you own assa-hole. Now *Dat's* a-racing!" Then he'd punctuate with either a colorful Sicilian hand gesture or a twelve-inch hip thrust.

Little Sid Muscatelli enjoyed Italy, too, even if he didn't exactly work out as a racing mechanic. In fact, rumor has it he poured oil in radiators, dropped washers down carburetors, and cross-threaded every bolt he got his hands on. During one crucial pit stop, Sid Jr. yanked the right-side tires off the leading Ferrari—worn right down to the damn canvas—switched them around, and put them right back on the car. The poor driver tore off in a cloud of rubber smoke while the fresh tires were still sitting there on the curb! Plus he wound up smearing everything he touched with blood (his own, natch) but fortunately it didn't show because the cars were painted bright red anyway. On the other hand, Sid was funny and likable and had a unique talent for negotiation. His skill with hotel owners, restaurateurs, and local hookers made him more than welcome even after the team learned not to let him *near* the damn race cars.

And now all three of them worked for Carlo Sebastian, Alfredo and Giuseppe doing the hands-on mechanical stuff while Sid Jr. ran the parts and Customer Excuses departments. To tell the truth, I envied the hell out of those guys on account of Carlo's Ferraris were so beautiful and exotic and, well, *hot*.

By mid-August, Barry was finding plenty of stuff for me to do over at Westbridge, mostly because Vito got fired for stealing parts to do side jobs at home (often on Westbridge customers' cars!) and then threatened to flatten Barry's nose with the lead mallet when he was questioned about it. Which meant I started taking the two-hour train-and-bus ride into Manhattan every morning so I could arrive just after lunch. Barry insisted on that, since it meant he only had to pay me for half a day. No matter how late we worked. And some nights we worked *late*.

I didn't have much in the way of a proper tool set, what with Butch's stuff still stuck under the workbench at the Sinclair, but Big Ed let me borrow a few things out of his Sears Shopping Spree collection and Sylvester would let me dip into his battered old toolbox whenever I needed something special. Fact is, I didn't need much in the way of sophisticated equipment anyhow, seeing as how I was the new guy and therefore got stuck with all the grunt jobs (grease and oil, cleaning parts, tire mounts, rusted exhausts, etc.) while Sylvester and the regular foreign-accented Westbridge crew handled all the heavy assembly work and fine-tuning. Every day I'd arrive to find a fresh assortment of Jags and MGs lined up with shit lists stuck under their windshield wipers, and my initials would inevitably be penciled in next to all the stuff you could train a damn monkey to do. To tell the truth, it was really getting me down. Hell, I figured I was at least as good as anybody in the shop (except for Sylvester, of course) but Colin and Barry were afraid to trust me with anything complicated on account of I was so young and only had a couple months' experience on English cars. Besides, you always need *some*body to clean filthy transmission casings in the parts tank or remove all the gooey, smelly Cosmoline gunk from the new cars and then mount the bumpers and windshields and such. You could fit a lot more Jags and MGs in the hold of a ship if they didn't stand any higher than the fender line and were shorter by two bumpers, and they definitely needed that sticky Cosmoline coating against the salt air so's they wouldn't start rusting away to nothing until they were safely in the hands of their new owners. And I was the guy who got to do it all. Lucky me.

But at least I got to hang around a lot of neat sports cars, and I was learning a lot about how the English put their cars together. Or *almost* put their cars together, as was more often the case. But it was a great education, even if I was putting in a lot of hours for a guy earning part-time pay. Most usually, I'd spend the afternoons (right through the heat of the day, natch) attending to oil changes and such for Colin and Barry's "boulevard" customers, and we wouldn't even *start* on the racing stuff until well past what normal people consider dinnertime. Barry would usually pack it in around twilight, but sometimes he'd let Sylvester and me stay a little later to finish this or that after he was gone. That was always kind of fun, on account of we'd talk while we worked, and I came to appreciate that Sylvester Jones was a pretty interesting guy. Bitter as hell, but *interesting*. He knew all sorts of stuff about mechanical gizmos and life in general (like Butch, you know?) and also like Butch, he didn't get along with many people at all. In fact, Sylvester carried around an extensive mental list of people who could bring him boundless joy by simply stepping in front of a fast-moving steam locomotive. Right at the top of that list were all the mean cracker sergeants he'd endured in the service, the shifty black dice jockeys he shot craps with two or three times a week, a conservative 97 percent of the white population in general, damn near all his relatives, and always and most especially, Colin St. John. "You look in the fuckin' dictionary," he told me. "You'll see ol' Colin's picture right next to the word 'asshole.' Ah ain't lyin'."

Also like Butch, Sylvester invested a lot of creative energy into imagining terrible things that could happen to the people he didn't like. "Sheee *it,* son, they oughta put all them cracker sergeants in a big ol' hydraulic press..."—he'd hold his arms out like the jaws of a giant bench vise—"...an' then you jus' pull the damn lever an' let it *ease on down*..."—he'd slowly bring his arms together—"...until you hear all them cracker skulls pop like ripe watermelons..."—at this point he'd add some really ingenious and disgusting popping noises—"...and when you done, alls you got lef' is a bad smell an'a big ol' smear of cracker grease." It was beginning to dawn on me that Sylvester and Butch really had an awful lot in common, and it was too bad they would've gotten into a fistfight if you ever sat them down together for a glass of beer.

Naturally, Barry wouldn't think of trusting Sylvester or me with a shop key, so he'd padlock the office and overhead door and set the alley door to latch itself behind him. Then he'd quietly remove the cash drawer (like we didn't know what he was doing, right?) and take off. So we had to be careful not to get ourselves locked out if we went into the alley for a smoke or a little fresh air. And you *needed* a little fresh air now and then on a steamy August night with all the damn doors locked and no breeze except a sad little hamster wheeze off the wall fan up by the service counter. Once Barry was gone, Sylvester'd most usually go down to the corner liquor store and buy us a six-pack (I'd chip in, of course) and that always helped. But we had to leave the empties in a trash can behind some other building so's Barry wouldn't know we'd been drinking in his shop. Not that he didn't, but you don't want to insult a guy by leaving the evidence right out in the open so you have to deny it. Anyhow, we'd both be pretty wrung out by the time we finished, and afterward Sylvester'd generally give me a lift to the Port Authority bus terminal on his way home (or to some gin mill or crap game in Harlem or wherever the hell else he might be headed) and it was always neat riding through the late-night Manhattan streets in Sylvester's rusty old Plymouth. We'd have the windows down and vents rotated backward to get a little breeze through the interior, and Sylvester'd most usually have one beer left that we'd pass back and forth and hide down below my knees anytime we drove past a cop car or saw one out walking his beat. There was always something electric about those rides through Manhattan on a warm summer night, even if I was just on my way over to the damn Port Authority in a rusty old Plymouth with a surly black grease monkey at the wheel. It made me feel real mature and experienced, you know?

The bad part about my new job at Westbridge was how every damn minute seemed to be spent either working on cars or getting to and from work, and it was all I could do to just flop down at my apartment and grab a few winks before the damn alarm rang and it was time to get up and do it all over again. Why, it was like my old man's stupid chemical plant job! Only it took longer to get there and the pay was worse. Lots worse, in fact. Plus I was working nights and weekends, too. I suppose the smart thing would've been to find myself a place to stay in Manhattan (in fact I did sleep right there in the shop a couple times when we worked real late, or if Sylvester maybe bought us two six-packs instead of one) but somehow I knew that my deal at West-bridge was just temporary. It was one of those things you just sort of *feel*. Besides, the talent turnover at Colin and Barry's shop gave me lots of reasons to feel that way. Much as I liked being a Racing Wrench right in the heart of the biggest, most exciting city in the world, I knew in my heart that I was just a kid from Jersey who didn't really fit in. When you got right down to it, I *belonged* back at an ordinary corner gas station on the wilderness side of the George Washington Bridge. And preferably Old Man Finzio's place, since that's where Julie was. . . .

Truth is, I wasn't seeing much of Julie at all, since I didn't really have the time, money, or motorized vehicle to take her on a proper date—not even to the Doggie Shake or the drive-in—and I wasn't so sure she would've been interested anyway. After all, she'd surely gotten a giant, economy-sized load of grief from Old Man Finzio after he caught us out behind his station, and the way her mother made a point of always answering the phone just so she could hang up whenever I called left no doubt that she'd been filled in as well. But, gee whiz, it wasn't like Julie and me were really *doing* anything, you know?

Things weren't much better around my folks' house. I'd broken down and told them I got fired from the Sinclair one Sunday evening (right in the middle of my mom's famous pineapple-glazed ham with candied yams and all the fixin's) and after that, things got pretty tough with my old man. Oh, my mom was still great—she always was—but my dad and me got into one of those deals where we couldn't be in the same room for more than thirty seconds without getting into a big enormous fight about something. Or even nothing. You remember how mad he got when I quit his stinking chemical plant job so's I could go work at Old Man Finzio's? Remember how it was such a stupid, dumb, dirty, low-life, shitty-ass excuse for a job? Well, now he was even *madder* on account of I wasn't working there anymore! Can you believe it? Plus he was angry that I'd got myself fired—like it was *my* fault, right?— and even more pissed off about how Cal and me damn near burned down my aunt's garage. As you can imagine, that had been pretty hot news all over the neighborhood (ranking just behind General Motors' announcement that they were going to offer air-conditioning on selected new models) and even his rank-and-file union buddies had heard about it. So every time I went over to cadge a free meal or get my mom to do my laundry or even just raid the damn refrigerator, my dad would start hollering at me. For no reason at all, you know? And that would get me mad right back at him, and pretty soon we'd be snarling and spitting and howling back and forth like a pair of damn alley cats. My mom knew from watching her stupid birds that there was no sense trying to separate two males of any species once they've decided not to get along (especially if they happen to be father and son) so she'd generally go down and do her ironing or sneak upstairs to fluff up the pillows a couple hundred times just to get out of the line of fire. Most usually, it'd start with something simple and stupid, like if he caught me gnawing on a cold chicken leg or wolfing down the last slice of my mom's Dutch apple pie. *"So,"* he'd snarl, *"you think you can just waltz in here anytime you feel like it and take any damn thing that strikes your fancy, don't you?"*

"What?!" I'd snarl right back, making sure he got a real good solid look at whatever I was chewing. *"Y'mean I'm not even allowed to EAT here anymore?"*

"YOU earn a goddam living! Or at least that's what you CLAIM, smartass! Why don't you go out and buy your OWN damn food for a change?"

"I DO buy my own food! All the time! I just come over now and then t'see how you and Mom are doing. That's what a son is SUPPOSED to do, isn't it?"

"Yeah. Sure. You touch my heart. That's why I always catch you with your goddam friggin' nose in my refrigerator!"

"Oh, so now it's YOUR refrigerator."

"Sure, it's MY refrigerator, you insolent little piece of shit. Who the goddam hell you think PAID for it."

"MOM!!" I'd yell upstairs, *"YOU BETTER STAY THE HELL OUT OF YOUR HUSBAND'S REFRIGERATOR."*

"CUT THAT OUT!" he'd bellow even louder.

"YEAH, WHY SHOULD I?"

"BECAUSE I SAID SO!"

I must admit, he had me beat on bass resonance and sheer, windowpane-rattling volume (he'd had a lot of high-level training at his job) but whenever he threatened to shout me down, I'd simply march over to the refrigerator, take out one of his beers, lever off the cap, and drink it right there in front of him—real slow and deliberate, you know?—just so's I could watch him sputter and change colors. Sometimes he'd even haul back like he was gonna belt me, but we both knew I was too quick for him and he'd pretend to think better of it (like he was doing it for *my* benefit, right?) and mutter something like, "You're pretty goddam cocky for a kid that can't even hold on to a job as a goddam gas station grease monkey," while shaking his head as if I was the worst damn person in the world.

That's when I'd wipe the last of his beer off my chin, look him right square in the eye, and agree with him. It drove him *nuts.* "You bet your ass I am," I'd sneer, and then walk out real quick before he forgot I was too fast for him and took a swing at me. You've probably gone through shit like that with your own family. It happens to every kid, just as sure as chicken pox and puberty.

My buddy Cal was having family trouble, too. Seems his folks found out about Giant's Despair and Brynfan Tyddyn via the well-known family grapevine (most likely that sweet old sap-collector lady from Vermont) and they took away what was left of his MG and grounded him for the rest of the summer. Not that Cal was likely to *stay* grounded, but it was tougher to get around without his TC or the spare set of keys to his mom's new Packard. That Cunningham driver dropped Cal's dead MG in front of my aunt's house the Monday morning after Wilkes-Barre (right about the time I was getting fired over at the Sinclair, in fact) but a couple days later a tow truck with New York plates appeared out of nowhere and hauled it away. Not that the TC was in any shape to drive, since it was at least an engine block, connecting rod, and several other important pieces (such as fenders, headlights, windshield wipers, and a windshield for them to wipe) away from roadworthiness.

I talked to Cal a couple times, and of course he tried to make it sound like everything was rosy and that he didn't really care much one way or another. But if you listened close, you couldn't miss the hollow ring to his voice. Like people whispering in the hallways of intensive care wards and such. *"Everything's gonna be fine, Buddy. This'll blow over. No problem at all. You'll see."*

The screwy part is I *believed* him. I knew how desperately Cal wanted—*needed*—to go racing again, and that he'd do whatever it took to get himself back behind the wheel. But I was realistic enough to know it wouldn't be anytime soon, no matter what Cal said. Truth is, I was feeling pretty much alone in the world, what with Cal serving time at Castle Carrington and Julie more or less off-limits and Big Ed sulking all the time about those S.C.M.A. membership committee assholes who didn't want anything to do with him (at least when he wasn't busy sulking about how Carlo Sebastian wouldn't sell him a Ferrari or that there wasn't anybody he trusted to take care of his cars at the Sinclair anymore) not to mention how my folks' house had turned into a battleground of ugly skirmishes between my dad and me. The only thing left in my life was working at Westbridge and getting to and from work at Westbridge, and that is not what you could call a well-rounded existence.

So I decided to drop over by Butch's place, just to see how he was doing and ask if maybe he'd like to join me for the trip to Grand Island. After all, he had a car (albeit not much of one) and besides, I thought he might enjoy it. Hell, just getting away from Marlene for a few days figured to do him a world of good. Plus he could pick up and go at the drop of a hat because he didn't have much of anything else to do. Which was really pretty sad if you stopped to think about it.

Butch and Marlene lived in an ugly little clapboard house behind the chemical plant where my dad worked, and it had pretty much gone downhill ever since Butch got hurt (not that it was ever anything out of *Better Homes and Gardens* before that). Truth be known, Mean Marlene was not what you could call a real persnickety housekeeper—not hardly!—and Butch didn't help any on account of he could never resist any motorized contraption that needed "just a little fixing up" to be "good as new" again. So Butch and Marlene's front lawn looked like one of Big Ed's scrap yards, what with cracked engine blocks, seized compressors, burnt-out space heaters, rusty outboard motors, orphaned hand-crank washing machines, and even a couple big industrial wall fans scattered all over, each and every one waiting for Butch to find the spare time (and parts) to do "just a little fixing up" so's they'd be "good as new" again.

Marlene was gone that day (she'd got herself a job waiting tables someplace) and I found Butch out on his rickety front porch with the guts of a used carburetor spread out on a three-legged card table he had propped up against the railing. He seemed real pleased to see me—he even smiled!—and when I asked him how he'd like to go up to the races with me, he damn near jumped out of his wheelchair. "Hell, *yes!*" he whooped, slamming his lump hand down so hard that little brass carburetor parts jumped every which way. "Why, I been stuck in this friggin' place s'damn long I'm about t'go stark raving buggy! Marlene drives me nuts. Sittin' on this damn porch drives me nuts. The stink off that friggin' chemical plant drives me nuts. Hell, it's about burnt the damn hair right outta my nostrils. See?" He tilted his head back to show me the inside of his nose.

"So you wanna go?"

"You bet your damn *ass* I do!"

"That's great," I told him. "Just great. Why, it'll be just like the old days, you know?" Not that Butch and me really had much in the way of Old Days. At least not road trips. About the farthest we'd ever gone was across the Williamsburg Bridge to pick up some hydraulic jack parts in Brooklyn. But it sounded good.

About then Butch's old Ford came clattering up the street with Mean Marlene at the wheel, and right away I began having second thoughts. I mean, no way was that heap going to, ah, *blend in* with the polished-up MGs and Jaguars and whatnot at Grand Island. And besides the cosmetic shortcomings, it was banging and popping something awful and listing over to starboard like a garbage scow taking on water. Looked like a couple busted leaves in the right rear spring (or maybe they'd just gone soft and sagged a few inches) but whatever it was, it made that old Ford look pretty damn comical. At least if you weren't planning to take a cross-country road trip in the damn thing. "Say," I mumbled, giving the Ford a serious professional eyeballing, "you think that old crate'll *make* it?"

Butch's eyes narrowed down to slits. "Hell *yes* that car'll make it," he snarled. "Why *wouldn't* it? Y'fergettin' who put that damn thing t'gether? Y'fergettin' who taught you every goddam thing you *THINK* you know about automobiles?"

"No, Butch, I . . ."

"Besides," he added, squeezing off an insider wink, "if the sonofabitch breaks, we'll just up an' *fix* it! After all, we're goddam mechanics, ain't we?"

10

GRAND ISLAND

THERE WAS a lot of stuff to do around the Westbridge shop come race week, and it seemed like the instant I'd get done changing the oil in an XK120 or checking the spoke tension on an MG's spare or packing cans of brake fluid and chassis grease in the back of the parts van, Barry'd be right there with another three-page shit list of things that required immediate attention. In fact, you had to be impressed with the way he kept everything straight while the entire shop crew was scurrying around like the last passengers on the Titanic. It was a tremendous amount of work, and I wound up pulling tandem all-nighters Tuesday and Wednesday, and daybreak Thursday found me still hard at it, helping Barry and one of his foreign-born grease monkeys load damn near everything in the shop into the parts van. Then he lowered the overhead door and drove off, leaving me to take the damn hour and a half bus-and-train ride back to Jersey. It didn't even occur to the sonofabitch to offer me a lift. Then again, maybe this was just another sterling example of the *freedom* and *independent thought* that came along with employment as a Westbridge racing mechanic.

It was straight-up noon by the time I got over to Butch's place, and another hour before we got done packing his stuff and dropping by my apartment so's I could grab the three *s*'s (shit, shower, and shave) and do the same. I reckon it was mid-afternoon when we finally hit the road in Butch's ratty old Ford, taking off across most of New Jersey and virtually all of New York toward Grand Island, which sits in the middle of the Niagara River about seven miles north of Buffalo. The S.C.M.A. had cooked up a deal with the local city fathers to put on a race as part of the Grand Island Centennial Celebration. They could do that kind of thing because lots of the S.C.M.A. regulars were the city-father type themselves. Or at least their fathers or grandfathers were. In any case, the S.C.M.A. races stood out as unquestionably the most exciting feature of the entire festival weekend. Unless you're partial to high school marching bands and pie-eating contests, that is.

But it was one whale of a long drive to get there—almost 400 miles—and I had to do it pretty much solo on account of there was still no way Butch could operate a set of pedals. We tried having him sit behind the wheel to steer while I kind of angled my feet in from the passenger side and worked the clutch, gas, and brakes for him—he really seemed to get a charge out of that—but after we damn near ran up the backside of a gravel truck outside Paramus, I decided that maybe wasn't such a good idea. So I wound up doing all the driving while Butch sat there in the passenger seat with a road map spread across his lap, smoking cigarette after cigarette and telling me what road to take and how far we were from the next town and yelling at me to "get the goddam lead out" whenever we got bottled up behind a slow-moving truck. But every now and again we'd get a clear stretch of road, and then Butch'd make me run that old Ford as fast as she'd go. And I was happy to oblige, mashing down on the gas until it just about put a dent in the firewall. The damn thing'd shake like a paint mixer at anything much over 45, but that didn't bother Butch and me. Not one bit. I can't say exactly how fast we went (the speedometer needle waved all over the dial) but I'd hazard to say we touched 75 or 80 a couple times on the long downhill slopes. Believe me, that's god-awful scary *fast* in a rattletrap like Butch's old Ford.

We followed New Jersey 23 up through Paterson, Hamburg, and Colesville to Port Jervis, then northwest on Route 97, kind of running along the Delaware River. It was real pretty country, what with thick green forests and the river running all blue and frothy down below and these huge limestone rock formations rising up on either side. It reminded me how much handsome, free-roaming space there is in this country once you get outside the towns and cities. I kept wishing I had Julie there to share it with me, since old Butch was hardly the type to appreciate fresh air and fine scenery. At least to say anything about it, anyway.

Around seven we stopped to eat at a little railroad-car diner near Damascus, and that's where Butch and me had our first major difference of opinion. He didn't want me to haul his wheelchair out and roll him into the restaurant. "Gimme them goddam crutches," he growled. "I ain't about to be wheeled around ever'where like a friggin' tea cart." Against my better judgment I went along with him, and it took Butch about forever to hobble and scrape and stumble his way across the parking lot and up the three little steps to the door. I caught myself looking around the diner real sheepish—as if I was *apologizing* for something, you know?—and I'm sure glad Butch didn't see me. I mean, why should I give two shits about what a bunch of truck drivers and hash-house waitresses think in some broken-down roadside diner?

Turns out I must, though, because after we ordered I swallowed hard a couple times and told Butch what was on my mind. "Look, Butch," I said, talking real soft so none of the coffee-and-doughnut jerks who were craning their necks to listen in on our conversation could hear, "I don't mind pushing you around in that wheelchair. Honest I don't." I saw his eyes start to squint down, but I kept after it. "We'll cover a *lot* more ground that way. Really we will. You'll see."

Butch wavered for a moment, and just about the time I expected him to uncork both barrels and let me have it, he sagged back in his seat and rolled his eyes up toward the ceiling fan. "Yeah, I s'pose," he sighed in barely a whisper, staring up at the slowly rotating blades. "But what a damn pain in the ass."

"It sure is," I agreed solemnly, and took myself a king-sized bite out of a hamburger that tasted an awful lot like coal tar.

After dinner we gassed up, added a quart of oil, tossed a couple more in the backseat (just in case, right?), and stopped at a liquor store for a cold sixer of beer. But the jerk behind the counter wouldn't sell it to me on account of I wasn't twenty-one, so I had to haul out the wheelchair and roll Butch inside just so's he could hand over the cash. Naturally, Butch got hot about it and called the counter guy a couple nasty names—in several different languages, in fact—but the weasel behind the cash register didn't have any shame and yelled right back at him, wheelchair and all. "Now lissen here," he screeched like a rusty gate hinge, "I ain't about t'jep-or-dize *my* liquor license over a couple broken-down, beer-guzzling stumblebums. No sir."

Well, that did it. Butch exploded up out of that wheelchair with every intention of giving the jerk a well-deserved sock in the nose. But of course he couldn't keep his balance, and if I hadn't grabbed him by the scruff of the neck, Butch would've fallen right through the big glass cigar case next to the register. Boy, what a mess *that* would've been! Then there was nothing to do but wrestle Butch back into his wheel-chair, snatch our beer and change, and hustle our buns the hell out of there before the guy could retaliate. It was a pretty ugly scene (to say the least!) and made me think about what Marlene had to put up with every day of the year. No question my friend Butch Bohunk had himself one *very* short fuse.

We drove along in silence for an hour or so, just sipping our beers and listening to all the rasping, rolling, grating, thumping, whistling, and gyrating noises Butch's old Ford made, and it wasn't until fifteen miles east of Binghamton that I finally got up the nerve to throw my two cents in. "Look, Butch," I said, measuring my words carefully, "you really gotta watch that temper of yours. It's gonna land us in some serious trouble one of these days."

"Mmmph," Butch snorted. "How many other little sissygirls they got back home at the Palumbo household?"

"Hey, I *mean* it, Butch. Nobody's gonna take a sock at *you*, right? So who stands to catch hell, huh?"

Butch opened up his pocketknife and levered the caps off our last two bottles of beer. "Y'know," he sighed, taking a good long pull, "I ain't been in a decent fistfight since I got messed up in my accident. Prob'ly never will again. I reckon I miss that more than fuckin'. Honest to God I do."

We finished off our beers and Butch smoked himself another cigarette as we drove into the last of the sunset between Binghamton and Elmira, and it must've been pretty handsome, since neither of us said much of anything until the final smudges of purple and raspberry-orange faded from the sky. I was so tired that Butch tried another stint at driving, but working the pedals for him was even tougher than handling the car solo, and I was thankful when he finally pulled over at a little roadside grocery to buy another pack of cigarettes and let me take the wheel again.

Butch kind of nodded off to sleep after that, and you'd have to say that was one of his greatest talents: He could sleep *any*where. In damn near any position. And I'm talking a *real* sleep, not one of those closed-eye fakes you pull when you're riding the knife-edge between asleep and awake and trying to kid yourself into dozing off. You could tell it was the McCoy because he'd start snoring like surf rolling in and every once in awhile snort or chuckle or mutter into his shirt collar as he dreamed of sonofabitch Marine sergeants, broken Fords, big meaty women, and splendid fistfights.

All I could do was keep driving, and that can get pretty monotonous after dark, what with that endless dotted centerline coming at and at and at you through the jiggling blobs of headlamp light. I eventually got so damn woozy that I must've missed a turn and all of a sudden there weren't any highway signs anymore. Or highway, for that matter. Not only was the centerline missing, but the road itself had gone from smooth and straight to rough and swervy. The pitching and bouncing woke Butch up, and right away he wanted to know where the hell we were. "Jesus, Palumbo, where the hell *are* we?"

"Uh, I'm, ah, not exactly sure, Butch. . . ."

"Whaddaya mean, *not exactly?*"

"I mean I, uh, kind of lost the highway."

"Whaddaya mean, *lost* the highway?" He was starting to sound a little upset.

"Well, we're, ah, not *on* it anymore."

"How d'ya know?"

"Well, uh, first off, they don't generally make state highways outta dirt, do they? Besides," I added, pointing out the windshield, "state highways most usually don't have barns built at the end of them, either."

Sure enough, there was a big old wooden barn dead ahead, completely blocking the road. I slowed to a stop, but before I could so much as grab reverse, this Pa Kettle type in oversized bib coveralls came gimping out of nowhere with a shotgun under his arm. *"What's yer business?"* he demanded, waggling his shotgun at us to make sure we recognized what it was. Which we most certainly did. *"Yew boys here after my chicken aigs agin'?"*

"Uh, we, ah, kinda got ourselves lost off the main highway," I tried to explain. But the farmer had apparently formed a pretty solid opinion about us already—no question we *looked* the part of poultry thieves in Butch's old Ford—and raised his shotgun up to shoulder level.

"I'll give ye jest thutty seconts t'get off my proppity!" he shouted, glaring down the gun sight. *"Thutty seconds, y'hear?"*

"Gee whiz, mister, could'ja maybe just tell us where the main highway is?"

"Back where ye came from, idjit!" the farmer yelled, clicking back the hammers on both barrels. *"Now GIT!"*

Have you ever tried backing a rickety old Ford with a plywood slab over the back window down a rutted and totally unfamiliar dirt driveway in the middle of the night? With a shotgun pointed your way? If you have, it will come as no surprise that I managed to hit a haystack, a ditch, and a decent-sized manure pile in quick succession before sideswiping the gate clear off the old geezer's fence as I whipped us around backward onto the public right-of-way. As you can imagine, the farmer didn't appreciate that at all and let loose a blast from the shotgun to properly register his displeasure. *"Jee-ZUS!"* I yelped. "The sonofabitch is *shooting* at us!" and hammered the gas to the floor.

But Butch didn't seem upset at all. In fact, he was laughing his ass off. *"Haw-haw-haw-haw!"* he bellowed, eyes wide and wild as a kid on Christmas morning. *"Haw-haw-haw-haw-haw!"* Why, he was whooping it up so hard he damn near choked on it. "Aw geez, Buddy," he gasped as we sped out of range, "I ain't had this much fun in *ages!*" No question Butch loved a little raw-boned excitement, and I guess you never get much of that when you're stranded in a damn wheelchair.

But we were still lost. And I mean *LOST.* All I knew is that we were on some strange, pitch-black country back road heading hell only knows where, and the sky was all overcast so we couldn't make out the moon or stars or *any*thing to help get our bearings. Not that it would've done much good, since the pavement swooped uphill, downhill, left-right through S-curves, Y-intersections, and assorted switchbacks until neither of us had any idea whether we were pointed north, south, east, west, up, down, or sideways. Every now and again we'd come to some nowhere backwoods intersection marked with a little hand-painted wood sign reading COUNTY ZP ALT or APPLESAP SPRING RD or something similar (none of which were on our map, of course) and it was about then I noticed that the fuel gauge was registering dead empty. Oh, *great!* Of course, you never really know about fuel gauges until you've done a little experimenting and run a particular automobile bone-dry once or twice, but this one certainly looked like it meant business, what with the needle pointed over toward the hopeless side of *E*. Still, it seemed awful soon to be out of gas, and I wondered if we'd maybe picked up a little hole in the tank. Like about the size of a shotgun pellet?

Now the Marine Corps always told Butch it was important to have a backup contingency plan on tap for emergency situations, and I'm proud to say he knew exactly what to do. He had me pull over to the side, shut off the motor, and explained as how we were going to spend what was left of the night right there in his old Ford (which, you'll recall, had run through a rather substantial manure pile earlier that same evening and smelled distinctly of cow shit). But Butch figured there wasn't any sense using up the last fumes in the tank just to stumble around in the dark looking for a gas station that most likely wouldn't be open till morning anyway, and I had to agree. "We bunk right here," he told me, sounding none too happy about it.

"You think we'll be, you know, *safe* out here?" I'm basically a city boy—born and raised around Passaic—and like most city boys, I always imagined it'd be real peaceful out on a farm-country back road in the middle of a pitch-black farm-country night. But it's nothing of the kind. There's all sorts of hooting and mooing and cackling and rustling in the bushes going on—*big* stuff, too—and I swear, every time a damn twig snapped or owl hooted or frog burped I'd jump like I'd grabbed the business end of a hot coil wire. I tried rolling the windows up, but that just turned up the manure smell off the undercarriage even worse. No question we took a pretty healthy chunk out of that farmer's fertilizer supply. "Jeez, Butch," I grumbled as we tried to settle in for the night, "I'm real sorry about all this."

"Aw, don't worry about it," he said, trying his best to shift into a comfortable position. "Why, I ain't had this much fun since I can't remember when."

"Hey, thanks a lot, Butch."

"No sweat, Buddy. Reminds me what life *useta* be like. Just wish we had us a bottle of something to keep us company. . . . Saaay, wait a minute! Take a look under the seat, willya?"

So I reached under the seat (jeez, there was all *kinds* of stuff down there!) and rummaged around until I located a half-empty pint of sloe gin in a wrinkled paper bag. "Haw! I *knew* it!" Butch beamed. "I knew old Marlene'd have a li'l nip bottle tucked away someplace. Lemme see it." Butch took a pull and I had a sip and then we more or less polished

it off, passing it back and forth without a word while we listened to all
the frogs and crickets and whatever the hell else was out there dancing
around in the darkness.

Butch fell asleep right on cue as soon as the bottle was empty (like
I said, it was a gift) but it was already coming up light when I finally
dozed off. And I swear it didn't seem fifteen minutes before some local
rooster started crowing his ass off and blasted me wide awake again. A
thick, heavy fog had settled in around us like an enormous cloud that
was just too damn heavy to float, and looking out the windshield you
couldn't see much past the fenders. And was it ever *quiet*. I can't ever
remember a morning that ghostly silent and liquid still. Why, you could
almost hear the dew puddling up on the leaves. Then old Butch unloaded a good-morning fart that could've easily blown up a half dozen
party balloons, and that more or less broke the mood. I think it would've
topped ten seconds if you'd had a watch on it. "Hey, asshole," Butch
growled, opening one eye an eighth of an inch, "you waitin' for a damn
engraved invitation t'get yer God Damn ass in gear?"

"No, Butch, it's just I—"

"Well, I gotta crap, see, so you better start findin' us a place where
I can do it." He let loose another monster fart to show he meant business, and then began fishing around in his pockets for his breakfast
cigarette. So I fired up the Ford and we took off, barely creeping along
on account of the fog. We were still disastrously low on gas, not at all
sure where we were going, or even what damn direction we were
headed. But no more than a mile up the road we came to a nice, wide
asphalt two-lane with a freshly painted stripe down the middle and
even a stop sign facing our way to mark it as a major highway.

Seeing as how we had no idea where west might be (or north, south,
or east, for that matter), we flipped a coin and turned right when it
came up tails. Naturally, I took it real easy and made sure to coast on
all the downhills in order to stretch whatever fuel we had left as far as
it would go. Not that you could've gone any faster, since the fog was
like a wad of cotton wrapped around us and I had to navigate off the
centerline and the gravel at the edge of the road. Every now and then
we'd break into a clear area where we could see the sky, and since it
seemed a shade or two lighter over to our right, it was better than even
money we were headed north. Then the road would dip down into a
hollow and just like that we'd be back in the soup again. The gas gauge
couldn't have read any emptier, and just about the time I expected the
motor to start sputtering, we broke out of a heavy fog patch in a tiny,
two-bit town named North Java, which consisted of a general store
(closed), a pay phone (not working), and a roadside vegetable stand
where some oversized amateur grease monkey was stuffed under an

ancient Dodge pickup, trying to fix a leaky oil pan at 5:30 in the morning.

"Say, buddy, where's the nearest gas station? We're kinda lost. . . ."

"Lost, eh?" he answered in a chipmunk's voice. "Where yew boys headed for?"

"Grand Island. Near Buffalo."

"Buffalo, eh?" The big guy with the tiny voice sniggered. "then I guess ye could say yew boys . . ."—you could see he thought this was awful damn funny—". . . that yew boys'r *ON A BUFFALO HUNT!*" and he let go a high, ear-piercing cackle that damn near fluttered the shingles on the vegetable stand's roof.

"Ah, look here," I tried to explain, "we're also about outta gas, see, and—"

"Outta gas?" he said. "*Outta GAS??* And *lost,* too? Why that's real sad, boys." He was starting to giggle again. "Real, real sad."

"Yeah," Butch snarled, glaring at him, "an' I gotta find me a can soon. You understand me? *Real* soon."

"Weeeell," the big guy said, scratching at the scraggly beard around his chins, "I figger the nearest gas station is, oh, mebbe thutteen or fourteen miles."

"*I ain't gonna make it!*" Butch groaned, a hint of panic rising in his voice. I can't say as I'd ever heard a sound that helpless or pitiful out of Butch before, and it was just a little scary.

"Weeeell, I got me a one-holer out back there. Ye kin use it if ye like." He looked us over again and added, "Fer a dime, anyways."

Butch looked at me and I looked back at Butch and we both understood this was no time to haggle. So I ran over and handed the guy his lousy dime and then did my best to help Butch to the outhouse. We couldn't use the wheelchair on account of it was on a hill with bushes and rocks and stuff and just this little beaten-down dirt path to the door, and I couldn't believe how that mountain-sized local jerk just stayed there under his damn truck like a denim-covered compost heap and let Butch and me struggle it out by ourselves. Why, I had to damn near carry him a couple times and we had a hell of a time getting his pants down and trying to swing the damn door open and lever him over the stinking hole. And I do mean stinking. Then there wasn't any paper, so I had to run back down and beg some off the guy under the pickup. He wanted an extra nickel for that. It was starting to dawn on me how incredibly difficult (*and* humiliating) it was for a guy in Butch's condition to do the simple little everyday things that everybody else on this earth takes for granted. Made you wonder how people like him keep getting out of bed every morning, you know?

As you can imagine, we'd had it up to *here* with the moneygrubbing lardass under the Dodge, but since the needle on the Ford's gas gauge was resting against the peg like a fallen timber, we were about out of options. "Say, buddy," Butch asked, trying to work up a friendly smile, "y'think you could maybe fix us up with a gallon or two of gas?"

The guy under the pickup pretended like he didn't even hear. He just kept working away on his oil pan gasket, taking the bolts out the hard way by flopping a box-end combination wrench over and over in very tight quarters, an eighth of a turn at a time. You can always spot amateurs by the way they never use the proper tool. "We'd be happy to pay for it," I added sheepishly.

That got the guy's attention. He jiggled out from underneath the oil pan, kind of squirming along on his back because he was just too big to roll over and crawl out (and that Dodge was up on cinder blocks so it had damn near two feet of ground clearance!) but it was easy to see why when he grabbed the front bumper and hauled himself upright. Jee-*zus*, what a monster! He was wearing the biggest damn pair of coveralls I'd ever seen outside of a Barnum & Bailey sideshow attraction, and sported one of those goofy hayseed beards like a fur halo around his pumpkin-sized face. But although he may have *looked* like some sort of hulking, back-country hick, he sure as hell understood an open wound of economic opportunity when he saw one. "Suuuure," he smiled, filling up the entire passenger-side window with his head. "I might could provide ye a leetle gas. Ye got enny cash money on you?"

Butch flashed him two wadded-up singles.

"Help ye'self," he grinned even wider, gathering up the money in a melon-sized hand. "Take all ye want. . . . Up t'two gallons, that is."

"Two gallons!" Butch wailed, but I gave him a shot in the ribs to shut him up. After all, the mammoth vegetable-stand bumpkin from North Java had us by the short hairs and knew it. I mean, can you imagine paying a whole damn *dollar* for one lousy gallon of gasoline?

Naturally, we didn't have anything like a proper siphon hose, so I had to take one of our empty beer bottles, climb under the pickup, undo the fuel line, fill the bottle, put the hose back on, crawl out, empty it into the Ford, and then do the whole deal all over again. And again. And again. I noticed a damp spot while I was under the Ford, and sure enough we'd picked up a pinhole leak in the seam around the brass bung on the bottom.

"Hey, no problem," Butch said, and turned to the guy in the over-filled coveralls again. "Say, you got any hand soap around here?"

"Hmm. Might have. Cost ye, though."

"How much?" Butch asked, his eyes narrowing.

"Oh, I'd say about twenty cents?"

Butch's nostrils flared. "Howzabout a dime, huh?"

The big guy rolled his eyeballs skyward and thoughtfully pulled on his beard, mulling it over. "Naw," he said at last, "times bein' how they are, I don't see as how I could see my way clear t'sell enny soap fer less'n twenty cents. Supply and demand, don't ye know. That's the American Way."

Butch glowered at him, but in the end dug a dime and two nickels out of his pocket and handed it over. The big guy rummaged through all the two-by-fours and linoleum tile scraps and stub rolls of tar paper in the back of his pickup until he came up with a small, dirty chunk of Ivory. "I use it fer soapin' wood screws," he explained, "but it's almost brand-new. Bought it just last month. Honest I did."

Butch wiped it on his shirt a few times and then had me crawl under the Ford and rub it where the fuel was weeping out. I'd never heard of that trick before, but it worked like a charm. Then it was back to crawling under the pickup, filling the beer bottle, crawling out from under the pickup, pouring it in the Ford, crawling back under . . . you get the idea. Naturally, fuel went all over the place (mostly on me!) and even after a dozen trips the needle on the gauge hadn't so much as budged. But the pickup guy must've figured we'd gotten our two gallons' worth, because he asked if he could maybe take a look at that beer bottle just as I was about to slide under his Dodge for the ump-teenth time. I handed it over without thinking, and he just hauled off and threw it as high and far as he could. It rainbowed up over the telephone lines and came down dead center in the middle of the high-way, shattering like ice. "Nice doing business with ye, boys," the big guy cackled, and waddled back over to finish the oil pan job on his pickup, taking each bolt out one flat at a time.

Boy, were we *pissed!* Not only had the sonofabitch screwed us out of two dollars for what should have been about fifty cents' worth of gas, but he'd rubbed our damn noses in it as well. Still, there was nothing you could do short of taking a swing at him, and as a general policy I never pick fights with people who outweigh me by more than twice. So the asshole *had* us, and there was nothing left to do but put my ears down, drop my tail between my legs, and take off.

SHIT!

Butch said he would've dragged the fat bastard out by the heels, kicked him until blood ran out both ears, and taken our goddam money back. Then he yanked out another Pall Mall and started fumbling around for a match, but I had to stop him on account of I reeked of gasoline and the last thing that old Ford needed was a major interior fire. As we drove off, it occurred to me that stuff like that never hap-pened when I was traveling with Big Ed. In fact, just the opposite. Pull in someplace in a gleaming new Jaguar that costs more than what most

poor lunch-buckets earn in a year and folks simply can't do enough for
you. For *nothing!* But show up lost and out of gas in a rusty, broken-
down Ford sedan and they'll screw you every time. And act mean as
hell while they're at it. Like the enormous vegetable-stand butcher from
North Java said, it's the American way.

We stopped a little later in East Aurora for gas, and even managed
to borrow a hose to spray off the undercarriage so the Ford wouldn't
smell so much like cow manure. Or at least not as bad, anyway. Afterward we ate breakfast, got ourselves as cleaned up as you can get in a
street-corner coffee-shop men's room, and took off again for Grand
Island. The weather had cleared up considerably, and we enjoyed a nice
drive through Spring Brook, Cheektowaga, and Eggertsville, but ran
into a hellacious traffic jam once we got near the toll bridge over the
Niagara River to Grand Island. Sports cars and family sedans full of
racers, fans, centennial celebrants, and general curiosity-seekers were
backed up bumper-to-bumper for more than a mile, mostly because the
S.C.M.A. registration tent was the first thing you came to on the other
side of the bridge, and it was taking five to ten minutes for each car to
go through the necessary red tape before it could either enter the paddock or be on its way. Which of course meant most of the Jags in line
were steaming merrily away, but since Charlie Priddle was in charge,
there was no way you could even *think* about parking your car in the
paddock *first* and then walking back out to the S.C.M.A. tent to register.

It took damn near an hour to get across and signed in with the
Westbridge crew, and then the armband people didn't want to let us
in on account of we didn't have one of Charlie Priddle's precious little
stickers on the windshield (not to mention that they were less than
impressed with the general presentability, style, and lingering manure
odor of Butch's old Ford). But instead of turning around and fighting
our way back, I pointed to Butch's wheelchair and rolled my palms up
in the well-known New York *what-can-you-do* shrug. The armband
people looked at Butch, looked at the wheelchair, looked at each other,
and gathered together for a quick behind-the-hand powwow about
what should be done. After an incredible amount of nodding, finger
pointing, head shaking, mustache tugging, and elbow scratching, they
agreed to let us through, but only after we *promised* to hide the Ford
behind something large and opaque where nobody could see it.

We found the Westbridge truck parked along a stretch of snow
fencing on the back row of the paddock, and naturally everything was
up for grabs trying to get the cars ready for practice. To tell the truth,
Barry didn't seem too thrilled to see me once he got a load of Butch,
his wheelchair, and our ratty old Ford (not to mention that I wasn't
looking particularly chipper myself that morning) but he had us park

it more or less out of sight behind the truck, and from that moment on, my day at Grand Island turned into a total blur. Why, if I wasn't tapping knockoffs and checking tire pressures on a TC, I was changing oil on an XK120 or chasing a filter out of the parts truck or pulling a windshield off or synchronizing a set of S.U.s that had gone out of balance on the trip up from Manhattan. And I can't tell you how many times I found myself crawling around on my hands and knees trying to find some damn bolt or clip or cotter pin that had rolled off a fender and dropped in the grass.

Of course, the more cars we got ready, the more came roaring in off the circuit steaming hot and spewing oil and brandishing symptoms of all sorts of new mechanical maladies we had to track down and repair. And we weren't just working on Westbridge customer cars, either, since racing was a blood serious commercial venture as far as Barry Spline was concerned, and he stood ready and willing—clipboard in hand—to tackle any damn English sports car problem in the paddock. As long as the job paid cash, that is.

So there was just no end to it, one thing after another, and it didn't take long to realize that I was about the only honest-to-goodness mechanic Barry had on hand that weekend. I guess the other designated crew guys either got lost or sick or wised up and quit at the last minute, and seeing as how Barry was not real keen on bringing Sylvester Jones to the races, he and I were the only Westbridge representatives in the paddock. Which meant my old friend Butch came in real handy, wheeling around as best he could to put tape over headlights and paint numbers on doors with shoe polish, not to mention doing bench work like fixing bum fuel pumps and sticking distributor plates. We set him up in the shade of the parts truck with an old outhouse door laid across two sawhorses and a little tray of hand tools, and I swear Butch was happy as Old King Cole, cursing in five or six different languages while he fiddled away with contact points and carburetor packing gaskets and this and that. Wheelchair or not, Butch turned out to be quite an asset. Sure, he couldn't do *big* stuff anymore, and he still had a hell of a time making that lump of a right hand do what he wanted, but Butch could take something apart on his makeshift workbench and tell you in two seconds if it could be lashed up or field dressed or jury-rigged somehow to make it through the weekend. Oh, Barry didn't much appreciate how he cursed at everything and the way you had to keep bringing him this or that, or especially his habit of *fixing* things instead of simply demanding new parts (many of which Barry had readily available at his special, 50 percent-over-retail Race Weekend prices). But even Barry Spline had to admit that Butch was a big help to us that Friday at Grand Island.

While the three of us were slaving away on a Jag with a slipping clutch, an MG with a jammed starter, an Allard with its exhaust system coming adrift, and another MG with bent pushrods thanks to an over-enthusiastic owner who apparently didn't know what a tachometer was for, who should pull in next to us but Skippy Welcher and Milton Fitting, accompanied by more damn racing gear than you have ever seen in a two-seat automobile. It's a wonder the rear springs didn't collapse from sheer exhaustion. Squire Milton set about unloading Skippy's massive collection of vital racing stuff—stacking it in a neat, perfectly aligned row along the fencing—while The Skipper waltzed over to negotiate himself a deal on a new oil filter element for his ex-everything XK120. Naturally, Barry was up to his eyeballs in a bewildering array of British car problems, but that made no difference at all to Skippy. No sir. It wasn't like The Skipper didn't *care* if you were desperately busy, but more like he never seemed to notice. "So, tell me," The Skipper asked, his eyelids flickering ominously, "exactly how much would'ja charge me for an oil filter for my Jag?"

"With or without an oil change?" Barry gasped, straddling the transmission of the XK120 and pulling desperately with bloody, grease-blackened fingers to get it separated from the block. Sweat beads the size of ball bearings were rolling down his cheeks.

"Well," Skippy mused, thoughtfully stroking his chin, "why don't you just give me a price *with* the oil and with*out* the oil. I'm perfectly capable of changing it myself, you know. Or at least my squire"—he twitched in the general direction of Milton Fitting,—"can do it for me. He's really the expert at that sort of thing. Changing oil, I mean. Does it for me all the time. Uses real *vegetable* oil, too. None of that crappy mineral stuff. *Never* use mineral oil in a Jaguar. Gums up the works. We tried it once. *Hah!* Gummed up the works, just like I told you. But, of course, we didn't know any better then. Why, you should've seen how that..."

And that's about when I stopped paying attention and went back to installing Butch's rebuilt starter on the TC. There was a point at which you could more or less stop listening to what The Skipper was actually saying and let it all turn into a kind of whining, gyrating background noise. The kind a dry speedometer cable makes if it's got a bad kink in it.

We had extra trouble that day when all the Allard drivers started dropping by to complain about skittish handling, and no question the brutes were a real handful on the narrow, bumpy, high-crowned pavement at Grand Island. "Why, the car's simply *uncontrollable*," one of the slower guys whined, dabbing his forehead with a cowboy bandana, "and you know how terribly, terribly serious things can be...*out there....*" He let that last part dangle like a carcass on a meat hook while staring off in the general direction of oblivion, and my personal opinion was that people like him really had no business racing. Especially in hairy-chested equipment like an Allard. Hell, if all you wanted was to parade around in goggles and driving gloves and put on airs at the beer parties, you could embarrass yourself just as thoroughly in an MG TC or one of those pretty little Crosley-engined Siatas. Why pick something that scared you half to death?

But since all the other Allard guys were singing the same tune (although not whimpering so much) and since they were also mostly Westbridge customers (and *cash* customers, at that), we wound up checking every damn Allard shock, spring, wheel nut, steering knuckle, idler arm, and tire pressure in the whole blessed paddock. But we couldn't find anything wrong, and the inescapable conclusion was that it was some sort of backbone difficulty with the drivers. It sure made me wish Tommy Edwards was on hand to show those crybabies how a *real* race car driver makes the best of things and gets on with the job at hand. But Tommy was missing that weekend. Something about trying to keep his marriage together.

We had to work late into the evening to get that XK120 clutch job buttoned up, and when we were done, Barry Spline packed up his gear, bid us good night, and took off for town in one of the customer MGs (on a strictly professional evaluation test-drive, you understand), leaving Butch and me to pretty much fend for ourselves. The sonofabitch didn't even ask if we needed a couple dollars for dinner or maybe a room with a decent shower and clean sheets on the bed. What a guy. But Barry was a stickler about never getting your weekend pay—not one cent of it!—until the job was complete, and that meant back at the Westbridge shop in Manhattan on Monday. Or even Tuesday, if he could get away with it.

Then again, you couldn't really blame him, since race mechanics with fresh wads of cash in their pockets have sort of a reputation for frequenting quaint, small town drinking establishments and subsequently calling to get bailed out of quaint, small-town jails at 3:30 in the morning. And even if your crew persons managed to avoid encounters with the local police or unpleasant complications with prematurely developed high school girls, they still wouldn't be worth dog shit come the next day. So no way were you going to get dime one out of Barry Spline until after the last spark plug, oil filter, spool of wire, and can of brake fluid were safely restocked in the Westbridge parts department on Monday morning.

Butch and I made the best of things and set up camp in the parts truck, moving the compressor and most of the larger boxes outside and gathering up newspapers and shop rags and such to make a sort of half-assed mattress. Luckily, we also gathered up several free beers and a couple hefty snorts of rye whiskey from various mechanically bedeviled sportycar types still hanging around the paddock, and I'd have to say Butch and me slept like newborn babies that night.

Come Saturday we had more car trouble when one of the MGs started popping out of second gear and another had the needle-and-seat jam in the rear carburetor and leak fuel all over the exhaust manifold, resulting in a brief but spectacular engine fire. There wasn't any serious damage, but cleaning up after a fire (and, worse yet, a fire extinguisher) can be a pretty messy business. And how. Plus we had the usual prerace checking of fluid levels and tire pressures and beating a final make-sure tap on the knockoffs, not to mention continued moaning from the Allard drivers, who were coming in off the circuit with their eyes popped open like fried eggs. No question those cars were a handful here, leaping and pounding from one bump to the next like shallow-hull speedboats in choppy water. In the end, the Allard drivers decided to have a major sit-down with the S.C.M.A. armband squad after Saturday morning's final qualifying session, and the upshot was that they all volunteered to withdraw their entries and not run in the race later that afternoon. *Volunteered,* can you believe it? No way would Tommy Edwards have gone along with a program like that.

The races started after lunch, and that's when you suddenly run out of stuff to do. So I asked if Butch and me could go watch the races and Barry said ok, just so long as we checked in every now and then and came back to help load up at the end of the day. Fact is, old Barry was in a pretty agreeable mood, and you could see why when you caught a glimpse of the bulge in his back pocket. That was all folding money—more than an inch thick of it!—and I doubt many of those bills had President Washington's or Lincoln's picture on them. Yes sir, the Westbridge Motor Car Company, Ltd., had itself one *very* successful weekend at Grand Island. And without laying out a lot of extra cash for mechanics' expenses, either.

Anyhow, I loaded Butch up and we headed over by trackside to find ourselves a decent vantage point, and right away I discovered another Big Convenience about pushing somebody around in a wheelchair: You don't have to shove your way through a crowd. Why, people move aside without even looking at you. In fact, they make a big point of *not* looking at you, sort of aiming their eyeballs up and to the right as if they recognize a famous circus trapeze act or a rare species of South American fruit bat just a few feet above your left earlobe. Which means you can finesse yourself a much better than average spectating spot with a cripple and a wheelchair.

The track at Grand Island was a lot like Bridgehampton, what with 3.7 miles of narrow, bumpy blacktop stitched together in a big, uneven rectangle. There were uphills, downhills, two bridge crossings over Spicer Creek, a few fast, sweeping curves down East River Road, and four 90-degree rights to string it all together. Butch and me set ourselves up across from turn one, where Whitehaven Road teed into East River, and it was easy to see why the Allard guys were having problems. Not only was the surface narrow and ripply, but there were also a significant number of solid objects close by the roadside that a slightly out-of-control sports car might easily collect. Like spectators, for example.

Fact is, they didn't have much at all in the way of crowd control at Grand Island. Not hardly. Oh, they had the usual tire and sparkplug company banners strung up to keep people back, but those came down early, and afterward the fans pretty much wandered wherever the hell they felt like wandering. Even *right across the damn track* if some ignoramus thought he could make it between race cars! The armband types tried their best to stop them, but all they could do was holler and wave and jump up and down like kids with busted coaster wagons, and that didn't do much good. Even with the P.A. announcer alternately begging, pleading, insisting, and *demanding* that spectators stay the hell back. But there were only a handful of loudspeakers, and what with the engine noise and echo effect from one to the next, it all came out pretty garbled. Sure, if you stood smack-dab in front of one and listened real close, you could make out: *"KEEP OFF THE COURSE! PLEASE!! CLEAR THE RACECOURSE!!!"* But if you stepped back even a few feet, it sounded like they were broadcasting Polish through a window fan and no way could you understand a word of it. Not that anybody was much listening, seeing as how everybody wanted to get down *close,* you know, so they could *feel* the hot shock wave of exhaust on their shins as the cars thundered past just a few feet in front of their noses. It was *nuts!* And believe me, I know, because Butch and me were right down there in front with the rest of the goofballs.

The first race was a ten-lapper for rank novices, and it was pretty entertaining, what with lots of flailing elbows and cars squirreling all over the place. A guy named Bob Ryberg won in a blue XK120M similar to Skippy Welcher's (except I don't believe it was *ex*-anything) and our boy Carson Flegley was in there, too, hustling his black TD along in an agitated manner toward the back of the pack. He was one of those white-knuckle types who hang on to the wheel like they're dangling off the landing gear of a Sopwith Camel while it's strafing enemy trenches. I'd picked up enough from Cal and Tommy Edwards to know that was no way to drive a racing car. But you had to hand it to Carson

for being so damn determined, even if he was all jerks and edges and
had the bad rookie habit of turning in early, missing his apex, and then
having to square off the end of the corner to keep from skating into
the dirt. That *never* works. He ultimately dropped two wheels off, tried
to horse it back in line, and wound up snapping back the other way
and mowing down a row of mailboxes. Right in front of us! That caused
one of the local cops to have a chat with the S.C.M.A. officials about
getting the spectators the hell away from that corner. So a couple of
them ran over and started shouting and shaking their fists until they'd
herded us twenty or thirty yards up Whitehaven Road. Right in the
middle of the braking zone. On the next lap, some overeager doofus in
a green Jaguar locked all four and looped it through a plot of staked
tomato vines just a few feet from where we were standing. So now the
cop and the armband people were a little perplexed as to exactly where
they should tell us not to stand. Not that it made much difference, since
no matter what they said or did, it wouldn't be five minutes before
another wave of fans rolled in and filled up the space again. The crazy
part was that nobody except the cop and the armband crew seemed the
least bit worried. Like we were somehow all *in* on it—right along with
the drivers!—and trusted them not to do anything so brave or foolish
as to put their lives (not to mention *ours*) in jeopardy. Which made no
sense at all if you'd spent any time around an S.C.M.A. paddock and
met some of those assholes face-to-face. I mean, people like Carson
Flegley and Skippy Welcher didn't exactly fill you with a sense of cool
confidence and self-control. Not hardly.

But in spite of the spins and Carson's trip through the mailboxes,
there was no serious damage, and the program moved on to a ten-
lapper for small-bore production cars. The field included lots of
Porsches and MGs and a couple of those nifty Italian Siatas that looked
like miniature Ferraris but sounded more like power lawn mowers.
Two of them were running up front, dicing it out hammer and tongs
with a couple Porsches and a supercharged MG, when all of a sudden
the cars stopped coming around and everything got real quiet. *Spooky*
quiet. I thought the P.A. announcer maybe said something about an
"accident," but you couldn't make it out, so now everybody was standing around mumbling and shrugging their shoulders and trying to figure out what the heck was going on. Then a white Cadillac ambulance
whooshed by—siren wailing, mars lights flashing—and you could see
some poor guy stretched out in back with a doctor bent over him. The
ambulance disappeared up the road, heading toward the bridge, leaving
behind a silence so deep and empty you could hear water moving in
the river a half mile away.

We waited the better part of an hour for the S.C.M.A. to get things squared away, and then—like nothing had happened!—the smallbore cars came out to finish their race. Tom Hoan won it in a supercharged TC, but he was pressed hard by some guy named Hansgen in one of those pretty little Siatas. No question he was getting all there was out of that car, and I made a mental note that this Hansgen guy might be worth keeping an eye on. All in all, it was a pretty decent contest. But of course nobody much cared, since all they wanted to know were the latest rumors and whispered grisly details about The Big Wreck and what happened to the poor guy they carted off in the ambulance.

We got part of the answer between races, when a local tow truck came groaning up East River Road dragging the remains of a Porsche coupe behind it. Jee-*zus,* what a mess! The roof was all flattened down with big clumps of turf hanging off it, the hood and decklid were ripped clean off, both doors dangled open, and every piece of glass was shattered. The left-front wheel was missing entirely and you could see the left-rear was folded way underneath the fender, so the Porsche was kind of wobbling and skittering along behind the tow truck, making ugly noises like chalk screeching on a blackboard. It was a total—no doubt about it—and you couldn't help wondering and worrying how badly the guy was hurt.

Or maybe if he wasn't hurting at all anymore.

Naturally, the accident put everything way behind schedule, and the S.C.M.A. had to shorten the big-bore race and the Grand Island Centennial Grand Prix finale in order to finish before dark. Neither was much of a show, since Creighton Pendleton the Third was on hand with his new 4.1 Ferrari and waltzed off to easy victories in both heats. What with Tommy Edwards home and all the other Allard drivers too chickenshit to run, nobody could so much as catch a whiff off his tailpipes. Far as I was concerned, watching Creighton Pendleton and the gorgeous, chestnut-haired Sally Enderle taking another victory lap in that bright red Ferrari of his was getting a little stale.

After the checker, I wheeled Butch back to the paddock and helped Barry load up, and we overheard a lot of loose talk about the guy who crashed the Porsche and how it happened. The general gist of it was that he got a little loose through Ferry Bend (by far the fastest turn on the circuit) and compounded things by making about the biggest single mistake a driver can make when his car starts getting away from him: He lifted his foot off the gas. Once that happens, it's usually all over but the cleanup, since no mere mortal is quick or subtle enough to catch it when a car snaps back the other way. Especially a Porsche. Anyhow, the car shot off the road backward, hooked a rut all funny, and went into a series of violent end-for-end flips. The driver damn near came out on the second one, and that's how his left arm got caught between the roof and the pavement when it crunched back down again. On the next roll, eyewitnesses said his arm cracked in the air like a damn bullwhip. It was a real nightmare, no lie.

Late word from the hospital said he had multiple fractures of his left arm and right leg, a couple cracked ribs, all kinds of cuts and bruises, and a severe concussion. Far as I could see from the remains of that Porsche, he was damn lucky to be alive. Worse yet, the S.C.M.A. didn't have any accident insurance at Grand Island—not one penny!— so the paddock officials were passing the hat to sort of help the guy out with his hospital bills.

But by far the luckiest people were the spectators down at Ferry Bend. Somehow that Porsche managed to cartwheel down the track at better than 80, bouncing off the scenery and shedding wheels and chunks of hardware every which way, and yet *never got into the crowd.* And those people were pressed in five- and six-deep along both sides of the road! If you ask me, it was a genuine miracle. Honest to God it was. In fact, the only injury of any kind was a bruised knee some guy got off the front wheel after it tore loose and went bouncing down the road on its own. But just imagine if that Porsche had flipped into the crowd. Jee-*zus,* arms and legs would've gone flying like bowling pins!

It made you sick inside just to think about it.

11

HOME GAMES AND ROAD GAMES

IT TOOK Saturday night and all day Sunday to make it back from Grand Island, and along the way Butch and I pooled our resources (if you can call four dollars and eighty cents "resources") and rented ourselves a tourist cabin at a cheap mom-and-pop place east of Binghamton. It needed paint and a few windowpanes, but at least the beds were clean and there weren't any bugs. But I kept having dreams about Julie, and what it might be like if she came up to the races and we wound up sharing a room like the one Butch and me were in. Or better yet, a little nicer. Then the scene would shift and we'd be at the racetrack, and that's when everything started to turn all strange on me—like it does sometimes in dreams. I'd be over by the parts truck, trying to fix three MGs and two Jags and the brakes on Tommy's Cad-Allard like some wrench-wielding cartoon octopus, and meanwhile, Julie's just standing there like she's waiting for a train that's five hours late. Barry Spline's there, prancing up and down like a damn drum major—clipboard in hand—cheerfully lining up even more cars to fix. Then, right out of nowhere, Creighton Pendleton comes screaming up and whips his Ferrari around in a magnificent figure-eight powerslide, showering gravel that sparkles like rhinestones, coming to a perfect halt directly in front of Julie. Damn near runs her over, in fact. So Creighton jumps out like he wants to make sure she's OK, and next thing you know, the two of them are sort of smiling and giggling and talking in whispers, and I can't do a thing about it because I'm stuck in the background like a piece of stage scenery, fighting with a frozen-up water pump on some piece-of-shit MG. Every time I take off a nut or undo a hose clamp, it seems to grow another one. And another one after that. And by now Julie and Creighton are nuzzling into each other and even kissing (and *French,* at that!) but I can't say anything on account of I'm holding the new water pump gasket in my mouth. You know how it goes in bad dreams. I want to run over and make them stop, but it turns out my wrists are shackled to the damn exhaust manifold, and I realize I can't go *any*where until the job is finished. So I try working faster. And faster. And pretty soon I'm spinning wrenches so fast my hands are nothing but a raw-knuckled blur. But it's no use, and in the end all I can do is stand there by that stinking MG with my guts turning to jelly while Creighton Pendleton the Third roars off into the sunset with *my* girl next to him in that blasted bright red Ferrari of his....

I told Butch about my dream over coffee and a couple scrambled eggs the next morning, and he thought it was colossally stupid. After all, what would a handsome, bucks-up, well-bred asshole like Creighton Pendleton want with some blue-collar carhop dolly from Passaic? Especially when he already had a magnificent, rich, classy girlfriend like Sally Enderle? Why, he probably wouldn't give somebody like Julie a second look. And that got me even more upset.

Not that I was getting to see much of Julie since I'd been fired from her uncle's gas station. In fact, I wasn't seeing her at all, what with my endless work-and-travel schedule as a highly skilled (albeit highly underpaid) Westbridge race mechanic. And it occurred to me, as we headed toward home that quiet Sunday morning, that I really *missed* seeing Julie. Why, I even missed working at Old Man Finzio's gas station, in spite of him being about the orneriest old fart I'd ever met in my life. I was on my own hook at the Sinclair, running jobs and figuring stuff out for myself instead of playing bottom-of-the-totem-pole grease flunky at Westbridge. So by the time we reached Jersey, I knew I wanted to quit my fancy-ass race mechanic job in Manhattan and move back into my old life. Problem was, I'd come down with a pretty serious case of the racing disease, and once you get a dose, there's just no getting rid of it. Real life is just so damn dull and predictable by comparison. But I had this hot little kernel of an idea in my head that there might be some way, what with Big Ed and Carson Flegley both hot to trot and living close to Passaic, that I might be able to make it all come together at the Old Man's Sinclair.

After I dropped Butch and his rusted-out Ford off in Newark and took the bus back to Passaic, I stopped at the corner grocery and put my very last dime in the pay phone to call Julie. Sure, I could've done it for free in my Aunt Rosamarina's house, but that phone always came with an extra set of ears and at least four arrogant felines staring you in the face while you were trying to carry on a private conversation. Which is why the pay phone at the corner grocery had become my personal command center ever since I'd moved into the space over my aunt's garage. I mean, there was no way a guy earning race mechanic's wages at Westbridge could afford a frivolous luxury such as his own private phone. Besides, what good would it do, since I was hardly ever home to answer it?

I remember dialing up Julie's number and kind of shuffling back and forth from one foot to the other while I waited through the silence and desperately tried to figure just what the hell to say. Especially if her mom answered. But I lucked out and Julie picked up the phone herself, and it sent a wave of cold, tiny shivers through my system when I heard her say, "Hello?"

"Uh, er, hi, Julie...."

"Buddy?"

"Uh, yeah, ah..."

"Where *are* you?"

"Uh, at the grocery store over by my apartment, actually. Right between the rye bread, mayonnaise, and piccalilli."

"What on earth are you doing there?"

"Well, uh, I guess I'm sort of calling *you*, aren't I?"

There was a long pause, and I got this feeling like maybe her mother had just breezed through the room. "Listen, Buddy," she whispered, her mouth right up against the receiver, "you stay right there at your place. You hear me? I'll be over in a little bit." And she hung up—*click!*—before I could say another word.

I had to grab the bread rack to keep from keeling over into the condiment shelf. Julie Finzio was actually coming over to my apartment... *COMING OVER TO MY APARTMENT?!* And I instantly realized I'd better get my ass over there and tidy up so Julie wouldn't think I was some kind of major-league slop hog living in a walk-up garbage dump. I ran across the street and bounded up the stairs three at a time, and when I finally threw the door open, I was shocked to discover it was even worse than I remembered. Then again, I hadn't been using it for much except to flop for a few hours every couple nights, and I can't say as I was ever a persnickety housekeeper. Which is undoubtedly why the place reeked from the remains of a decomposed peppers-and-egg sandwich and some well-aged carryout coleslaw I'd somehow neglected to throw out. Not to mention that several layers of used coveralls were decorating what I laughingly referred to as my "furniture," and orphan socks were scattered thither and yon like they'd been having some sort of Walt Disney ankle dance party while I was gone. And a quick glance in the mirror confirmed I was not looking all that presentable myself. Fact is, the last time I'd been real intimate with a bar of soap was when I stopped up that gas tank leak on Butch's old Ford. Fortunately, it took Julie more than an hour to sneak out of her mom's house, and that gave me just enough time to rush around my apartment like an electrified crazy person, throwing windows open and chucking old garbage and the worst of the coveralls into the trash out back. I mean, I could always go back for them later, right? I even sneaked into my aunt's house and gleeped the fan out of her kitchen window and a couple of those sachet things out of her linen drawer to maybe make my apartment smell a little nicer.

Lord knows anything would've helped....

Now Aunt Rosamarina normally didn't approve of me coming into her house unless I knocked first and waited for her to open the chain lock a quarter inch so she could verify that I was indeed her nephew Buddy and not some escaped mental patient cleverly disguised to look and sound exactly like me. But it was Sunday evening, so I knew she'd be in the midst of one of her sherry-soaked Sunday night bubble baths, which included one bottle of lilac-scented bubble bath, one bottle of light cream sherry, and about twenty-five gallons of extremely hot water. She'd lay there in her tub for hours on end, and she could get herself *very* relaxed on your typical Sunday evening. In fact, I don't believe she even knew I was in the house that night.

I set my aunt's fan up in the window with those sachet things dangling in front of it on an old shoelace, and I must admit my apartment was starting to look and smell almost as good as your average tenement slum. The only problem was the bed. I mean, it looked so damn *obvious,* sitting there smack-dab in the middle of the floor. It seemed as if that bed had somehow inflated itself—like a blow-up beach toy!—until it filled up half the room. And it didn't help that the bedclothes looked like they'd been dragged through a swamp and subsequently run over by a bulldozer. It goes without saying that I didn't have any fresh sheets or pillowcases, and, seeing as how time was growing desperately short, I finally just grabbed the whole mess with both hands and flopped it over—mattress, sheets, socks, magazines, half-eaten doughnuts, and all!—and covered it with the wool Army blanket my mom gave me for cold winter nights.

With the apartment more or less squared away, it was time to rip off my clothes, stash them under the sink, and take a lightning-quick shower in my eighteen-by-eighteen metal stall. I banged the shit out of my knees and elbows on account of the temperature would fluctuate from Just Right to Ice Cold and back whenever my aunt reached her toe up to run a fresh stream of hot water into her bath, and there is just no place you can jump inside an eighteen-inch Sears shower stall without bouncing off the damn walls. The neighbors must've thought I'd taken up the kettledrum, you know? And of course I didn't have a bar of honest-to-goodness bath soap on hand (no surprise) so I resorted to a bottle of dish soap I had under the sink. At least it figured to make me smell nice, even if I felt a tad on the slimy side.

I was just drying myself when I heard a gentle knock on the door. Jee-*zus!* It was *Julie!* I scrambled to wrap the towel around me as the door swung open, then damn near dropped it when I saw Julie standing there with the soft evening sunlight flowing in around her like some sort gauzy halo. She was wearing that sleeveless yellow sweater I liked so much and her hair was all done up in springy black curls. And boy, did she ever look *great!* "Jeez, Buddy," she smiled, looking down at my towel, "you didn't have to *dress up* or anything...."

"Uh, sorry, Julie. It's just I was, uh, sorta trying to get the place cleaned up a little, see, and I, uh ..."

"You call *this* cleaned up?" she laughed, her eyes sweeping around the room. "Jesus Christ, Palumbo, you've been trying to get me up here for months, and now I can't for the life of me imagine why."

"W-Well," I stammered, "I just got back from Grand Island, see ..."

"Don't worry about it," Julie grinned as she Waltzed herself inside. Just like *that.* With me standing there in a towel and everything! She came straight up to me, put her hands on my shoulders, and gave me a hot little peck on the cheek. "So," she said, "how've you been?"

"Oh, I dunno," I gulped. "I guess I been OK. How'bout you?"

"OK, I guess. I've kinda missed you, though. Sort of, anyway...."

"I've kinda missed you, too."

"Oh, *really?*" she snorted. "That's news to me, Palumbo."

"Look," I tried to explain, "I been real busy with the traveling and all ..."

"I guess *so!* In fact, you been so damn busy you can't even find the time to call me or ask me out on a frickin' date, haven't you?"

"Aw gee, Julie, your mom always answers and hangs up on me...."

"*Oh?* And how would *you* know? You haven't so much as *tried* to call for at least three weeks."

"Aw, it hasn't been *that* long...."

"Like hell it hasn't. The last time my mom hung up on you was three weeks ago Friday. August 8th, to be exact."

"Are you *sure?*"

Julie nodded, and I knew better than to argue. Women possess an uncanny memory for precise dates, times, and circumstances whenever they require such information to make a male of the species feel guilty and/or apologetic. "Well, y'gotta understand," I said lamely, a slow burn working its way up my cheeks, "I been real sorta, you know, *busy,* see, and ..."

"So, I guess that means I'm just not *important* to you anymore. Is that it?"

"No, Julie, it's just ..."

"Or maybe it's just I'm not real good company, huh? I guess I must *bore* you." She wasn't really scolding me, but more sort of teasing me the way girls do when they think you deserve to squirm a little. "Gee,

Buddy," she continued airily, "it's too bad this just doesn't *mean* any-thing to you anymore. . . ." And she leaned in real close so her lips were right up against my ear and whispered, "*Isn't* it?"

Jee-*zus,* her breath went through my system like the hot rush of air through a subway tunnel on a warm summer night. I put my arms awkwardly around her and prayed she wasn't paying much attention to the hard, hungry lump rising up underneath my towel. "G-Gosh, Julie," I mumbled into the top of her head, "I've really missed you. Honest I have."

"You have? Really?"

"Uh-huh," I nodded, nuzzling gently against her curls. "Fact is, I can't tell you how good it is to see you again. Honest, Julie. Why, it makes me feel . . ."

"I can *see* how it makes you feel," she laughed, shooting me one of those dirty-girl winks she'd picked up from the movie magazines.

As you can imagine, that turned me the color and temperature of a freshly baked beefsteak tomato. I embarrass real easy, no lie. In fact, I can get embarrassed just thinking about getting embarrassed, if you know what I mean.

"*So,*" Julie continued, kind of wandering over and sitting herself down oh-so-casually on the edge of my mom's Army blanket, "how've you been, Palumbo?"

"Aw, OK, I guess."

"*Really?*"

And that's when I felt this god-awful big sigh come out of me, like the last bit of air leaking out of a bad tire. "No," I finally admitted, looking at the floor, "not really. I've been working my goddam ass off at Westbridge—for *nothing!*—and I've just about *had* it with that piece-of-shit race mechanic job over in Manhattan."

"You have?"

"Uh-huh. Why, it's got to where it just isn't worth it anymore, you know?"

"I sure do," Julie nodded, leaning forward on the edge of the bed and resting her chin on her hands.

I didn't have the slightest notion what to do or say next. In the flutter of a heartbeat the room got *very* quiet. So quiet it was almost deafening. "Uh, gee," I finally asked, "can I, er, *get* you anything, Julie?"

"Well, what've you got?"

My eyeballs took a quick rotational inventory. "Well, um, when you get right down to it . . . ," I admitted helplessly, rolling my palms up-ward, "*. . . nothing.*"

We got a pretty good laugh off that.

"So," I asked her, "how're things going over at the Sinclair?" I was still standing in the middle of the room with my towel wrapped around me, trying to figure out how to get myself over to the bed without having it look like I was actually trying to get over next to her. "How's that new mechanic working out?"

"Which one?" Julie laughed.

"Whaddaya mean, *which one?*"

"Well, we've had three since you left. . . ."

"You *have?*"

"Uh-huh."

"But, gee whiz, I've only been gone a couple weeks."

"Well, you know what they say about good help being hard to find. Too bad you left, Palumbo."

"If you remember, I didn't so much *leave* as got my ass *fired,*" I reminded her.

"Yeah," she smiled, "and it was a pretty nice ass to have around, too."

All by themselves, my legs carried me over to the edge of the bed and sat me down beside her. And Julie didn't seem to mind one bit. In fact, it almost seemed *too* easy, you know? "So," I said again, my voice cracking a little around the edges, "your uncle's been having some wrench trouble?"

"And *how!*" Julie laughed, tossing her curls back. "The guy who came right after you wasn't too bad, but my uncle caught him stealing parts out of the storeroom to do side jobs and fired him on the spot."

"That must've been a pretty ugly scene."

"Oh, it was. And then we had this big fat guy from Clifton who didn't show up half the time."

"That's nice."

"Uh-huh. And the last one was even worse."

"What could possibly be worse than stealing parts or not showing up?"

"How about dropping a customer's car off the lift?"

"Yeah," I had to agree, "that would be worse."

"It was actually pretty funny. Honest it was. He was trying to fix the exhaust on Mrs. Muccianti's Pontiac, and he had it hanging off the side of the lift—"

"So he could get at the pipe, right?"

"Right, so he could get at the pipe. But then one of the bolts was rusted or something, so he went and got this big, long, uh. . . ."

"This big, long breaker bar."

"Right. This big, long breaker bar. And he hooked it up on the bolt and started yanking and pulling—"

"And pulling and yanking." I could almost *see* it, you know?

"Anyhow, he's leaning on it for all he's worth, and then something snaps and he goes sprawling one way while Mrs. Muccianti's Pontiac topples off the other."

I imagined a little cartoon soundtrack of trash cans falling down flights of stairs. "So what happened then?"

"Well," Julie giggled, "the car sort of landed between the lift and the wall. On its side, you know? They couldn't get the lift down because the car was under it, and my uncle wound up having to drag it out of there with the tow truck before they could flop it back down on its wheels again. It was a hell of a mess."

"I bet he was real happy about *that*."

"Oh, he was downright thrilled."

"What did he do?"

"Well, for starters he chased that poor guy down the block with a monkey wrench. Wouldn't even let him back in the shop to get his tools. The guy had to find a traffic cop to make my uncle let him get his toolbox. It was pretty funny, honest it was. At least if you weren't my uncle or Mrs. Muccianti...."

"Did it do a lot of damage to the Pontiac?"

"Oh, not too bad, considering. It put a little pavement rash on the side and most of the glass got broken and a bunch of gas and oil spilled all over. My uncle couldn't even light a cigarette inside for the rest of the day."

"Now *that's* serious."

"Yeah. It was the guy's first job, too."

"His *first* car?" I asked incredulously, my eyes flickering like birthday candles. "That wasn't exactly real professional of him, was it?"

"No, I guess not," Julie agreed. "I think maybe he was a little stiff, too. You could smell it on him."

"You'd be surprised how much of that goes on in the wrenching business."

"No, I don't think I would, Buddy."

"No, I guess not."

And then all of a sudden we were just sitting there looking at each other again, so I kind of leaned in and kissed her. Not one of those wet, steamy, Hollywood kisses, but just a nice, gentle kiss that was all soft and warm around the edges. The kind of kiss that makes your toes curl. "You know, Buddy," Julie sighed, "I bet you could get your old job back if you really wanted it."

"You think?"

"Yeah, I do. Big Ed comes around asking for you all the time. He won't let anybody else *touch* his cars. Not even the Cadillacs. I think he's taking the Jaguar over to some guy in Englewood, but you can tell he's not real happy about it. And this skinny guy in a black suit keeps dropping by with one of those MG things."

"That's gotta be Carson Flegley."

"Yeah, that's him. He looks kind of like, I don't know . . ."

"Like an undertaker?"

"Yeah, that's him all right. Anyhow, he asks about you all the time, too. And that rich kid with the other MG . . ."

"Cal Carrington?"

"Right. The handsome one. He's been by once or twice himself. Even gave my uncle a couple dollars for some spotlight you guys stole off his tow truck."

Good for him, I thought.

"Anyhow, you really oughta drop by and see how things are. My uncle hasn't been feeling too good lately, and—"

"Hasn't been feeling good?" I asked, surprised I cared much one way or the other. "Why, that old fart never acted like he felt good a day in his life. How the hell can he tell the difference?"

"He's been going to the doctor a lot."

"He has?"

"Yeah. Twice last week."

"You know what's wrong?"

Julie shook her head. "But you know my uncle. He wouldn't go *near* a doctor's office unless he thought he was pretty sick. That's why he needs a really solid mechanic to help out around the station. Somebody he can *trust,* you know?"

"Oh, sure. And he's really gonna trust *me,* right? Gee whiz, Julie, you were there when he fired me. Hell, you were the damn *reason* he fired me. . . ."

"I wouldn't be surprised if that's all blown over, Buddy. Especially now that he really *needs* somebody. Besides," Julie added, looking at me out of the corners of her eyes, "I don't think he gives two shits about what I do or who I do it with. Not really. He just doesn't want to have to *look* at it."

"Or have it happen on company time."

"That either."

"Which reminds me," I said, unleashing a little of the old hairy eyeball myself, "what *have* you been up to lately?"

"And what business is it of *yours?*" Julie asked, arching her eyebrows. "You think I should just wait by the stinking phone so I can be there whenever the great Buddy Palumbo gets the urge to call? Is *that* the way it's supposed to be?"

No question she was yanking my chain—hell, she had every right to!—but you couldn't miss how the gleam in her eye was saying something completely different from the words coming out of her mouth. "Aw, Julie," I whimpered. "You know it's not like that. Not at all."

"So *you* say."

"Aw, c'mon, Julie. Let's make up."

"Yeah? What for?"

"*What for?* Why, so we can start hanging around together. That's what for."

"Oh? Hanging around together? And just what exactly does *that* include?"

"You know. Going out together and stuff. You haven't been going out with anybody, have you?"

All of a sudden the temperature dropped about twenty degrees. "A lot you care," Julie sniffed. You could tell she was avoiding my eyes.

"But I *do* care," I told her. "I care a *lot*. So c'mon, Julie, *tell* me. Have you been going out with anybody else or what?"

"Why should I tell *you?* You don't tell *me* about the girls you've been running around with at those races. Not that I really want to know...."

"There's nobody, Julie. Honest. Nobody at all."

"Really?"

I looked her right in the eyes and nodded. "Hell, Julie, I don't have time to sit down and take a decent crap on a race weekend, let alone chase after girls."

"Honest?"

"Absolutely. And believe me, the girls they have at those races wouldn't be interested in some greaseball automobile mechanic from Passaic. Not hardly."

"So you haven't been seeing *any*body?"

I shook my head. "How 'bout you?"

"Oh," Julie sighed, looking down at where her legs poked out from underneath her skirt, "I went out a couple times with that David Sweeney guy who used to manage the kitchen at the Doggie Shake on nights and weekends."

"You *did?*" I gasped, my insides going all hollow on me.

"Yeah, *sure* I did," Julie growled, sticking out her jaw. "Why the hell shouldn't I? Huh? Why?"

She had me there. "B-But, Julie," I protested, "if he's the one I'm thinking of, he's gotta be *at least* thirty years old...."

"He's twenty-eight," Julie said flatly.

"And he's half *bald,* for Chrissakes."

"No, he isn't."

"*Sure* he is."

"Well, maybe just a little bit. On top."

"*So,*" I asked, trying to act real suave and Continental about it, "did'ja have a good time with this David Sweeney guy or what?"

"Oh, we had a *swell* time," Julie mumbled into the shoulder of her sweater. "Not only was the jerk half bald, he turned out to be half octopus, too. . . ."

"Half octopus?" I pretended like I had no idea what she meant.

"You know. The way he was trying to get his hands into everything all the time. Our last date he invited me to the damn wrestling matches, and *we* turned out to be the main event."

The bastard, I thought, my guts flopping around like a carp on a fishing pier. I mean, what right did *he* have trying to get away with the same kind of stuff *I* was trying to do with Julie? I mean, she was *my* girl, wasn't she? Well, *wasn't* she? "So, uh, how many times did you go out with this David Sweeney guy, anyway?"

"Jeez, Buddy, does it matter? I mean, the guy turned out to be a fourteen-carat jerk, ok?" She looked down at her knees again and added softly, "Besides, I'm not seeing him anymore."

"But you see him at work, don't you?"

"Nah, he's not there anymore. I guess he took a job as lunch hour manager at some sit-down dinner place on the New York side. Up near Scarsdale, I think. The jerk doesn't even live around here anymore."

I could tell by her voice that this David Sweeney character hadn't exactly worked it out with Julie ahead of time that he was planning to pull up stakes and leave town, and it got me more than a little curious as to exactly what went on between them. On the other hand, here was Miss Julie Finzio, right where I'd always dreamed and wished and hoped and imagined her, right here in the apartment over my aunt's garage—right on the damn *bed,* for gosh sakes!—and it seemed better to concentrate on the here and now rather than hashing over the details of some phantom boyfriend who was (hopefully) past tense now anyway. "So," I said, sliding my arm around her, "you been seeing anybody else lately?"

"Well, I'd like to see more of *you,* Buddy"—she looked down at my towel—"that is, I'd like to see you *more often.*"

"I'd like that, too," I agreed, and moved in for another kiss. It was a hot one this time (for both of us—I could tell!) and pretty soon we were all wrapped up in each other and even stretched out fully parallel-to-the-ground horizontal on my bed. Why, she even let me run my hand up underneath her sweater and unhook her bra! And she knew exactly what I was doing, too. I'm *sure* of it.

But just as I was getting to Full Frothing Hormone Alert, Julie stopped me like she always did (what else?) and said that she really had to be getting along before her mother started missing her. But the truth is, I didn't feel too bad about it (at least once I got over the usual whimpering, pleading, teeth gnashing, and nervous-system aftershocks) seeing as how I'd been treating her like dogshit ever since the day I got fired from the Sinclair, and I couldn't believe how incredibly *nice* it felt to have her back again. And her front, too. . . .

For the very first time, that sort of thing seemed like it might be in the cards for us, and it had my internal juices on full boil. After all, we'd gone further that Sunday than we'd ever gone before, and that meant I could probably go back again anytime I wanted. That's the way it worked. It was like your hands were commando squadrons trying to occupy hostile territory—fingers stealthily creeping a tentative quarter inch at a time, constantly on the lookout for enemy opposition—but once you'd managed to conquer a particular plain, peak, hilltop, or valley, you could always go back and occupy that spot again. Every time you made out. It was kind of an unwritten law, you know? Of course, you had to follow the same careful, tedious maneuvers and remember not to skip any of the preliminaries, but so long as you played by the rules and made sure to keep your girl happy and content the rest of the time, you could maybe even go for a little more. So there's no doubt I had quitting on my mind when I rolled into Westbridge just precisely past noon that Monday morning. All during the bus-and-train ride into Manhattan I'd been planning and rehearsing what I was going to say. By far the most satisfying would've been the time-honored *"Screw you, I QUIT!"* outburst, punctuated with a few choice Italian hand gestures and a quick, pithy recap of how much *fun* I had sleeping in the damn parts truck and how much I appreciated the opportunity to work full-time for part-time pay. But that really wouldn't have been fair. After all, I'd taken this lousy job with my eyes wide open (bugged out, in fact) and besides, I was still desperately sick with the racing disease, and no question Colin St. John and Barry Spline were right in the eye of the storm where that was concerned. Like I said once before, you never want to burn your Westbridges.

I thought about trying the old *"better deal somewheres else"* gimmick, but the truth is you only pull that one out of the bag when you're trying to get a pay raise or increased benefits at the place you're already work-ing. Not that you had to worry much about employee benefits at West-bridge, on account of there weren't any.

The last and most diplomatic option was the old *"personal reasons"* routine, which is always the favored line of bullshit when you're trying to stay on good terms with the people you don't want to work for anymore. So I planned to trot out another bogus horror story about my poor, sick old Aunt Rosamarina back in Passaic. But the entire speech slipped my mind the instant I walked in and saw Tommy Edwards all huddled in a corner with Barry and Colin St. John. No question something *big* was brewing on the racing front, and right away I felt this ratlike gnawing in my gut because I wanted desperately to be in on it. "Hey, sport," Tommy called out as soon as he saw me, "how's the young master mechanic these days?"

"Oh, pretty good," I allowed. "Still a little tired from the weekend, though."

"Grand Island?"

I nodded.

"Damn. Sure wished I could've made it. Had some, ahh, *personal* business to attend to. . . ."

"I heard."

"Oh *really?*" Tommy said through lightly clenched teeth. "And pray tell what exactly did you hear?"

Barry and Colin glared at me like four Lucas P200s on high beam.

"Well, er, aahh," I stammered, trying to figure out what to say next, "I just sorta heard, well, what I mean is, I heard . . ."

"Oh, what the bloody hell," Tommy sighed, shaking his head. "It's probably all true enough, whatever it was."

"It, uh, it wasn't really anything," I mumbled into my shirt while my face changed color like a traffic light.

"Oh, that's all right, sport," Tommy told me, putting his arm around my shoulder and mustering up a hard-won smile. "Race paddocks are worse than the bloody military when it comes to rumors. Might as well put your personal business on a bloody full-page ad in the Sunday *Times*." He let out a long, weary sigh. *"Women,"* he observed to no one in particular, "sometimes I wonder why the good Lord ever saw fit to make them with heads. . . ."

"Amen to that, brother," Sylvester sang out from the back of the shop, and everybody broke out laughing.

Then Tommy asked me how things went at Grand Island, and it was a pretty nice feeling that he thought enough of my opinion to ask. "It was OK, I guess," I told him. "Some guy flipped a Porsche coupe and got hurt pretty bad."

"I heard."

"And those other Allard guys chickened out and wouldn't run in the race on Saturday afternoon."

"I heard that, too," Tommy said evenly, his nostrils flaring just a bit over his salt-and-pepper mustache.

"Think *you* would've run?"

Tommy leaned back against the parts counter and thought it over. "Well, I reckon it's not entirely fair to pass judgment, is it? After all, I wasn't *there*. . . . "

"True enough, true enough," Colin agreed diplomatically.

"But on the other hand," Tommy continued, a nasty little edge coming into his voice, "why on earth would anyone take a sports car all across the length and breadth of New York State and then not *race* the silly thing. I mean, what *for?*"

"Bloody 'ell *right!*" Barry growled, and spit in the waste can for emphasis.

Then we just stood there for awhile, listening to the clicking of ratchet wrenches in the back of the shop. "So," I finally I got up the nerve to ask, "what are you guys up to, anyway?"

Tommy looked at Barry and Colin and then back at me. "Oh," he said with a mysterious little swirl in his voice, "I suppose you could say we're scheming up a little surprise. . . ."

"Mind letting me in on it?"

"Letting you in on it? Why, my young mechanical genius, you're *part* of it."

"I *am?*"

Tommy nodded. "Indeed you are, sport, indeed you are." He looked around at the other two. "You and I are going to take a little trip together."

"We *are?*"

"Righto," Colin grinned. "First thing tomorrow, in fact."

"Jeez," I asked breathlessly, "where are we going?"

"All in good time, mate," Barry advised. "All in good time. We'll be taking a run over ter the warehouse later this afternoon. Yew'll see for yerself."

"Righto," Colin nodded. "Indeed you shall. Let's just say I need you to help transport a couple of rather, shall we say, *special* Jaguars to Wisconsin. Assuming you can afford the time, that is."

And just that quick, I forgot all about giving Colin that speech I'd rehearsed and stumbled all over my tongue telling him how happy I'd be to oblige.

"You'll need a jacket, a change of clothes or two, and a toothbrush," Tommy told me. "And I'd recommend a pair of sunglasses and a hat with a decent brim."

"And be sure that bloody 'at fits *tight,*" Barry added with a quick-silver grin, "or yer'll lose it for sure."

I was under a much-abused MG TC a few hours later when Colin came over to tell me it was time to go, and the truth is, I was only too happy for the interruption, since the owner of this particular MG thought it was an XK120 and tried to make the poor thing perform accordingly. Especially from stoplights. You hate working on cars like that (even though they're a guaranteed gold mine) because the jerk who owns it is only going to beat the shit out of it all over again when you give it back to him. I mean, what's the point? And it's never long before the asshole comes rolling back in (for the umpty-umpth time) to complain about yet another weary mechanical component that has finally given up the ghost and burst, bent, broken, shattered, snapped, melted, cracked, kinked, crumbled, fractured, or some ugly combination thereof. Worse yet, these types always throw in a little off-the-cuff lecture about what a horribly designed, poorly engineered, and indifferently assembled pile of crap their car is, and moreover how the damn valve float is preventing them from revving it to the last digit on the dial so they can blow it properly sky-high the way God and Nature intended. People like that don't deserve neat cars.

Anyhow, I was fighting to get the MG's corduroy-finish flywheel separated from its crankshaft flange, and the damn thing just didn't want to cooperate. Which made perfect sense, since as soon as I fixed it, the poor thing would be back in the pitiless hands of the jerk who owned it, and you couldn't hardly blame it for not wanting to go. So that flywheel was hanging on like Grim Death, and I was doing my level best to finesse it off rather than resorting to an outburst of violent, Old Man Finzio–style beating, heating, prying, and cursing. And that's when I caught sight of Colin St. John's neatly pressed pants cuffs making their way across the concrete like John Wayne's P.T. boat in the movie *They Were Expendable*. "I say," Colin's voice echoed down from the rafters, "it's time for that run to the warehouse we spoke about earlier. Let's be quick about it."

"Sure," I grunted, trying to gently *pop* that flywheel loose with two long screwdrivers coming in from either side, "be right with you."

Colin's lighter clicked open, followed by the usual wet, sucking sounds as he fired up his pipe. "I believe my intention was *now*, Mr. Palumbo," he puffed impatiently. So there was no choice but to lay my tools down and slide out from under, leaving that flywheel wedged all catty-wumpus on the crankshaft flange. Any decent mechanic *hates* to leave a job hanging like that. It's just not natural, you know?

Barry had me clamber into the backseat of Colin's daily driver (which was a light blue Morris Minor that particular week) and believe me, the backseat of a Morris Minor was never designed to hold anything so large as a full-grown human being. Barry made me put three layers of newspaper and a fender blanket under me so's I wouldn't soil the upholstery. That was important, on account of Colin always disconnected the speedo cables on his daily drivers so he could sell them as brand-spanking-new automobiles when he was done with them.

Once they had me packed in the back like a canned ham, we took off across town to the meat truck garage where Colin stashed his new Jaguars so that every one gracing his showroom floor could be *"absolutely, positively the LAST ONE in the country."* Along the way, the Morris developed a serious stumble and gas smell, and when it got so bad the engine would hardly run, Colin pulled over so Barry and me could take a look under the hood. I mean, we *were* two of the best damn British car mechanics in New York, weren't we? The raw fuel pouring out the overflow vent was a pretty good indication that the needle and seat were stuck, but we didn't have any tools—not even a damn adjustable crescent wrench!—to undo the lid and fix it. So Barry took the tire iron out of the trunk and gave that Morris a good, solid *whap* on the float bowl lid. And that cured it! Honest it did! And I'll always consider that one of the most endearing features of those cars. Sure, they had their share of mechanical gremlins. And Lord knows they wouldn't climb a 10 percent grade with more than two people on board. But, like other British cars, Morris Minors had so damn much *character* going for them. And they could be wondrously easy to fix. Sometimes all it took was a good, hard rap on the knuckles.

With the carburetor problem sorted out, we continued on to the meat truck garage, and along the way I kept trying to figure out what was going on and precisely how *I* fit into the picture. "So," I said, "could'ja maybe give me a little hint or something about where exactly Tommy and me are going?"

"As I said," Colin answered, looking at his nails, "you are transporting a pair of rather *special* XK120 Jaguars across country for me."

"Oh? And what's so damn 'special' about them, huh? Are they like the one Skippy Welcher owns?"

Colin looked at Barry and Barry looked back at Colin. "Oh, I should think they're a bit more special than that," Colin yawned, eyeballing me in the rearview mirror. "Wouldn't you say so, Mr. Spline?"

"I believe I would," Barry agreed, grinning over the seat back like the Chesire cat. No question my curiosity glands were pumping overtime when we pulled up in front of Colin's warehouse.

"I reckon this is one trip you'll remember for a rather long time," Colin allowed as Barry unlocked the overhead door. "For a rather long time indeed."

We drove inside and Barry lowered the steel door behind us. It seemed pitch black after the bright sunlight outside, so Colin flipped on the headlamps. We followed their dancing blob of yellow light between towering rows of sleeping meat trucks, made a tight U-turn with a rubbery screech off the tires, and headed up a bare concrete ramp toward the second floor. "The cars you and Tommy are taking to Elkhart Lake are up here," Colin explained casually, lighting his pipe again.

"Elkhart Lake?"

"Righto, Elkhart Lake. Ever heard of it?"

"Yeah," I said, "sort of."

"I thought you might. As I said, they're a rather *special* pair of XK120s."

Barry was grinning so hard I thought his teeth would shatter. But before he could say a word, we came over the top and there dead ahead, frozen in the headlights, were two of the lowest, sleekest, liquid-smoothest puddles of aluminum ever to rest on a set of wire wheels. One was a green so deep and dark it almost seemed black, and the other was a gleaming silvery-gray. You could tell right off they were Jaguars on account of the grilles and the unmistakable bronze cat-head medallions just above them, but right there any resemblance to the Jaguars I'd known came to a shuddering halt. They were built lower and lighter and hugged tighter to the ground than any ordinary, road-going Jag 120, and you could tell from the low plexiglass windscreens and the slick covers faired in over the headlamps to cheat the wind that these were purpose-built racing cars. A pair of naked exhaust pipes ran down their rocker panels and dumped into a set of "mufflers," that weren't much more than a couple of empty tomato cans stuck on as an afterthought. Like you were really going to drive something like this on the damn *highway*, right? "Jee-*zus*, Barry," I gasped, "what the hell *are* those things?"

"This," Barry patted the dark green one on its rounded hood, "is a Jagyewhar XK120C. I reckon it's about the best bloody long-distance racer ever built."

"Indeed it is," Colin chimed in. "No doubt about it. Why, a C-type like this won the twenty-four hours of Le Mans last year . . ."—he paused to suck a little more fire through his pipe—". . . and on its maiden attempt, as well."

"That really got the attention of the bloody Germans and h'Italians," Barry beamed, "and they would've made it two in a row this year except the bleedin' new h'erodynamic bodywork wouldn't let enough air to the bloody radiators. Put the whole bleedin' team out before nightfall. But they were bloody well *fast* enough to get the job done, make no mistake about it."

"Wow!" I said, looking the cars up and down. The only place I'd seen curves like that before was inside Julie's angora sweater.

"Now, you must understand," Colin continued, looking me squarely in the eye, "these are the only two Jaguar XK120-C competition models in the entire country, and our aim is to have them racing at Elkhart Lake this coming weekend. Tommy will be driving the green one for us, and *you*"—he stared at me so hard my joints went solid—"are to deliver the silver one into the hands of Mr. Ernesto Julio. He'll be bringing his own driver from California. Do you understand?"

I nodded, not really sure that I did.

"We need ter get a little break-in mileage on the drivelines, mate," Barry explained, "and h'its always a good idear ter log a few miles and make certain nothing's about to fall off before yer race the bloody thing."

"Now, Tommy *personally* selected you for this trip—Lord only knows why—and I want you to be *extremely* careful." Colin poked me in the chest with his pipe stem. "I'm sure I need not mention that these cars are not only *very* expensive, but also *totally irreplaceable*. Do you understand me, Mr. Palumbo?"

That I understood.

"Right, then. Take the Morris back to the shop and we'll meet you there in a bit. And from this moment on, I want you to do absolutely *every*thing and *any*thing Tommy tells you. Is that clear?"

"Uh-huh."

"And should you, in any way or for any possible reason, manage to harm one of these automobiles, I want you to remember one simple thing. . . ."

"What's that?"

"Make bloody well sure you die in the wreck. It'll be easier that way. . . ."

12

CROSS-COUNTRY BY C-TYPE

I SHOWED up at Westbridge early the next morning with my toothbrush, spare jeans, three T-shirts, and a few pairs of socks and underwear that I'd picked up over at my mom's house (she always seemed to have a little clean stuff waiting on a kind of haphazard, stock-rotational basis), along with the Brooklyn Dodgers baseball cap I'd picked up at Woolworth's just to aggravate my old man. Like I've said, he was a *big* Yankees fan. I had all the stuff packed in a white cloth laundry bag on account of the only suitcases we had at my folks' house were a couple of those big old straw-colored jobs you see down by the bus depot, and I sure didn't want all the S.C.M.A. racing types to see me with one of those things. Not to mention they would *never* fit into the luggage space of a C-type Jaguar (of which there really isn't any as you or I might normally recognize it).

Barry told me to not even bother starting in on that MG flywheel again since we'd be leaving as soon as Tommy showed up, so I got myself a mug of coffee and kind of sneaked back to straighten things up around that poor TC. I knew they'd have to hand the job over to another mechanic—probably Sylvester—and there isn't a wrench-twister in the world who likes jumping into a project some other knucklehead has torn apart. I mean, you never know what's been done and what hasn't or where to find all the bits and pieces and the inevitable coffee can of nuts-and-bolts hardware you need to screw it back together. And I hated the idea of Sylvester sliding underneath and finding I couldn't even remove a damn flywheel! So I decided to give it one more try, and wouldn't you know, I didn't so much as nudge the ring gear and that stubborn old flywheel fell right off in my hands. Just like *that!* Stuff like that happens every now and then, but nobody except a seasoned auto mechanic can appreciate what an awesome and mystical experience it is.

I knew right away this was going to be one *very* special day.

Tommy Edwards showed up a few minutes later carrying a small R.A.F. duffel with his helmet and track gear in it and a well-worn leather bag with tooled-in initials for the rest of his stuff. He had me put together a tool kit and a bunch of emergency spares to carry along, and it was tough figuring out exactly what to bring and what to leave behind. I mean, there's nothing in the way of an actual trunk on a C-type (you hardly need your toothbrush or an extra pair of socks when you're rocketing down the Mulsanne straight at Le Mans!) so all the Jaguar designers provided was a little nook-and-cranny space around the spare and a kind of makeshift shelf along the rocker panel plus whatever you could stuff into the footwell. I ultimately settled on a spare for each car, a set of cold racing plugs screwed into the neat little machined aluminum block the Jaguar race shop bolted to the doorsill for exactly that purpose, another set of warm-up plugs, some richer jets and needles for the carbs (not that I really knew when, how, or why I should put them in), a case of 40-weight Castrol down in the passenger-side footwell of both cars, a small scissors jack, a couple blocks of wood, a flashlight, a clipboard, a stopwatch, a spare point set, condenser, distributor cap and rotor, two cans of brake fluid, two oil filter elements, a knockoff hammer, a basic three-eighths-drive socket assortment, a set of British Standard combination wrenches, two tins of gear oil, a tub of wheel-bearing grease, a small, bullet-shaped grease gun, three flat-blade screwdrivers (a regular, a stubby, and a monster), two Phillips-head screwdrivers (regular and stubby only), three sets of pliers (a regular, a needlenose, and a Channel-Lock model), one set of all-purpose Vise Grips, a feeler gauge, a hacksaw, a rat-tail file, and enough bailing wire, rope, twine, and electrical tape to rig a frigate. Barry threw in a spare set of brake shoes—just in case, you know?—and some miscellaneous engine stuff that came in a box with the green car. For what reason I couldn't imagine, since what was I going to do with a set of crankshaft end-play shims at the damn racetrack?

I guess it seems crazy that Tommy Edwards and I took off from the heart of Manhattan on Tuesday, September 2nd, year of Our Lord nineteen hundred and fifty-two, heading for Wisconsin in the latest, fastest, and certainly most overloaded pair of Jaguar automobiles in the Western Hemisphere. The trip was over a thousand miles, and those C-types didn't have much in the way of mufflers, tops, windshields, or heaters. Not that you exactly *needed* a heater in a Jaguar racing car. Just the opposite, in fact. And I must admit I was nervous as Tommy and me wheeled out into Manhattan street traffic for the very first time. The growling, liquid-silver C felt so taut and eager that it seemed likely to scoot right out from under me if I didn't keep a tight rein on it. A hair-trigger racing clutch didn't help matters, on account of it had exactly two operational modes: totally disengaged and full-squirt forward. It worked like a damn toggle switch, and you'd best have a little room up ahead before you lifted your foot toward the Point of No Return. Plus the C-type's engine was a bit high-strung for city work and would go all soft and fluffy if you lugged it or let it idle too long at stoplights.

So you had to do a little judicious foot juggling to keep the C rolling along in mellow harmony with the taxicabs and buses and those damn delivery trucks that could whip out of an alleyway when you least expected it or stop wherever they pleased to unload sixty or seventy dozen ladies' straw hats and matching handbags just in from the sweatshops in Panama. Right in the middle of the street! Then again, that's the way they've always done things in Manhattan, and probably always will. The best I could do was just follow Tommy in the green Jag, trying to keep up and make everything mesh, but not really doing too good a job of it.

We crossed the George Washington in heavy midday traffic, and I pulled up next to Tommy at a stoplight on the Jersey side and asked if we could maybe take a little side trip over by the Doggie Shake so I could tell Julie where I was going (and incidentally make all the rank-and-file lunch customers choke on their malteds when we cruised up in our C-types!). I'd tried to call her the night before to explain as how I hadn't exactly quit my job at Westbridge, but she was working and there was no way I could get over to see her on account of I had to go over to my folks' house to get clothes and stuff. Ok, so maybe I *could* have got over there if I'd really wanted to, but the fact is, I thought she might be a little upset about my not quitting Westbridge so I could come back to work at her uncle's gas station, and even more disgusted about my sudden, drop-everything trip to Wisconsin. The good news was her mother didn't hang up on me (for the first time in ages) although she wasn't exactly real friendly, either.

"Yooda gas station boy, right?" she rasped into the receiver (as if she hadn't been hanging up on me every time I'd called for the past five weeks, right?).

I allowed as how I was, and kindly asked if perhaps Julie might be at home.

"She's a-notta home. She's a-work."

"Well then, I wondered if I might leave her a short message...."

"Lissen, gas station boy," she hissed through her teeth, "you gotta anything t'say to my Joolie, you teller youself, OK?"

Then she hung up the phone. *Click!*

Still, that conversation represented a real breakthrough in my relationship with Julie's mom. I mean, we were at least *talking* again, you know?

Anyhow, Tommy and me cruised up past the Teterboro Airport toward Passaic and stopped in at the Doggie Shake about the time the stragglers from the lunch crowd were finishing off the last of their french fries and they about fell off their stools when we growled up the drive in those two brand-new Jaguar racing cars! Unfortunately, Julie wasn't around, but we decided to fortify ourselves for the trip with a couple cheese-and-mushroom burger baskets and toasted our adventure with a root beer float apiece (which we had to hold in our hands on account of there's no place at all to hook a window tray on a C-type Jaguar). Tommy insisted on treating, and left the girl a whole dollar tip, too, just to make sure word would get back to Julie. And *how!*

After lunch we picked up the New Jersey Turnpike near Palisades Park and Tommy motioned me to the side at the tollbooth to ask how I was doing. "Everything shipshape, sport?" he yelled over the burble from the side pipes.

"Yeah. I guess so. I'm still having a little trouble with the clutch in traffic."

"You'll get used to it," he laughed. "Here, take this." He tossed me a crumpled cigarette pack with a twenty-dollar bill wadded up inside. "That's for tolls and anything else you might need along the way."

"Gee whiz, *thanks!*"

"Right then," Tommy grinned. *"Tally ho!"* He revved the green Jag's engine up to about four grand, deftly unloaded the clutch, and rocketed away with wheel smoke churning off the tires.

"All right," I said to the shell-shocked kid in the mirror, "like the man said: *Tally ho!*" and left my own two bucks' worth of Dunlop's best on the concrete.

We were on our way!

On the turnpike, the C-type really came into her own, running along at an effortless 75 or 80 without breaking a sweat. Why, you could even take your hands off the wheel and she'd still track like she was on rails! I'd never driven anything like that in my life, and comparing it to a standard-issue XK120 was like comparing an XK120 to a Nash or Henry J. It was that much faster and lower and tighter and lighter on its feet. And the Jersey Turnpike was a really fantastic stretch of road for a car like that, what with four lanes and a posted limit of 55. But you could see pretty far ahead so there wasn't much worry about cops as long as you kept your eyes peeled. Plus everybody we passed—and we were passing *everybody!*—looked at us like those Jaguars were two flying saucers freshly swooped down from outer space! Kids plastered themselves against the back windows of bullet-nosed Studebakers and puffy women in flower-print sundresses occupying the front seats of Buick Roadmasters craned their eyeballs around their husbands' profiles to get a better look. Sometimes they'd even hazard a sneaky wave. And the husbands never noticed, on account of they were too damn busy gaping at us themselves. Why, some of them got so mesmerized they veered clear off the edge of the pavement or drifted perilously close to the divider median. To tell the truth, it was downright intoxicating, and it even got worse when Tommy decided to "blow the carbon out" a few miles south of Elizabeth. I heard him downshift to third at about 75 and watched the rear end squat as he buried the gas and the green Jag instantly howled off into the distance. Why, there was nothing I could do except drop down to third myself and floor the throttle. I mean, what choice did I have? A few seconds later we were weaving through light traffic at over 100, and I'd be a damned liar if I didn't admit we were up over 120—*two miles a minute!*—before we hit the redline in third and upshifted to top! I had my fingers wrapped around that fancy wood-rim wheel in a white-knuckled death grip, praying on one hand that Tommy'd ease off and hoping in another devilish corner of my brain that he'd keep his foot hard in it all the way up Wisconsin! I finally chickened out around 130 or so, and no question that was as fast as I'd ever gone in my life. But old Tommy kept the pedal down clear through 5500 in top, which worked out to roughly 145 miles an hour. Give or take a few. On the blessed New Jersey Turnpike, for gosh sakes! In the middle of an ordinary, lunchbucket Tuesday afternoon.

Well, so much for "taking it easy on the cars."

The 1952 edition of the *Rand McNally Road Atlas* will tell you it's precisely 88 miles from New York to Philadelphia, and that it should furthermore take you about three hours at a reasonable and proper rate of travel. But Tommy and me were hauling into the northern outskirts of Philly a full hour ahead of the advertised Rand McNally numbers— and that's only because Tommy had to ease off and wait for me a bunch of times because I got nervous as hell at anything much over 90. Especially in traffic! But Tommy didn't think a thing of it. "Bloody great road, isn't it?" he hollered over the exhaust as we pulled up to a stoplight in Elkins Park. "But the one coming up is even better. You'll see."

Sure enough, we picked up the Pennsylvania Turnpike at Conshohocken, and that turned out to be the most fantastic stretch of highway I'd ever seen. Of course, it helped that I was wheeling a C-type Jaguar! It started off like the Jersey Turnpike—except that the speed limit was 70 miles an hour. *SEVENTY MILES AN HOUR!* I couldn't believe it! And of course Tommy automatically added another 40 or 50 whenever he thought we could get away with it. But he'd always slow it down a few notches when we came up on traffic. "No need to frighten the populace, sport," he told me later. "It's impolite."

We flew past King of Prussia and New Centerville and Valley Forge in quick succession, and that last one got me thinking about how we once fought a bunch of Englishmen like Tommy for the right to run this country—beat them out of it, too—and now here I was, some wise-ass gas station kid from Passaic, following an actual British fighter pilot on some kind of modern English commando raid on these same United States, ripping through the historic gut of our country in a brand-new Jaguar racing car that made the size, weight, speed, and handling capabilities of your average American road barge absolutely laughable by comparison.

The Pennsylvania Turnpike stretched 105 miles from Philadelphia to Harrisburg, and we covered it in well under two hours (instead of the 2:45 Rand McNally suggested) and that included a lot of in-town stuff north of Philly before we ever hit the turnpike. I couldn't believe we didn't get shagged by the cops, but Tommy was real sharp at spotting the black State Trooper Fords with their gumball machines on top, and he always got us hauled down to a reasonable pace so we didn't come swooping past them like a couple of ground-hugging Sabre jets. Even so, one of them pulled us over just outside Harrisburg, but it turned out he just wanted a closer look at the cars. Tommy motioned for me to stay put while he undid the nose on the green car and tilted it up to show the cop what was underneath. The guy was so impressed (as much with Tommy's accent as the hardware under the hood, I think) that he fired up his siren and mars light and led us on an exclusive three-car parade into the town of New Cumberland for dinner. He even turned out to be a pretty neat guy (for a cop, anyway) and you could tell he really got a charge out of those cars and couldn't get enough of Tommy's racing stories. Neither could I, come to think of it, on account of the way Tommy told them. I mean, most guys tell racing stories just to impress you (and anybody else within earshot) and sometimes the harder they try, the more you wish they would maybe go find somebody else to try to impress. But Tommy always made it seem like he never did anything especially brave or daring or clever, but rather that he just happened to luck into the right car at the right time whenever he did well. Which naturally got you imagining that maybe you could've done the same—*no problem!*—if you'd just happened to be there instead of him at Bridgehampton, Watkins Glen, or even the twenty-four hours of Le Mans.

It was past six when we finally rolled out of Harrisburg, full-up with two excellent fried chicken dinners and two fresh tankfuls of the best gas we could find, ready to take on the magnificent 196-mile run through the Appalachians from Harrisburg to Pittsburgh. The wide, smooth, four-lane Pennsylvania Turnpike climbed and dove and swooped its way up steep inclines and scary, bobsled-run descents, and the view was absolutely spectacular, what with the sun inching down into the horizon ahead of us, painting the hillside forests with a rich, golden light and filling the valleys below with deep, purple-tinged shadows. I'd never seen anything so breathtaking in my life. Not that I could pay much attention, since Tommy had the bit between his teeth and was hustling us along at well over 100, slicing clear across two lanes (at least when there wasn't any traffic!) through the corners to make the arc wider so we could maintain our speed. I had to drive my ass off just to keep up! But at least I wasn't clutching the wheel in a death grip anymore. In fact, me and that C-type had gotten pretty friendly by then, and I'd even grown more or less accustomed to Tommy's hellish rate of progress.

Why, 100 miles an hour seemed almost normal.

We arrived at the Breezewood toll plaza just after dark, and I must admit I'd never seen a town anything like it. From a distance, it looked more like one huge, ultramodern gas station rather than any kind of ordinary live-in, go-to-work, church-on-Sunday rural community I'd ever seen. Why, it was nothing but a quarter-mile concrete shelf set right next to the turnpike, and from one end to the other it was all filling stations and motels and burger drive-ins and glass-and-linoleum sit-down restaurants—one right after the other!—all of it bathed in an eerie, lavender-tinted fluorescent light. Why, you could see it for miles as you descended down the mountains, and all those cafés, drive-ins, gas stations, and motels did a cracking business on account of Breezewood was the perfect (and only!) convenient stopping place for quite a distance in either direction. It was also an average motorist's one-day trip out of New York City, so the greater majority of your rank-and-file vacation travelers stopped there. I'd never seen anything like it before.

But we had plenty of gas left in our Le Mans–sized fuel tanks, so we cruised right on past Breezewood and headed for Pittsburgh. Now, the so-called travel experts at Rand McNally figured it should take your average lunch-bucket jerk in his Ford, Pontiac, or DeSoto five full hours to cover the distance between Harrisburg and Pittsburgh—including the normal pee, gas, and dinner stop in Breezewood—but Tommy and me were hell-bent on beating the living crap out of Mr. Rand and Mr. McNally's ideas about just how long it should take to drive from one place to another. So we set our sights on Pittsburgh, a good 100 miles away, and Tommy seemed determined to make it in less than an hour. But he did ease off to a safe, sane, and relatively sedate 80 or so whenever we came up on traffic. After dark, those Highway Patrol cruisers start looking like every other pair of taillights until you're too damn close to do anything about it!

Outside of that, the darkness didn't make any difference to Tommy.

Not at all. But it sure as hell bothered *me,* barreling headlong into this endless, churning blackness and trying like hell not to lose Tommy's taillights (which sometimes got so far ahead they turned into two little rat's eyes that threatened to vanish into nothing if I didn't keep my foot in it). Every now and again we'd come to one of those amazing tunnels the Pennsylvania Turnpike engineers carved clear *through* the mountains, and all of a sudden the exhaust noise would quadruple—exploding off the walls!—while the death-ray yellow glare through the plexiglass headlamp covers raked through that tunnel like streaking, electrified halos, damn near showering sparks off the concrete. Then we'd burst out on the other side and all the noise and light would blast off into space again. I have to admit charging through those tunnels gave me the willies (not to mention taking blind curves at 90 with nothing but a tender little strip of guardrail between me and the yawning black emptiness on the other side) and I remember wishing once or twice I had Cal along to take the wheel, on account of I was getting a little tired and sloppy and not incidentally scaring myself silly.

As you can imagine, I was wrung out like a used dishrag by the time we rolled into McKeesport, just a little southeast of Pittsburgh, soaking wet from perspiration with my bottom half damn near melted off from the heat coming through the Jag's fire wall and my top half just as damn near frozen. But of course I didn't notice any of that while we were driving—no time to think about it, you know?—and it seemed like we were barely crawling as we grumbled down the exit ramp at a meager 45 or so and headed into town. I swear I could've gotten out and walked alongside, it felt so blessed slow.

Tommy found us a little tourist motel just off the turnpike, and although the DELUXE CABIN ACCOMMODATIONS advertised on the sign in front turned out to be six tiny, white clapboard sheds not much bigger than your average outhouse, at least they were clean and even had a few geraniums planted in window boxes to make them look sort of homey. A young, pimply-faced attendant came barreling out like his shirttails were on fire the instant he got a load of Tommy and me tooling up in the C-types. *"Jiminy!"* he gulped. "What the heck *are* those things?" So I explained to him as how they were the very latest and fastest Jaguar racing cars in the whole damn world, built way over in Coventry, England, and how we were on our way to this big race in Wisconsin—just breaking them in with a little cross-country run, you understand—and furthermore how the guy in the green car was none other than Tommy Edwards, one of the top racing drivers in the whole blessed universe. I was kind of pleased at the way the guy's jaw dropped another notch with each new tidbit of information, as if it was a hydraulic jack and I was working the handle. But I could tell from

Tommy's expression when I went into the part about what an Internationally Renowned HotShoe Driver he was that it was maybe about time for me to shut up. "Look here, sport," he said to the pimply motel guy standing in front of us with his mouth hanging open like a dead carp, "you think you might have a place for us to sleep tonight?"

"Huh?" the guy said, looking back and forth from Tommy to me to the two sleek Jaguar C-types and back to Tommy like the whole bunch of us had just beamed down from outer space.

"A room," Tommy explained. "You know, like those over there. We'd ever so much appreciate a place to clean up and get a good night's sleep."

The guy sputtered for a moment, trying to get his thoughts together and jaw back up to normal speaking position, but then he exploded in all directions like a busted radiator hose. "S-Sure!" he gushed. "Y-You bet. Why, y'can have *my* room if you wannit. It's a little bigger'n the others, see. Even has a kitchen in it. I got food in the icebox, too." He looked around over both shoulders and added in a whisper, "I even got a couple beers in there."

That sounded pretty good to me, but Tommy wouldn't hear of it. "No need for that," he told the kid, "but thanks anyway. Ever so much. One of your regular cabins will do quite nicely." Then Tommy turned to me and asked, "You don't mind bunking together, do you, sport?"

"Suits me," I said, feeling pretty special that he didn't mind bunking with me.

"Tell me," he asked the motel guy, "you think there might be a secure spot where we could park the cars overnight? They're quite valuable."

"They're the only XK120C Jaguars in the whole country," I added (as if the motel kid had any idea what that meant).

"You just leave them right there, sir," the kid gushed, kind of snapping to attention and fussing to get his shirttails tucked in. "*I'll* keep an eye on 'em for you. Glad to help. I even got some towels out back in the linen box. They're not dirty or anything. I can put a couple over the seats if you'd like. For the dew...."

"You sure it's not too much trouble?"

"No, *sir!*" the kid said, grinning like an idiot. "No trouble a'tall. Heck, I'm stuck here in the office all night anyway. It'll give me something to do."

And so Tommy and me left the two rarest, sleekest, most valuable Jaguars in all of North America parked on the gravel drive outside that little motel office in McKeesport, Pennsylvania, and headed off to bed. As Tommy unlocked the cabin door, I glanced back and saw the motel guy pulling a chair out of the office and setting it down on the gravel right next to the Jags, and I wouldn't be surprised if he spent the whole damn night there. In fact, after he waited an hour or so to make sure we were asleep, I bet he even climbed over the door panel of one of those cars (no way you could find the latch-pull on a Jag if you didn't know where to look) and sat himself down behind the wheel. It's hard to resist an opportunity like that—especially for some teenage motel clerk from McKeesport, Pennsylvania.

One of the things you have to get used to if you're going to pursue a career as a Full-Fledged Professional Racing Mechanic (or even a part-time Full-Fledged Professional Racing Mechanic) is that you wind up sharing a lot of strange, unfamiliar rooms—not to mention other, less formal sleeping quarters—with a bunch of strange, unfamiliar people you don't really know all that well. Truth is, it can make you pretty damn uncomfortable. But bunking with Tommy Edwards was no problem at all. He insisted I wash up first, and when I came out with a terry-cloth towel wrapped around me, he had this little silver flask set out on the nightstand with two small silver shot glasses beside it. "Have a quick snort of brandy?" he asked, pouring both of them right up to the top. "Cheers," he grinned, and clinked the glasses together. "You did a pretty fair job out there today, sport."

"Aw," I said, looking down at the carpet.

"No, really," he said, tossing back his brandy. "Nicely done."

"Thanks," I told him, taking a slow sip off the rim of the other shot glass. The liquor tasted all crackly-hot like a wood fire, and it must've been some pretty expensive hooch, on account of it didn't burn my gut too much on the way down.

"Now finish up and let's get some sleep." So I drank the rest and Tommy screwed the two silver shot glasses back on top of his nifty silver flask and headed into the bathroom. I waited until the door closed to take off my towel and find a pair of undershorts to sleep in, but I guess that's only normal, you know? And it occurred to me, as I eased between the sheets, that Tommy was about the only racer I'd met who could take just one drink and pack the bottle away—with plenty left!—instead of continuing to knock 'em back until the whole damn thing was gone. By the time he came out of the shower, I was fast asleep.

Tommy roused me about 6:30 on account of there was heavy over-cast and he wanted to get some miles in before it rained. "I reckon we'll have breakfast in Ohio," he allowed as we carried our stuff out to the cars. The motel guy had kept towels over the seats all night—changing them every now and then like field dressings on a wounded soldier—and it looked like he'd spent quite some time wiping the cars down and even polishing them a little, since you could smell fresh wax and there wasn't a single bug splat on either one. Tommy wanted to give him a little something for his trouble, but the guy wouldn't hear of it. In fact, he insisted on giving us free coffee and half of his morning sweet roll.

"Say, sport," Tommy asked as we were about to pile into the cars, "feel like swapping mounts for a spell?"

"Huh?"

"You know. You take this one and I'll try the silver one."

"Sure. Why not."

So I hopped into the dark green C-type and Tommy sat down behind the wheel of "my" car and we took off. This time it was easy to fall into that 85- to 110-mile-per-hour rhythm on the turnpike, and I was amazed all over again how stable and solidly planted the C-type felt at speed—just loafing along with a fingertip touch on the wheel—and the only way you could tell how fast we were going was when we zoomed past some off-to-work local in a three year old Ford sedan and scared the poor bastard halfway off the road. In the distance ahead I could see thick gray smoke like an ascending shadow rising off the Pittsburgh steel mills and filtering into the lighter gray overcast of the sky. That of course got me thinking about my old man's union job at the chemical plant. Only this was steel country, and somewhere out there beyond the guardrails, a million stone-faced union guys were punching time clocks at foundries and mills and forges and rolling plants and getting down to work. It sent a shiver through me, and I remember pushing the gas all the way to the floorboards as if I could somehow accelerate away from that feeling and leave it behind. It was guilt, I suppose. I mean, here were all these worn-down guys in worn-out coveralls, shuffling into work like a legion of zombies, what with their clunky tin lunch boxes and thermos bottles of thick, black coffee and morning-edition newspapers rolled up under their arms. And here *I* was, streaking across Pennsylvania at two miles a minute in one of the fastest, rarest, sexiest, most valuable sports racing cars in the entire world. Fact is, I felt like I'd *escaped* from something, you know?

The last tollbooth on the Pennsylvania Turnpike was at a little town called Petersburg near the Ohio border, and there were big, dusty-orange road graders and all sorts of construction equipment scattered all over since they intended to one day make that road run clear across the belly of America, like a piece of kite string tied around its waist. But now the four-lane ended a little southeast of Youngstown, and it was a lot tougher making decent time once you got off the turnpike. Not to mention that the country gets ironed down pretty flat once you roll down the Appalachians and head west into the plains. Don't get me wrong, it's still nice to look at—especially the peaceful, yawning

farmland and the neat little brick-and-clapboard towns you pass
through, what with their homey village squares and solid county court-
houses and slender church spires pointing quietly into the sky—but it's
not near so dramatic as the mountains in Pennsylvania.

Still, you get to do a lot more actual *driving* on town-to-town two-
lane blacktop than you do on the turnpike, where it's usually just "foot
down in fourth and follow the centerline" unless you see a tollbooth or
a lurking Highway Patrol cruiser up ahead. On the two-lane, you had
to work harder and concentrate, what with slowing for towns and accelerating out of them, braking and downshifting for the occasional tight
curve or switchback, and, best of all, pulling out to pass. That was *fun*
in a C-type Jaguar! A quick blip down to third (or even second!) and
a hard punch on the throttle were all it took to leave the local pickup
yokels, out-of-state family vacationers, and cross-country truckers gasping in your wake. And what a sound when you pulled the cork on that
barely muffled Jaguar six! Why, we were passing three, four, even five
at a time, slicing in and out like supercharged fighter planes buzzing a
transport convoy. I'd never felt so strong or quick or devilishly clever
in my entire life.

I did manage to notice a few subtle differences between the green
car and the silver one. Not anything you could actually reach out and
put your finger on, but a sort of hard-to-pin-down contrast in *feel*.
That's one of those mysterious things every mechanic understands, even
though it makes no reasonable sense: No two cars are ever *exactly*
alike—even if they're built side by side in the same damn factory by
the same damn hands out of the same blessed parts bins. And it's especially true of race cars, which tend to be more hand-fitted and are
always affected by the old mechanical/genetic "luck of the draw" as far
as valve seat finish and timing mark accuracy and friction losses in the
bearings and perfectly meshed gears and dead-nuts wheel alignment
and a kazillion other tiny details are concerned. Far as I could tell,
the green car was just that infinitesimal bit *quicker* and *tighter* than the
silver one. Not that anything was *wrong* with the silver C-type. Far
from it. It's just that the green car, for whatever collection of minute,
accidental, and totally unintentional reasons, wound up feeling the more
spirited and athletic of the two. And so it made perfect sense that Colin
St. John was selling the silver car to Ernesto Julio to take back to
California and keeping the green one for himself. What else would you
expect?

Tommy and me stopped for breakfast a little after eight, and over
eggs, toast, and bacon, we compared notes on the two cars. I was pleased
to discover he'd felt the same things I did and figured "his" Jaguar was

definitely the stronger of the two—albeit not by much. Then Tommy pulled out a couple folded-up highway maps and worked us out a route for the rest of the trip. He figured we had a choice of heading north and picking up 224 south of Youngstown or taking a jog south to U.S. 30 near Lisbon. We decided 224 looked like our best bet, because it cut straight across the state all the way to Tiffin, right near the Indiana border, and I felt proud as all getout that Tommy wanted my opinions. Then again, I *was* the only native American on this trip (not that I had the slightest idea what I was talking about, seeing as how I'd never been much west of Trenton before).

Route 224 turned out to be painfully slow going after the high-speed freedom of the turnpike. The official limit was only 50, and while Tommy was never particularly concerned about posted speed limits, it did slow the cars we were trying to pass, and you have to be a little more careful on a two-lane so's you don't pull out to pass a meandering local egg truck and catch twenty tons of interstate Peterbilt right in your face. Still, our C-types made a pretty easy job of it. You could pop down to third and be around your average John Doe road obstacle in no time at all. On the other hand, you had to be patient, on account of sometimes the road was blind up ahead or maybe you were stuck behind a gravel hauler or a tanker truck and couldn't see. Remember our Jags were right-hand drive, and that made pulling out from behind any decent-sized truck a true religious experience. We had a few close calls, but I guess that goes without saying. Every once in a while we'd hit an empty stretch and Tommy'd run us up to 120 or so, but not very often on account of you had all these little roadside vegetable stands and cider stops, not to mention that Route 224 ran right smack through the center of towns like Western Star, Leroy, Homerville, Ruggles, and Delphi, and the last thing the local populations needed or expected were a pair of Jaguar racing cars streaking through the landscape at damn near the speed of light. So Tommy and me would slow down to 40 or so and grumble along on the idle jets in third. But they were pretty little towns, and it was neat how everybody looked at us with their jaws dropped open and eyes bugged out. Especially the high school girls hanging out on Main Street, enjoying a little five-and-dime window shopping or maybe a chocolate ice-cream soda during those precious last few summer days before school started up after Labor Day. We passed some boys in muddy sweatshirts and cleated shoes coming home from football practice, carrying their helmets loosely at their sides while they bragged and wisecracked about what they'd done (or were planning to do!) with those girls we saw up on Main. But all those small-town football heroes stopped dead in their tracks when they got a load of Tommy and me in our C-types. And it occurred to me, as I smiled serenely back at them, how much older, wiser, and infinitely more mature I'd become compared to those poor hicks.

It took us over five hours to cross Ohio, and to tell the truth, it got pretty blessed dull, what with towns popping up one after the other and the truck traffic and all. So just past Tiffin, Tommy decided to reroute us sort of free-form northwest, heading off 224 and trying all the nameless, unnumbered little county roads for variety. They turned out to be wonderful, high-crowned country lanes that ran through rolling fields and shady valleys, past lopsided barns with matching farmhouses, bored-looking herds of dairy cows, and the inevitable car-chasing farm dogs you find all over rural America. Of course, none of those mutts had much of a chance against our C-types, but I've got to give credit to one particular golden retriever, who took a shortcut across an alfalfa field and made a real race of it for damn near a mile. I suppose taking those back roads cost us a little time, since you had to back off at regular intervals on account of every rise or bend in the road might be hiding a stray cow or a slow-moving hay wagon. But they were great places to drive, and you could feel as how the Jags were enjoying it every bit as much as Tommy and me. Of course, we had a hard time keeping ourselves pointed in the right direction, what with all the unexpected swoops and turns and unusual intersections, but every time we came barreling up to one, Tommy'd glance left and right, make a snap decision, and in less than a heartbeat have the revs up, clutch out, and smoke squealing off the tires. And sometimes he'd hesitate for an instant before deciding which way to turn, and I'd have to lock the damn brakes to keep from sliding right into him! No doubt Colin would've gotten pretty upset if he'd been there to see it. But Tommy always seemed to know where I was, and he'd roar out of the way just as I skittered up behind him with the car all up on tiptoe. Then I'd snatch second, fishtail through the intersection, and charge up through the gears after him—right on his ass!—like we were racing each other at some place like Bridgehampton! Sure, I got scared once or twice that I was going to slide into a ditch or a fence post, but I was starting to get a little confidence, too. Like maybe I really *could* get the hang of this after all.

We ran into light rain as we crossed into Indiana, and at first it was kind of refreshing. But then it got hard to see (those short racing windscreens weren't much good in the wet), not to mention we had water streaming over the dash cowling and around through the door seams and even up through the footwells. On top of that, my Dodgers hat turned out to have the exact proper aerodynamic shape to leak a stream of cold, dirty rainwater right down the back of my shirt. Pretty soon the sky got so dark we had to put the lights on—not that it helped much—and I must admit I felt relieved when we finally found ourselves face-to-face with a numbered highway again. It was Route 8, just outside of Auburn, which is where they built those stylish, superexpensive Auburn automobiles before the depression set in and more or less dried up the market. Those were some pretty magnificent machines—especially the supercharged Speedster models—and not even Ferrari or Rolls Royce ever built cars with more class and elegance. They were about the last American cars you could really be proud of, those Auburns, Cords, Duesenbergs, and V-12 Packards from the twenties and thirties. But then times got tough and the war came and I guess there simply wasn't much need for cars like that anymore. Or maybe there just weren't many drivers left who were up to the scale and style of those cars.

Anyhow, Tommy found us a gas station (a Sinclair, in fact) and the owner was only too happy to let us park the Jags inside and give them a couple oil changes while we waited for the storm to pass. He even made me a deal on a pair of dry coveralls and a used rain slicker since my mom's laundry bag was more or less floating in the Jag's footwell, so my clothes were thoroughly drenched. Then he lent us an umbrella and directed Tommy and me across the street to a little corner place called, naturally enough, The Auburn Grill, where we each had a bowl of homemade beef stew and a slice apiece of some very decent Dutch apple pie—à la mode, natch. It wasn't quite as good as my mom's, but amazingly close for some two-bit Indiana coffee shop smack-dab in the middle of nowhere.

It took the better part of an hour for the rain to slack off, and during that time Tommy and I had quite a conversation about how he got started in racing and what it took to do something like that properly. "Oh, I don't think a bloke's got to be particularly *brave* to be a racing driver," he allowed, thoughtfully stirring his tea. "Not really. Foolhardy will often do just as well."

"Aw, you're just saying that."

"Oh, I suppose. But it's really nothing like you'd imagine from reading all the tabloid stories or watching those dreadful Hollywood movies. Not at all."

"It isn't?"

"Oh, good heavens *no!* Why, they paint it up all blood and guts and devil-take-the-hindmost. 'A fair fight and may the best man win,' and all that sort of rubbish. Utter nonsense."

"Really?"

"Why, of course. It's the bloody *cars* that win races," he said matter-of-factly. "The drivers can only *lose* them. . . ."

"I don't get it."

"Well, the bloody truth of the matter is that a driver is always limited by what his machine can do over any given stretch of road. His job is simply to bring it up to that level and keep it there for the whole bloody race." Tommy took a long, thoughtful sip of tea. "But of course you never can."

"You *can't?*"

"Oh, of course not. Why, you're constantly making mistakes and screwing things up here and there. It can't be helped."

I couldn't believe what I was hearing, you know? After all, I'd seen Tommy Edwards drive, and far as I was concerned, he was about the most perfect damn race car driver in the galaxy.

"Trust me, Buddy," he said evenly, looking me in the eye, "there's no such thing as a perfect race. Or even a perfect lap. Why, there's hardly even such a thing as a dead-nuts-perfect corner. You're always seeing little things you could've done just that wee bit *better.* . . . "

"Wow," I said, letting out a low whistle.

"In fact, I reckon the better you are at it, the more you see each and every race as a bloody grim collection of errors, mistakes, and missed opportunities."

"Even when you *win?*"

Tommy nodded. "Of course. Sometimes even more so."

I shook my head, trying to make sense out of it.

"The saving grace is that you're up against other blokes who put their pants on one leg at a time and generally tend to be just as bloody stupid, pig-headed, and ham-fisted as yourself. So at least you've got a sporting chance. It's a little like fighter piloting that way."

"You did that in the war, didn't you?"

"Oh, a little here and there."

"What was it like?"

"A bit scary, actually," Tommy laughed. "But also quite exciting. More than anything I've ever done, when you get right down to it. Here's you in your aircraft and there's the other fellow in his, and it all comes down to who has the better machine and the skill, instinct, nerve, and patience to exploit it. You need to concentrate and stay cool when the other bloke is getting hot under the collar."

"And you gotta be *fast,* too," I added.

"Oh, I suppose," Tommy reluctantly agreed. "But the graveyards are full of young chaps who tried to get by on brass balls and lightning reactions. It's a deadly combination."

"It is?"

"Absolutely. Experience is probably the most important thing—seat time, don't you know—because you can't *think* about what you're going to do in the heat of battle. You've got to *know*. By the time you've thought your way through a situation, it's generally over. . . ."

"Wow."

"In fact, I reckon that's what I love about racing. It's exactly the same—you and your machine against the other bloke in his—except you're on the ground instead of in the sky and none of the participants necessarily have to get killed in a motor race. But the feeling of speed, concentration, and outright competition is quite similar."

"So that's how you got started?"

"I suppose it is. . . ."

"Right after the war?"

Tommy nodded. "I reckon I needed something to, well, *replace* the war, you know? It sounds rather silly, but there just isn't much out there in civilian life to compare. Not just the air battles, but simply being a *part* of it. Being, you know, a 'member of the club,' so to speak. That's what I found again in motor racing."

"Well, you're sure plenty good at it."

"Oh, please," Tommy laughed, turning a little pink around the ears, "I'm just a bloody journeyman, really. Lots of brute muscle and experience but not too awfully much talent or finesse."

"Why, you're absolutely *great!*" I told him.

"It's nice of you to say so, but I think 'good' might be a bit more accurate."

"What's the difference?" I asked.

"Well, let's just say that a 'good' driver is one who can win with the best car. After all, that's what he's supposed to do."

"And a *great* driver?"

"That's easy. He's the fellow who can win even when some other bloke has the best car."

ELKHART LAKE

THE VILLAGE of Elkhart Lake sits on the shoreline of a beautiful, spring-fed lake where the water's so blessed clear you can see bottom at twenty feet. The surrounding countryside is all rolling farmland and thick forests and sunshiny meadows full of honeybees and wildflowers and that sort of thing, which naturally makes for some mighty fine sports car roads. Elkhart Lake hosted its first-ever S.C.M.A. road race in July of 1950, using about three and a half miles of local country back roads west of town and God only knows how many kegs of local Wisconsin beer. The event wasn't big or well publicized, but everybody had a great time and so word spread and more people came the following year. This time they made the circuit over six miles long and ran it right smack-dab through the middle of town, and once again everybody enjoyed the hell out of themselves and made plans to come back and bring their friends along, too. All of them.

And I could see why when Tommy and me took a left off Highway 67 and followed the little overhanging sign that pointed the way into town. It was late Thursday afternoon, and already the place was chock-full of MGs, Jaguars, OSCAs, Allards, and Lord only knows what else. Seeing as how most of the heavy-duty sportycar activity was happening either on the East Coast or out in California, Elkhart made a perfect middle ground for everybody to hash out once and for all (or at least until next year) who had the fastest cars, the quickest hot-shoe drivers, and the best-looking girlfriends.

Anyhow, Tommy and me followed County A into town, crossing a set of railroad tracks across from Schuler's Bar and turning left on Lake Street, past the IGA grocery and Gessert's Soda Shop across the street from the train station where all the rich meat-packing families from Chicago and brewery families from Milwaukee used to get off for their summer vacations back around the turn of the century. Elkhart Lake was a peaceful, homey sort of place, and I liked the look of it right away.

A couple blocks from the train station, Lake Street curved hard left and ran along the shoreline of about the prettiest little fishing and swimming lake you ever saw, and that's where we made an abrupt U-turn and pulled our Jags up to the curb in front of the green-and-white awning that marked the office of Siebken's Resort Hotel. It was right next door to the Osthoff Resort Hotel and directly across from the entrance to Schwartz's Resort Hotel, and those were where all the racers stayed. In fact, it was hard to tell exactly where one Lake Street resort hotel ended and the next one began, since they were all made up of the same sort of clean-looking, white clapboard buildings with rolling green lawns all around and matching green shutters on the windows, and it was hard not to think of them as a set. Oh, Schwartz's had the bigger beach and an elevated front porch with shuffleboard courts and a beautiful view out over the lake, while Siebken's had an outdoor bandstand and rooms done up with genuine antiques. The Osthoff was the official S.C.M.A. headquarters for the weekend, but a lot of the racers liked the food at Siebken's better. Not to mention the bar.

Tommy steered us over there for a quick one before we even checked in, and it seemed like everybody we'd ever met was crowded in around the tables and packed three-deep at the bar, drinking local Milwaukee beers like Schlitz and Blatz and Pabst Blue Ribbon while swapping tall tales about their heroic drives up to Elkhart from places scattered all over the whole damn country. I saw Creighton Pendleton and two of the Muscatelli brothers shooting the breeze over by the far door, and directly behind them was the gorgeous Sally Enderle. She had herself draped over the top of the big Wurlitzer jukebox, checking her reflection in the chrome while she halfheartedly punched in "Come on a-My House" by Rosemary Clooney and "Your Cheatin' Heart," the brand-new Hank Williams song. That seemed like a good reason to mosey over myself and check out the music, just kind of casually leaning in over her shoulder like I didn't particularly recognize who she was (as if you could mistake Sally Enderle for any other female on the planet—especially when she was wearing a halter-type midriff top and one of her snug-fitting pairs of shorts). I've noticed only well-built, evenly tanned women can wear stuff like that properly, and I must admit Sally Enderle qualified with honors on all counts. Anyhow, there I was, leaning in over Sally's shoulder, pretending to check out the music selection (and incidentally getting a spectacular peek down the front of her halter top) when she suddenly rotated around and put the two of us nose to nose and eyeball to eyeball. She was so close I could smell the delicate scent of her perfume and feel a breeze of heat across my cheek every time she breathed. "Uh, hi there," I smiled, my voice cracking just a little, "remember me?"

"Hello?" she said, looking at me like I was a closet door.

"You're Sally Enderle, aren't you?"

She gave me an invisible nod, and it was about then I realized I was wearing the same damn clothes that had been lying in a pool of

dirty water at the bottom of the C-type's footwell all Wednesday afternoon, not to mention that I hadn't had a shower or combed my hair
or brushed my teeth since about 10 P.M. the night before. Then again,
here was the gorgeous, chestnut-haired Sally Enderle—right smack-dab
in front of me!—and there was no turning back now. "Uh, w-well," I
stammered, kind of stumbling over my tongue, "don'cha remember?
I'm the guy who blew up that TC at Giant's Despair."

A little two-watt flicker of recognition come up in her eyes. "Oh?"
she said, dropping it down to a watt and a half. "So you're the one
who blew his TC up at the starting line."

"Uh, not quite."

"You didn't blow it up?"

"Oh, I blew it up all right. Sky-high. But it wasn't exactly, uh, *my*
MG."

"Oh?"

"Nah. It was Cal Carrington's car. You know Cal?"

You could see that Cal's name rated about twenty-five watts with
Sally Enderle. "So," she wanted to know, "if it was Cal Carrington's
car, why on earth were *you* driving it?"

"Well, see, Cal's sort of my, uh, *friend,* you know? Besides, I work
on it a little for him every now and then...."

"Oh, that's right," she said, looking past my left earlobe to see if
there was maybe anyone more interesting along the bar to talk to,
"you're that *mechanic,* aren't you?"

"Uh, yeah. You could say—"

"Excuse me," Sally interrupted, "but I think I see somebody I
know." Before I could say another word, she'd taken a quick, dainty
step around me. "Bye now," she called back over her shoulder. "See
you again sometime...."

Which left me standing all by my lonesome in front of that big
Wurlitzer jukebox, staring into the turntable like I was looking over
the edge of the Grand Canyon, my ears glowing about the same brilliant
red as the illuminated plastic panels on either side. I naturally pretended
like I was going over the songs real carefully (as if anybody was even
looking, you know?) and wound up playing a couple of the syrupy,
dreamy-soft Nat King Cole tunes that always seemed to get Julie in the
mood, followed by a repeat spin of that new Hank Williams tune.

Just about everybody I'd ever seen at the races seemed to be in
Siebken's bar that particular late-summer afternoon, and I even noticed
my old asshole-buddy Charlie Priddle over in the corner with a couple
of other armband types, embroiled in a *very* serious discussion about the
scoring procedures for the so-called Monte Carlo Rallye to Elkhart
Lake. It was obvious the thing hadn't been very well organized (what

with whole entire cities used as checkpoints and much of the scoring done on the honor system) and most of the teams drifting into Elkhart had no idea even where to turn in their time sheets. Which was just fine with the rallye committee, since they really had no idea how to score them anyway. Fact is, the whole idea of the Rallye to Elkhart Lake was to get sports car enthusiasts from all over the country together in one place at one time for a few too many drinks and some lively conversation, and most didn't expect anything more than the phony Monte Carlo Rallye license plates and matching dash plaques they got for entering. But Charlie had his eye on the big, silver-plated loving cup on display for the winner, and he was doing his level best to make sure it wound up on his mantelpiece back home—right next to that fine first-place mug he "won" so convincingly at Giant's Despair. By God, he'd read the rules for that damn rallye, and they plain-as-day specified a substantial handicap based on the age of the automobile. And now, seeing as how the scoring was a hopeless shambles, and furthermore seeing as how he'd arrived in unquestionably the oldest automobile entered (supposedly the same 1914 Stutz that Barney Oldfield once drove), there wasn't a shred of doubt in Charlie Priddle's conniving little mind that *he* should be declared the winner. Even though one of the Porsche guys thought he saw Charlie and a couple local piano movers unloading the Stutz from a flatbed in Fond du Lac, less than forty miles away. Anyhow, Charlie and the other armband types looked to be taking the matter *very* seriously.

I recognized a few of the MG guys from Giant's Despair guzzling beers along the bar, so I leaned in and joined them for a round. They were mostly talking about some brilliant idiot from Detroit who'd stuffed a Ford V-8 into his TC, and moreover how the short wheelbase, narrow track, skinny tires, unfortunate weight distribution, and little pie-plate brake drums would surely make it a handful around a road circuit. "Whoever winds up driving that contraption better stock up on Brave Pills," one of them advised, and the rest of them clinked their mugs in solemn agreement.

Even old Skippy Welcher came trolling through Siebken's—Milton Fitting in tow, natch—searching desperately for any free pair of ears that would have him. I made sure to keep the back of my head pointed his way, and headed for the john pronto when I thought The Skipper recognized me and started muscling his way through the crowd in my direction. Who should I run into coming out of the men's room but my old English-accented traveling companion, Tommy Edwards. "Hey, Tommy," I said, "where've you been?"

"In there," he smiled, "shaking hands with the prime minister."

Some guy in a bright red polo shirt hailed us from the bar and

bought Tommy a drink. "What took you so damn long to get here?"
he asked. "Why, we've damn near used up all the booze while we were
waiting."

"Took us three bloody hours to get through that blasted hometown
of yours," Tommy groused as the bartender poured a tall gin and tonic.
"And those new C-types don't much fancy city traffic."

"I expect not," the guy grinned. "But are they *fast?*"

"We'll find out later this weekend, won't we?" Tommy grinned
right back. "Buddy," he said to me, "I want you to meet Eddie Dearborn, the fastest damn Allard driver in the whole bloody country." He
shot me a wink. "Or at least that's what he *tells* people, anyway...."

"At least that's what I tell people when *you're* not around, you
worthless, no-good, crumpet-eating piece of dog meat. Say, is this kid
old enough to drink?"

"Sure he is. But I'm not quite so sure about *you*...."

"Hell, I was *born* old enough to drink. Everybody knows that. *Hey,
Doug!*" the guy in the polo shirt yelled, *"Get us another one!"* And in
no time at all I had a frosty mug of beer in front of me.

"So," Tommy asked, "who figures to be quick?"

"Well, there's you and there's me...but that goes without saying,
doesn't it?"

"Right," Tommy agreed, clicking their glasses together. "Perhaps
we ought to simply flip a coin right now and save everybody a lot of
needless wear and tear on the motorcars."

"Don't think we'll be able to talk Cunningham into it. He brought
the whole blasted Le Mans team this time. Two roadsters and a coupe.
And just wait till you take a gander under the hoods...."

"Oh? What're they running?"

"I'm not gonna tell you. Why spoil the surprise? You'll see for
yourself soon enough. But he's got Johnny Fitch in one of the roadsters
and Phil Walters in the coupe, and Briggs is gonna handle the other
car himself."

"Fitch won here last year, didn't he?"

"Sure as hell did. Ran away from everybody."

"And what happened to you?"

"Me? I broke a wheel bearing. You know that."

"Well, that's not the way *I* heard the story," Tommy said, slipping
me a wink.

"You're obviously misinformed, Edwards. But then, we've come to
expect that sort of thing from you—*Hey, Doug! Three more down here!*—
why, I'm amazed we won the damn war with people like you as our
allies. Probably would've made out better with the damn krauts."

"I'm sure. But no matter how you try to change the subject, Mr.

Dearborn, Buddy and I are not leaving until we hear all the grisly details about last year's race and your famous wheel-bearing failure."

"Aw, it just broke. You can ask anybody."

"I have. They all say you collected a bloody hay bale."

"Of course I did!" Eddie howled, banging his palm on the bar. *"How'dja think I broke the damn wheel bearing?!"*

Needless to say, we got a pretty good rise off that, and as I recall, Tommy and me never exactly got around to getting cleaned up or going out to a proper dinner that evening. We just stayed there at Siebken's, drinking beer and shooting the breeze and wolfing down a couple fat roast beef sandwiches right there at the bar. They were served on thick black bread with lettuce and tomato and horseradish mustard and about a quarter-pound slab of Wisconsin Swiss on top, and did they ever taste great after our long day on the road.

It must've been eleven by the time Tommy went to check us in, and I meanwhile took an unsteady stroll down the sidewalk to get our stuff out of the Jaguars. There were sports cars of every type imaginable parked up and down the street, but even so, those two C-types had collected themselves quite a crowd. They were glistening there in the half-light like a pair of well-oiled panthers, and, as anybody who knows anything can tell you, there's a very special feeling when you see a bunch of gawkers gathered around—talking in hushed tones and peering at the dashboard over the red-tipped glow of cigarettes—and you're fortunate enough to be that one-of-a-kind guy who waltzes through the crowd, casually pops the door, and hauls his own personal luggage out of footwell. Even if that "luggage" is just a soggy old laundry bag. "Say," one of the cigarette glows asked, "this is one of those new Jaguar competition jobs, isn't it?"

"Yup."

"Boy, I never seen one before."

"Nobody has," I said like it didn't mean anything to me. "These are the only two in the country."

"Wow! Are you one of the drivers?"

"Well, uh, *sort* of. I mean, I drove it *here*. . . ."

"But are you gonna *race* it?"

"Nah," I told him, pretending like it didn't make any difference. "Tommy Edwards is driving the green one for, uh, *our* shop, and some West Coast hotshoe is gonna be in this one."

"Oh? Y'know who he is?"

"I dunno. He drives for some big, important wine guy from California. They're taking the silver car back there after the races. Gonna race it out there on the coast."

"That's gotta be Ernesto Julio."

"Yeah. That's him."

"Then the driver must be Phil Hill."

"Who?" I said, like I'd never even heard of him (although the name sounded awful familiar, and I was sure I'd heard it once or twice before).

"I saw Phil drive out at Torrey Pines last July. Lapped the whole blessed field. Believe me, Tommy Edwards is gonna have his hands full with that guy."

"Oh *really?*" I said down my nose. I mean, obviously this West Coast jerk had never seen Tommy drive. But there wasn't much else to say—the gauntlet was already down, you know?—so I gathered up our stuff and headed for the office. On the way, who should I spy huddled in the shadows but our old buddy Creighton Pendleton the Third, standing real close and talking in whispers with one of the fresh-looking hometown cocktail waitresses I'd seen serving drinks in the bar. Or at least that's who I thought she was, but it was definitely *not* Sally Enderle. Not unless she'd suddenly grown a couple bra-cup sizes and sprouted a blond ponytail. I even glanced into the bar to make sure, and there was Sally Enderle over by the jukebox, smiling and laughing and knocking back shots of Peppermint Schnapps with a bunch of prep-school types as if she didn't care one way or the other where the hell Creighton Pendleton might be.

Made you wonder what the hell he could be thinking. I mean, to have a sleek, spirited, high-class girl like Sally Enderle on a string and then take a chance fooling around with some underage local nobody, well, it just didn't make sense. Especially seeing as how Sally was right there on the other side of the wall, no more than thirty feet away. Then again, maybe old Creighton was trying to make some kind of point with her. Or maybe he was just one of those compulsive-chaser types who simply can't resist going after fresh meat whenever and wherever they come across it, just so's they can rack up another kill.

I went looking for Tommy after that, and finally caught up with him in a quiet little wood-paneled bar they had hidden under the stairs in Siebken's main office building, right behind the restaurant. It was more of a brandy-snifter kind of place than the big, noisy, beer-keg tavern across the yard, and that's exactly what Tommy was sharing with this incredibly tan older guy wearing a billowy white silk shirt like you'd expect Errol Flynn to wear in one of those Hollywood pirate movies. I'd never seen a male person dressed like that except maybe at a Halloween party, so I knew right away the guy had to be from California. I mean, nobody from Jersey ever dresses like that. At least not in public. "Hey, sport," Tommy called over, "pull up a bit of rail and have a nightcap with us."

I stepped up to the bar and Tommy's elegant-looking friend lit

himself a pencil-thin black cigar and nodded for the bartender to pour
me a brandy. He was about fifty or so, and looked pretty damn tough
in spite of his longish silvery-white hair and puffy silk pirate shirt. But
he didn't talk much. In fact, he hardly said anything. "So," Tommy
asked, "how are things out by the cars?"

"Aw, some wise-ass said you were gonna have your hands full with
that jerkoff California Hotshoe in the other Jag."

"Oh *really?*" Tommy said, arching his eyebrows up like Eddie Cantor. "And did he happen to mention who the blazes this fellow from
California might be?"

"I dunno. Some guy named Hill, I think."

"Hmmm. I don't suppose that would be Phil Hill, would it?"

"Yeah. I think that's him."

"I see." He turned to the guy in the white silk shirt. "You ever
heard of him?"

The guy with the skinny black cigar gave an elaborate New York–
style shrug. But you could tell he was fighting real hard not to laugh.

"Well," I continued, wondering what the hell was so damn funny,
"the guy said this Hill character's won a bunch of races out on the West
Coast. Says he lapped the whole field at some place called Torrey Pines
back in July."

"Do tell," Tommy said like it didn't mean anything at all to him,
and the guy in the pirate shirt nodded.

I drained the last of my brandy and the guy next to Tommy pointed
for the bartender to pour me another. "So," I asked, "you ever run
against this Phil Hill character?"

"No," Tommy said evenly, "not wheel-to-wheel, anyway. But I understand the bloke's been building himself quite a reputation out west."
He turned to the guy with the silver hair again. "You know anything
about this Hill fellow?"

The pirate shirt raised itself up in another fully orchestrated shrug.

"Aw, don't worry about it," I told him. "Tommy'll show 'em *all*
the quick way 'round come Sunday. Won'cha, Tommy?"

"Well, I'll certainly give it my best," he allowed through a perfectly
chiseled grin.

The guy with the silver hair couldn't contain himself any longer
and burst out laughing like the lid blowing off a pressure cooker. I saw
Tommy laughing right along with him, and somehow knew I was the
butt of the joke, even though I had no idea on earth what it was all
about.

"Buddy," Tommy laughed, clapping his hand on my shoulder, "I'd
like you to meet the chap whose car you've been abusing so thought-
lessly for the past three days." He stepped back so I was face-to-face

with the guy in the pirate shirt. "Buddy," Tommy said with a flourish, "shake hands with Ernesto Julio." The guy stuck out a tanned, muscular hand with a carpet of coarse silver hairs on the back and two fat gold rings on the last finger.

"So," he growled in a threatening voice, "Tommy says you beat the living crap outta my car on the way up here...."

"N-No, sir," I stammered. "I never did. Not even once. I took it real nice and easy the whole way."

"*Bullshit!* You kept up with this guy, didn't you?"

"Uh, sure I did. Of course. I just followed along behind Tommy and did whatever he did the whole way here."

"Then I *know* you beat the shit out of my car! Why, I bet you wound it past the goddam redline every chance you got!"

"No, sir, Mr. Julio, I never did. Not even once."

He leaned in so close our noses were almost touching. "Oh, yeah?" he snarled. "Not even *once?*"

I looked down at the empty brandy snifter in my hand and kind of shuffled my feet around on the floor. "Well," I admitted, "maybe just once or twice...."

"*Good!*" he bellowed, slapping me on the back. "That's exactly what the goddam things are for! Right, Tommy?"

"Right!" Tommy agreed, tossing off the last of his brandy.

Ernesto Julio insisted on buying us one last round and spent the whole time beating me up about how I'd messed up his car—boy, did he ever know how to put the needle in! Afterward, Tommy and me staggered off to bed. And I do mean staggered. Along the way, I asked if he really thought he'd have any trouble with that Phil Hill guy from California. "Well, he's won quite a few races now, hasn't he?" Tommy acknowledged with a steely little edge to his voice. "Then again, we didn't come all this bloody way to run second, now did we?"

"Hell *no!*" I agreed, leaping up the stairs three at a time and damn near falling through the railing. "We're gonna beat the living bejeesus out of *everybody!*"

I awoke Friday to the dull, scratchy thump of hay bales being unloaded from a flatbed and piled around a lamppost, and the sound skittered around in my skull like a three-pound rat trying to claw its way out of a bowling ball. My head hurt something awful and my body felt like lumps of putty held together with a few rusty cabinet hinges. I made my way unsteadily toward the john to get one of Butch's infamous morning-after cocktails (two aspirin with a Bromo-Seltzer chaser) and

I was fortunate to find the necessary ingredients right there on the sink. Obviously, somebody was looking out for me. Then I crawled back to bed, covered myself with the soft, puffy down comforter, and waited for the medicine to do its work.

Fact is, I was surprised I didn't feel worse. After all, we'd damn near closed the bar the night before, and that after a long, hot day's drive up from Chicago and not much in the way of dinner. But at least Tommy made me take a quick shower before I flopped into bed, so for a change I didn't wake up feeling like I'd been rolled in oatmeal and road salt the night before.

Truth is, I'd slept better than I could ever remember, and it wasn't just the brandy. There was something about the clean, fresh country air wafting in off the lake and the gently oscillating hum of the old brass ceiling fan that made our room at Siebken's perfect for summer sleeping. And the smell of freshly baked blueberry muffins and hotcakes on the griddle made it the perfect place to wake up in the morning, too. Even with a hangover. Tommy was already up and gone, and as I looked around, I couldn't help but notice what a bright, cheery sort of place it was. Sunlight filtered in through gauzy, flower-print curtains that matched up perfectly with the wallpaper and the comforter on the bed. Fact is, it felt more like a guest room in somebody's house than a hotel room, and I kept thinking that it was the exact sort of room I wanted to share with Julie some day.

I finally rolled out and headed downstairs around eleven, still a tad rocky but not near so bad as that gruesome morning at Brynfan Tyddyn. A quick pants check revealed I still had that crumpled-up twenty Tommy tossed me at the entrance to the New Jersey Turnpike, so I went to the dining room and ordered myself a man-sized plate of scrambled eggs, pancakes, toast, hash browns, a side of corned beef hash, and drank two tall glasses of orange juice and about a half gallon of coffee to clear my head and settle my stomach. Siebken's dining room was an airy, happy-looking place with windows that opened up like a sunporch and the smell of homemade bread and cakes drifting in from the little basement-level bakery across the way. No question it was going to be a gorgeous day, what with bright sun peeking through leaves that were just starting to show their first hint of autumn color and a nice, soft breeze blowing in off the lake. There were about a dozen other racing people around the room—some on breakfast, some already into lunch— and I couldn't believe how quiet and relaxed it felt there. But out on the street, you could hear the muffled bustle of activity as S.C.M.A. workers and a bunch of local volunteers piled up hay bales and strung lengths of snow fencing to keep the race cars and the expected crowd of spectators away from each other.

After breakfast, I took a little stroll up Lake Street toward the train station, and I swear you could hardly move what with all the cars and people and tootling horns and all-purpose confusion going on. The State Police had sent a couple cruisers over to help the local cops, but those guys looked as baffled as everybody else. I mean, there was really no place to *send* anybody, you know? So a couple chamber-of-commerce types made a deal with some nearby farmer to turn his field into a temporary parking lot, and by midafternoon nobody but bona fide S.C.M.A. types were getting anywhere except on foot. But they kept coming anyway, and you couldn't miss the prickly tingle of anticipation gathering on that crowd like static on a thick wool blanket.

From the curb in front of the train station, you could see how the "race circuit" came rolling in on County J, swept hard right around Schuler's Bar, headed through town on Lake Street—past the barber shop and the IGA grocery and the start/finish line right in front of Gessert's Soda Shop—then continued a few blocks underneath the trees and between the lampposts until it made a second-gear left between Siebken's and Schwartz's and disappeared off along the shoreline. I decided to take myself a little hike and maybe see where the circuit went from there.

A couple random MGs and Jags rumbled past as I walked along the edge of the road, obviously out trying to learn the course while dodging spectators and other race cars and all the armband people piling up hay bales and stringing up oil company banners (not to mention the local townfolk who were busily setting up lemonade stands and brat-wurst grills and nickel-a-cup beer tappers in their front yards). It was kind of neat to watch all that feverish prerace activity, and yet be able to turn my head an inch or two and see sailboats gliding effortlessly across the water and hear the *putt-putt* echo of a fishing boat trolling the shoreline across the way. The noonday sun made Elkhart Lake glisten like a silver wedding platter, and no question this was one hell of a perfect location for a sports car road race. No two ways about it.

A flesh-shredding howl suddenly blasted up behind me, and next thing I knew Creighton Pendleton's Ferrari exploded past at 70 or so with bare inches to spare. Why, it damn near blew me out of my shoes! I shook my fist at him, and you couldn't miss Sally Enderle's chestnut hair whipping the wind above the passenger side of the windscreen. She even flipped me a little backhand wave as they disappeared around the bend. Or maybe it wasn't a wave after all. Anyhow, I'm sure they were both laughing their asses off.

I followed the road down another couple hundred yards, curving gently to the right past Fireman's Park public beach, and while I was squinting my eyes to get a better look at the many promising young dairy-farmerette types sunning themselves on the beach, who should pull up silently behind me but a familiar black TD with none other than Cal Carrington and Carson Flegley in the cockpit. Cal was at the wheel, so it should come as no surprise that he crept right up behind me and let fly with the air horns (Carson'd bought himself a set like the ones on Big Ed's Jag) and they had to about peel me out of the trees afterward.

"How y'doin', Buddy?" Cal said through a wicked smile.

"I'll be fine after I take a couple of your teeth out."

"Aw, c'mon. We were just having a little fun."

"Yeah, just a little fun," Carson added like some kind of pasty-faced parrot. Fact is, Carson looked even pastier than usual, and you couldn't miss how he had his arms pressed damn near rigid against the dashboard cowling. Obviously, Cal had been showing him the quick way around the circuit.

"Hey, asshole," Cal grinned, "you lookin' for lost parts or something?"

"Nah. Just thought I'd take a little walk after breakfast t'see what's going on."

"Breakfast? Hell, it's past noon, Buddy. And on a weekday, no less. Why, I always thought you were a blue-collar working stiff."

"Didn't you hear? One of my rich uncles died and left me his whole blessed estate."

"Gee whiz, Buddy," Carson asked, sounding serious as a heart attack, "what're y'gonna *do* with it all?"

"Well," I said, looking just as serious right back at him, "I reckon I spent about half of it in the bar last night. . . ."

"Yeah," Cal cackled, "and he's gonna buy himself another beer with the second half tonight!" We got a pretty good laugh off that. Even Carson Flegley. Once he got the gist of it, anyway.

"So," Cal wanted to know, "who you with this time?"

"Tommy Edwards. We brought those two new Jaguar C-types out from New York."

"You rat-bastard sonofabitch! You mean you actually got to *drive* one of them?"

"Sure did," I nodded, modestly digging my toe in the grass. "Tommy and me took off from Westbridge on Tuesday. Just the two of us. And believe me, those things are *fast!* Why, we were hardly under a hundred from one end of Pennsylvania to the other."

"You lucky bastard," Cal growled. "I'd give my left nut to drive one of those things. My right one, too, come to think of it."

"You're just jealous."

"You bet your sweet ass I am."

"M-Me, too," Carson sputtered, head bobbing up and down.

"So, Cal," I asked, "you got any racing plans this weekend?"

"You know me. I *always* got plans. . . ."

"*Dreams* is more like it," Carson sniggered behind his hand.

"*Wet* dreams is more like it," I added for amplification.

"Ah, screw you both."

Now it was my turn to laugh. "No, really," I said when I was finished, "you got anything lined up?"

"Maybe. One of the MG guys from Detroit built a TC with a Ford V-8 in it, and he's having a little trouble making it go."

"I heard about it in the bar last night."

"Yeah, that's the one. Seems it doesn't want to go around corners. Or slow down, for that matter. But I think the guy is maybe just a little frightened of it."

"It's scaring the living crap out of him!" Carson nodded enthusiastically.

"Anyhow, a couple of the guys from Giant's Despair recommended he ought to let *me* give her a try. Just to see if I can do any better."

"I'm sure you would."

"So am I."

Like I explained before, Calvin Wescott Carrington never had any noticeable deficiencies in the balls or confidence departments.

"So, you planning to walk your way around the whole damn circuit today?"

"Can't say as I've really thought about it."

"Well, don't. Hell, it's six and a half miles, for gosh sakes! Your dogs'll be dead tired before you get halfway around. Why don'cha just hop in with Carson and me? We can all take a couple quick laps together. C'mon."

I looked at the big Cheshire cat grin spread across Cal's face and the chalky pallor on Carson's cheeks and I can't really say it sounded like such a great idea. Even though I trusted Cal completely when it came to driving, that didn't necessarily mean I wanted to be a first-person eyewitness when he showed off his stuff. Especially as the third full-sized human being in a two-passenger MG. "I dunno," I said hesitantly. "Doesn't look like there'll be room for all three of us."

"Aw, c'mon. We'll make room. And I'll take it nice and slow. Honest I will."

"Honest?"

"Cross my heart," Cal promised, crossing his heart. So I climbed in and Carson did his best to make his skinny little body even skinnier and we took off. "You know what's great about this?" Cal asked. "If I slide off the road and get us killed, we got our own undertaker on board to take care of things."

"I guess that's why I like hanging out with you, Cal. You always think ahead."

"Well," Cal shrugged as he wound the MG out in second, "*somebody's* gotta look after things. . . ."

Thanks to normal traffic and all the racers out learning the circuit and the armband types piling up hay bales, Cal could never really get up a good head of steam. For which I was thankful. But it was awesome anyway, and I could only imagine what those roads might be like under flat-out, balls-to-the-wall racing conditions, when you could use both lanes and not have to jab the brakes because you were about to ram the back end of a hay wagon. From Fireman's Park, the circuit continued to bend gently around to the right, kind of easing and then tightening again as it passed under the trees in front of the Quit-Qui-Oc Golf Course and Pine Point Resort on the other side. They called that section "Wacker Wend" after a wealthy Chicago-based S.C.M.A. racer named Freddy Wacker, who helped fire up the idea of bringing sports car racing to Elkhart Lake back in 1950.

The road curved slightly left out of Wacker Wend and climbed an easy hill past the entrance to Sharp's Cottages, then it was hard on the brakes for a 90 degree right-hander into a diving, climbing, roller-coaster corkscrew combination through Hammil's Hollow, followed by a long straightaway past the old country schoolhouse where even the tiddlers got up to some mighty impressive speeds. A downslope at the end got the cars going even faster, and then hard braking for another 90-degree, T-intersection right. It was called "Kimberly's Korner" after Gentleman Jim Kimberly, another obscenely rich S.C.M.A. racer who was buzzing Wisconsin in a light plane with Freddy Wacker when they "discovered" Elkhart Lake. Kimberly's Korner led to another long straightaway where the more powerful cars could tickle an honest 150 (!!!) as they whizzed past Hayssen's Farm and the electrical power station. At that point, the road made a lazy, downhill swoop to the right, followed immediately by a tighter uphill sweep to the left, and Cal allowed as how a good MG driver could take the whole section flat-out in top without lifting, but that it'd be a real white-knuckler in a Jag or an Allard. "It's places like this," he explained matter-of-factly, "that separate the *real* racers from the ribbon clerks. You gotta keep your foot down and thread that needle—lap after lap!—and it's places like this where you see the difference between the duffers and the Real McCoy."

"You do?"

"Absolutely. Hell, it's *easy* to be a hero in second gear. But take a really *fast* bend—where you gotta stay cool and smooth and hold your line even when your hands feel like strangling the damn wheel— *that's* where you see what a driver's really made of. Know what I mean?"

Yeah, I knew what he meant. Only knowing it and being able to actually *do* it were two entirely different things. And always will be.

After that fast, hair-raising right-left combination came a little more upgrade and then another long, downhill slope through acres of rolling farmland with a gentle kink near the bottom and a hard hairpin right at the end, just across from the entrance to Broughton Marsh. Ahead was yet another long straightaway, but steep uphill so you couldn't muster the kind of speed you could on the other two. You were climbing toward this peaked crest in top gear—totally blind!—and the only thing visible on the other side was this huge pine tree sticking up like it was planted smack-dab in the middle of the damn highway! Cal said you had to just aim straight for it and keep your foot down on the loud pedal, but I knew I could never go over that crest flat stick without grabbing a quick security stab on the brakes! The cars would get all up-on-tiptoe over the top, then plunge into a sweeping, gut-wrenching, right-left-right bobsled run through the forest into town. I couldn't imagine what that stretch might look like at racing speeds. Especially since there were trees and fence posts and country mailboxes and plenty of other ugly stuff just a few feet off the roadway. It looked scary as hell, and it seemed impossible that the faster cars could *average* over 100 (!!!) on that 6.5-mile loop around Elkhart Lake.

Wow!

I met up with Tommy, Ernesto Julio, and the two C-types later that afternoon in the parking lot of the Osthoff, where just about everybody was waiting in line for the S.C.M.A.'s technical inspection. Ernesto's hotshoe California driver was nowhere to be seen, but he had his mechanic along to open the hood and such so he wouldn't get dirty. Not that he was a sissy or anything, but nothing looks worse on a billowy white silk shirt than a grease smear or a fresh palm smudge of exhaust pipe dust. His mechanic was a smooth-cheeked, crew-cut young Californian named Chuck Day, who chewed big wads of bubble gum and stood in a perpetual concave slouch. He didn't say too much, and I wasn't real impressed when I heard he was one of those West Coast hot-rodder types who run souped-up old Fords out on the dry lakes in the California desert. I mean, what was the point in *that*? Especially compared to racing Ferraris and Jaguars clear through the night at exotic places over in Europe. But Tommy seemed to get on with him real well, and I began to understand when I discovered he was also

Ernesto Julio's personal airplane mechanic. I mean, this guy didn't look a day over nineteen! But apparently he'd done a tour in Korea taking care of Sabre jets for Uncle Sam, and you had to be impressed with stuff like that.

Anyhow, we got to know each other a little while we were waiting for the armband types to crawl up, over, under, and around each and every car like it was the first damn Jag 120 or MG TC they'd ever seen in their lives. Not that it wasn't important, since they were checking stuff like tire wear and wheel spoke tension and making sure nobody had any serious oil leaks or loose parts that might fall off and wind up squarely in the lap of the next poor fish to happen by. In other words, they were going over stuff that any self-respecting wrench would've checked and double-checked before even rolling out of his home garage. But you could never take that sort of thing for granted. I mean, I'd worked on Cal's TC, remember?

Tommy thought tech inspection was more or less a bunch of bullshit. He figured it was *your* bloody responsibility to make sure your machine was raceworthy, and he especially didn't like the part about the seat belts. Thanks to a brand-new rule, the S.C.M.A. tech crew was making sure every car had a set of seat belts, and furthermore that those belts were absolutely, positively anchored to the frame rails. "If I'm about to go tumbling ass over-teakettle down the bloody race track, the last thing I need is a large chunk of iron strapped to my backside." A lot of drivers felt the same way—that you were better off getting thrown out and taking your chances on your own. So some guys never bothered to fasten them when they sat down to drive, even though the regulations were pretty damn specific about requiring them. The tech people also checked your driver's gear, making sure you had a proper helmet and goggles and leather-palmed driving gloves, and finished up by dipping everybody's driving outfit in a big washtub filled with a smelly borax solution that supposedly rendered them flameproof. Or at least more flameproof than they were before.

Tech was going particularly slowly because we had the standard-issue S.C.M.A. Major Flap About Something going on to gum up the proceedings. In fact, we had several (hardly surprising, since this was *the* big East-West shoot-out and we had Charlie Priddle types from all over the country gathered together to make mountains out of every available molehill). The first big controversy was about Magnafluxing certificates. Now Magnafluxing is an excellent testing procedure developed by the aircraft industry to find cracks and flaws in ferrous metal parts—including cracks and flaws that may not be visible to the human eye. Anyhow, some well-meaning but thoroughly misguided people on the S.C.M.A. competition committee decided it would be a grand idea

for all the hubs and spindles and steering knuckles and such that make
up a race car's suspension to be Magnafluxed on a regular basis. Just to
make sure there weren't any hidden cracks that might cause a wheel
to suddenly part company with the car (like the one on Cal's ratshit
TC did at Bridgehampton). Now this was actually a pretty good idea,
but it didn't take into account that you had to dismantle everything and
get the parts all squeaky clean before you could send them out for
Magnafluxing. Not to mention that you had to wait a few days (or
sometimes longer) for them to come back. And then you still had to
reassemble everything and run fluid back through the brakes and reset
the alignment and whatnot before you were done. Which was of course
no problem for the big-buck guys with hired mechanics and spare cars
to drive while the work was being done. But it was a real problem for
the poorer rank-and-file racers who used their MGs and such for daily
transportation. Which made you wonder why the S.C.M.A. competition
committee suddenly decided to *require* Magnafluxing certificates for
every single car at Elkhart Lake. They spelled it out for everybody to
see in very small print in the fifth paragraph of the supplementary
regulations on the back of the entry forms. Problem was, a good two-
thirds of the cars showed up without the necessary paperwork.

So now what do you do?

Do you send people without the required certificates home? Even
if "home" is Montreal or San Luis Obispo or Lake Charles, Louisiana?
And what about all the bullshit stories from drivers who *swear* they left
their certificates back in their bureau drawers—even when it's obvious
their cars have never been apart since the day they left the damn factory? Or do you simply smile and wink and look the other way when
the same exact set of papers begins magically reappearing with eight or
nine different MGs? Or do you (as Charlie Priddle strongly favored)
come down like the Wrath of God on every single one of them, just so
they'd learn their lesson and never dare do it again? Charlie had a
surprising amount of support from some of the jerks who *had* their
certificates (like that asshole Skippy Welcher, natch) and figured anybody without the proper paperwork ought to be barred from racing
and sent home. Or maybe just to bed without supper.

Fortunately, we managed to squeak the C-types through on account
of they were brand-new and everybody wanted to see them run. So
when Tommy explained as how "Jaguar Magnafluxes *everything* on their
race cars, even the bloody wood rims on the steering wheels," the tech
people clucked their tongues in agreement and gave us our sticker.
But it was tougher for some of the other guys, and by the time hard-
liners like Charlie Priddle reluctantly agreed to let everybody run

(just this *once*, mind you) they'd made sure to change their minds and reverse directions enough times to piss off everybody in the paddock.

No sooner had the Great Magnafluxing Debate reached an uneasy resolution than we had another major flap about scheduling. Seems the official weekend schedule called for a hundred-mile small-bore race called the Kimberly Cup on Saturday and two races for the big-bore cars on Sunday. The first was a hundred-miler called the Sheldon Cup for cars up to four liters, followed by the big 200-mile feature for any cars over 1950cc that wished to compete. Naturally, there were a lot of guys who wanted to run both (like Tommy Edwards and that Phil Hill guy who drove for Ernesto Julio) and they suggested that maybe the organizers could switch the Sheldon Cup to Saturday, run the small-bore race Sunday morning, and leave the feature where it was. That way the Saturday spectators would see some of the bigger cars, the small bore guys would get to play in front of the Sunday crowd, and the drivers of the big iron would get to rest up and give the cars a decent once-over instead of running back-to-back on Sunday. This of course made too damn much sense for the organizing committee to accept without a monumental argument, and it was only after extensive lobbying, taking of sides, meetings in the hotel, and even a few strongly worded petitions that they finally agreed to change the schedule.

"Makes it clear why so bloody many of us drink, doesn't it?" Tommy laughed as he headed off with Ernesto Julio to celebrate their victory. "Look after the car then, will you, sport?"

"Sure thing."

"And pop by for a quick one when everything's squared away."

That left Chuck Day and me standing there with the two C-types, and before either of us could say a word, this enormous Fruehauf semi with Florida plates wheeled up in front of the Osthoff. It was gleaming refrigerator white with just a little checkered flag on the doors and the name "CUNNINGHAM" spelled out underneath in simple block letters. Everybody in tech stopped dead in their tracks and stared at it, slack jawed, like it was a live brontosaurus out for a stroll. It got so quiet that all you could hear was the distant *putt-putt* echo of that fishing boat trolling along the weed beds on the other side of the lake. The big semi eased to a halt with a shuddering sigh off the air brakes, and all of a sudden everybody was rushing over to get their first glimpse of the fabulous Cunninghams, just back from the twenty-four hours of Le Mans and the twelve hours of Rheims over in France. They were the only true American team trying to challenge Ferrari and Jaguar and the rest over in Europe, and although they hadn't actually *won* anything yet, they'd proved beyond any doubt that they could run head-to-head with the best of them.

A well-drilled squad of crewmen in crisp white Cunningham coveralls sprung into action and quickly unloaded two mean, broad-shouldered C4R roadsters and an incredibly evil C4RK coupe. All three were painted the American racing colors (refrigerator white with wide blue racing stripes) and they all had bulging fenders and yawning, bottom-feeder grilles and cast-alloy wheels that looked modern as a flying saucer. The Cunninghams were about halfway between the anvil-heavy bulk of an Allard and the low-slung grace of our C-types, but had the unmistakably wide, squatted-down stance of an all-American fullback. And when one fired up, you couldn't miss the deep bass grumble of a hefty Detroit V-8. That was the best thing about them: They looked and felt and sounded 100 percent American.

Chuck Day and I wandered over for a closer look, and you had to be impressed with the neat, sanitary job they'd done. And when they popped the hood on one, my eyes about popped out on stalks. Stuffed inside was the biggest, baddest V-8 ever to roll off a Detroit production line: the Chrysler 331 FirePower. It was brand spanking new in 1951, and most of us pump jockeys figured it to be the undisputed King Kong of American V-8s. Why, it had enormous valves and hemispherical combustion chambers—just like a Jaguar!—so it breathed a lot deeper than your average, garden-variety sedan engine. It was a *big* sucker, too, what with huge chrome valve covers and cylinder heads the size and heft of granite tombstones. And the particular FirePower V-8s underneath the bulging hoods of those Cunninghams had all the latest go-faster equipment, including special manifolds with four Zenith carburetors and tubular-steel exhaust plumbing and bright blue Scintilla magnetos sticking up off the back of the block.

Wow!

The most incredible thing was that one individual human being could afford to bankroll the entire operation. Briggs Cunningham had single-handedly managed to gather up some of the best hands and cleverest brains in the country, opened himself up a shop in West Palm Beach, Florida, and set about building real world-class American sports cars! It took more than just an obscene amount of money to do something like that. You had to have *spirit* and *patriotism* and a special *sense of commitment*. Which is why everybody in the whole S.C.M.A. was pulling for Briggs and his team. Sure, it would've been easy to carp about somebody with the colossal wherewithal to launch his own personal racing team and compete even-up with the best in the world. But most Stateside racers were *proud* that somebody had the guts and simoleans to take a little homegrown American iron across the Atlantic and keep the Brits and Italians (not to mention the French and Germans) honest. Even though Briggs's team could pretty much steamroller the opposition at every Stateside event.

Which is precisely why Creighton Pendleton and his crew were trying to get his 4.1-liter Ferrari dropped quietly down into the Sheldon Cup race on Saturday afternoon to run against the 3.4-liter Jaguar C-types. Sure, he said he'd still run the Sunday feature (and why not, since odds were he'd win his class), but what Creighton really wanted was an *overall* win—the kind that the Fred Average types in the spectator areas could understand—and there wasn't much chance of that happening Sunday afternoon unless John Fitch, Phil Walters, and Briggs Cunningham all took a wrong turn and drove all three C4Rs down the boat ramp at Fireman's Park. Problem was, the rules were pretty darn specific that the Sheldon Cup was for cars up to 4000cc's —*period!*—and Creighton's Ferrari was known to be a 4.1. But somehow he and his crew thought there might be a way around that little detail (after all, the rules had proven themselves to be engraved in putty two or three times already that particular Friday afternoon) and so you had a smiling, freckle-faced Sid Muscatelli explaining in the most reasonable of voices that the extra 101cc was only a lousy 2.5 percent, and if you bothered to measure the actual *piston* instead of the *bore,* why, they'd almost nearly be there, right? Of course, what Sid didn't bother to mention was that our C-types (which everybody figured as the cars to beat in the Sheldon Cup) had a hell of a lot less at 3442cc's all told.

To the complete amazement of ignorant and politically naive persons like myself, the Powers That Be (led by—you guessed it!—Charlie Priddle) decided it was in the best interests of everyone concerned to let Creighton Pendleton III and his oversized Ferrari run in the Sheldon Cup on Saturday afternoon! They came to this conclusion on the grounds that, well, who the hell needed grounds? The truth of it was that Charlie and his cohorts had lost two big ones already that Friday afternoon, and everybody in the upper echelons of the S.C.M.A. hierarchy felt it was time to let them win something, if only to keep all the racers properly off balance.

14

YOUR CHEATIN' HEART

THE OFFICIAL end of the S.C.M.A.'s Monte Carlo Rallye to Elkhart Lake was scheduled for six o'clock Friday evening, and the organizing committee's Grand Plan was to have all the entrants parade their MGs and Jags and Porsches and such down the middle of Lake Street while the local high school band played Sousa marches and cheering fans waved and whooped and threw fistfuls of confetti. But seeing as how most all the contestants had long since rolled into town, and furthermore how the scoring had been abandoned as an impossible mess, most everybody was over at the Quit-Qui-Oc Golf Course, where Mr. Briggs Swift Cunningham was hosting a quiet little barbecue for a couple hundred of his close personal friends. It wasn't any sort of *official* gathering, but it was pretty hard not to get an invite if you had anything whatsoever to do with the races. Heck, I even got one.

It was quite a spread, what with four 55-gallon oil drums slit lengthwise and propped up on angle-iron legs to serve as charcoal grills and half a dozen guys in white aprons doling out barbecued chickens and full slabs of spareribs. Next to the grills were big buckets of molasses baked beans and three kinds of potato salad and two kinds of coleslaw, plus fresh-baked bread from a bakery over in Sheboygan and a whole table full of apple, cherry, peach, and blueberry pies still piping hot from the ovens at Siebken's. To wash it all down, they had trash barrels filled with crushed ice and bottles of soda pop, not to mention six highly popular beer tappers scattered around at strategic locations. Thankfully they kept it real informal, which was nice for dirty-fingernail types like me who weren't used to casual, spur-of-the-moment parties that cost more than I made in a year. But at least there was something to celebrate, since this was the first time anybody had seen the Cunningham team since they got back from Europe. They had the three C4Rs laid out right in the middle of the eighteenth putting green, the roadsters on either side and the coupe hunkered down between them, with an American flag planted solidly in front of them and a couple colored floodlights shining down from someplace up in the trees. Looking at them made your chest sort of swell up. Honest it did.

Briggs Cunningham was there, too, walking around from one person to the next, quietly making sure each and every one of them had enough to eat and drink. And in return, each and every one of them would thank Briggs personally—not just for the party, but also for building those tough-looking Cunninghams and taking them overseas to show the rest of the world that Americans had the know-how to build something besides fat, chrome-encrusted four-doors with automatic transmissions and mushy steering.

I ran into Cal and Carson Flegley in the beer line, and you could see Carson was starting to get a little edgy on account of practice was scheduled to start the next morning and his laps with Cal had pretty much convinced him that he was in over his head. And naturally Cal was stoking the fire, since the S.C.M.A. had decided to award a special trophy to the top-finishing stock MG in Sunday morning's rescheduled smallbore race, and Cal was pretty damn certain he could win it if only Carson would let him drive. "Sure," Cal remarked offhandedly, "that blind hill coming into town looks a little scary at first. Can't see a damn thing over the top. Heck, there might be a car stalled or sideways or even flipped clear over smack-dab in the middle of the road. But you gotta take it flat in top anyways. Only way to get a decent lap time. 'Course, you *could* lift—even tap the brakes, just to settle the nose a little—but the fast guys'll leave you so far behind it won't even be funny." Carson swallowed hard a couple times, his Adam's apple bobbing up and down. "And then there's that swoopy section just past the power station," Cal added with a cavalier wave of his hand. "You really can't afford to lift off there, either...."

"Y-You *can't?*"

"Hell *no!* Not in a bone-stock MG, anyways. Not if you wanna be, you know, *competitive....*"

That's when I decided I should wander off before I inadvertently started sniggering and gummed up Cal's game. I mean, I wanted to see Cal drive almost as much as he wanted to do it. After all, Cal was *my* driver, and it seemed like some little fragment of the glory reflected back on me whenever he did well.

I saw Tommy over talking with Ernesto Julio and Chuck Day, and with them was a small, thin, quiet young fellow with hollow cheeks, wiry hair, and quick, darty eyes. "Hey, sport," Tommy called out. "Step over and meet Phil Hill."

I walked over and shook hands. "So," I said with just the hint of an edge in my voice, "you're the guy who's supposed to beat my friend Tommy here, right?"

Phil Hill shrugged and didn't say anything.

"Well," I continued, with maybe a few too many beers for inspiration, "I think you're gonna find that's a pretty tall order. Especially in equal cars...."

"Equal cars?" Ernesto Julio howled, rolling his eyes. "Are you trying to tell me Colin St. John didn't keep the fastest one for himself? Hell, that's what *I'd* do."

"Sure, we kept the best car," Tommy allowed through a crocodile smile. "But from what I've heard, we'll bloody well need it. Old Phil here's been building himself quite a formidable reputation out on the coast. Haven't you, Phil?"

Phil Hill looked down at the ground like he'd maybe dropped something and shrugged again. Of course, this was all part of the game, putting the old needle in and trying to work the other guy around a little before you actually had to go out on the track and run wheel-to-wheel with him.

Later I wandered over to take a closer look at the cars. The Cunningham team had them all polished up and gleaming like huge china figurines, but if you looked closely, you could see the little telltale dings and stone chips left over from their European campaign. I remember touching my fingers to the nose emblem of that wicked-looking C4RK coupe, and for just an instant an electrified shiver went through me, as if I could hear the war cry of that enormous Chrysler V-8 thundering down the midnight straightaways at Le Mans.

A dance band fired up over next to the clubhouse, and they were pretty decent even though they played mostly older, slower songs like "The Tennessee Waltz" and "Goodnight, Irene." I noticed Sally Enderle standing over by one of the beer tappers, all by her lonesome, and I decided to casually wander over and say hello and maybe see how long it would take her to shoo me away. But she actually seemed glad to see me. "So," she said through a wavering smile, "how's the mechanic who blows up other people's MGs doing?"

"Me?" I said, looking around like there was maybe somebody behind me. "Oh, I'm OK, I guess."

"Yeah? Me, too. I feel *great!*" She rolled her head back until she was looking straight up at the sky, and I noticed she had to hang on to the beer tapper to keep from toppling clear over. "Take a look up there. You ever seen so many stars?"

I had to admit I really hadn't, and then it turned all heavy and quiet between us, like cement setting up. "So," I asked, just trying to make conversation, "y'think Creighton's all set for tomorrow? That's quite a machine he's got there, yes siree. And where the heck is he, anyway? Haven't seen him around all night. . . ."

Sally looked me up and down like she was trying to figure where some bad smell was coming from. "Maybe he decided to turn in early," she snapped, glaring so hard her eyeballs seemed to vibrate. "Do I look like his damn keeper to you?"

"Oh, n-no, Sally," I mumbled. "A'course not. I just sorta, you know..."

"Lissen, Bub," she growled, pointing her chin into my face like an automatic pistol, "you don't need to wonder anything about me at all, understand?"

Boy, I could feel my ears burning.

"And as for Creighton's Ferrari, why don't you try getting your information from one of the other mechanics. You all speak the same inane language, don't you?"

Geez, I couldn't figure out what I'd done, you know?

So I left her standing there by the beer keg—steam rising from both ears—and wandered over to where my buddy Cal was tangled up in a major discussion with some of the MG guys about maybe getting himself a few laps in that Ford-powered TC. Boy, Cal could work somebody over so smooth and polite and *reasonable* that the poor sap never knew his pocket was being picked, his barn burned, and his family sold off into slavery until a day or two later. In fact, some of them never felt it at all. I figured it might be best not to butt in and maybe spoil Cal's pitch.

Truth is, I was feeling pretty tired (after all, I'd really tied one on the night before, and it didn't make sense to do it all over again when the real meat of the weekend activities weren't due to start until early the next morning) and so I left the party early and headed back to Siebken's to get some sleep. But first I wandered out on the eighteenth green for one last look at those magnificent, all-American Cunningham race cars. Boy, they were something, all right. And that's why I made a detour around the food tables to give my own personal "thanks so much" to Briggs Cunningham before I left. After all, there were plenty of guys in the S.C.M.A. who had piles of money to spend, but most of them just *bought* stuff with their money. Briggs Cunningham *made* things. You had to respect the hell out of something like that.

Just as I turned to leave, the guy fronting up the band leaned into his microphone and said, "We've got a request from a very pretty lady out there," and rolled into a better than average rendition of "Your Cheatin' Heart." When I looked back, I was surprised to see it was none other than the lovely Miss Sally Enderle making her way unsteadily back from the bandstand.

Your cheatin' heart...will tell on youuuu....

The music trailed off behind as I headed up the darkened road toward Siebken's, and it was an absolutely perfect sort of late-summer

Friday night, what with a hint of fall chill in the air and a wash of silver-blue light beaming down from the fattest damn harvest moon I'd ever seen. And was it ever *quiet*. So quiet you could hear water lapping against the docks down by the lake and the faint echo of laughter and Hank Williams music from the party. The only other sound was the soft shuffle of shoe leather against the asphalt. It was hard to believe that, in less than twelve short hours, this same silent stretch of Lake Street was going to be lined ten- and twenty-deep with spectators and this same pavement was going to shudder and squirm under the wheels of the fastest, noisiest, hairiest collection of sports cars in the whole blessed country.

I could hardly wait.

Morning came while it was still purplish dark outside, barking through the flower-print curtains with the sound of an MG engine popping and banging and backfiring through the carburetors. Obviously, someone had switched the plug wires around—just for the fun of it, you know?—and now the intended victim was waking everybody and his brother up at four-goddam-thirty in the morning. You got the impression that this individual wasn't particularly, um, *mechanically inclined,* since he kept shutting it off, waiting a few seconds, and then cranking the damn thing all over again. As if the stupid motor was going to magically stand up, clear its throat, and start to run properly again. I looked over and Tommy was still out cold, so I decided to take a quick run downstairs and see what I could do before this jerk's popping and banging woke up all the racers.

Turned out it was a nice red TD from Grosse Pointe, Michigan, and the owner (who looked more or less like he'd been to bed already, but not to sleep) thanked me plenty after I switched the number two, three, and four spark-plug wires back to their proper order. "Hey," the guy said, wavering back and forth like one of those blow-up punch-me clowns, "thangsannawfullot."

"No problem," I told him. "Now go get some sleep."

"Saay, dinneye meetchoo at Gianssdesspair?"

"Yeah, most likely. I was there with Cal Carrington. He was in—"

"I *remember,*" the guy said, drawing back in inebriated awe. "He drove that unnertakerguy's black TD, dinn'he?"

"That's right. Carson Flegley's car. He's trying to work a deal to drive it again in the race Sunday morning."

"Boy, I sure hope he gettsa shot," the MG guy said, pulling himself up more or less upright, "but he'll sureashell blow me in th'stinkin' weeds iffy does." The MG guy blew out a long, wheezy breath that smelled of hard liquor and cigarettes. "Still, I kinna hope he gettsa shot, y'know?"

"Yeah." I agreed, wondering just what exactly was holding this guy upright.

"Yup, that Cal Carrington fella's really somethin' *special* behind a steering wheel anna gas pedal, iddn'ee?"

"Yeah, he sure is," I agreed for the third time. "He said he's trying t'get a run in that V-8-powered TC later today, too."

"Y'mean *Robby's* car?"

"Who?"

"Why *Robby!* Robby Bernard. He built th'damn thing over'n Grosse Pointe Shores. Not more'n five miles from my house."

"Really?"

"*Sure* he did!" Then he leaned in close and whispered, "But jus' between youanme, he didd'n so much *build* it as have th'guy at the gas station do it for him. I think he mostly jus' bought th'parts, y'know?"

"I sure do."

"Iffya want, I think we might fix it real easy so's your friend Cal gets t'drive. I mean, Robby's scared hisself about ghost-white already, an' nobody's even got a full-tilt run yet. I'll put in a good word, no problem. Iss'tha least I can do."

"Hey, thanks," I told him as he plopped unsteadily behind the wheel, "that'd really be swell of you."

"Oh, no," he said, sticking the lever in first, "thank *you!*"

There was no way I could go back to sleep—especially since the S.C.M.A. armband types were already out in the early-morning half-light setting up flag stations and rechecking hay bales and putting up a few last gasoline company signs. It made me wonder what the hell they got out of it, you know? I went over and talked to some of them—even helped string the big PURE OIL banner over the start/finish line in front of Gessert's Soda Shop—and although they were overworked and underrecognized and making wisecracks all the time about how early it was and how lousy they had it, underneath you could tell they were all happy as hell just to be there. In spite of carping and grousing like some of my old man's union buddies, every last one of them had a spring in their step and a sparkle in their eyes rather than the standard-issue slow shuffle and dead-fish look you normally get out of grunt-level working stiffs. Especially the guys with seniority.

I wandered into the Osthoff and grabbed a free cup of coffee and one of the sweet rolls they had out for the S.C.M.A. workers, and then decided to take myself a little stroll and watch race morning begin. The sun was just starting to peek up all yellow-gold over the eastern horizon, and all along Lake Street local church groups and privateer townfolk were setting up their sandwich, snack, and lemonade stands, and a few early spectators were already straggling in from the temporary parking areas on the outskirts of town. I had this crazy notion to walk all the way around the circuit. Backward, in fact, since I was already pretty familiar with the section between Schuler's Bar and the golf course. So I headed north, past the IGA store and the railroad station and on up that bobsled run of a hill that the faster cars would be descending at three-digit speeds in a scant few hours. You never realize how long and steep a hill is until you try to walk it on foot, and I was out of breath by the time I reached the top. In fact, I was more than ready to abandon the notion of doing the whole blessed 6.5 miles. But I went a little bit farther, just so I could get out of the shadow of the trees and feel the sun coming up clear and fine across rolling acres of prime Wisconsin farmland. Boy, was this ever one beautiful place to hold an automobile race!

When I turned to head back into town, the sight of that blind hilltop with the pine tree growing out of it stopped me dead in my tracks. That's the view the drivers would have as they rocketed up out of the hairpin at Dicken's Ditch, winding out in second, third, and fourth as the road curved gently to the right and strained uphill. The faster cars would be well up over a hundred here, and it looked like that damn pine tree was smack-dab in the middle of the road on the other side. How a guy could gather up the moxie to flat-foot it over the top was simply beyond me.

By the time I got back into town, the place was filling up with spectators and most all the racers were busily monkeying around with their cars. Every now and then you'd hear one start and settle into a cold, lumpy idle, and most usually it wouldn't be thirty seconds before some idiot was snapping the throttles open and winging that poor chunk of iron clear to the redline—with no load!—before the damn oil was even warm. Some people just have no mechanical sympathy whatsoever. And it's amazing how many of them wind up in racing.

I found Tommy, Chuck Day, Phil Hill, and Ernesto Julio having themselves a big country-style breakfast over in Siebken's dining hall, and what with the place being mobbed with racers and officials and Skippy Welcher making a complete pest of himself by corralling every passing waitress so he could complain about how slow the service was and how his melon wasn't ripe and how they'd only cooked his sunny-side-up eggs on *one* side, well, it took us damn near forever to finish our meal. I had a thick blueberry waffle that was about the best I ever had outside of my mom's kitchen (who knows, maybe even better) and some swell corned beef hash with an egg on top. Boy, did that ever hit the spot! There's something about the night air in that particular corner

of Wisconsin that makes you want a monstrous, heaping, Sunday-style
breakfast every single day of the week.

There was a drivers' meeting behind the Osthoff at eight ayem, and
naturally it started a half hour late and you couldn't hear what anybody
was saying, what with a few race crews doing a little last-minute engine
tuning not fifty yards away and several hundred little private conversations going on all over the place. The gist of it was that the S.C.M.A.
was real pleased to have everybody there, and that—above all—they
wanted a *safe* weekend. Everybody knew the event was under a micro-
scope after the crowd-control problems and the near-disastrous Porsche
crash at Grand Island.

Practice started a half hour late at 10:30, and we had Tommy and
Phil right up toward the front in the C-types so's they wouldn't get
caught in the MG T-series traffic. And I gotta admit, those two Jags
looked pretty damn swell as they pulled out onto Lake Street and roared
away, their race-tuned sixes blaring like the meanest, mellowest horn
section you ever heard in your life. The stream of cars behind them
just went on and on, charging one after the other out of the Osthoff
parking lot like snarling animals through a cattle chute. If you knew
your engines, you could even close your eyes and pick 'em out by sound.
An MG. Another MG. A Jag 120. A Crosley-powered Siata. Another
MG. Another Jag. Creighton Pendleton's howling Ferrari. The lumpy,
inboard motorboat burble of Eddie Dearborn's Cad-Allard. But something was missing. Sure enough, those three Chrysler-powered Cunninghams were sitting patiently off to the side, ticking over at a deep,
grumbly idle, obviously in no hurry to join the last cars trickling out of
the parking lot. It took me awhile to catch on, but then I understood.
They were waiting for the wail of the first cars to come echoing downhill toward Schuler's Bar about four and a half minutes later. Only
then did the Cunninghams clunk their heavy-duty truck transmissions
into first and rumble out onto the circuit in close formation—with five
whole miles of open track in front of them instead of bogged down in
a bunch of traffic. Made a lot of sense, you know? Then again, these
guys had the legs on everybody when it came to experience and team-
work.

After the first lap, I kind of moseyed my way up to the hard left
in front of Siebken's for a closer look-see, and it was pretty interesting
to watch all the different driving styles through there. I was happy to
see that Tommy and Phil Hill were running in close company, well out
front of the main pack, and for awhile it even looked like they were
maybe closing the gap to the Cunninghams. Those C-types were obviously quick as the dickens, but it looked to me that Tommy was trying

a lot harder, getting it full-lock sideways and damn near nicking the hay bales every time through. But damn if Phil Hill wasn't hanging right with him, lap after lap, looking so smooth and unruffled that you wondered if they'd somehow swapped paint-jobs. I mean, we *knew* the green car was the faster one, didn't we?

Too bad that Phil Hill character didn't seem to know it.

Creighton Pendleton was his usual controlled, arrogant self behind the wheel, and you got the impression that his 4.1-liter V-12 had a little something in hand for our 3.4-liter C-types on this long, fast racetrack. In fact, he seemed to be gaining on them once he got through the slower cars. Just as promised, Tommy's friend Eddie Dearborn was pretty damn exuberant with his Cad-Allard, and that MG monstrosity with the Ford V-8 under the hood looked clumsy, nose-heavy, and darty as all getout. In fact, Robby Bernard pulled it in after a half dozen laps with the engine steaming and the brakes about gone, and you couldn't miss that he looked pretty relieved to have it safely back in the paddock.

No question the most impressive cars were the Cunninghams, looking solid, powerful, and totally unperturbed as they rumbled around the circuit in formation, carving through traffic with ease and leaving everybody behind at the end of the long straightaways. Somebody said they were topping 150 on the fast downhills into Kimberly's Korner and Dicken's Ditch. Eventually, pros Fitch and Walters eased away from Briggs himself in the second roadster, but not by much. Then again, you could tell they were nowheres near flat-out yet, wisely saving the last few r.p.m.'s and inches of pavement for Sunday afternoon, when it counted.

All the drivers were mightily impressed (or perhaps "awestruck" might be a better word) by the circuit at Elkhart Lake. It was big and fast and terribly scenic, and about the only complaints were how narrow it was for passing and how little room for error there was in some of the really fast spots. But that's exactly why ace drivers like Tommy and Cal and Phil Hill and John Fitch and Phil Walters liked it so much. It separated the men from the boys.

In fact, that's exactly why Robby Bernard decided to step out of his Ford-powered MG and let my buddy Cal have a try. That poor guy looked like he'd aged ten years for every lap he was out in that contraption! Cal found me underneath the Westbridge C-type, doing a little between-sessions fluid check and nut-and-bolt inspection. A decent mechanic does that every time a car comes in off the track (and if he doesn't find anything wrong, that just means he did his job properly the last time!). Anyhow, Cal wanted me to take a look at that V-8-powered MG before he went out in it, just to make sure nothing was about ready to snap, fracture, fall off, burst into flames, or blow sky high. I was flattered, of course, but also a little nervous. I mean, who wants that kind of responsibility?

Fortunately, it looked reasonably sanitary, and I figured if Cal could drive that ratty old TC of his without worrying about it, this thing should be a piece of cake. The guy who shoehorned the motor in fabricated some pretty nice engine mounts and the welds looked like something old Butch Bohunk might've done. Why, that Ford fit like it almost belonged, except that it had to run without the side cowlings to make room for the heads and exhaust plumbing. But most of the quicker MGs were running without the side panels anyway, so it really didn't make much difference. The engine had been modified by a speed shop in Detroit, and it had finned aluminum heads and a specially cast three-carburetor manifold from some California hot-rod place named Edelbrock. They were beautifully made all right, but I really wondered if this particular MG needed extra any power.

"How's it look to you?" Cal asked.

"I dunno," I said, giving him about half of an OK shrug. "Looks like they did their homework."

"That's good enough for me," he grinned, and jumped in the driver's seat.

The officials split up the next sessions into "slow cars" and "fast cars," and they stuck Cal in the same group with the Cunninghams and Allards and Creighton Pendleton's Ferrari (not to mention our two new C-types!) and not even Cal Carrington could make that MG V-8 shine against that sort of opposition. But he did pretty good, running about the same pace as the quicker XK120s while having to pump the brakes three or four times before every sharp corner. And then he didn't come around. I feared the worst, but was tremendously relieved when the Ford-powered MG reappeared at the other end of Lake Street, trundling along at little more than walking speed with the right-front wheel crabbed in. He pulled into the lot behind the Osthoff and sailed right past where me and the rest of the MG guys (including the car's owner) were standing. *"Help!"* Cal laughed as he steered past us again on another slow lap around the parking lot, *"this damn thing doesn't have any brakes left at all. . . . "*

Sure enough, the guy who built it ran the left-side exhaust a little too close to the master cylinder, and it got the brake fluid so hot it actually boiled (so *that's* why Cal had to pump the brakes!) and finally the seal gave up and the brake pedal flopped clear to the floor with no effect whatsoever. "Except," Cal explained wryly, "for a fresh little dimple in the seat upholstery on the driver's side."

It happened in the worst possible place—at the end of the long, fast, downhill run to Kimberly's Korner—where the track came up the stem of a T-intersection and there wasn't much of anyplace to go. Fortunately, Cal had the presence of mind to grab a big handful of emergency brake and swing the wheel from one side to the other to slew off some speed before purposely yanking it hard left and spinning the car to use up the momentum. Truth is, he was lucky to keep it from flipping right over! And he knew it, too. But somehow he got away with it and brought the car home with no more than a limp brake pedal and a bent tie-rod from where he tapped a hay bale right at the end of the spin. He was pretty unhappy about that. "Boy, if I'da had two more feet of asphalt—*two stinking feet!*—I wouldn'ta hit *anything!*"

Now, you'd think a hair-raising experience like that would dampen a guy's enthusiasm. But not my buddy Cal. No sir. The first thing he wanted to know was if we could get the brakes fixed and the wheels pointed more or less straight in time for the race that afternoon. "Gee whiz," I asked him, "aren't you a little, you know, *scared?* I mean, that coulda been a pretty damn serious wreck."

"Yeah," he shrugged, "I 'spose it could at that."

"That car coulda flipped right over on top of you. . . ."

Cal's face lit up in one of his patented rich-kid grins. "But it didn't, did it?" And that seemed to pretty much settle things as far as Cal Carrington was concerned.

We had about an hour before the Sheldon Cup race, and seeing as how Tommy's C-type was running just fine, me and some of the MG guys decided to see if we could maybe fix Robby Bernard's V-8-powered TC so Cal could run it. They liked seeing an MG running faster than most of the Jaguar 120s. And who could blame them? Still, the MG/Ford combination was lumped in the same class with our pair of C-types and Creighton Pendleton's Ferrari, where it really didn't have a prayer of picking up a trophy. "What's the point?" I asked Cal as I leaned my head under the fender to have a look at that bent tie-rod.

"Hey," he grinned, patting that mongrel MG on its radiator cap, "it's a *ride.*"

As you can imagine, it was no simple truck to fix the damn thing, because you couldn't really get at the master cylinder without pulling off the exhaust pipe on that side, and everything was still hotter than a barbecue grill down where we needed to be working. So we soaked down a couple shop rags and applied them a little at a time so as to cool things off a little without causing all the castings to shatter like a bunch of heavy-duty Christmas ornaments.

Fortunately, one of the MG guys had a rebuild kit for the master cylinder, and somebody else scrounged me up a couple empty tomato cans out of the trash, which I transformed with a hammer and a pair of tin snips into a cheesy pair of heat shields for the exhaust. They surely wouldn't have won me any awards for engineering excellence or fine craftsmanship, but it looked like they might get the job done. As for the bent tie-rod, the best we could do was heat it up with a torch we borrowed from the Cunningham trailer and kind of pry and hammer it more or less straight again. I did the fine adjusting with some kite string and a yardstick we borrowed from the Osthoff's maintenance man, and if I do say so myself, those wheels looked pretty damn straight when I was finished. Especially if you held your thumb out in front of your eyes and squinted real hard.

Come race time all the cars drove around to the train station parking lot and waited while a bunch of S.C.M.A. grid marshals fought with the drivers and crews about who belonged where. To tell the truth, the starting positions were pretty much pulled out of a hat, and some painfully slow guy in a new Nash-Healey somehow wound up on the pole. But right next to him was our old buddy Creighton Pendleton and his slightly oversized Ferrari. The second row consisted of Cal in the Ford/MG hybrid and a guy from Cincinnati in a J2 Allard with an Ardun Mercury under the hood. Phil Hill's C-type was back on the third row, right next to Tommy, and I must admit, those two C-types looked really sleek and modern compared to all the other iron on the grid. Some of the guys toward the back were upset about being behind obstacles like Skippy Welcher's ex-everything XK120M, and bitched about it right up until the engines fired. But it did them no good as the field rumbled off for a slow pace lap to get everybody settled in and all the mechanical bits up to operating temperature.

After the field arced out of sight in front of Siebken's and growled off into the countryside, I had my first real chance to take in the enormous crowd that had assembled five- and six-deep all the way down Lake Street and damn near as many lining the hill from Schuler's Tavern up toward that blind crest another half mile away. I have no idea how many spectators were actually on hand that day (somebody said it was over a hundred thousand!) but wherever you went, you had heads and torsos and elbows poking at you from all sides.

The field came around and reformed down the middle of Lake Street, and then the starter (it was that same doofus in the Great White Hunter getup I remembered from Bridgehampton) climbed a little wooden podium on the side, looked everybody over like a high school math teacher before a big exam, and gave 'em the green. Engines roared, tires squealed, and there was quite a bit of jockeying for position as the field thundered down toward the hard left in front of Siebken's and the fast guys struggled to find a way around that Nash-Healey. But you could see they were being pretty careful, too, on account of the spectators pressed in along both sides and the fact that there wasn't anything in the way of an escape road. As the last of the stragglers disappeared from sight, you could hear the unmistakable, wild-animal howl of Creighton Pendleton's Ferrari leading the pack through Wacker Wend, climbing the gentle hill, and then braking and downshifting for the sharp right into Hammil's Hollow. After that it got pretty quiet for a minute or so, and then you could pick up the echo of the cars as they passed the public boat launch on the other side of the lake. Sounded to me like Creighton's Ferrari, the two C-types a few seconds behind and running in close company, another gap, and then a whole freight train of cars one right after the other. I figured Cal and the Ford/MG to be some-where in that bunch. After that it got quiet again, and then you could make out the faint yowl of the Ferrari and the two C-types climbing the long, steep hill toward the blind crest with the pine tree growing right smack-dab in the middle of it. No question Creighton and at least one of the C-types gave it a big lift just before the hilltop—maybe even a stab at the brakes?—but the other C-type went over flat stick. You could hear it.

When they roared back through town, it was Creighton in front with Phil Hill in the silver Jag all over him, then about a two-second gap back to Tommy in the Westbridge C-type. And then just a huge, empty space with nobody in it. On the very first lap! When the rest of the field poured into town, it was an Allard and two of the quicker XK120s and some guy in a Frazer-Nash and our boy Cal in that over-powered MG all in a clot, followed by more Jag 120s and another Allard and a whole bunch of cars bottled up behind that stupid pole-sitting Nash-Healey. "Pretty good race," a familiar voice said, and I turned to find Chuck Day standing next to me, casually chewing gum and shield-ing his eyes from the afternoon sun.

"Yeah," I agreed, "that Phil Hill is doing a hell of a job in the silver car."

"He doesn't exactly poke around, does he?"

"Not hardly. And we figured that was the slower of the two cars."

"It was."

"How's that?"

"I said it *was*."

"Oh?"

Then the field came by again, and Phil Hill was still right on the Fer-rari's ass, but the gap back to Tommy Edwards had grown by another second or two. And Tommy looked like he was really *trying,* getting it all hung-out-to-dry sideways through the right-hander in front of Schuler's Tavern. "Jeez," I said, "he's really pushing it pretty hard, isn't he?"

"Yeah. Maybe even a little too much."

There was something to that. "So," I asked Chuck Day after the cars passed, "what did you mean when you said the silver car *used to be* the slow one?"

"Aw, it wasn't nothin', really. Phil just complained after first practice that the green car had more suds, so we sorta poked around until we found the problem."

"Oh? Mind letting me in on it?"

"Sure thing," he shrugged. "It was no big deal. Turns out they just made a little mistake at the factory."

"A mistake at the Jaguar factory race shop?" I asked incredulously.

"Yeah. They had the timing mark on the flywheel two teeth off, so it was running about 5 degrees retarded. Cams and ignition both. No big deal. . . ." Well, *he* could say "no big deal," but believe me, it took one hell of a sharp mechanic to figure that one out. I mean, he'd never even *seen* a damn C-type before!

The race between Creighton Pendleton and Phil Hill turned out to be a genuine classic. Phil's Jag was all over that Ferrari like a wet laundry bag, but the Ferrari had just that little bit extra in the horsepower department so Creighton could pull away enough on the straights to keep the Jag from ducking underneath going into the corners. And he made it extra tough by driving more or less down the middle of the road, so there really wasn't much space for overtaking. Meanwhile, Tommy was slipping farther and farther back, losing the odd second or two every lap no matter how hard he tried. And it must've been double tough on him since he still thought he had the faster of the two C-types. Maybe that's why he was trying so damn hard and slowing himself down.

Cal was putting up a pretty good effort in the Ford-powered MG, hanging on behind the quickest of the Jag 120s but slowly losing contact. And then he didn't come around anymore. I was worried, of course, but figured it was probably OK on account of they didn't red flag the race or send out an ambulance or anything. Apparently, he was just parked somewhere by the side of the road with mechanical problems again. Or at least that's what I hoped.

When the leaders thundered past with four laps to go, you could see Phil Hill had dropped back about five or six car lengths instead of hanging all over the back of the Ferrari. "You watch," Chuck grinned. "Phil's been setting him up. This is the lap he gets past." And, sure enough, the silver C-type was solidly in front the next time around. He stayed there all the way to the checker, too.

After the race, they towed Cal in with the right-front end of the MG/Ford somewhat rearranged. "What happened?" I asked as they dropped it off the hook.

"Aw, th'damn brakes went out again."

"They *did?*"

"Yeah. Pedal went right to the floor heading into Dicken's Ditch."

"Wow."

"Lucky for me there's an escape road there."

"Sure is," I agreed. "But then, why'dja crash it?"

"Aw, there was some idiot photographer squatted down right in the middle of the damn escape road. Can you believe it? I had to damn near drive up a tree to keep from hitting him." It turned out Cal had most likely saved that photographer's life, on account of he came charging down the escape road at a hundred-plus with no brakes and had the presence of mind to wait and see which way the guy was gonna jump before he yanked the wheel and swerved the other way. It would've been real easy to make a snap decision and turn the car one direction or the other, and if the poor lensman happened to jump the same way, he would've found himself pretty much *wearing* the front end of Robby Bernard's Ford-powered TC.

I looked underneath to see what happened to the brakes, and was relieved to discover it had nothing to do with the work we'd done before the race. No, this time the brake pipe on the back axle had busted, and it didn't take Sherlock Holmes to figure out why. Somebody'd left the little brass nut off that holds the brake line T-fitting to the axle, and so the brake line was getting a nasty little twist thrown into it whenever the axle moved up and down. It was only a matter of time.

One of the MG guys brought us over a couple cold bottles of Pabst Blue Ribbon and Cal gave us a thrilling eyewitness account of the super-duper passing move Phil Hill pulled on old Creighton Pendleton. "Creighton was kinda hogging the middle of the road so there was really no safe way around—I mean, the pavement's pretty narrow there and you're going awfully fast—and so Phil just kinda sat there on his bumper and worked him over for about eight laps, darting and feinting around in his mirrors. After he had Creighton good and worried, he dropped back a few lengths and took a run on him down the backside between Kimberly's Korner and where I was stranded up by the hairpin. He had it timed just perfectly, got himself a nice little boost coming up in the Ferrari's slipstream, made like he was gonna pass on the outside, then whipped around the inside at the little kink going into the braking zone. *Without ever lifting his foot off the damn floorboards!* Boy, what a pass!"

After helping get Robby Bernard's MG loaded up so they could haul it down to some garage in Cedarburg where a guy named Kovacs could fix just about anything—even on a Saturday afternoon—I went wandering around in search of Tommy Edwards. But he was nowhere to be found. I located the green C-type easy enough (parked right where it belonged next to the silver one) with Phil Hill, Chuck Day, and Ernesto Julio standing in the middle of the usual crowd that gathers around winners like flies on fresh dogshit. Ernesto had brought out a case of his special private-stock California wines and even had honest-to-goodness wine glasses and some stiff in a tux to do the opening and pouring. Some guys are just real handy with money.

"Anybody seen Tommy?" I asked.

Everybody shook their heads and kind of looked off the other way. But before I took off to go looking for him in the bar, I had myself a glass of red and a glass of white (in different glasses—the guy in the tux insisted!) and made sure to congratulate Phil Hill on a hell of a drive and a really nice win. He looked down at the ground and shrugged and thanked me in a quiet, almost apologetic voice, and right then I knew this guy was going places.

I located Tommy over in Siebken's bar, and he'd obviously already had himself several stiff drinks. But they weren't exactly cheering him up. In a single afternoon, it seemed like he'd changed from a guy who could drink all night and never show it to a guy who could get himself righteously stiff on four or five watered-down scotches. He had a grim look on his face, and it didn't help much when I explained about the timing marks and how Chuck Day had made the silver car at least as fast as the green one. But Tommy just wasn't interested. Far as he could see, he'd been beaten by another driver in a lesser car, and that had never really happened to him before. It had never even happened in an *equal* car. And that's why it didn't help much when I told him the silver Jag was running a whole lot better come race time.

The official weekend program listed a "Concours d'Elegance and Motoring Fashion Show" for 7:30 Saturday evening, and that gave me just enough time for a couple commiseratory drinks with Tommy and a quick run back to the room to shower and put on some clean clothes. Only I didn't exactly *have* any on account of I'd put the best stuff I had on that morning, then spent most of the day crawling around under Robby Bernard's overstimulated TC. Fortunately, Ernesto Julio overheard me moaning about it in the bar (he'd come over to buy Tommy a few more drinks, which he really didn't need) and nothing would do but that I go up to his room and take whatever the hell I wanted out of his closet. "Hey, no problem," he told me. "Take any damn thing you want."

"You sure? Even one of those pirate shirts?"

"Pirate shirts?"

"You know. Like the one you were wearing in the bar under the stairs the other night?"

"Why not?" he shrugged, rolling his palms up. But then he leaned forward and stared at me eyeball to eyeball. "That is, if you think you're man enough to pull it off. It's easy to look like a damn sissy in an outfit like that. Especially if you don't have the balls to wear it properly. *Capiche?*"

I told him it was a risk I was willing to take. So I went up to Ernesto Julio's room and borrowed myself a puffy silk shirt and a pair of freshly pressed tan slacks that were only about two sizes too big and headed back to my room for a major cleanup before I dared to put that stuff on. Fact is, I spent better than twenty minutes in the shower, trying to get most of the grease out from under my fingernails. When I came out of the bathroom, I saw Tommy stretched out on the bed in his driving suit, staring up at the slowly rotating ceiling fan. "How're y'feeling?" I asked, like he'd been sick or something.

Tommy waved one of his hands halfheartedly through the air. "I'll be fine after a hot bath and some dinner," he sighed, his voice all heavy with liquor. "You run on along. I'll be down in awhile." So I put on Ernesto Julio's shirt and pants and headed downstairs to see just what a Concours d'Elegance and Motoring Fashion Show could possibly be.

"Concours d'elegance" is a French phrase that means prettying up a car so that it's too damn nice to drive, and you would simply not believe all the spiffed up cars they had on display under a string of party lanterns down Lake Street. There were the usual MGs and Jaguars and Porsches and such you expected, all polished and gleaming in the soft yellow light, but there were other cars, too. Huge, magnificent-looking Rolls Royces and Bentleys and even a V-12 Lincoln Continental. I noticed a gorgeous metallic blue Alfa Romeo coupe that some designer guy named Brook Stevens had just brought back from Italy, plus one of those flamboyant, supercharged 540K Mercedes convertibles that were such a hit with the Nazi bigwigs during the war. There was a really nice Model T next to an old Overland, an older Mercer, and of course Charlie Priddle's antique Stutz. Across the way, a slippery, boat-tailed Auburn Speedster was parked beside a Murphy-bodied Duesenberg and this block-long, liquid-smooth French thing called a Delahaye. They may have been designed more for pulling up in front of fancy restaurants than screaming around corners, but those cars were sure as hell magnificent to look at. I spent the better part of two hours there, just walking up and down, taking it all in. A lot of people—and especially women—simply don't understand the magic of automobiles. But there it was for all to see, spread out down the middle of Lake Street like a damn smorgasbord.

About 9:30 they started wheeling the cars away while a clot of official S.C.M.A. judges huddled by the starter's podium, trying to puzzle out who should go home with the trophies. Personally, I couldn't see how anybody could judge one of those cars as *better* or *nicer* or *superior to* any of the others. I mean, they were *all* beautiful. Every single one. And the owners had worked so hard primping and preening and polishing them—the real hard cases going over the damn engine compartments with scouring pads and toothbrushes and Welcher Wax-out cotton swabs to make them as immaculate as humanly possible. In fact, the lengths some of them went to seemed almost *silly*. But a lot of those *concours* types took it awful damn serious, and you could tell by the steely look in their eyes and the granite-hard thrust of their jaws that they wanted to *win* just as surely as any of the drivers entered in the actual races. Maybe even more so.

I grabbed myself another beer and one of the fine local bratwursts (complete with dark mustard and sauerkraut, natch) from one of the church group refreshment stands, then moseyed down to where they were setting up a twelve-piece dance band from Chicago. But first they announced the *concours* winners, and suddenly everything made sense seeing as how they gave trophies out to just about *everybody*. Why, they had almost as many classes as they had cars in the show! Charlie Priddle of course got another big first-place mug (plus a special award for oldest car in the show) and so he was happy as a hyena on a fresh carcass. Tommy always called Charlie "a bloody pot collector," and I was sure beginning to see why.

The official program listed, and I quote, "Dancing in the Streets" as the main activity commencing at ten P.M. on Saturday evening, and I must admit the band fired up right on schedule. There was quite a crowd left over from the *concours*—racers and spectators alike—and it didn't take very long before we had fox-trots and waltzes and jitterbugs and even polkas and irregularly shaped square dances going on from one end of Lake Street to the other.

I'd never seen anything like it.

I dropped into Schuler's Bar on the corner for a quick refill, and who should I notice over in the back corner but Creighton Pendleton and that blond-ponytail dolly from across the street. I kind of wondered what old Sally Enderle might have to say if she got wind of what was going on, and suddenly it seemed like the most excellent of notions to maybe see if I could find her. So I headed back toward the resorts, working my way through all sorts of frantic dancers and intense, nose-to-nose conversations about oil viscosities and spark-plug heat ranges and proper inflation pressures for various brands of tires. And all the while, that twelve-piece band filled the air with party music and the string of lanterns swayed in the breeze and there was whooping and shouting all up and down Lake Street like 4th of July fireworks going off.

I eventually found Sally hanging on the end of the bar at Siebken's, working on about her seventh or eighth sloe gin fizz. "Say," she said, looking strangely happy to see me, "you clean up pretty good for a grease monkey."

I'd forgotten about Ernesto Julio's white silk pirate shirt. "Hey, thanks," I told her, kind of pulling my shoulders back, "d'ya think I can buy you a drink?"

"Sure. It's a free country."

So I bought her a drink—another sloe gin fizz—and we shot the breeze for awhile about the *concours* and the "fashion show" she and most of the other wives and girlfriends attended over on the back steps of the Osthoff. "It was okay," she said, not sounding particularly impressed, "but they didn't have much that *I* liked." You got the impression that Sally Enderle was pretty damn picky about where she got her clothes.

"Say," I said, thinking about Creighton Pendleton the Third and that blond ponytail sitting in the back of Schuler's Bar at the other end of Lake Street, "you maybe wanna go outside?"

"What the hell for?" Sally asked, sounding bored already. She was pretty blasted, no question about it.

"I dunno. Maybe we could, you know, maybe, uh, *dance* or something. . . ."

"*You* know how to dance?" she said down her nose.

"Sure," I told her. And I actually did. I mean, you don't grow up in a household with four older sisters without learning how to lead.

Sally sucked the remainder of her sloe gin fizz through her cocktail straw and thought it over. "Nah," she said at last, "I really don't feel much like dancing."

"Oh," I said, looking down at where my dirty tennis shoes were poking out from under the perfectly creased bottoms of Ernesto Julio's slacks.

"*Say!*" she yelped, jabbing me in the arm. "Y'know what *I'd* like to do?"

"What's that?"

"Go for a swim."

"Go for a swim?"

"Uh-huh."

"You mean *now?*"

"I mean *right* now!" she said, slapping her hand down on the bar.

"B-But," I stammered, fumbling for words, "I haven't got a bathing suit. . . ."

"*So?*" she snapped. "Neither do I. At least not with me. And I'll be damned if I'm gonna run all the way back t'the goddam room just t'get one. Not just t'go take a l'il dip. I mean, who the hell *needs* it?" Sally Enderle was drunk all right, no two ways about it. But there was something else, too. Something I couldn't quite put my finger on. "Lissen," she hissed, "don't be a damn party pooper. *C'mon.* It'll be *fun!*"

My guts went hollow as an echo and all these little alarm bells I didn't even know I had started going off in my head. But I heard myself say, "Sure. Why not?" and next thing I knew, Sally Enderle grabbed my hand and dragged me out into the night. Not that I put up much resistance. She ushered us down the darkened side of Lake Street past the Osthoff, and I guess it should've felt like some kind of dream come true—out there all alone on a perfect summer night with the beautiful, rich, and incredibly sexy Sally Enderle—except I was nervous as hell and also feeling kind of dirty-sneaky rotten at the same time. Like I was somehow *cheating* on Julie Finzio, you know? Even though Julie and me weren't engaged or going steady or even exactly dating each other at the time.

Sally led me through a little gate in a chain-link fence and down a steep, narrow flight of steps toward the beach. You could hear the sounds of the street party and a loud bunch of drunks on the front porch of the Osthoff fading behind us, and down below, the water was lapping at the shoreline and you could see the reflection of that fat harvest moon floating in the water like a bucket of quicksilver spilled toward the horizon. We were having a little trouble with the steps on account of it was so dark and we were both pretty bombed, but we finally made it down to the bottom. Sally leaned her head next to mine and whispered, "Last one in's a monkey's uncle!" directly into my ear, then ran her tongue up and down the lobe for emphasis. Geez, where do women learn that stuff, anyway?

But there was no time to think, because Sally was already unbuttoning her blouse and shimmying out of her shorts. I yanked Ernesto Julio's silk shirt up over my head (I even think I heard a little *rrriiipppp* when I did it) and fumbled to get out of my shoes and pants. There was a splash behind me as Sally took two quick steps and dove headfirst into the water. And I stood there for a second with my thumbs hooked into the waistband of my Jockey shorts, wondering if I really wanted to take them off. "*C'mon,*" Sally urged with a nasty taunt to her voice, "don't be *chicken.* . . ."

"H-how's the water?" I stammered while my head, heart, and fingers fought each other back and forth for control.

"Just dreamy. C'mon. Jump in."

"Sure I will," I heard myself say.

"Right. Sometime before Christmas. Haw!" She rolled over in the water and took a couple slow strokes toward the swimming raft parked about fifty yards out from shore. "C'mon, chicken. What've you got to lose? *Bock-ba-bok-bok-bok!*" Sally could do a particularly humiliating chicken cackle.

So I stripped off my shorts and dived in after her. I mean, why the hell not, you know? The water was pitch-black and icy cold, and it occurred to me, as I followed her out toward the raft, that I'd never been an especially good swimmer, and that this was exactly the kind of situation your parents, teachers, camp counselors, and church clergymen warn you about while you're growing up. I mean, all I needed was to drown out here in this cold, black water while skinny-dipping seriously drunk and butt naked with somebody else's rich girlfriend. If Julie or her uncle or mom, or even my dad ever found out, they'd *kill* me. In fact, they'd take turns. . . .

I was about full up with lake water by the time we got out to the raft, but at least I wasn't cold anymore. In fact, the water felt all warm and velvety around me. Sally was hanging off the corner of the raft, and I kind of hand-over-handed my way along the edge until I was right there next to her. "So," she said, turning around so I could feel her up against me, "you made it."

"Yeah," I gasped, trying to move in a little closer.

"Not so fast, bub," she said, pushing me away.

"Huh?"

"I said *not so fast*. You understand English, don't you?"

"Uh, sure I do, Sally. I just don't, y'know, don't exactly *understand*, see . . ."

"It's simple," she whispered through a wicked, teasing smile. "I'll let you do anything you want to me—anything at all—if you can just do one simple thing."

"What's that?"

"Beat me back to shore!" she laughed, and took off full steam ahead toward the beach. Well, there was no way I could catch her—no way at all—but I must admit I gave it about the best damn try of my life. In fact, I was probably two or three heartbeats from full cardiac arrest by the time I finally crawled out of the water and lay back gasping on the sand. "Aw, poor baby," Sally cooed, kneeling over me and kissing me teasingly on the forehead. She was still stark naked, and as I looked up at her fabulous body and felt the water droplets falling off it, some-

thing hot and strong and desperate rose up inside me like the gathering swell of a great wave. I reached up and put my arms around her neck and drew her down into a kiss. She let me do it, too. In fact, she even helped a little. But then she stopped me. "Not here," she whispered, "we don't have a towel or a blanket or anything, and I don't want to get sand in my thing."

"Huh?"

"C'mon," she whispered urgently. "Follow me."

And so I did. We wrestled on about half of our clothes and scrambled up the steep wooden staircase and across the street to the deep shadows around the far-side door of the Osthoff, then up the stairs to the second floor and down the hall to her room. Or Creighton Pendleton's room, to be more precise.

It was a hell of a nice room—nicer by far than the one Tommy and I had—and even with the lights off, I could see well enough to check it over while Sally went into the can for a few minutes to do whatever it is girls like Sally do before they plan to have sex. Then she came out, pulled her blouse up over the top of her head, shimmied out of her shorts, and jumped under the covers. "So," she said evenly, looking at me standing there in the middle of the room like a damn cigar store Indian, "you planning to come to bed or what?"

"S-Sure," I told her. "But I think I gotta use the can first. You think it's OK?"

"Boy," Sally laughed, "you really know how to sweet-talk a girl, don't you?"

"Uh, well, geez, I . . ."

"Go ahead," she laughed, shaking her head under the covers, "and put a hustle on, willya? I'm cold."

So I went in the bathroom, closed the door, and damn near jumped out of my skin when I saw Creighton Pendleton standing there in the mirror right behind me! But it was only his blue Dunlop driving suit, draped over a hanger on the back of the bathroom door. Boy, did that scare the shit out of me!

Naturally it took me forever to get my body to cooperate and let some of the excess beer out, and when I finally flipped off the light and went back into the bedroom, it was like the temperature had changed. But Sally knew what to do about that once I got into bed with her. No question she'd had a lot of experience at this sort of thing. But for some reason, it was all so *unreal*—like I was watching a movie or something and not actually there in person, staring down at the beautiful Sally Enderle with her chestnut hair plastered down all wet and stringy over the pillowcase, listening to the sounds of the party winding down a few blocks away and wondering if I was going to hear the telltale *thump-*

thump-thump of Creighton Pendleton's footsteps down the hall and the icy-fingered click of a key sliding into the lock. Here I was, exactly where I'd hoped and yearned and fantasized about being one day— never for one single second believing it could actually happen!—staring at the illuminated alarm clock dial on the nightstand while I humped away like a bored cocker spaniel, wondering why I didn't feel like the luckiest guy in the world.

I left that room as soon as it was over. Maybe even a little before. I mean, you know how everybody says you're supposed to feel all melty-soft and dreamy afterward, and maybe just lie there and smoke a couple cigarettes, watching little phantom neon lights pulsing and flickering on the insides of your eyelids and listening to the sounds of the street-dance party filtering in from two blocks away. But I didn't feel that way at all. In fact, I felt kind of sick to my stomach and clammy all over, not to mention seriously worried that old Creighton might pop through the door at any moment. In fact, maybe that's what Sally had in mind all along. Maybe I was just the sacrificial lamb in this deal. Or maybe it was enough that I helped her muss up the sheets and left a few telltale wet spots behind. Hell, there was no telling what she had in mind. Worst of all, I couldn't stop thinking about Julie. I mean, it made no sense at all! Wouldn't you know it, just then the band swung into a slow, jazzy version of "Your Cheatin' Heart," complete with a long, mournful saxophone solo. Before it was over, I'd put Ernesto Julio's torn pirate shirt back on and beat it out the door. Sally didn't even roll over to say good night.

I crept down the side staircase, kind of sneaking along in the shadows, and headed straight over to Siebken's. But the place was so loud and boisterous it made my head pound, and the truth was I didn't much feel like talking anyway. So I left half a beer on the bar and headed off down the street. The crowd had dwindled down like toward the end of a big family wedding, and the band was mostly trudging through slow dance numbers and sappy old big-band tunes from the forties. I went into Schuler's to see if maybe Creighton and the ponytail were still there, but of course they were gone. So I ordered myself a snifter of brandy—just like Tommy would have—but the bartender wanted to see some I.D. before he'd pour a drop. Naturally I didn't have any in the pockets of Ernesto Julio's pants (or any that exactly said I was twenty-one in the pockets of my pants, either), but I'd gotten so used to being served when I was with the racing people that I got a little indignant about it. So the guy threw me out, you know? There was nothing to do but head back to the quiet little bar under the steps at Siebken's. But I stopped along the way and asked the bandleader to play "Your Cheatin' Heart" one more time.

"We just played it five minutes ago," he said with a forced smile.

"Yeah, I know. But it's for someone, you know, *special.* . . ."

He didn't look too convinced.

". . . And I just *gotta* hear that sax solo again."

Well, that of course got the sax player looking at the bandleader like a sad beagle puppy, and he eventually caved in. "Okay, we'll play it. Right after the next song. It was a request, too." And he tapped the music stand with his baton and the band took off into "Some Enchanted Evening" from *South Pacific.* They played it really lush, and as I walked slowly with each other down Lake Street, looking at the leftover partygoers talking softly and slow dancing under the warm, yellow lantern light and the sports cars from all over parked nose to tail up every available driveway and down every side street, I realized it really *was* an enchanted sort of evening, even if I was personally feeling a little lost, confused, soiled, and melancholy.

Your cheatin' heart . . . will tell on youuuu. . . .

That's the last I heard as I headed through Siebken's empty dining room to the quiet little bar under the stairs. It was full of people I didn't really know, but that was OK because the walls of that place always seemed to absorb all the chatter and you could somehow be alone with your thoughts even with a lot of other people around. I had a couple snifters of brandy, but they didn't seem to do much, and then I decided to take myself a little walk down past the Osthoff and that steep wooden stairway Sally Enderle and me had taken down to the beach only a few hours earlier. It felt like some kind of dream—like it never even happened, you know?—but I could tell from the hollow, empty feeling in my gut and the smell of her coming up from Ernesto Julio's shirt collar that it was true, even if it didn't seem like it. The band had stopped playing over in front of Schuler's and you could tell the party was finally breaking up, and the night was getting all black velvety quiet again.

But I wasn't ready to go to bed. So I walked on up past the Quit-Qui-Oc Golf Course and then farther up the road to the sharp right into Hammil's Hollow, and, honest to God, I just kept walking and walking all the way around the whole damn six and a half miles. It took me more than two hours. But I hardly felt it, because I had things to think about. Only I couldn't. It was like trying to wrap my fingers around something made out of the predawn mist.

I finally got back to town about four in the morning, and everything was dead quiet except for a little breeze rustling through the trees and a faint, threadlike squeaking off the party lanterns still swaying gently to and fro over Lake Street. I still didn't feel sleepy, but there was nothing to do but go back to the room. I was pretty damp from my long walk and all the other things that had happened, so I stepped in the shower and turned the hot tap up until I could hardly stand it and went over my body again and again until my fingers were wrinkled like prunes and the bar of soap was worn down to nothing. But no matter how much I tried to clean myself, I still felt scummy all over.

15

A NIGHT ON MICHIGAN AVENUE

IT DIDN'T seem like I was asleep for more than two minutes before I was awakened by engines firing and Charlie Priddle's irritating voice booming through the loudspeakers outside my window, calling for all drivers in the Kimberly Cup smallbore race to get themselves to the grid. Gee whiz, it was almost ten ayem! I hopped in the shower again just to wake myself up, threw on my dirty jeans and T-shirt, and carefully folded duds. Ernesto Julio's Cinderella clothes and set them gently on the windowsill. I made a mental note that I really ought to have them cleaned and pressed (and maybe have that little rip mended) before I gave them back. At least I felt a little more like myself again in my old wrenching clothes. I went downstairs and bummed a cup of coffee from the back door of Siebken's kitchen, then wandered out front to see the first race.

The smallbore contest looked like it would boil down to a scrap between a bright red OSCA driven by a guy named Bill Spear, one of the quicker Porsches, a couple heavily modified MGs, and a highly regarded little homebuilt from the West Coast based on parts from a small French sedan called a Simca. To tell the truth, I wasn't too interested. But then I recognized Cal's familiar old polo helmet sticking up out of Carson Flegley's black MG TD about halfway down the pack, and all of a sudden I was right up on the fences, shouting and waving my arms and yelling for Cal to *"Give 'em hell!"*

And did he ever. He charged right down the inside into that first hard left and immediately picked up three or four positions, and by the time they completed lap two, he was up to about tenth or so and easily leading all the other stock MGs. In fact, he was having a hell of a scrap with one of the modified TCs that should've been a whole lot faster. Only Cal more than made up the difference, and you could see he was really enjoying getting under this guy going into the corners and passing him only to have him scream past on the straightaways so he could do it all over again! The guy in the hopped-up MG didn't seem to be enjoying it one bit, and you could see he was getting more ragged and desperate each lap as he tried to hang on to Cal through the twisty bits. Finally, he lost it in a big way—right in front of me!—getting into one of those ugly left-right-left-right deals and snapping into a spin when he simply couldn't steer fast enough to keep up anymore. The MG plowed into the fencing right smack-dab in front of the Osthoff Hotel! The car wasn't really going all that fast by the time it hit, and about all it did was knock some people over. But there were a few cuts and bruises and one lady got a broken leg when somebody fell on her. So they waved a bunch of yellow flags and ambulances came wailing in from all directions (no question they were prepared for the worst at Elkhart that year) but most people said they'd seen worse at high school football games.

Anyhow, that Spear guy's OSCA ultimately won the race, and my buddy Cal took the trophy for best finish by a truly stock MG and afterward acted like it was nothing special at all. I was coming to understand that about really great drivers: Given any sort of competitive machine and decent opportunity, they *expect* to win.

They got the mess in front of the Osthoff mopped up pretty quickly, and everything was back in place in plenty of time for the thirty-one-lap Elkhart Lake Cup at 12:30 P.M. But it was kind of a letdown after all the close dices we'd seen in the other heats. Simply put, nobody could keep up with the Cunninghams. In fact, Creighton Pendleton didn't even make the grid with his Ferrari. Somebody heard he'd had some valve spring problems, but I was right there when they loaded it on the trailer, and it sounded healthy as all getout to me. There were a couple nicely finished local specials called Excaliburs that looked an awful lot like Sabre jets, but they were just cut-down Henry Js underneath and not really up to the challenge. But they looked neat as hell, and the guy who built them—that industrial designer out of Milwaukee named Brooks Stevens—wanted to mass-produce them as a sort of all-American answer to the MGs and such from overseas.

Tommy and Phil Hill rolled out with our C-types, and, along with Eddie Dearborn's rambunctious Cad-Allard, they looked to be the only possible threat to the Cunninghams. And I must admit Tommy didn't look that sharp, what with his face all pale and drawn like he had a bad case of stomach flu. When the race finally started, it was the three Cunninghams thundering away at the green and roaring away from the field in close formation. Johnny Fitch in the number three roadster and Phil Walters in the evil-looking C4RK coupe soon pulled away from Briggs himself in the other roadster, and you could see those two were just sort of playing with each other at that stage, mindful that 200 miles is a long, long way, and that it's all too easy to use up a race car in short order if you really start flogging it. Phil Hill drew a fourth-row starting position and had to do a little fancy footwork to slice through traffic, but then he reeled in the third-place Cunningham and even managed to pass Briggs after being bottled up for a few laps. Then he took off after the leaders, and you could see that he really had the bit between his teeth. But the Cunningham team signaled their drivers that the C-type was after them, and right away Walters picked up the pace and passed Fitch, and then Fitch turned up the wick and repassed Walters, and the gap to Phil Hill's C-type began to grow.

But it wasn't really Phil's fault, on account of the tin-can muffler had burned through on the inside where you couldn't see it, and the way the air came down the side of the car and up over the door was putting all the fumes directly into his face. At first he didn't realize what was happening or why the road seemed to be wobbling and staggering away from him all the time. But he figured it out after Briggs repassed him for third place, and he spent the last hundred-odd miles with his head hanging over the driver-side door, trying to get a little fresh air and clear out the cobwebs. Meanwhile Tommy worked his way through to a boring, solitary fifth overall after a brief skirmish with Eddie Dearborn in his brutal J2X Allard.

So it turned into a pretty dull procession, with Fitch running a few seconds ahead of Walters (but neither one of them really pushing it to the limit), then a long gap to Briggs in the third Cunningham, another long gap to the woozy-but-recovering Phil Hill, and yet another thirty seconds back to Tommy in our Jag. Fact is, the only race worth watching was between a few standard-issue Jag 120s back in the pack, but I didn't know any of the drivers, so it really didn't mean anything to me.

After the races, I helped Tommy load our stuff into the green Jaguar and we said our good-byes to Ernesto Julio and Phil Hill and Chuck Day and I wound up giving Ernesto Julio his clothes back all wadded up in a ball. But he didn't seem to mind. "Have a good time in them?" was all he said, and I told him I did.

There was a big awards banquet scheduled for 6:30 that evening, but a lot of folks who had twenty- or thirty- or fifty-hour drives home were packing up and heading out just as soon as they could. The spectators had already leaked off down Route 57 toward Milwaukee, and it appeared the big S.C.M.A. victory bash was going to look more like a wake for a poor relation.

Tommy hadn't said much of anything all day, and you could see he was having trouble coming to terms with the way Phil Hill had smoked him. Plus all the hooch he'd packed away hadn't helped matters. But he disappeared with a couple of guys from the Cunningham team after checking us out of our room, and when he came back an hour or so later, he had a little of the old sparkle back in his eye and some small portion of the customary military snap to his step. "I say, sport," he said through a tight grin, "I need you to do me a bit of a favor."

"Sure thing," I told him. "Just name it."

"I have to go someplace right after dinner."

"No problem. I'll give you a lift. Doesn't matter to me."

"No, you don't understand, sport. I need to go somewhere with one of my friends from, well, nevermind from where. But the point is I need you to take Creighton's car back to New York for me."

"*Creighton's* car??"

"Of course. He owns the green C-type. Didn't you know?"

"I don't get it. I thought that car belonged to Colin St. John."

"Well," Tommy explained, drawing close, "it's all supposed to be terribly hush-hush, but Creighton owns the green car. Bought it sight unseen, the way I heard it. But the bloke wanted to know if it was faster than his Ferrari before he took a chance with it. Smart move, that. Didn't want to burn his bloody bridges with Carlo Sebastian and the Muscatelli brothers. So he asked Colin to keep things quiet and find somebody decent to drive it for him, and Colin rang me up to see if I'd be interested."

"Wow."

"Yes sir, he's a pretty shrewd customer, that Creighton Pendleton is. But he didn't bloody figure on the second car. Didn't bloody figure on it a'tall. And I'm sure old Colin quite forgot to mention it during the negotiations."

"That sounds like him. So now what happens?"

"Well, *I* go take a hot shower, get myself some dinner, and head for the airport. As for the rest of it, I suppose Creighton'll have Colin St. John sell the Jag before anybody else finds out he's owned it. Then he'll most likely write Carlo Sebastian a rather huge personal check and buy himself whatever the next hot new Ferrari turns out to be."

"You don't think he'll keep the C-type?"

Tommy shook his head. "I expect not. Oh, it's a wonderful driving car, and possibly the best in the whole bloody world over distance, but it's just not powerful enough for our kind of racing. At least, not on tracks like this one, where torque and top-end power are at such a premium. You need yourself a real brute of a car with a god-awful monstrous engine if you want to run with the Cunninghams...."

"But aren't they in a different class?"

"So what? Classes aren't what's important. At least not to somebody like Creighton Pendleton. Or myself either, come to that. People like us need to be *in there,* you know?"

"In there?"

"Right. You know, scrapping it out at the front of the pack and that sort of thing. That's why I'm going back to my Allard first bloody chance I get."

"You think your Allard is faster than a C-type?" I mean, that just didn't sound right. Why, the Jaguar looked a whole generation lower and lighter and sleeker and, well, *more refined* than any blessed Allard I'd ever seen.

"Oh, maybe not *now,*" Tommy allowed, "but mark my words, my young mechanical friend, it *will* be...."

"I don't get it."

"Nor should you, Buddy. Nor should you," Tommy grinned. "Just remember what your fine president Mr. Roosevelt once said."

"You mean about there being nothing to fear but fear itself?"

"The other Mr. Roosevelt. Theodore. Do you recall?"

I shook my head. I mean, all I knew about Teddy Roosevelt was that he had buck teeth and wore spectacles and led some calvary charge up San Juan Hill.

"Well," Tommy whispered with an exaggerated wink, "Mr. Theodore Roosevelt advised that one should speak softly and carry a big stick, and I believe I've discovered exactly where such a bigger stick might be found."

"I'm still lost."

"No matter. This is still the time for speaking softly, my young friend. Just get that Jaguar of Mr. Pendleton's back to New York without a scratch, don't let on to anyone that it's his car, and be ready to put some bloody long hours in the next few weeks before Watkins Glen." And with that, he handed me a neatly folded wad of twenty-dollar bills.

"Geez, Tommy, what's *this* for?"

"Road emergencies. Bed and board. Phone calls. You know. But I'd actually appreciate a bit of change back when I see you again in Manhattan." He shot me a wink. "But not too awfully much."

And without another word, Tommy Edwards lifted his leather overnight bag out of the passenger-side footwell and headed back into the Osthoff. "And by the way, sport," he called back over his shoulder, "do try not to get arrested."

I decided not to hang around for the big victory banquet, and after Tommy made his mysterious exit, I just flat couldn't wait to get back on the road and home to Jersey. I wanted to see Julie, you know? In fact, I took off with every intention of driving straight through without stopping for food or gas or even to take a damn leak. But that notion faded a little south of Milwaukee, when I about dozed off at the wheel and came to the sudden realization (as I narrowly avoided putting the C-type into a ditch!) that I was tired as hell and desperately in need of some sleep. Driving solo in the green car was lots different from chasing after it in the silver one, and without Tommy out there in front like a carrot on a stick, it wasn't near so much fun. Sure, people still stared at me goggle-eyed out of their Nashes and Plymouths, but I was past getting excited about it. It was just hot and cramped and uncomfortable, and I couldn't believe I'd never noticed it on the way out from New York. Of course, we'd been traveling damn near the speed of sound when Tommy was leading the way, and I was afraid to go much more than ten over the posted limits on my own. I mean, what the hell was I going to tell a cop if he stopped me?

I was past dead tired by the time I reached the suburb of Winnetka about forty minutes north of Chicago, and you should have seen some of the houses there along the lakefront on Sheridan Road, all lit up with columns and archways at the end of long, gated driveways. Why, you could almost *smell* the antique Oriental carpets and wall safes hidden behind oil paintings and perfectly straight teeth on all the kids. It was a world you could never even dream of breaking into from the outside, and I knew it.

But I could maybe sneak a little peek into that life every now and then through racing. And that's why I decided to put myself up for the night at one of those big, fancy, downtown hotels on Michigan Avenue in downtown Chicago. I told myself it was just so's I'd have a safe place to park the Jag, and I figured that old Tommy would probably go along with a story like that. So I followed the ghostly sweep of the Palmolive beacon down the Outer Drive into Chicago, and stopped just about smack-dab in front of it at the Drake Hotel. The doorman was all dressed up in gold braid and brass buttons, and once he got a look at the C-type, he didn't need any excuses for my grubby T-shirt or ragged windbreaker or dirty tennis shoes. "Will you be spending the night, sir?" was all he said, and when I told him to be extra-careful with the car, he bristled and said, "Of *course,* sir," with a little touch of frost in his voice. So I tipped him a whole dollar, just to melt the ice. And it worked like a charm, just the way Big Ed always said it did.

My room at the Drake Hotel cost more than an entire week's pay as a Westbridge race mechanic, but I didn't care. The bed had silk ruffles and you could look out the window and see the Outer Drive arcing gracefully northward toward the suburbs and the searchlight sweep of the Palmolive beacon as it rotated through the low-lying clouds at regular intervals. It was well past 10:30 (which meant it was almost midnight back in Passaic), but I decided to take a chance and call Julie anyway. She answered the phone herself, thank goodness, and I can't tell you how great it felt to talk to her again. She seemed pretty happy to hear from me, too. "So, how've y'been?" I asked.

"Same as always. How'bout you?"

"Yeah. I guess."

"I haven't heard from you in quite a while, Buddy."

"Yeah. I know. I been real busy...."

"That's what I figured. The girls told me you stopped by the Doggie Shake with that English guy on your way out of town."

"Tommy Edwards."

"They said he's pretty cute."

"Cute?" Somehow "cute" was not exactly the sort of word I would have ever used to describe Tommy Edwards. But then, girls have their own private language when it comes to stuff like that.

"So where are you?"

"In Chicago. At the Drake Hotel." And I told her a little about my room and the swell view out my window.

"Sounds nice," she whispered dreamily. "I almost wish I could be there with you...."

"So do I, Julie, so do I," I heard myself whisper back while all sorts of new thoughts and feelings swirled around inside me. Or maybe they were just urges. Sometimes it's hard for a guy to tell the difference. Anyhow, we kind of hung there on the phone line for the longest time—not saying a thing—just sort of running up my long-distance bill and listening to each other breathe and maybe even pretending a little like we were actually alone together in that wonderful and perfect hotel room overlooking Lake Shore Drive in Chicago.

After we hung up I didn't feel much like sleeping, so I took the elevator downstairs and went for a stroll up Michigan Avenue toward the Chicago River. It was chilly that evening, and I had to zip up my windbreaker and pop the collar up around the back of my neck. But it was a nice walk anyway, past all the fancy shops and the Tribune Tower, which looked like a big, empty stone cathedral. Across the street was the Wrigley Building, all lit up and glowing like carved ivory, and every minute or so the Palmolive beacon would sweep across the sky above it. Fact is, I'd always thought Manhattan was about the prettiest city in the world, especially the view across the Hudson from the Jersey side around Englewood Cliffs. But as I walked across the Michigan Avenue Bridge to the other side of the Chicago River and watched one of the late-night party boats pulling in at the dock down below, I had to admit it didn't have all that much on this town.

I noticed a bustle of taxicab activity and people in fancy evening clothes going through a plate-glass revolving door just up the street, and the marquee sign above it read THE LONDON HOUSE. As I walked up that way, I could hear jazz music pumping out in waves every time the door went around. So I thought I'd maybe duck inside and have a listen, you know? But the doorman took one look at me and nodded for me to just keep moving. Didn't even want to check my I.D. or anything. Not that I had any to show him. And that was the problem coming back from a race weekend. I'd somehow forget that I was just a dumb, underage, blue-collar grease monkey from Passaic, and it always took a few rude awakenings and long looks in the mirror before I remembered who I was again. But I slept real well at the Drake anyway, and even left my clothes inside the hollow front door so's the butler service would wash 'em for me. And you know what? They were back in that door, clean and fresh as hospital sheets, by 7:30 the next morning!

I treated myself to breakfast from room service and ate my first-ever serving of eggs Benedict at the antique white table over by the window looking out over Lake Shore Drive. It was pretty good, too. And they brought a morning edition of the *Chicago Tribune* along with my breakfast tray, so naturally I thumbed through to see what they had to say about the races up at Elkhart Lake. I found it eventually, a little half-column item buried on the last page of the sports section, just below a piece about some stupid polo game that nobody on the planet cared about. And this was the biggest sports car race in the whole damn country! Plus it was the first time anybody in those parts got a chance to see the Cunninghams that were carrying the American colors into battle against all the big-time European teams overseas. Why, the Elkhart Lake Police Department estimated the crowd at over *135,000!* That had to be more than any other sporting event all weekend. But I guess that just didn't mean much to the *Chicago Tribune.* Or maybe they simply didn't *know* anything about automobile racing (except for the Indy 500, of course) and I suppose newspaper reporters don't feel comfortable unless they're writing about something they know and understand and maybe even used to do themselves back when they were little kids and hadn't yet discovered that they weren't really any good at it. Which is probably why that *Tribune* sports section was chock-full of dumb-ass stick-and-ball stories about the Cubs and the White Sox— neither of whom were worth dogshit that year. But the worst of it was how that tiny little story in the sports section was written. The headline went something like this:

RACER CRASHES FENCE; 8 INJURED

So thank you, Hal Foust, *Chicago Tribune* sportswriter, for picking out the most telling, important, and newsworthy fact of the entire weekend, and then going on to write three full paragraphs about a few skinned knees and bruised elbows and the one stinking broken leg before getting into anything at all about the damn races. Which is probably why poor old Hal Foust's story was buried way at the back of the *Tribune* sports section. After all, nobody got killed. And a couple bumps and scrapes just didn't rate any large-type headline coverage.

No question that stupid *Tribune* story was upsetting my digestion, so I put the paper down, poured myself another cup of coffee from the big china pot, and looked out at the last of the Monday-morning rush hour traffic jam and the swarms of suits and ties shouldering their way along the sidewalks to work. In a strange way, it reminded me of the union stiffs filing in through the front gate at my old man's chemical plant. Only the clothes and the haircuts were different. And so I took a moment to just say "thanks" to nobody in particular for being able to go to the races and work on sports cars until all hours of the night and then sit up here on a damn Monday morning looking down on all those poor slobs who were heading off to do the same damn thing they did last Monday morning and the Monday morning before that.

I didn't check out until after the traffic cleared, and I must say I was a little flabbergasted at how much it cost to get your shirt cleaned, pants pressed, and eggs Benedicted when you had them hand-delivered to a fancy-ass hotel room overlooking Lake Shore Drive. Sure put a dent in that wad of twenties Tommy gave me for the trip home.

Still, I was in a hurry to get back and see Julie again, so I pushed it pretty good from Chicago to Fort Wayne and on across the rest of Indiana and Ohio toward Pittsburgh and the beginning of the Pennsylvania Turnpike. But it was a long, *long* drive, and not nearly so much fun as the trip out from Manhattan. There was an incredible amount of heat coming through the firewall and a cold wind whipping in over the top of the windscreen and I'd lost my Brooklyn Dodgers cap someplace so my face got sunburned all morning and the back of my neck even worse all afternoon. And no matter how fast I dared to drive, it seemed to take absolutely *forever* to get from each little two-bit farm town to the next, even though I never stopped except to fill up a couple times and do a quick kidney tap in the gas station rest rooms. Even so, it was getting on toward midnight by the time I saw the purple and orange flames of the night-shift Pittsburgh steel smelters licking the sky off to the southeast.

No question I was tired. But when you've been traveling like that for eleven or twelve hours straight, you get sort of lost in the droning, rolling rhythm of it. Sometimes to the point where it's damn near *impossible* to head up the next exit ramp and stop. Then I came up over the top of this hill a little after one and there was the town of Breezewood again, sitting down there in the bottom of the valley like a tin platter of fluorescent light. It was built to be a convenient overnight stop about halfway between Chicago and New York, and it suited me fine to use it for exactly that purpose. I found an all-night gas station right next to a little blond-brick strip motel, and the kid inside agreed to keep the Jag in the service bay overnight for fifty cents. He probably would've done it for nothing. In fact, I thought he looked a little *too* eager, so I lifted up the nose and pretended to check the oil and water, but actually removed the distributor rotor and slipped it into my pocket. It didn't figure you could find spare ignition parts for a Jaguar C-type in the middle of the blessed Appalachians at two in the morning. Not hardly.

Tired as I was, it took me a long time to doze off to sleep, on account of I still had the rumble of the highway pumping through me and the no-longer-mellow growl of that barely muffled Jaguar six vibrating in my ears. But I must've fallen asleep eventually, because I remember waking up early the next morning when some dumb tourist cut off a big eighteen-wheel Diamond-T and the trucker leaned on his entire collection of air horns to register his displeasure.

It was not the sort of noise you could sleep through.

There was no drifting back for a few more winks once I was awake, and I really wanted to be on my way again. I was maybe even a little homesick, you know? Which sounded pretty nuts on account of I was hardly ever home even when I was home (if that makes any sense) but somehow it was nice just knowing it was there in case I ever took a notion to drop by. Plus I really wanted to see Julie again.

So I checked out and walked across the lot to the station where I'd left the C-type, figuring I'd maybe drive an hour or two before stopping for breakfast. But right about then a Ford pickup come rolling up the westbound ramp, and hitched behind was a flatbed trailer with a dirt-track sprint car on top. You could tell they'd been driving all night, on account of it was well past sunup but they still had the headlamps on, and when the rig made a big, wide turn and pulled up in front of the Cozy Cup Coffee Shop, I decided maybe I'd go over and have a slug or two of java and a chocolate-covered doughnut myself before heading east again. So I whipped the C-type around in a fast, screechy arc and brought it up to a perfect halt right next to the tow rig with the dirt-track sprint car hitched to the back.

I always thought those oval-track cars were neat, and no question I had more in common with the dirty-fingernail types who hung around that kind of racing than all the rich playboys and black sheep of wealthy families you found on the sportycar circuit. The flatbed trailer had a Texas plate on the back and the sprinter on top was painted a garish bright red with metallic blue trim and white pinstriping. Kind of sharp, actually, but it didn't take much inspection to see it had a lot of rough miles on it. It wore a big, gold-leaf "77" on the tail and the name "WIN-SOME SPECIAL" spelled out on the hood in matching letters. There were clods of dried clay and fresh oil spatters all over the nose and wind-screen, and when I looked inside the narrow, low-cut cockpit opening, I couldn't help but notice how the driveshaft ran directly beneath the driver's seat—right under the family jewels!—and they had the shifter on the *out*side because there simply wasn't any room for it inside the cockpit. The steering wheel was enormous and mounted close and up-right so the driver could really lean his shoulders into it. No question it took a lot of moxie to climb into a thing like that and sling it around a rutted dirt oval like a damn rodeo rider on a mean bull. So I took special notice of the smaller gold-leaf lettering below the cockpit that read: *"Sammy Speed."* What a perfect name for a racing driver!

Two guys in jeans were staring at me and the C-type through the front window of the Cozy Cup, so I went in, sat down next to them, and ordered myself a cup of coffee and some French toast. One of them was short and wiry, with brown, leathery skin and those special, long distance fighter-pilot eyes with lots of crow's feet at the corners. The other guy was kind of pale and pudgy-looking, and right away I figured him to be the mechanic. "That's a pretty nice rig you got out there," I observed, just trying to make conversation.

"You think so?" the pudgy guy grinned. "Tellya what. We'll swap it fr'that sweet little foreign job you just rolled up in. Right here and now. Whaddaya say?"

"Well, if it was up to me, I just might," I told him. "But it's not my car."

"Do tell." He'd already sussed I was just another wrench-twister.

"Yup, just taking it back home for a friend of mine. An English-man, actually."

"That an English car?"

"Sure is," I told him. "It's an XK120 Jaguar competition model."

"I've heard of 'em. Won that big twenty-four-hour race over in France, didn't they?"

"That's right," I said, really impressed.

"I never seen one before. At least not in the flesh. How'bout you, Sammy?"

The wiry guy with the leathery skin shook his head. "Can't say as I have."

"Well," I explained, "they're really *something*. I'm just bringing this one back to New York from the races up at Elkhart Lake."

"Where?"

"Elkhart Lake. Up in Wisconsin."

"I never heard of it," the pudgy guy allowed, pulling the last half of a used five-cent cigar out of his pocket and lighting up. "You ever heard of it, Sammy?"

"Can't say as I have."

"How long is the track?" the guy with the cigar wanted to know.

"Six and a half miles," I told him. "Up over hills and down through valleys and all over the whole blessed countryside."

"Isn't that something!" the guy said, shaking his head. "You ever run on a track like that, Sammy?"

Sammy Speed shook his head. "Nope. Can't say I've ever had the opportunity." Then I noticed that special little race driver spark light up in the corner of his eye. "But I'd sure as heck like t'try it. In a minute. All's I'd need is a chance."

"He would," the pudgy guy grinned. "And I bet he'd do real good at it, too."

"A car's a car and a track's a track," Sammy Speed allowed. "All's a decent race driver needs is an opportunity."

"Amen to that, brother," his mechanic agreed. "By the way, I'm Spud Webster and this here's Sammy Speed. You prob'ly ain't heard too much about him yet. But you will. Count on it."

"That your real name?" I asked. "It's a pretty good name for a race car driver."

Sammy Speed looked down into his coffee and didn't say a thing. "Aw, don't mind him," Spud grinned. "He's a little embarrassed is all. Aren'tcha, Sammy?"

"Aw, g'wan," Sammy growled, "leave it alone."

"His real name is Sammy Slowinski," Spud whispered, leaning in like it was some big government secret, "but he tells people he had it legally changed."

"Aw, I do not," Sammy snorted, pretending like he was angry. "I just do it for my work, see." You couldn't miss the little twitch of a smile at the corner of his mouth. "I mean, who's gonna hire a race driver named *Slow*inski, huh?"

"Yeah," Spud agreed. "It's like all those Hollywood movie stars, you know? They make up names for themselves all the time."

"Yup," I nodded. "They sure do."

"No reason why a race car driver can't do the same thing, right?"

"No reason at all."

"Glad we agree on that. How'bout you, Sammy?"

"Can't say as it makes much difference t'me one way or the other," he yawned. "Just so long as I get t'drive some decent cars."

"So," Spud asked, "how'd you guys do up at that road race in Wisconsin?"

"Well," I said, kind of backpedaling around the truth, "*my* driver had a few little problems—you know how that goes—but our, um, *teammate* from California won the race on Saturday and finished fourth overall and first in class on Sunday."

"*Really?*" Spud said, obviously impressed. "What's one of those sportycar races pay to win, anyway?"

"Ahh, well, actually," I said, trying to properly explain it, "they don't pay *anything,* see. In fact, the S.C.M.A. specifically *forbids* prize money at their races."

Sammy Speed and Spud Webster looked back and forth at each other like something had just gone wrong with their ears. "Then how can y'make a damn living at it?" Spud wanted to know.

"Well, *I* make a living preparing the cars and hustling 'em back and forth to the races and fixing 'em when they break."

"But how 'bout the *drivers?*"

"Well, *they're* generally the ones who pay me t'do it. Or actually, they pay my boss, see, and he takes 85 or 90 percent and gives me what's left."

Spud took a long drag off the stub end of his cigar and shook his head. "But how do the drivers earn a damn *living?*" he wanted to know.

"Well, most of these guys already *have* money. Lots of it, in fact."

"So they actually *pay* to race?"

"And they can't win *anything?*"

"Yup," I nodded. "That's it exactly."

Sammy Speed shook his head and laughed. "I guess it takes all kinds to make a world, doesn't it?"

"Well, Sammy," Spud grinned, "y'gotta understand that it's one a'them sit-down-to-pee *European* sports, see?"

"I guess. . . ."

The waitress poured us another round of coffee, and I decided to ask about their car and the kind of racing they did. "Well," Spud allowed, "we got us an old Diedt chassis with a Meyer-Drake on twin Riley carburetors, and we run about the whole damn Triple-A circuit. Or we will this year, anyway. Next May we'd really like to try and qualify for the Indianapolis 500, but we prob'ly need a little better car for that. Maybe a year-old Kurtis or something if we can afford it. . . ."

Sammy Speed rolled his eyes, and I got the idea that things were running just a little tight moneywise out on the old Triple-A dirt-track circuit.

"So," I asked, "where're you guys coming from?"

"Aw, we just got done with the big mile track up by Syracuse. Jack McGrath won that one. Sammy here finished fifth, I think. . . ."

"Seventh," Sammy corrected him.

"OK. Maybe it was seventh. But we don't really have the best setup for those long tracks. Not enough power. And the tires was shot. We were gettin' a little low on tire money. . . ."

"Yeah," Sammy Speed sighed. "You could say we've hit us a sort of dry patch the last couple races."

"That's too bad."

"Hey, it happens to everybody now and then."

"Yeah," Spud agreed. "I always figured that was one of the big differences between car racing and most other sports."

"How's that?"

"The odds stink." He took a final drag off the last half-inch fragment of his cigar and explained. "Now, you take a look at most of your popular stick-and-ball sports, and half the people who play get to go home winners after every game. *Half* of them! But you go to a car race—especially a big-time event like the Indy 500—and, even if you're lucky enough to qualify, the odds start out at thirty-three to one and get worse from there depending on how your equipment stacks up."

"So why do it?" I asked without thinking.

Sammy Speed looked at me like I didn't have a brain in my head. "Y'do it because someday you're gonna catch a break and get a chance in a really competitive car, and that's when you show 'em all that you *belong*."

"Then you're *in*," Spud nodded, grinding his cigar stub out in his saucer.

"So, where'd you guys race before Syracuse?"

"Hmm. Lessee," Spud mused, thinking it over. "We ran the week before at Du Quoin, Illinois. I think it was Chuck Stevenson won that race. Sammy was up to fourth, but we lost a cylinder. Plug wire shorted out. Damn insulation melted, y'know? Anyhow, that would've been Sunday, I think. The day before we were up by Detroit for a hundred-miler. Sammy did good up there and finished third. . . ."

"It was fourth."

"OK, *fourth*. Billy Vukovich won that one for J. C. Agajanian. Drove his ass off, too."

"He's a wild one," Sammy Speed agreed with a mixture of awe and defiance. "Someday I'm gonna have *me* a car that good. Then we'll see what's what. . . ."

"Your time'll come, Sammy. No doubt about that."

"Nope. No doubt a'tall." You couldn't miss the fierce look of determination in Sammy Speed's eyes.

"Where was I?" Spud asked. "Oh yeah. Detroit. The week before that was the Milwaukee State Fair, and two weeks before that was

Springfield, and, geez, I can't remember it all straight without my note-book. It's out in the truck. . . ."

"So that's all you guys do? Just go around to the races?"

"Yup. We're on our way to Denver for a race on the twenty-eighth, and I'm hoping we can maybe stop home in Fort Worth t'give the old crate a little rebuild and a few fresh parts. She's pretty wore out right now—the race car and the tow wagon both—and it wouldn't hurt t'check in on my wife an' see if I'm still married. Then we'll haul on up to Denver for the race at Centennial Park, head south when that one's over for the race in Phoenix. If the money holds out, anyways. But that's the last one on the schedule. Fr'this year, anyway. And, like Sammy says, we got some irons in the fire for a little better sponsorship deal and maybe even a newer chassis and engine fr'next year. . . ."

"Yeah," Sammy sighed, rubbing his eyes. "That'd sure go a long way toward putting a few more beans on the table."

"Might even get us in the first couple rows at Indianapolis come next May. That's where the *real* money is."

"Wow!" I said, giving the two of them a low, respectful whistle. "I can't believe you guys actually make a full-time living off this!"

"Neither can we!" Spud laughed.

"Well," Sammy allowed with a tough, weary edge to his voice, "we been at it three whole seasons now, and somehow we're still at it."

"Yeah," Spud grinned, shooting me a sideways wink, "only just *puh-leez* don't ask us how."

16

ANOTHER HOMECOMING

I HAD a lot to think about during the long drive across Pennsylvania and New Jersey. It was a beautiful September day, and the green C-type was running sweet and turning heads everywhere it went. But I couldn't just lean back and enjoy it, on account of I was coming to understand that I would never amount to more than a grunt-level working stiff at Westbridge, and the fact it offered me a chance to rub shoulders with a bunch of rich, stylish people with entirely too much time on their hands and money in their pockets didn't necessarily mean any of it was going to rub off on me. Sure, I loved the exotic cars and the excitement of the races, and no question it was rewarding to put your time and effort into a machine and then have some topflight hot-shoe like Cal or Phil Hill or Tommy Edwards really put the spurs to it and finish up front. There wasn't anything like that in everyday life.

But after meeting Sammy Speed and Spud Webster—two guys who were out there on their last couple nickels, rolling the highway from one dirt-track bullring to the next, trying like hell to break into the bigtime before they went broke and make an actual *living* out of automobile racing—well, all of a sudden those rich sportycar guys started looking like a bunch of lah-de-dah Play Racers. It was all about *money,* see, and I was coming to understand that poor, dull, blue-collar grunts like me generally wound up working for the Colin St. Johns and Barry Splines of this world, or wound up living hand-to-mouth on the road like Spud Webster and Sammy Speed. Or—worse yet—wound up with a lifetime position as some rich dork's Personal Racing Squire like that poor geek Milton Fitting was for Skippy Welcher. And here I was, heading back across the Appalachians in one of the two rarest, fastest, most valuable sports cars in the whole damn country, thinking on and off about Julie and how this really wasn't what I wanted to do with the rest of my life. Sure, I wanted to stay around the racing, but I wanted to earn a decent damn living at it, too! It was a shame my old man wasn't around to hear all that stuff going through my head. I mean, it sounded a lot like all that "responsible adult" garbage he used to lecture me about after the ninth inning was over and there was no beer left in the refrigerator. Then again, who wanted to give him the blessed satisfaction? It made me wonder just what the hell was going on inside of me, you know?

No question some of the glamour had faded during the long road trips and sweaty garage nights and rocky mornings-after. Especially after seeing the look in Sammy Speed's and Spud Webster's eyes when they talked about tire money and how far they were from home and all the nights they'd slept in the back of the truck just so's they'd have enough gas and coffee money to make the next event. And I came to realize I was coming down with a pretty serious touch of the Racing Disease myself, where the days start running together and you're forever swallowed up by the thousands of little details that have to get themselves handled before the next green flag falls and turns the cars loose again. And all of a sudden I saw how a bright, eager, enthusiastic young guy could turn himself into a haggard, bleary-eyed, weak-willed chunk of meat stuck at the end of the socket ratchets and box-end wrenches that actually got the work done. On the other hand, who the hell wanted to make a living doing dumbass tune-ups and brake jobs on the ordinary Fords, Chevys, and Henry Js that all the ordinary rank-and-file lunchbuckets of this world drove to work every morning and out to grandma's house for dinner every Sunday afternoon? But where was the damn *future* in being a race car mechanic?

I did a lot of deep thinking as the C-type and I tooled our way east across New Jersey. The one thing I tried *not* to think about was my night with Sally Enderle up at Elkhart Lake. Not that you could really call it a night, since the entire episode took less than an hour. Truth is, I kind of wished it never happened and wondered if Sally felt the same. And it dawned on me that Sally Enderle probably didn't much care one way or the other. And that, more than anything, was why I felt so, you know, *cheap.*

So my strange experience with Sally was sitting there in the back of my head like one of those old licorice tins eight-year-old boys hide under their mattresses for their mothers to find, usually full of month-old night crawlers or collections of mouse feet from old traps in the basement. But anytime I caught myself starting to wonder and worry over Sally Enderle, it was no problem at all to start myself wondering and worrying over something else. By the time I finally rolled into Passaic around 6:30, I knew exactly where I wanted to go. I headed straight over to the Doggie Shake to see if maybe Julie was on duty. And for a change, I was in luck. From almost a block away, I could see she was standing outside the curb-service window, shooting the breeze with the other girls and waiting for the next burger baskets and root beer floats to come out of the kitchen. I pulled over and did my best to straighten my collar and pat down my hair, then gave the C-type a modest bootful and came swooping into the lot in a reasonable facsimile of a hellacious powerslide. Boy, you should've seen the way everybody jumped up and jammed their noses against the window! That's a thrill you never outgrow in a really sexy sports car, no matter how long you've had it or how many miles you've covered together.

But Julie Finzio wasn't the type to let herself get snowed by any goddam automobile—not even a low, sleek, obscenely expensive racing car like that C-type! She took her own sweet time meandering over to say hello. "So," she said like I was driving a damn Nash Rambler, "what'll it be tonight, stranger?"

Still, you could see in her eyes that she was pretty damn impressed with the Jaguar—not to mention happy to see me!—and there was no question I felt exactly the same about her. But no way would a girl like Julie allow herself to go all soft and mushy with the other Doggie Shake girls watching through the front window. Especially when I'd been off someplace without her for the past couple days. Or at least not without busting my hump for a few minutes to show me how things were. "So," Julie asked again, pretending like it was all she could do to keep from yawning, "you planning to eat something here tonight, or did'ja just drive up to show off your damn car?"

"I came to show off the car, of course," I shot right back. "After all, guys who drive cars like this don't generally eat dinner at dinky roadside drive-ins."

"I'm sure they don't," Julie sighed. "And maybe someday you could see your way clear to introduce me to one of them. I've always been real partial to dumb guys with money." She looked the Jag up and down. "What the heck does one of these things *cost,* anyway?"

"I'm not sure," I said, casually inspecting my nails, "but I heard it's around six or seven times as much as your average, run-of-the-mill Ford or Chevrolet." That was actually a bit of an exaggeration, since it was more like four or maybe five times as much. But guys always tend to pump stuff up when they're talking to girls as a matter of routine procedure. I think it has to do with glands or something.

Julie let out a low whistle. *"Wow!"* she said in little more than a whisper. "Then I guess the guy really *is* rich, isn't he?"

"Most of those sportycar people are."

"And dumb, too."

"How can you tell?"

"That's easy. He's lettin' a bozo like you drive it!"

"Well, maybe he inherited the money and doesn't care."

"Must be."

I was staring so deep into Julie's eyes that it reminded me of those dark tunnels Tommy and I raced through on the Pennsylvania Turnpike. "So," Julie asked without moving her eyes one-thousandth of an inch, "you actually know how to drive this thing or what?"

"Sure thing!" I grinned. "Why, I can drive any damn thing with four wheels and an internal combustion engine."

"Oh, of course!" she laughed, rolling her eyes.

"Hey, don't take *my* word for it. Hop in an' see for yourself. Lemme take you for a quick spin around the block...."

Julie glanced over at the crowd watching us from inside the Doggie Shake. "I dunno, Buddy," she said, backpedaling a little. "I'd love to. Honest I would. But I'm not so sure Marvin'd go for it...."

"*Marvin?* Who the hell is *Marvin?*"

"He's the new night and weekend manager. He's the owner's cousin or something. Anyhow, I'm not so sure he'd like me taking off in the middle of my shift."

The little hairs on the back of my neck sprung to attention. I mean, who the hell was this Marvin character, anyway? Why, I still got P.O.'d every time I thought about that David Sweeney guy who used to manage the kitchen at the Doggie Shake and had the nerve to take Julie out a couple times when I was all tied up over at Westbridge. Not that I had any business feeling that way, you understand. Especially not after what happened with Sally Enderle up at Elkhart just a few short days before. And of course the instant I started thinking about it, my ears started burning bright cherry red and I caught myself staring into the Jag's driver-side footwell like I'd lost a screwdriver or something down there.

But Julie didn't seem to notice, and I can only assume it was because I was so blessed sun- and windburned from riding cross-country in the C-type that she couldn't tell the difference. Anyhow, she went inside to see if she could maybe go for a spin around the block, and I felt real relieved when I saw Marvin the Night Manager waddle out from behind the counter. Why, he didn't stand an inch over five feet and must've weighed 230 or so—a real bowling ball with legs!—so he didn't figure to be much of a threat with Julie. And he was obviously putty in her hands, since it didn't take her more than thirty seconds to convince him to let her go. Just once around the block, you understand. I must admit my heart skipped a beat when I saw Julie take off her yellow-trimmed Doggie Shake apron and matching car-hop cap and head out the door toward where I was parked in the C-type. Jeez, you really should've seen her smile and the sparkle in her eyes!

At least until she tried getting into the car, anyway. I still had all the racing gear and my dirty clothes and such piled next to the passenger seat and packed into the footwell, and all Julie could do was assume a sort of deeply reclined hammock slouch with her legs arched up over

Tommy's track gear and the boxes of spare parts we'd brought along from Westbridge. "You comfy?" I asked her.

"Oh, sure, Palumbo. Like I'm about to give birth."

"Great!" I said, patting her on the knee. "Now hang on!" And with that, I punched the starter button and watched Julie jerk damn near upright as the exhaust pipes exploded to life just below her left ear. She struggled to keep herself up as I reversed out of the parking slot, but flopped right down again when I snicked the lever into first, gave her about 4000 r.p.m., dumped the clutch, and left two smoldering black stripes all the way down Fremont Avenue. I took it clear up to the redline in first, snapped the shifter back *hard* into second, and gave it one more blast before backing out at around 60 and dropping her gently into fourth. Julie's eyes were bugged out like a goldfish on a living room carpet.

"Jee-*zus*, Palumbo," she gasped. "Is this thing ever *fast!*"

"I'd say so!" I nodded enthusiastically. "And you know what else it can do?"

Julie shook her head.

"It can *stop!*" And I proceeded to double-clutch down to second, whip around onto a side street, yank her *slap!-slap!* left-right up an alleyway between two buildings, and jammed on the brakes so hard the car damn near stood on its nose! We were behind the loading dock of Martino's Appliance Store, and before the Jag even rocked level again, I reached over with both hands, grabbed Julie by the shoulders, and planted the Kiss of the Century right smack on the center of her lips. And she kissed me back, too! "Jesus, Buddy," she gasped when we came up for air, "what the hell was *that* all about?"

"I dunno," I told her, my face turning red again, "I guess I just kinda, you know, *missed* you or something...."

And I guess I really did, too.

I kept the Jag overnight in my Aunt Rosamarina's garage, and drove down to Westbridge early the next morning with every intention of quitting. Julie'd told me how her uncle was still having some health problems that he wouldn't talk about, and she'd already kind of greased the way for me to come back to work at the Sinclair if that's what I wanted—and as a Management Trainee, no less. I guess the Old Man had been through another couple more "professional automobile mechanics" (the latest one tried to steal the station's customers so he could work on their cars as side jobs at home) and Old Man Finzio was well past ready for somebody he could actually trust. So I made a point of dropping in on him early that morning before I headed across the bridge into Manhattan. Believe it or not, the Old Man seemed almost happy to see me, and I even thought I detected the faintest wee glimmer of a smile. But you could never be sure about that kind of thing. Anyhow, he ran his eyes up and down the green C-type and gave it a grudging nod of approval. "Well, well, would'ja just look at this here," he rasped. "Looks like one a'them famous international racing mechanics I heerd so much about."

"Aw geez, Mr. Finzio, it's just me. Buddy Palumbo."

"Well, so it is. So it is. Didn't hardly recognize you."

"Must be the car."

"Yeah, that must be it all right." He pulled a wrinkled-up Camel out of his back pocket and lit it up. "So," he wheezed, trying hard not to break down in one of his coughing jags, "what brings an important guy like you around to a little old streetcorner gas station?"

"Well," I told him, sticking out my hand, "I came t'see if maybe I could get my old job back." Now, the truth of it was that I didn't so much want my old job back as to maybe put together a deal for a *better* job. One where I could fix and maintain a lot of fancy European sports cars right there at the Sinclair. One where I could wind up *running* the shop one day, and running it the way *I* thought a really high-class foreign car shop ought to be run. I had this idea in the back of my head that I could bring in enough high-dollar sports car work to make a really decent living there at the Sinclair. I mean, there wasn't anybody else in the area doing it, and every day you were seeing more MGs and Jags and such all over the place. You could charge plenty on those cars, too—lots more than you ever could for Dodges and DeSotos and Buicks—and most of those sportycar customers were only too happy to pay if you could just do the damn work properly and get it finished on time. Why, I might even get a few racing customers so's I could keep heading off to places like Bridgehampton and Elkhart Lake every now and then. Only this time *I'd* be the one who finished up the weekend with a wad of tens and twenties and fifties in my back pocket instead of Barry Spline, you know? And, judging by the yellowish-green tinge to Old Man Finzio's complexion and the ugly noises going on inside his chest, he was gonna need somebody to run the place for him.

But you had to be careful about what you said and how you acted around the Old Man. I mean, he'd kicked the shit out of enough sick, crippled-up, old mongrel dogs in his lifetime to know that the last thing you wanted to be was old and sick and crippled-up. In fact, I'd have to say that morning was the first time I ever recognized pure, cold-blooded *fear* drifting around like a mist in Old Man Finzio's eyes. It wasn't fear of being sick or even fear of dying, but that Worst-of-All Fear of winding up helpless and having to rely on other people. The thought of it had turned the Old Man all withered-up and trembly inside, right below the surface where you could see it plain as day if you knew him well enough.

Anyhow, we shot the bull back and forth for a couple minutes, and he allowed as how he'd "think it over" about letting me come back to work there at the Sinclair. Maybe. If I asked him real nice.

So I did.

Needless to say, Barry Spline didn't take too kindly to my plan to pack up and leave Westbridge. "Where's yer bloody sense of *loyalty?*" he wailed, his nostrils flaring. "Why, we've one bloody race ter go yet h'at Watkins Glen—*the biggest bloody race of the whole bleedin' season!*—and that's when yer decide yer wanter run h'ome t'bleedin' momma!"

"Gee whiz, Barry," I told him, "it's not like *that.*"

"Oh? And just 'ow is it then? We got ourselves the biggest bloody last-minute project of the whole bleedin' year t'finish up fer Tommy Edwards, and yer not plannin' t'be around t'do yer bleedin' share."

"How's that?" I asked, just a little curious as to what the project might be.

Barry curled his lip at me. "Can't bloody tell *you,* mate. Why, h'its top bloody secret!" He snarled, spitting on the floor behind the parts counter for emphasis.

"Really? What *is* it?" In spite of all my thinking and planning and plotting and considering, I was still a sitting-duck sucker for an interesting race car project.

"Can't give any bleedin' information h'out t'somebody like yerself 'oo won't even be around t'lend a bloody 'and...."

"I don't get it."

"Well, why not just take yerself a bloody look 'round the back of the shop, eh?" Barry growled, and walked into the office.

So I did, and it didn't take long to find Sylvester Jones bent over a huge, gaping hole in the middle of Tommy's Allard. "What's goin' on?" I asked.

"How th'hell should *I* know?" Sylvester snorted, fiddling with the fuel and oil lines on the firewall. "They tells me t'pull a damn engine and I *pulls* a damn engine. Even if th'damn thing is running jus' fine as can be. Sheee-*it!* It don't make no damn differents t'me...."

Sure enough, the hot-rodded Caddy V-8 from Tommy's Allard was sitting against the back wall, trickling a little blackened oil and brackish water onto the floor. It made me wonder what was up, you know? I mean, no question that was one *fast* Cadillac engine sitting there against the wall.

About then Colin St. John came rocketing out of his office like a launched torpedo. *"So!"* he snapped in an icy voice, "I understand you're planning to leave us today. Is that the case?"

"Well, er, uh," I mumbled into my collar. "It's just I, uh, I . . ."

"Don't mumble, young man," Colin growled disgustedly. "Let's have it. Spit it out."

"Well, see, it's like this," I told him, hunting around for words like a guy pretending to look for change in his pockets when he knows he doesn't have a cent to his name. "I been doing a lot of thinking, see . . ."

"And?"

"And, well, Manhattan is just so blessed far away from *home,* you know. . . ."

"So *that's* why you're quitting?" Colin demanded, drawing himself up like there was a guywire pulling on the top of his head.

"Well, I kinda got a girlfriend, too, and she's been tellin' me she's plain sick of never seeing me anymore and never going out to movies and stuff. . . ."

"But you've had this girlfriend all summer, have you not?" Colin snapped.

"Well, yeah. Sorta." I could see he wasn't buying it. "And, well, I also got this opportunity to run this gas station back in Passaic, see . . ."

"Oh, I *see* all right," Colin snorted. "In fact, I see *perfectly.* You have an opportunity to take the skills and knowledge you have accumulated right here—*in this very shop!*—and use them to leave us in our time of greatest need so that you can go into business against us." Colin looked down his nose at me like I was a smear of road slime. "I do have that all properly accurate and correct, don't I?"

"Well, uh, geez, Mr. St. John, if you put it *that* way. . . ."

"Oh? And could you perhaps explain some *other* way to put it? My understanding as of ten minutes ago is that you plan to simply take your leave—on a moment's notice!—leaving us in a lurch with the biggest, most important event of our entire summer season at hand, not caring in the least that we have undertaken a *major* engine project on your supposed 'friend' Mr. Edwards's Allard. . . ."

"Uh, gee whiz, Mr. St. John . . ."

". . . A project that will undoubtedly *not* be completed in time for Mr. Edwards to race at Watkins Glen because of your sudden and capricious departure." Colin stared at me with a look of withering disdain and sadly shook his head. "You *are* planning to leave us," he asked me point-blank, "aren't you?"

"Uh, well, gee whiz, a'*course* not, Mr. St. John," I heard myself say, "I mean, you'd have to be a real heel t'do something thing like that. . . ."

"Indeed," Colin agreed softly, and just like that, I realized old Colin

St. John had somehow maneuvered things around and turned the tables on me. Again.

"But I'm still planning to leave after Watkins Glen," I threw in lamely, trying to salvage some small, tiny fragment of self-respect.

"That will be fine with us," Colin agreed coolly. "As a matter of fact, we usually terminate all our race mechanic positions after the last event of the season anyway." He said it like they had maybe two or three dozen race-weekend grease monkeys working there at Westbridge instead of just me. And so, without really thinking about it, I'd somehow agreed to stay on at Westbridge two more weeks until the race at Watkins Glen was over.

I went across to the sandwich shop where I could at least be alone and called Julie's mom's house. But there was no answer, so I called the Sinclair and told Old Man Finzio I'd given my two weeks' notice at Westbridge (like that's what I'd planned to do all along, right?) and would be coming back to work at the Sinclair on Monday, September 22nd. He didn't much more than snarl and grunt once or twice, and it was actually kind of nice to hear him sounding like his nasty old self again. "Say, lissen," he said before hanging up, "y'oughta call Big Ed sometime. He's been droppin' by with that fancy-ass English sports car of his, lookin' fer you. . . ."

"Oh?"

"Yeah. Couple times at least. Y'oughta give him a call over t'the scrap yard."

"Okay. Sure I will. Thanks."

Then the Old Man hung up on me, which was his way of saying good-bye.

So I rang Big Ed up at his scrap yard over by the Jersey shore, and he right away dropped what he was doing as soon as he heard it was me on the line. "Hey, long time no see," he said around his cigar. "Whaddaya been up to?"

"Aw, not too awful much. Just workin' my ass off down at Westbridge. But I been goin' to lotsa races and stuff all summer."

"So I heard. I see a couple a'those high-flyer friends of yours over at the meetings every now and then, see."

"Meetings?"

"The S.C.M.A. meetings over in Manhattan."

"You mean you got *in*?" I couldn't believe it, you know? I mean, last I heard, Charlie Priddle was still Head Man on the S.C.M.A.'s membership committee (not to mention just about every other committee they had) and he'd made it pretty clear he'd sooner take his liver out with a pair of needlenose pliers than let somebody like Big Ed Baumstein into the club.

"Naw," Big Ed groused, "I didn't get in. But I started showing up at the damn meetings anyway. Just to piss off that Charlie Priddle asshole, y'know?"

"What a swell idea."

"Yeah, wasn't it though? But I'd just sort of hang around the bar and buy a few rounds for the guys before the actual meeting started in a private room upstairs. Charlie'd even put a guard at the door just t'make sure I couldn't get in. But I didn't try. Didn't want to give the little prick the satisfaction of having me thrown out. But I got t'know some of the other members pretty good. Even turns out we do a little scrap business here and there with some of 'em."

"Oh?"

"Yeah. Some of 'em actually hold down jobs and *work* for a living...."

"But you still can't get in?"

"Nah. Not unless I have that Priddle asshole fitted for a building foundation or a dock piling first."

"That's too bad."

"Nah, it isn't."

"It isn't?"

"Nah." And then it got real quiet on the other end, and I could almost see Big Ed's cigar making rolls and twirls and figure-eight loops right through the receiver. "I figgered a way so's I can race my Jaguar anyway, see."

"You *did?*"

"Uh-huh. And believe me, it's gonna piss off that Charlie Priddle jerkoff something awful. But there ain't a goddam thing he can do about it."

"Why, that's, that's..."—I was stumbling for words—"...that's just *terrific!*"

"Yeah, ain't it? Anyhow, that's where you come in."

"I do?"

"Yeah. I need for you t'come up to Watkins Glen with me next weekend. T'help get the car squared away and all."

"Sure, Big Ed. Glad to. I got a lot of experience at that stuff now. Honest."

"So I heard. Everybody says you do a good job."

Big Ed couldn't have made me feel any better if he'd given me a hundred-dollar tip. But then I remembered the deal I'd just made with Colin St. John. "Say, lissen, I got one little problem...," and I explained to Big Ed about my two weeks' notice at Westbridge and the big mystery project on Tommy's Allard.

"No sweat," Big Ed answered without skipping a beat. "I unnerstan' how stuff like that goes. Just see you find time t'go through my Jag before we leave. The guy I got on it now's got it screwed up so's it runs like shit. No lie."

"Shouldn't be a problem," I told him, taking a certain perverse pride in knowing his Jag was running poorly without my attention. "By the way, how'dja ever swing a deal so's you could race with those tight-assed S.C.M.A. types?"

"I ain't saying nothin'. Not to you or nobody else. But you'll see soon enough up at Watkins Glen." Big Ed took a long, slow drag on his cigar. "I got a nice little surprise worked up for those guys...."

It sounded like another of Big Ed's world-class ideas, and no question I wanted to be a part of it. "So what can I do to help?"

"Just get the damn car ready. I can leave it over by Old Man Finzio's if you want," he took a quick pull off his cigar. "Th'grapevine sez you're comin' back t'work there anyway."

"Gee whiz," I gasped, "how'dja know *that?*"

"That niece of his with th'big knockers told me. You know, Julie. The one you like so much."

"Oh, really?" I sort of choked. "And exactly when was that?"

"Last week, I think. Or maybe the week before...."

And that's when I started wondering all over again about who the hell was actually running my life. I mean, just as I was getting this notion that I was really Taking Charge of Things and becoming Captain of My Own Ship, I come to discover I'm just another below-deck slob with one oar in the water.

You ever wonder like that?

Back at Westbridge, I asked Barry what the big deal was with Tommy's Allard. "Yer'll see in h'about an 'our, mate," he answered with a mysterious wink. "Let's just say we need yer t'go on a little cross-town parts h'excursion with Colin and me, eh?" And sure enough, Barry came around an hour later and pulled me off the postrace inspection, lube, and oil I was doing on the green C-type. The rumor was it had been sold, and we had to get it all properly spiffed up for its new owner. I only had a little more to do—just the brake adjusters and a spoke check—and I really would've just as soon finished it. But Colin was in a big hurry because "we had to meet something someplace," and I must admit that sounded a little strange. It also seemed odd that we needed three people to go on a damn parts run, you know?

But it was never my business to ask questions around the Westbridge shop, so I packed up my tools and clambered into the back of the parts truck while Colin and Barry climbed in front and then did my best to stay more or less seated on the wheelwell while we shimmied and juddered our way across Manhattan and bounced across the Williamsburg Bridge into Brooklyn. It wasn't until we hit the Sunrise Highway that I realized we were on our way to Idlewild. But I still couldn't figure why we were going or what could possibly require three whole people and a parts truck to accomplish. So my curiosity glands were pumping overtime by the time Barry wheeled us into the airport, and they accelerated to Maximum Flow as we passed right by the passenger terminal and headed up a little access road that dumped us right out on the flight line. Jeez, I'd never been out on an airport flight apron before, and it was a little overwhelming. All around us, big four-motor DC6s and twin-engined DC3s were getting between-flight service and loading up with passengers and luggage. We even passed one of those incredibly graceful Lockheed Constellations (the ones with the three tail fins) done up in Pan American Clipper Service colors that had just returned from someplace tropical, judging from the flower-print shirts and oversize straw hats on the departing passengers. Then one of those double-decker Boeing Stratocruisers passed over on its landing approach—engines howling!—and it felt like an entire Manhattan skyscraper toppling over on us. I know *I* dived for cover (of which there wasn't any in the parts truck) and banged my head on the opposite-side wheelwell. "I say," Barry observed, "did'jer 'ave yerself a wee fright there, mate?" After which Colin and Barry enjoyed a nasty little chuckle at my expense. Real funny, right?

We followed along the perimeter of the field to a faded hangar with some ex-military freight planes and a few beat-up forklifts out front. "Wait here," Colin said, and went inside. So I sat there with the back door open and watched that monstrous Boeing Stratocruiser taxi past, and it was hard to believe that anything that enormous could get off the ground. It was scary just thinking about it. Plus I'd had enough ugly mechanical experiences with cars not to have the greatest faith in ivory-tower engineers who spend their workdays poring over drafting tables (not to mention clock-watching production workers who ultimately screw their stuff together) and you must admit that the sky is a little short on places to pull over and have a look-see if any problems crop up. So it was kind of scary watching those rivet-winged monsters charge down the runway—engines roaring—gaining speed and gaining speed as they strained upward. I swear, my heart stopped cold every time one of them lifted off the concrete and climbed into the sky....

"Ahh, Mr. Palumbo? Excuse me?"

I wheeled around and Colin was staring at me over the seat back.

"Everything's set. Come give us a hand now."

So I followed him into the hangar, and in the middle of the floor was a wooden crate about the size of a Frigidaire. I cocked my head so I could read the label, and sure enough it was addressed to Tommy

Edwards, c/o Westbridge Motor Car Company, Ltd., and the return address was someplace in Detroit. Hmmm. Well, the three of us could hardly budge it—not even with two air-freight attendants helping— and Barry had to back the truck right into the building so they could load it on with one of the forklifts. With a lot of grunting and shoving and cussing and sweating, we managed to get it levered into the back of the truck, and the weight compressed the springs so much that the front wheels damn near came off the ground! It didn't look real stable, so we took a bunch of rope and a piece of chain and kind of lashed it down, and then all three of us piled into the front seat to balance the load. On our way out, a thunderous whooshing sound passed over— like the noise Niagara Falls makes, only from the sky—and I looked up to see one of those fabulous British Airways Comet jets coming in from Europe. *Wow!*

It took damn near two hours to get back to the shop on account of Barry couldn't go much over 20 with that huge crate in back, and the three of us were wincing in perfect unison every time we went over a bad bump or dropped a wheel in a pothole and felt that thing lurch and bang against the floorboards. But we made it, and then it took damn near everybody in the shop to get that thing down on the floor.

"So," I said, wiping off my brow, "what the hell's *in* there, anyway?"

"Well, it's this way, sport," Tommy chuckled as he came through the door. "Let's just say it's that 'bigger stick' I was telling you about at Elkhart." Boy, it was great to see Tommy again, and I was happy to observe he had a little spring in his step and some of the old Tommy Edwards glint back in his eyes. No question he hadn't been himself through that whole business with Phil Hill and the two C-types at Elkhart Lake, and sometimes you worry stuff like that is going to be permanent. But you could see Tommy had his old confidence and enthusiasm back, and he could hardly wait for Barry to grab a crowbar and open that crate. The lid came off with a grating, chalk-on-a-blackboard sound as the nails creaked out of the wood, and that's when I found myself staring at the biggest, widest, meatiest damn automobile engine ever to come stomping out of Detroit. It was a hemi-head Chrysler, of course—just like the ones in the Cunninghams!—and it even had the same special intake manifold (only with Carter carbs instead of Zeniths) and a swept-back set of tubular exhausts like pipes off a monstrous church organ. *Wow!*

"Its got 'igh-compression pistons and oversize valves and a special, h'experimental camshaft," Barry said proudly, "and the lads who built it figure over *three hundred* horsepower at the bloody flywheel!" He nudged me in the ribs. "Give or take a few."

"So," I asked, "what exactly are you planning to *do* with this thing?"

"Why, you and me and Sylvester are going to shove it under the bonnet of Tommy's Allard, of course."

I stared into the big wooden crate, noting how the Chrysler's huge cylinder heads filled it from one side to the other, and how the smooth, streamlined exhausts fanned out underneath, and it occurred to me that this was one *hell* of a large motor to try and shoehorn in to a two-seater English sports car. Even a great, hulking example like Tommy's Allard. "You sure this thing will fit?" I asked.

"Well, Sylvester and me did a little preliminary measuring before Tommy ordered the bloody thing, and far as we can tell, it's going to be pretty bleedin' close all the way. Pretty bleedin' close indeed...."

"Boy, *I'll* say."

"Sheeeee-*it!*" Sylvester sighed, shaking his head. "This gonna be one hell of a fuckin' deal. You jus' wait an' see...."

And of course it was.

But Tommy was as excited as I'd ever seen him. "You just wait till we get this little beauty buttoned into the car," he gushed, patting the big Chrysler on one of its massive valve covers. "Then we'll see about those bloody C-types and Ferraris." He was like a kid on Christmas morning, you know?

But I couldn't see it. Much as I liked and respected Tommy, it seemed to me that his big, chunky Allard was starting to look like a dinosaur compared to the newer cars. Sure, you could always find some way to cram more horsepower under the hood, but you couldn't make an Allard any smaller or lower or lighter—in fact, that big cast-iron Chrysler was going to make it even heavier than before!—and far as I could see, lighter weight and better brakes and niftier handling were the things a driver was going to need if he really wanted to run even-up against the new generation of race cars from England and Italy and West Palm Beach, Florida. But Tommy didn't see it that way. After all, he'd always been the fastest guy in an Allard—won himself a lot of races, too—and no question he hadn't done as well in other cars. So he was developing into sort of an Allard hardcase, and it was blinding him a little to what else was out there. In a nice way, I tried to tell him as much. But he couldn't see it. "Oh, I don't know," he said quietly, smiling down at his new Chrysler FirePower V-8, "I reckon the C-type is better on overall balance. And Creighton's Ferrari is always danger-ous. But with this lump of iron between the frame rails, there's one race my Allard will *always* win."

"What race is that?"

"Why, the race to the next corner, of course!"

Right or wrong, Tommy'd decided if the car could do just that for him, he was a good enough driver to pretty much take care of the rest.

Needless to say, Julie was less than thrilled when I rang her up to explain as how I was staying on at Westbridge for another two weeks. "Yeah, *sure!*" she snorted into the receiver. "It'll be two more weeks, and two more weeks after that, and on and on until you're old as my frickin' uncle. You'll see. Those two English jerks are playing you like a damn violin!"

"No they aren't," I tried to tell her, "it's just we got a whole bunch of work t'get done before the races up at Watkins Glen the weekend of the 19th. I can't just ditch out on them, honey. It's just not right. But it's only two more weeks. Honest it is."

"Humph," Julie grunted. "And you expect me to believe that? Do I honestly look that stupid to you?"

"It's the truth," I pleaded. "Really it is."

But Julie wasn't exactly listening. You know how females can get when they're angry. Especially tough, streetwise, no-bullshit Italian types like Julie. *"So,"* she hissed, *"this* is the thanks I get for kissing up to my asshole uncle so's he'd hire you back on at the Sinclair...."

"But I *am* coming back to work at the Sinclair. Really I am. If you'd jus—"

"Well, thanks a lot, Buddy Palumbo. Thanks an awful lot."

"B-But, Julie..."

"Don't you 'b-but, Julie' *me,* you low-life, bullshitting jerk. Oh, *sure.* You just couldn't *wait* t'get back here to Passaic so you could come to work at my uncle's gas station and we could start spending a little time together...."

"Julie. *Please!* Listen to me! *I SWEAR TO GOD I WILL BE BACK AT YOUR UNCLE'S GOD DARN GAS STATION ON MONDAY MORNING, SEPTEMBER 22ND—BRIGHT AND EARLY—AND IF I'M NOT, MAY GOD ALMIGHTY STRIKE ME DEAD WITH A LIGHTNING BOLT!"*

"Just remember this, Palumbo," Julie snarled into the receiver. "If *He* doesn't, *I* will!"

It's a good idea to take Julie seriously when she says stuff like that. For your own safety, you know?

So now all Sylvester and Barry and me had to do was wrestle that monstrous Chrysler into Tommy's Allard and have it ready to roll in seven days so Tommy could drive it up to Watkins Glen Wednesday morning. And if that doesn't sound like an absolutely monumental task, you have obviously never attempted to change anything on an automobile from the way the manufacturer of record originally intended. Suffice it to say that we spent almost every minute that week buried elbow-deep in Tommy's Allard, doing our best to take care of all the countless mechanical mismatches and "clearance problems" that come with every engine swap. Although the general profile of the Chrysler's oil pan would more or less fit between the frame rails, certain of its other dimensions were trying to occupy space already filled with rather solid chunks of automobile. And of course none of the motor mounts were in the right place and the linkages didn't match up and the water pump outlet was on the wrong side and pointed in the wrong direction and, well, you get the idea. Fact is, we never could've got the job done if it wasn't for a Polish-born machinist from Brooklyn named Roman Szymanski.

Roman Szymanski was already a minor legend around East Coast racing garages by the summer of 1952. He was a pale, tubby-cheeked guy with thinning hair and thick bifocals, and he could be difficult to understand on account of he spoke so softly and only knew a few hard-object nouns and some of your more basic present-tense verbs in English. I guess he left Poland in 1938 with little more than the clothes on his back, and worked his way up to owning a tiny, back-alley machine shop in Brooklyn where he made parts for all kinds of industrial machinery. But then he got "discovered" by some local repair guys (including the Muscatelli brothers), who found out he could do valve jobs and bore cylinder blocks and regrind crankshafts and weld up cracked water jackets and straighten bent cams and rethread stripped stud holes quicker and cheaper and better than anybody in New York. Then somebody from Frick-Tappet Motors got him to make motor mounts and bell housing adapters and such for a few weirdass engine swaps, and all of a sudden Roman Szymanski found himself in the racing business. I guess he enjoyed it (although you couldn't hardly tell, since Roman never seemed to smile or frown or show much emotion) but he sure never had to hunt for customers after that.

I was over by his shop several times that week while we fought with the engine installation on Tommy's Allard, and it was amazing how he could look at something you were trying to do—like, fr'instance, mating up that Chrysler V-8 with the three-speed Cad/LaSalle transmission in the Allard—pull at his eyebrows for a couple minutes, take a few measurements, and in a day or two come up with *exactly* what was needed to get the job done. His lathes and drill presses were all pretty old and mostly German (in spite of the fact that he didn't care much for the Germans—not hardly!), but they were neat and clean and he kept them in perfect running order, and Roman could take those machines and make you damn near *anything*. Even with Roman's help, Barry and Sylvester and me ran into lots of problems. Like getting the exhaust pipes to clear the steering gear and getting the throttle linkage so it opened all four carburetors the same when you stepped on the gas. and cutting a few holes so the hood would close over those four little chrome-pot air cleaners. Plus we had a bunch of other customer cars to get ready and the green C-type to square away for its new owner (whoever it was), and meanwhile I was running back and forth to the Sinclair in Jersey so I could spin wrenches on Big Ed's Jaguar in the middle of the night and all day Sunday. He'd sweet-talked the Old Man into giving me a key, and I had to work my ass off to straighten out all the idiotic stuff that other mechanic had done. The main problem was the thermostatic actuator again, but the guy obviously didn't understand about that and tried to compensate by leaning out the carburetors. He even changed the damn jets! But I tracked it all down and got it fixed, and even reset the valve clearances (which is one *hell* of a job on a Jag twin-cam!) and adjusted the timing chain and then finished it off with new plugs and points and a razor-sharp tune-up. Then I test-drove it into Manhattan on Monday morning, and spent the next forty hours or so putting all the final little five-minute finishing touches on Tommy's engine swap.

But, like Barry explained as he punched the starter button and that big, honking Chrysler burbled to life early Wednesday morning, "H'its always the first 90 percent of a job like this that takes the first 90 percent of the time..."—we watched Tommy climb behind the wheel and charge off toward Watkins Glen in a thundering cloud of rubber smoke—"...but h'it's that last 10 percent of the job that always takes the *other* 90 percent of the time."

17

THE GLEN

THE MORNING we left for Watkins Glen I tooled Big Ed's Jag out of the Westbridge shop about 10:30 and drove across the George Washington to pick him up over by his scrap yard. It was a big, ugly place spread out over a couple of acres with a few rusty tin buildings and a high wood fence around it. But there must've been good money in buying and selling used industrial scrap, or Big Ed could never have afforded that monstrous house of his with the two stone lions out front. He had his bag ready so we were out of there in minutes, but we still had to stop by my folks' so I could grab a quick shower and snatch some clean clothes off the ironing board in the basement.

My mom was home and it was really nice to see her—even for just five minutes—and of course she fussed about how nobody in the family got to see me anymore. Right in front of Big Ed, too, so it was kind of embarrassing. But then she insisted he have a cup of coffee and try some of her famous Dutch apple pie, and there was really no way Big Ed could refuse. So he had to sit there and listen to my mom ramble on about how those darn blue jays were picking on all the poor little wrens and chickadees around the bird feeders out in the yard, and also about how worried she was about her favorite downy woodpecker on account of she hadn't heard him drilling holes in the telephone poles for several days. There was really no stopping her once she got started, but what with all her kids more or less gone (or just in and out for a few minutes) and my old man being a genuine five-star grump and not much of a conversationalist, my mom was almost like The Skipper when she got a run at a fresh pair of ears. But she was bright and pleasant, and no question her apple pie made listening to her pretty easy. I even took a slice along for the road.

Big Ed took over driving, and he was pretty damn impressed with how well the Jag was running. "Boy, you got this thing like brand spankin' new," he grinned, unwrapping another fancy Havana cigar. "What was the problem with it, anyway?" So I tried to explain to him about the starting carburetor and the thermostatic actuator and what the other mechanic had done wrong, but you could see I'd lost him before the end of the first sentence. But that was OK, since I was plenty tired and didn't feel much like talking. So I just laid back against that soft red leather, pulled my old Army blanket up over my shoulders, and drifted off to the sound of the tires on the highway and the rolling purr of that smooth-running Jaguar six.

We followed the same route Butch Bohunk and I took back in August on our way to Grand Island, and like always, it didn't seem as long the second time through. Besides, it was a beautiful early-fall sort of day, and it was nice just leaning into the seat back with the afternoon sun on my face and that green wool blanket pulled up around my chin. I thought a little about Julie and going back to work at the Sinclair, but mostly I remembered how it was on that Saturday morning back in May, sitting in this exact same seat in this exact same Jaguar while Big Ed and me headed out to Bridgehampton for the first sports car race either one of us had ever seen. Jeez, it seemed like ages ago, only at the same time like it was just yesterday. Or maybe the day before. The big difference was that now the yellow-orange fall colors and the smell of harvested fields and burning leaves were in the air instead of the fresh wet green of springtime.

We ate dinner at that same little railroad-car hash house in Damascus where Butch and me stopped on our way to Grand Island, and I really can't say why I told Big Ed it was a good place to eat, since I distinctly remembered that the burgers tasted like coal tar. But it was the only place I knew, and lots of times you wind up going back to the same lousy joints time after time just because they're familiar. Anyhow, Big Ed asked for the best thing on the menu and the waitress recommended chicken-fried steak, so we ordered a pair of them. While we waited for the guy in the kitchen to do his worst, I asked how Big Ed was planning to convince Charlie Priddle and the rest of the armband types to let him race. "It's kind of a surprise," he allowed, his cigar rolling from one side of his mouth to the other, "an' I don't want to take a chance and jinx it. You'll find out soon enough." And then he oozed out a mean little chuckle.

I couldn't wait, you know?

Our chicken-fried steaks were dry and tough and covered with a muddy-looking gravy that was about the same consistency as gear lube and didn't taste much better. But at least the portions were large, what with huge mounds of tasteless mashed potatoes and about a half pound of canned carrots and peas. On the way over to pay the bill, Big Ed let me know in no uncertain terms that *he* was going to pick out the restaurants from there on in. And I couldn't say as I blamed him. But in spite of the food, it was kind of neat going back there again, just so I could think back over all the stuff that had happened that summer and how much everything in my life seemed to have changed.

As we got ready to leave, who should come powering up in a

shower of gravel but Skippy Welcher and faithful squire Milton Fitting. But the amazing thing was what they were driving. Believe it or not, those of idiots were in the green C-type from Westbridge—*my* C-type, for gosh sakes!—and no matter how many times I rubbed my eyes, I couldn't get rid of the frightening, ridiculous, and thoroughly nauseating sight of Reginald "Skippy" Welcher at the controls of the ex–Creighton Pendleton (even though he'd never actually driven it) C-type that I'd personally chauffeured back and forth across half the damn country just two weeks before. To make matters worse, Skippy was wearing a set of those split-panel fighter-pilot goggles and a Union Jack scarf tied around his neck like some kind of Hollywood cowboy.

"What ho!" Skippy shouted, waving his fist in the air.

"What ho, yourself," Big Ed answered, staring at the C-type with eyes full of envy. He'd never seen one before. "Say, what th'hell *is* this thing, anyway?"

"The very latest and best out of Coventry, my good man!" Skippy spewed through a maniacal grin. "A work of high art. An instrument of destruction. A *singing sword!*" The Skipper's face was starting to seethe and pop like hot lava.

Well, as interested as Big Ed was in Skippy's new car, he'd also been involved in enough meandering and unending conversations with The Skipper to know that no automobile on earth was worth going through that again. "Well, see you at the races," he said, fumbling for his keys.

"Indeed we will!" Skippy replied, snapping off a two-fingered salute and one of his patented gold-tooth smiles. *"Tally ho!"* he hollered, popping the clutch and tearing off in a hail of gravel with the engine right on the verge of valve float. I swear, the bastard didn't upshift until he was damn near out of sight. And that's when I realized that he never got out to eat or gas up or even take a pee. He'd only stopped on account of he saw Big Ed's XK120 out front, and wanted to make sure whoever owned it had a decent opportunity to fawn and gape and drool over his new toy.

Big Ed had me take over for the final push up to Watkins Glen, heading up Highway 96 out of Owego, then picking up 234 at Van Etten for the last spurt through Swartwood, Alpine, and Odessa to the junction with Route 14 at Montour Falls. We needed gas anyway, so Big Ed had me turn off Highway 14 onto Main Street heading into the town. It looked like your average small-town street, what with a drugstore and a hardware store and a greasy spoon or two, except for the sheer rock wall at the far end of Main Street—tall as a skyscraper!—with a thundering, frothy-white waterfall tumbling down it like the water was pouring out of the sky! Just across the street was a little brick building with columns in front like miniature smokestacks, and inside were the offices of a local lawyer named Cameron Argetsinger who loved sports cars and more or less put the whole deal together to bring road racing to Watkins Glen back in 1948. It was actually the first place the S.C.M.A. ever raced—at least out in front of the public instead of up and down the driveways of their fancy East Coast estates—and just like Bridgehampton and Elkhart Lake, the local shop owners, bankers, and bartenders were only too happy to have them around.

Big Ed had booked us a cabin at the Seneca Lodge on the advice of a couple regulars he'd bought drinks for at the S.C.M.A. club meetings he couldn't attend on account of he wasn't a member. "It's a little rustic compared to some other spots around town," they advised him, "but the food is good and a lot of racers stay there because it's the only place to sleep that's within walking distance of the Seneca Bar." The obvious conclusion was that the best of the Watkins Glen racing parties happened around the Seneca Bar, and only those who stayed on the premises could stagger or crawl their way to bed afterwards.

The lodge itself was a big log cabin sort of place made up of a large, loud dining hall packed to the rafters with laughing, jabbering racers and a little lean-to bar off the back that was packed even tighter. It was hard finding a parking place in front on account of the lot was jammed bumper-to-bumper and fender-to-fender full of MGs and Jaguars and Porsches and Siatas and Aston Martins and BMWs and Ferraris and Maseratis and just about every other kind of low-slung, two-seater European sports car you could think of. Big Ed checked us in and we dropped our stuff in the cabin (which, as promised, was about as basic as you could get and still be considered an actual man-made housing enclosure) but the air smelled of pine needles and freshly harvested crops, and you could hear owls hooting up in the trees and little furry things rustling in the bushes, all of which made the Seneca Lodge a very pleasant and serene sort of place to be. At least until you ventured into the bar, anyway.

Still, it was a nice feeling, now that I'd been around all summer, how all the racing people chewing their steaks and bellied up to the bar flashed me quick little half-smiles of recognition. Everybody except Sally Enderle, that is, who made a real point of looking right through me as if I had been suddenly rendered invisible. Then again, I had no idea what I would or could have said if she'd done me the courtesy of acknowledging that I was indeed another English-speaking human being whom she might have had a brief, passing acquaintance with some time in the distant past. Like say eleven days ago at Elkhart Lake. But like I said, I was just as happy she was hanging on Creighton Pendleton's arm again and ignoring me the way people of my social class and cultural background deserved to be ignored.

Big Ed bullied us up right next to them, making it even tougher for Sally to look right through me. But she had a real knack for it, and could make her eyes take a quick detour around me each time she scanned the room for somebody important she needed to talk to. And it didn't take long for her to spot a likely prospect, pop up on tiptoe, wave gaily, and take off for some other corner of the room. It was hard to believe I used to think she was such hot stuff, you know? Sure, she still filled out a pair of shorts and a midriff shirt better than any female I'd ever seen this side of a movie screen, but, like old Butch always said about Mean Marlene, "I'd druther have a woman ugly clear through than pretty on the surface and ugly underneath. It ain't near so disappointing that way."

With Sally Enderle gone from Creighton's arm, Big Ed saw an opportunity to strike up a conversation, and he did it in the usual Big Ed Baumstein way by offering to buy him a drink. "Say, I'm Ed Baumstein," he said, sticking out his hand and even removing his cigar for the occasion. "Me an' Buddy here saw you win that big race at Bridgehampton back in May."

"How nice for you," Creighton allowed down his nose.

"Yeah. And I'd sure like t'buy you a drink. That was some pretty damn fancy driving you did up there."

"Was it?" He said it like neither me or Big Ed would know fancy driving if we saw it. But Creighton wasn't above taking a free drink when one was offered. Just so long as it didn't come with any strings attached and he only had to hang around until it was served. "Yes sir," Big Ed continued, not about to be brushed aside, "you did one hell of a job with that Ferrari of yours."

"Hmm."

"And boy, that's one hell of a car, too."

"Isn't it."

"Y'know, I'd like to get myself a car like that someday. One *just* like it, in fact."

A nasty little smile curled up around the corners of Creighton's mouth. "Well," he said into the swizzle stick of his tall gin and tonic, "why don't you buy yourself one then, hmm?"

"Aw, I tried. But it's tough to do." Big Ed knew he was getting hosed around, but he was after something and not about to spoil it by getting mad or giving up. "I tried buying one off that Carlo Sebastian guy, but he didn't have a car for me."

"Oh, really?"

"Nah. He said maybe I could get one someday—one of the *street* models, you know—but no way I could land one of the real racing jobs like you've got."

"And why is that?" Creighton was really jerking him around—just to see him squirm, right?—but Big Ed was a pretty shrewd customer, even if he didn't look it.

"Well, I figure there's only so many of those things to go around, right?"

Creighton nodded absently as the bartender placed a fresh gin and tonic on the edge of the bar.

"So guys like you—guys who've proved what they can do with 'em—get all the latest, hottest cars from Ferrari just as soon as they cross the Atlantic."

Creighton nodded again, his eyes starting to look around for a little better company to enjoy Big Ed's drink with.

"So anyway, see, I was thinking I could maybe *buy* that car of yours off you next time a new one comes over from the factory in Italy, y'know?" Creighton Pendleton the Third slowly rotated his head and looked Big Ed up and down as if seeing him for the very first time. "I'd give ya a good price for it, see, and you really wouldn't *need* it anymore, since you'd have your new one. Right?"

Creighton took a long, slow pull on his drink. "Well, Mr. Baumstein . . . "

"Call me Big Ed, okay?"

"Well, Mister, um, Big Ed, I'm sure that's a very intriguing proposal. But I'm afraid it's just not possible."

"Oh? And why's that?"

"Well, let's just say I've always had a little sort of, um, *arrangement* with Reggie Welcher, and he always gets first crack at my race cars when I'm done with them." Creighton was the first guy I'd ever heard call Skippy Welcher "Reggie," but it sounded just right when he said it. Like ivy climbing up old brick walls.

But Big Ed was not about to give up. "Well, I guess that's a pretty sweet deal for you. But what if somebody were to offer you, say, a little more money. . . ."

"A *little* more money?" Creighton asked, arching up one eyebrow. "And what exactly might that mean?"

"Oh, I dunno," Big Ed shrugged while cash register bells rang in his head like fire alarms, "let's just say enough to make it worth your while. . . ."

I could see Creighton was just jerking him around, trying to get Big Ed to name a figure just so's he could look down his nose at it. But Big Ed had made enough deals in his life—automotive and otherwise—to know that the first guy to name a figure *always* loses. So he tried the old Colin St. John turn-the-tables-on-'em maneuver that generally starts with playing dumb as a post and pretending that the fish across the table is ever so much smarter, shrewder, wiser, and more appealing to the opposite sex than you are. "Tellya what, Creighton," Big Ed said, ordering up another round of drinks, "I'm new to all this sportycar stuff and really have no idea what a car like that Ferrari of yours might be worth—new *or* used— so why don't you just tell me what it would take to get in line ahead of everybody else when you're done with it?"

Creighton Pendleton rubbed his perfectly chiseled chin and searched for the exact combination of words that would chop Big Ed off at the ankles like a stalk of celery. "Well, that's really a tremendous offer, Ed," he said with what sounded like genuine gratitude. "But I'm afraid I'll have to pass it by."

"You will?"

Creighton nodded, picking up the second of Big Ed's gin and tonics. "You see, it's not just a question of money between Reggie and myself. We've always had this, well, this *understanding* about my cars, you see. Reggie always gets them when I'm done with them. Simple as that. Price has never been an issue."

"It hasn't?"

"Absolutely not." Creighton took a quick sip of his drink. "I tell Reggie what I think the car is worth and he writes me a check. We never dicker over *price....* "

Big Ed had never heard of such a thing. And neither had I, come to think of it. In fact, I got the distinct impression it was just an enormous load of bullshit laid out for the purpose of fertilizing the notion that Big Ed and me were nothing but no-class, no-talent, Johnny-come-lately, goofball outsiders. Especially after I caught the snide glimmer flickering in Creighton Pendleton's dark, penetrating eyes. "Well," Big Ed grumbled, realizing he was headed up a dead-end street with no place to turn around, "you just keep it in mind, OK?"

"Oh, I surely will," Creighton assured him. "After all, it's a really *generous* proposition." He said "generous" like it was some kind of incurable medical condition. "Then again," he added as he polished off the last of his drink, "I've never had much of a head for business." He pushed his stool away from the bar, obviously preparing to leave. "But then I guess I've just never actually *needed* one...."

Come Thursday morning we had registration and technical inspection over by the courthouse in downtown Watkins Glen, and that's when I finally got to see Big Ed's top secret plan to race with the S.C.M.A.

He'd gotten one of the other members to enter his car (I'm not sure, but I think it might have been Tommy Edwards) and he presented himself at registration as simply the driver. Now there was always a lot of that going on, with guys like Colin St. John and Ernesto Julio and even Briggs Cunningham entering cars for other people to drive, so no way could any of the hard-line S.C.M.A. armband types say anything about it. But then there was the little question of what made Mr. Big Ed Baumstein think he was capable of operating an automobile at racing speed. Just *who,* the S.C.M.A. wanted to know, ever told Big Ed he had the qualifications to be a racing driver?

That's when Big Ed pulled out one of those fancy leather-grain folders like lawyers and insurance salesmen carry and produced a bona fide American Automobile Association racing license and a bunch of ironclad paperwork to go with it. Now the Triple-A sanctioned almost all the big-time oval track races (including the Indy 500) and Big Ed knew they cooperated with the S.C.M.A. in running the road races at Watkins Glen. It was already a matter of record that the S.C.M.A. accepted A.A.A. licenses, since that Phil Walters guy who drove for Briggs Cunningham had raced the Triple-A circuit for years. So Charlie Priddle and the rest of the S.C.M.A. tight-asses had themselves a real problem with Big Ed Baumstein, on account of there was no way they could keep him from driving without creating a hell of a red-tape procedural mess. And those guys knew what they were up against, since they absolutely lived and breathed red-tape procedural messes every day of the week. They couldn't refuse his car without refusing the other entries from the guy who made it (whoever that was) and they couldn't keep Big Ed from driving unless they also shot down one of the star hotshoes on the Cunningham team. And that wouldn't do at all.

So Charlie Priddle and his armband buddies were outmaneuvered, and they knew it. The only loophole was to try to find something wrong with the car, but I had that Jag in perfect order, and knew she was ready as the best of them. Not to mention we had quite a few friends among the drivers and mechanics by then. The truth was that Charlie Priddle and his wolf pack of armband police were only a small percentage of the rank-and-file S.C.M.A. membership, but they somehow wound up *running* the show on account of all everybody else wanted was an opportunity to fire up their damn sports cars and go *race.*

Tommy Edwards came over to congratulate us after we cleared tech, and then he kind of eased Big Ed aside and told him to watch himself and be careful and not do anything stupid on account of Charlie and his buddies would be circling like vultures, just looking for an excuse to yank his dubious ticket and send him packing. "Keep your eyes on the mirrors, sport," he advised Big Ed, "but don't *ever*"—he wagged his forefinger under Big Ed's nose—"don't ever even *think* about moving over to make room for an overtaking car."

Big Ed looked confused. "How's that?"

"When a faster car comes up behind," Tommy explained, holding his hands out palms down to illustrate like racers always do, "the poor bloke has no idea if you've seen him or what you're about to do."

"So?"

"So the safest thing for everyone involved is for you to just drive along on your proper racing line and let *him* worry about how to get around you."

"It is?"

"Absolutely. It's the only way a faster driver can be sure of where you'll be. If you take a notion to be a good sport and pull over to make room, he may well have already committed to passing you on that side. Do you see what I mean?"

You could see the gears spinning behind Big Ed's eyes while he thought it over. "Yeah, I see," he said. "You wind up in his lap."

"That's it exactly," Tommy smiled, and patted Big Ed on the shoulder. "Outside of that, just relax, have fun, glance in your mirrors every now and again, and don't do anything stupid."

"Hey, thanks," Big Ed told him.

"Oh, and try to get a little practice around the circuit today and tomorrow. There won't be any on race day."

"There won't?" I asked, wondering just what the hell guys were supposed to do if they'd never raced at Watkins Glen before.

"No, I'm afraid not. They can't close down the roads until early Saturday morning, and, what with three races on the schedule, there simply isn't time."

"But how'rya supposed to know which way the damn road goes?"

"Well, they *do* give three warm-up laps before each race on Saturday, but I don't reckon that's enough to really familiarize oneself with the circuit."

"Oh?" Big Ed said, looking just a little bewildered.

"Look, I've got an idea. Let's you and I take a quick lap or two right now."

"Right now?"

"Absolutely. I can show you around. Then you and the mechanical Boy Genius can go out for a few more laps this afternoon—not at speed, you understand, just to more or less get the *feel* of things—and maybe I can take you out again tomorrow morning for a little fine-tuning. How's that?"

Naturally, Big Ed couldn't thank Tommy enough, and by then I was pretty sure he was indeed the guy who'd entered Big Ed's XK120 for him. Not that he was saying anything about it, on account of there were more than a few S.C.M.A. bigwigs with their oh-so-blue noses out of joint because a guy named Baumstein was running around loose in their own private playpen. But you could see Tommy was getting something out of the deal, too, since he seemed to be gaining a lot of his old *Dawn Patrol* confidence back by acting as sort of tutor and racing maven to Big Ed. And I was enjoying the hell out of it, since every now and then Charlie Priddle would stalk past with a look on his face like he was having serious gallbladder trouble.

While Big Ed and Tommy were out learning the course, I took a little stroll down Franklin Street, which was the main drag through Watkins Glen and also served as the start/finish straightaway for the races. I ran into Cal and a few of the MG guys at a neat little clapboard coffee shop and I joined them for a cup or two of java. Turns out Cal rode up with Carson Flegley again, but this time Carson was bound and determined to drive the TD himself in the Queen Catherine Cup smallbore race, so Cal was once again out shopping for a ride. And he wasn't having much luck, either. The guy with the evil Ford-powered MG was a no-show after putting it into a spin, a ditch, and a tree trunk in quick succession during a "shakedown run" after they'd completed repairs following Elkhart Lake, and although he wasn't hurt, the car was going to need all winter to get back in shape again. "How're things goin' with you guys?" Cal asked while sopping up a few quarts of syrup with the last of his French toast.

So I told him about Big Ed's Triple-A license and the look it'd put on Charlie Priddle's face and all about shoveling that monstrous, fire-breathing Chrysler into Tommy's Allard and how I suspected that Tommy was the guy who entered Big Ed's 120 for him. I was happy to see Cal got as big a kick out of it as I did. "So," I wondered out loud, "you got any fish on the line yet this weekend?"

"Well, the prospecting hasn't gone too awfully well," he sighed, swirling the coffee around in his cup. "But we didn't roll in until two, and I've only had this morning to work on it."

"Something'll turn up."

"It sure better. I'm supposed to stand up at my sister's wedding this weekend, and all hell's gonna break loose at Castle Carrington when I get back."

"So?"

"So it'd be a damn shame to catch all that flack for *nothing....*"

I could see his point.

"Well," he grinned, snaking on his aviator sunglasses and flashing me all those brilliantly white rich-kid teeth, "time t'go to work. Wish me luck."

"Good luck," I told him. And I meant it.

"And say," Cal added as he eased up out of the booth, "you think you could maybe pick up the tab for breakfast. I'm a little, er, *financially embarrassed right now....*"

"You're *always* flat dead-ass broke," I told him. "Every damn time I see you!"

"I'm *never* broke," he corrected me. "It's just that my resources are generally tied up in high-yield but unfortunately nonliquid assets, and as a result I can find myself temporarily between money. Anyhow, can you pay for breakfast?"

"Yeah, why not," I agreed with a helpless laugh. "After all, why should a high-line, well-to-do person such as yourself be expected to carry any loose change in his pocket?"

"Thanks, pal," Cal said as he headed toward the door. "You saved me having to crawl out the damn men's room window again...."

After breakfast I finished my walk up Franklin Street and looked into the barber shop and the bakery and a bunch of dumb little tourist shops that sold ice cream and Indian curios and stuff. It was amazing how similar and yet how different Watkins Glen was from Elkhart Lake. Especially when you got to the far north end and looked out over Lake Seneca, which was huge, deep, steel gray, and serious compared to the cozy-looking water at Elkhart. It disappeared off to the north like a small ocean, and was wide enough east-to-west so you had to squint your eyes to make things out on the opposing shoreline. Down at the south end of Franklin Street was the entrance to the other big tourist attraction, a woodsy glen full of steep rock faces and tall, spindly waterfalls with a stone stairway that went all the way to the top and took more than an hour to climb. I know, because I did it.

After that I just wandered around looking at all the cars and people flowing into town. Traffic was tied up in knots with armband people unloading hay bales and Porsches and Jags and MGs double- and triple-parked while the owners jawed back and forth about where to eat and where to drink and where to buy ice, not to mention all the rank-and-file tourists making the rounds of the restaurants and curio shops and wandering right across the damn street whenever they felt like it. Big Ed said it took him fifteen minutes to drive the five lousy blocks from the north end of town to where I was waiting for him in front of the courthouse, and the gurgling noises under the Jag's hood left no doubt he was telling the truth. "Think I better shut it off?" he asked, staring bug-eyed at the temperature gauge.

"Well, it might be better to go around again if we can get a little

clear running outside of town. You shut her off when she's hot and
she'll get even hotter."

"She will?"

"Sure," I said, hopping inside. "You shut an engine off and the
water stops circulating and she climbs even higher. It's OK if you're
just gonna leave it cool, but you're prob'ly better off to see if we can
find a place to give her a run up to 40 or so and push a little wind
through the radiator."

That made sense to Big Ed, so he chugged us down toward the
south end of Franklin Street, past the gas station and the Glen View
Souvenir Shop to where the racecourse swept hard right and then
curved immediately left as it climbed up the long, steep grade of Old
Corning Hill. And all of a sudden we were *free*—out of all the traffic
and meandering pedestrians—charging up that hill as it curved gently
to the right and just kept climbing and climbing and *climbing!* Big Ed
wound the Jag all the way out in second and upshifted to third—foot
to the floor!—and you could feel that hill sucking the guts out of the
Jag's engine. Made you wonder what a TC or a TD would be like?
Why, you'd be lucky not to *lose* r.p.m., even with the throttle mashed
clear to the stops. And then I started thinking about the big, hot-rod
Chrysler we'd crammed into Tommy's Allard, and how maybe he knew
what kind of "bigger stick" he needed for a place like Watkins Glen
after all.

The road flattened out at the top and then dropped through a
shallow, tree-covered gully just past the Seneca Lodge, and then it
headed into some narrow, sweeping esses coming up out of the trees
and a pretty decent straight section with a gut-hollowing dip where the
road dived abruptly under a railroad bridge. We were doing maybe 65,
and you could really feel the Jag coming down on the springs at the
bottom and then getting all floaty-light as it rocketed off the hump on
the other side. It didn't help any to look over and see Big Ed's eyes
were wide as saucers and that he'd bitten off the business end of his
cigar and apparently swallowed the rest. And I could see why when I
looked up and saw the road take a flat, gentle sweep to the right and
curl back to the left ahead of us. That's where Sam Collier got himself
killed in Briggs Cunningham's Ferrari during the second lap of the
1950 race, and it was all too easy to see how it must've happened. Like
all the really dangerous spots at Elkhart, this was simply a nondescript
little bend in a narrow road. But it was approached at top speed in
fourth gear and the fast guys took it without lifting. Or at least they
talked about taking it without lifting. What made it so dangerous was
the penalty: There was simply no place to go if you misjudged it. A
solemn-looking grove of trees stood off to the left like a congregation

of green-cloaked monks with their hoods up and heads bowed in prayer. *Waiting* . . .

So I was pretty relieved when we came up on a bunch of small-bore racers out learning the course and Big Ed had to back off and fall in at the end of the queue. Especially after I saw what was coming up next. We'd climbed I don't know how far uphill since we'd left downtown Watkins Glen, but as we braked for the hard right at School House Corner, the track suddenly lost all that elevation in a *big* hurry. The roadway plummeted downhill through a series of wrenching, bobsled-run switchbacks with trees close in on all sides, pounded across a humpbacked stone bridge at the bottom, and started climbing again through another dense, green forest until it broke through at the top and the oiled gravel turned to hard-packed dirt. There was a dramatic, broadsliding right called Archy Smith's Corner and then hard on the gas down a long straight and over a bumpy railroad crossing that tossed the cars in the air so's you could see a foot of daylight under the wheels if the driver had the moxie to keep his foot in it. Then came another pavement change—to cement this time—as you passed the entrance to Glen State Park and found yourself cresting a gentle rise to one of the most spectacular and daunting sights in racing. There you are, way up at the top overlooking a carpet of treetops with Lake Seneca spread out all wide and deep and somber down below. You're entering Big Bend, which is a fast, endless sweep to the right taken in top gear with no guardrail at all and the fear of tumbling oblivion stuck under your left elbow like an armrest. It was another of those spots that separated the men from the boys, and I didn't need Cal or Tommy to point it out to me. The pavement changed yet again as the road descended into Watkins Glen like a hawk swooping out of the sky, and at the bottom there was a sharp left at Milliken's Corner followed immediately by a 90-degree right onto Franklin across from the Jefferson Hotel. It was 6.6 miles all the way around, and I'd have to say I thought Elkhart was scary right up until I took my first ride around Watkins Glen. The Glen wasn't as fast on lap average because of the tough climbs and the fact that there weren't so many long straights, but it was narrower, had steeper grades, ran over four different pavements, and was generally reckoned to be more demanding by the drivers.

Besides, people had died there.

We partied it up at the Seneca Lodge that night with Cal, Tommy, Barry Spline, and a bunch of the MG guys, and Cal was in pretty good spirits even though he hadn't located anything to drive. Then again, staying in good spirits and keeping his confidence up were never problems for Cal—especially when he had a minor-league snootful—and you had to keep that sort of appearance up if you ever expected people to hand over the keys to their race cars. I caught myself thinking what a sweet deal it would be if Cal could drive for that Ernesto Julio wine guy from California. Not that Ernesto didn't already have a super-duper driver in Phil Hill, you understand, but Cal was my friend.

Friday the Cunningham team arrived with their big transporter and freshly pressed white coveralls and set up an impressive bivouac in a roped-off corner of the Jefferson Hotel parking lot on Franklin Street. They had the same three cars and drivers, and you could see the cars had been painstakingly hammered out and touched up and hosed down and polished to a smooth, gleaming finish during the two short weeks since Elkhart. You could do that sort of thing when you had a lot of willing hands available (and moreover, enough cash to put paychecks in those same hands come the end of every week). Briggs did it all with a scale, style, and sense of commitment that put everybody else in the shade, and it says a lot about the guy that most everybody seemed to like him anyway.

Phil Hill and Chuck Day showed up with Ernesto Julio's silver C-type, which they'd left in Wacky Arnolt's warehouse in Chicago after Elkhart Lake, flew home to California, then flew back again ten days later to pick it up and drive it east for Watkins Glen. Seems there was some special deal cooked up for Johnny Fitch to drive it in the unrestricted Seneca Cup race Saturday morning before Phil Hill took over again for the big Watkins Glen Grand Prix feature later in the afternoon, while Fitch hopped back into one of the Cunninghams. I guess Briggs's team wanted a firsthand reading on the C-type from one of their own drivers, and Ernesto Julio was happy to oblige (with, of course, the unspoken understanding that Briggs would be the car's new owner if it got fetched up against a tree someplace). Phil Hill didn't seem too put out about it, and reckoned he'd have no trouble landing something else to drive in the Seneca Cup. I wished him luck, but I was actually a little depressed about it, seeing as how the presence of a known commodity like Phil Hill on the market cut the odds on a Seneca Cup ride for my buddy Cal Carrington even further.

And all the while, streams of cars and people kept pushing their way up Highway 14 into Watkins Glen, stuffing that little resort town until it was ready to burst at the seams. The drivers could hardly even practice by noon on Friday, seeing as how all the roads were clogged with people looking to get into town or looking to get out of town or looking for friends they were supposed to meet or trying to find a place to stay. And there were more people coming all the time! In fact, that was one of the hottest topics Friday night at the Seneca bar:

"I heard there's over *fifty thousand* spectators here!"

"I heard it's more like a *hundred* thousand!"

"That's what I heard too!"

"Hell, you can't get a room anyplace for a hundred miles!"

"Really?!"

"Absolutely!"

By closing time, it was up to roughly a half-million people (give or take a few) and there were no rooms available at any price in all of upstate New York....

Ernesto Julio arrived at the Seneca driving a brand-spanking new '53-model Packard Caribbean convertible in kind of a deep plum with creamy gray leather and it was unquestionably the first one that anybody had ever seen. The rumor was that he'd flown into Syracuse that afternoon, taken a cab over to a local Packard dealership, and *bought* that car right off the transporter—like I said, it was the very first one—just so's he'd have something nice to drive for the weekend. Truth is, the ten-day Garage Thrash I'd endured to get Tommy's Allard and Big Ed's XK120 ready had left me a little out of touch with the staggering flash, style, and wide-open money tap you found around sportscar racing. But it only took a couple hours in the field or a few drinks at the bar to get accustomed to it all over again. Why, these people talked about flying across country to pick up race cars and buying brand-new Packard convertibles and taking off for Europe or Palm Beach or Bermuda whenever their busy racing schedules allowed like it was *nothing*. And it was all too easy for a dumb, blue-collar grunt like me to get intoxicated with the smell and taste and feel of it and start to thinking like he was really a *part* of that life instead of just one of the damn supports holding it up.

The party in the Seneca bar was going full steam, but I didn't much feel like joining it. So I just kind of hung around in the parking lot, wandering up and down the haphazard rows of cars while a brilliant, icy-blue sliver of a moon climbed over the tree line, gleaming off the chrome grilles and jaunty fenderlines of all the MGs and Jaguars and Aston Martins and Ferraris and Porsches and Allards and OSCAs and Siatas and Frazer Nashes and even Ernesto Julio's brand new Packard convertible. They were all so wonderfully *different,* you know?

It was getting pretty cold outside, but the more I listened to the muffled whoops and hollers coming from the lodge, the less I felt like going in again. What I really wanted was to call Julie, but it figured to be pretty late and I was afraid her mom might answer. But damn if they didn't have a pay phone screwed to the wall right beside the stairway to the main dining room. And, wouldn't you know it, I had a bunch of loose change jangling around in my pocket too.

It rang and rang, and just about the time I panicked and went to hang up before anybody could answer, someone picked up the receiver.

"Whoozis?" an angry voice demanded from the other end of the line. It was Julie's mom all right, and, as you can imagine, she was not sounding exactly pleasant.

"Uhh, hi there," I said like I was handing her a dozen roses, "is Julie home?"

"Whaddaya mean, izza my Joolie home? A'course a'my Joolie's home. Why, it's past a'middanight, fer'Godda sake."

"Jeez, is it *that* late?"

"A'sure it is. Whattsamatta wit'you, anyways?"

"Uh, gee whiz, Mrs. Finzio, I ..."

Then there was a big commotion at the other end, and next thing I knew, Julie was on the line with me. And the funny part is, I knew it was her before she even said a thing. It was like I could just *feel* it, you know?

"Buddy?" Julie asked, still half asleep. "Is that you?"

"Yeah," I admitted, feeling stupid as hell since I really didn't have much of anything to say. "It's me."

"Is anything wrong?" She sounded a little worried. Really she did.

"Uh, n-nothing, honey," I told her. "Nothing at all."

"Then why are you calling so late?"

"I dunno," I mumbled, kind of shuffling around on my heels. "I just wanted to, you know, *talk* to you...."

"At twelve-thirty in the morning?"

"Gee whiz, is it *that* late?"

"Yeah, it sure is." Now she sounded sort of angry. But just a little bit, you know? "Say, have you been drinking?"

It being a race weekend, that pretty much went without saying. "Jeez, I'm sorry," I told her, sounding particularly lame. "Hope you're not sore about it."

"It's my mom who looks sore about it," Julie said with just the faintest hint of a laugh. And I could almost see her old lady standing there in her bathrobe—hair up in curlers, eyebrows arched, arms folded tightly across her chest—wagging her head disgustedly while sparks shot out of her eyes.

"Well, I guess maybe I better hang up and let you go back to sleep."

"I guess you'd better."

"Well, g'bye then."

"G'bye." She went to hang up, but I could feel her stop and wait for a moment. "Buddy?" she said softly, her mouth right down next to the receiver.

"Yeah?"

"Thanks for calling."

That sent a warm, soft sort of ache rolling through my system, and when I hung up and looked around again, it reminded me how *perfect* it would've been to have Julie up there with me that weekend. That very *minute,* in fact, standing there in the parking lot of the Seneca with the stars and the pine trees and that waning sliver of a moon overhead and muffled laughter filtering out from the bar. There was just enough chill to make us want to snuggle up together as we headed off to bed in our own little cabin. It sounded pretty damn good to me, you know what I mean?

I made my way back to the cabin wrapped in all sorts of dreamy-steamy fantasies about me and Miss Julie Finzio. But they disappeared the instant I opened the door and discovered Big Ed sprawled out on the bed like a sleeping hippopotamus and snoring up a storm. Jee-*zus,* I'd never heard a noise like that in my life! At least not from a human being, anyway. It was like thunder through wet gravel or maybe a slow freight passing over a creaky old railroad bridge, and so it took me a long, *long* time to drift off to sleep, and not one minute of it was that deep, pure, warm black hole that leaves you feeling rested and refreshed in the morning.

But no matter what, Race Day brings its own special buzz to perk you up, and I was up at the crack of dawn with my eyes popped open like fried eggs. Why, I didn't even have a hangover. It was overcast and damp outside, with a chilly dew beaded up over all the cars in the parking lot. You could smell hot coffee and frying pans full of sizzling bacon and hash browns over in the kitchen, and I decided it would be a great idea to have myself a real major-league breakfast feast, since this was probably going to turn into a very long day. But as I passed Big Ed's XK120, there was no missing the way the front bumper was right down on the grass and the dash cowl wasn't any higher than the MG parked next to it. Something was very definitely wrong, and it didn't take much investigating to reach the conclusion that all four tires were flat. It could've actually been kind of funny—at least after the initial flash of anger wore off—and certainly in line with the sort of pranks and hazing that rookie drivers get as a matter of general principle. Only the sonofabitch who pulled *this* stunt was downright malicious. Instead of just letting the air out (or maybe even unscrewing the tire valves and walking off with them), this rat-bastard had snipped the valve stems clear off with a pair of side-cutters, so I'd have to somehow get Big Ed's car up off the ground, pull all four wheels, find some way to truck them into town, locate a new set of inner tubes that would fit our 6.00 × 16 Dunlops, dismount and remount all four tires, get the wheels balanced, bring everything back, put them on the damn car, and then get Big Ed's Jag back down to the paddock before the roads closed for the first race. So much for breakfast.

But I got it handled, thanks to Tommy and Carson and especially Ernesto Julio, who didn't think twice about lending me his new Packard convert so's I could carry the tires down into town for repairs. In fact, he *insisted,* and actually seemed kind of happy about it—as if the opportunity to do noble, outlandish things didn't come around often enough in this life. "But what if I get it *dirty?*" I asked, eyeballing the virgin gray leather inside that plum-colored Packard Carribean.

"Oh, hell, Buddy, don't worry about it," he laughed. "That's what soap and water are for!"

And I had to admit, he was right.

I had all the wheels off and loaded in the Packard by the time Big Ed rolled out for breakfast, and I told him to just take it easy for an hour or so and that I'd take care of everything. I mean, the last thing I needed was a loud, monumentally pissed-off Big Ed Baumstein all over me while I was trying to get a big job done in a desperately short amount of time.

I got three inner tubes off Barry Spline (who was none too happy about getting hauled out of bed at 6:30 ayem) and the fourth out of the spare in the trunk. I couldn't just use the spare as it was, on account of Big Ed hit a pothole in Brooklyn a solid lick and bent the rim, and so no way could you use it on a race car. The Atlantic station down on Franklin Street had a mounting stand and a couple tire irons handy and a compressor to supply the air, and I sweet talked the pump jockey into letting me use them even though neither the owner or the resident grease monkey was on hand. "Y'know, I'll get my ass fired if th'boss ever finds out," the gas station kid told me while I worried one of Big Ed's tires off its rim. "Jiminy, I'm not s'posed t'let *any*body come in the shop. Not ever. And if—"

"Look," I told him, "this is an *emergency,* understand?"

"Yeah," he said, not sounding real sure about it, "I *guess* so. . . ."

After the kid helped me finish the job and load everything back into the Packard, I reached in my pocket and slipped him a folded-up dollar, passing it to him under my palm the way Big Ed used to when I worked on his Caddies back at the Sinclair. "Jeez, *thanks,* mister," the kid gasped, holding the bill out in front of him like it was a damn sawbuck or something. Truth is, I couldn't ever remember anybody calling me "mister" before.

I had Big Ed's Jag squared away in plenty of time to make it down to the paddock before they closed the roads, and a quick check with Tommy Edwards indicated everything was shipshape with the Chrysler-powered Allard as well. Tommy reminded me to keep an eye on Big Ed and whisper soothing words into his ear every now and then, seeing as how he was obviously getting a serious case of the prerace jitters.

You could tell by the way his eyes bugged out and how his stogie was hesitantly wobbling its way from one side of his mouth to the other.

There really wasn't much to do at that point except find a spot along the fencing to watch the races. Along the way, I saw my buddy Cal stalking around the paddock with an uncharacteristic scowl plastered across his face and his hands jammed deep into his pants pockets. I guess Carson Flegley had timidly held his ground about driving the TD himself that weekend, and since the only real practice sessions were the three warm-up laps before each race, there'd be no opportunity for Carson to change his mind and hand the car over even if he wanted to. Cal did manage to finagle a drive in some older guy's XK120 around closing time at the Seneca Friday night, and he was really looking forward to having a crack at a Jaguar. Only now that morning had arrived and the illuminating effects of the liquor had worn off, the older guy was having second thoughts. But of course there was no way he could come right out and *tell* Cal he was backing out of the deal. After all, that wouldn't be *gentlemanly*. So he'd come up with some cockamamie story about the oil pressure gauge fluctuating during the drive down to Franklin Street that morning, and while it would be perfectly OK for him—the owner—to blow the damn engine sky-high, he surely didn't want to put an innocent and honorable fellow like Cal in the uncomfortable position of being responsible for a devastatingly expensive repair bill. In fact, those were his exact words: "a *devastatingly* expensive repair bill," just so Cal would be sure and understand that he was doing it for Cal's own good.

"Aw, don't worry about it," I told Cal. "You'll get plenty more chances to drive in this lifetime."

"Yeah, sure," Cal snorted, turning the ends of his frown down even further.

"No, *really*," I told him. "I mean, everybody knows what a super driver you are. You'll get your shot."

"That's easy for *you* to say," he groused, nudging the gravel around with the toe of his Bass Weejuns. "*You're* not missing your sister's damn wedding back home just to be up here for the races. Jesus Christ, Buddy, my life may not *go* much past Monday morning. . . ." And then, without warning, that mischievous old rich-kid smile came out of nowhere and spread across his face like sunlight peeking from behind a cloud bank. "Aw, what the hell," he sighed. "Let's go watch the damn races and see if any of these jerkoffs can drive."

The first heat of the day was the Seneca Cup for "unrestricted" cars, and Cal and me worked our way toward the south end of Franklin

Street while the cars assembled on the grid for their three warm-up laps. Most of the heavy runners like the Cunninghams and Tommy's Allard and Creighton Pendleton's Ferrari and the standard-issue XK120s were saving themselves for the big Watkins Glen Grand Prix feature later that afternoon, so you had a field of mostly dinky little open-wheel Formula III cars and some strange hybrids like a Chrysler-powered Lea-Francis special and even a few stripped-down TCs running on alcohol fuel and breathing through Rootes-type superchargers. The prerace favorite was a rather notorious S.C.M.A. regular named George Weaver in a scruffy but blazingly fast 4.5-liter Maserati Grand Prix car he called "Poison Lil." It was from before the war, but under the scrapes and dings that thing was a real thoroughbred. It had a magnificent supercharged V-8 that ran on some exotic fuel blend that made your eyes tear and nose run, and it howled like a squadron of dive-bombers whenever he cracked the throttles open. Then again, the Maserati brothers were machinists by trade back in Bologna, and everything they made was beautiful to behold. Except for maybe some of the welds. But Weaver's car was getting a little long in the tooth by 1952, and there figured to be some serious competition from the silver C-type Ernesto Julio had so generously lent out to Cunningham driver Johnny Fitch for, um, "evaluation."

And that's exactly how the race played out. After three warm-up laps, the cars gathered down the middle of Franklin Street again, and when the Great White Hunter guy brandished the green, George Weaver lit the fuse and that supercharged Grand Prix Maserati took off like a scalded cat, leaving streaks of rubber all the way to corner one! Johnny Fitch was a little more conservative at the start, but began picking up the pace after a little familiarization and was right on Weaver's tail by the end of the third lap. Next time around, the C-type was in front by at least a hundred yards, and you could hear that the hard edge had come off the Maserati's engine note. It went out a lap later with clouds of expensive-looking smoke coming out of the tailpipes (head gasket was my guess) and it really wasn't much of a contest after that, as Fitch and the silver Jag led as they pleased the rest of the way home. But it was really something to watch that guy drive, and even Cal had nothing but admiration for the way he took the exact same line—down to the damn *inch!*—lap after lap. Fact is, it made you wish Skippy Welcher would've put Phil Hill in the green one, just so's we could've seen those two duke it out head-to-head in identical cars.

Next up was the Queen Catherine Cup for small-bore cars (which made you wonder who comes up with those names, anyway) and although it was a big field and there was the usual cut-and-thrust dicing among the stock MGs, the race for the overall win was once again a real snore. Bill Spear won going away in one of those handsome little OSCA MT4s, and Jim Kimberly (the same one from Kimberly's Korner at Elkhart Lake) finished second in another just like it. They were beautiful cars, those little OSCAs, and I heard from Barry Spline that they were built by the Maserati brothers—the same guys who dreamed up that awesome supercharged single-seater we saw in the first race— after they quit working for this big industrialist guy who bought them out when they were going bankrupt for about the fourth or fifth time. But the Maserati brothers didn't much like working for a big industrialist guy—it just wasn't their style, you know?—so the day their contract ran out, they packed up their machine tools and moved back to Bologna so they could live the way they wanted to live, build the cars they wanted to build, and go bankrupt every now and again whenever the mood struck them. Only problem was they couldn't use their own name on account of the big industrialist guy still owned the rights to it. So they called their cars OSCAs (which stood for Officiallizzone Specialliazzone Constructiazzzone Automobillinni or something in Bolognese) and even if they couldn't afford to build *big* race cars anymore, they built maybe the slickest, quickest, and most beautifully proportioned little ones you ever saw.

Third place in the Queen Catherine Cup went to that West Coast guy Roger Barlow in his blue Simca special, but he was way back and more or less cruising around on his lonesome. Fact is, except for a little MG dogfight halfway down the pack, the only interesting thing was watching our buddy Carson flog his black TD around. He was well toward the rear of the field, of course, and that got Cal to muttering about how *he* should've been out there instead. But I pointed out that at least Carson wasn't dead last (in fact, I think he may have had as many as five or six cars behind him, and at least half of those were running on all four cylinders!). Besides, he'd managed to keep it on the road, and you'd have to say that was a real improvement in his driving style. Better yet, he *finished* the damn race—his first ever!—and even managed to pass another car right there toward the end. As you can imagine, Carson was floating a good two feet off the pavement when he climbed out of his steaming TD afterwards, and I don't think I ever saw a face as happy and proud and satisfied with itself as Carson Flegley's when he pulled his helmet off. Why, he could hardly talk, and there was even a timid little swagger in his step as we headed over to get ourselves some ice cream. Cal Carrington even *bought* (can you believe it?) and that really put the icing on the cake. Carson had a grin hung across his face like it was hooked on his ears, and you could tell that—at least for those precious few moments of his life—he had indeed become the brave knight who slew the ferocious dragon, the courageous

private who single-handedly saved the whole platoon, and Rita Hayworth's favorite leading man . . . all rolled into one!

Things were running more than an hour behind by the time the
cars pulled out for the big Grand Prix feature race, and, what with all
the people milling around on Franklin Street and the general confusion
getting the cars lined up and the reports coming in from the corners
that there were spectators wandering across the racetrack, I kind of
wondered how they were going to get everything back in order for the
race. The three Cunninghams filled the first three grid positions, and I
was thrilled to see my guy Tommy chuffing out to take fourth slot on
the outside of the second row. But the joker in the deck was two rows
behind, as none other than our favorite lunatic Skippy Welcher pulled
up in his newly acquired C-type, waving to the crowd and flashing his
gold-tooth smile and revving that poor Jag's engine like there was a
special trophy for bending valves on the starting grid. Directly ahead of
The Skipper (and looking plenty concerned about it!) was Creighton
Pendleton in his blood red Ferrari, and next to him was Phil Hill in
the other C-type, staring straight ahead with no expression on his face
at all. He almost looked mean, you know, but it was really just concentration. Phil Hill knew the Cunninghams and Tommy's Chrysler/
Allard and even Creighton's 4.1 Ferrari had a lot more suds than his
"little" 3.4-liter Jaguar, and, what with the steep grade up Old Corning
Hill, there was no question he'd be lucky to just hold position for the
first half lap or so. You could see the wheels turning under his pudding-
bowl helmet as he went over the track in his mind, trying to figure out
exactly where and when and how he might sneak past those guys.

It was a good ten minutes before they got the rest of the field lined
up, and Big Ed Baumstein was one of the last. He actually should've
been five or six rows up from the back based on engine displacement,
but Charlie Priddle and his armband brigade decided it might be better
to start him at the end of the field where he couldn't do much damage,
and for once I had to agree with the wisdom of their decision. In fact,
it was a pity they couldn't do the same with Skippy Welcher.

I walked over to see if Big Ed needed anything, but he was pretty
much past talking by that point. He had on this shiny, fresh-out-of-the-
box racing helmet without a scratch on it (the sure sign of a rookie)
and he'd even had it painted the same creamy ivory-white as his car.
Truth is, that's about as far as I ever saw Big Ed go in terms of color-
coordinating his wardrobe. He was wearing a pair of those split-lens
aviator goggles, too, and through the glass you could see that the look
in his eyes was both fearsome and desperate.

It took another twenty minutes before they got all the crews and
wives and girlfriends and photographers and hangers-on cleared out of

the way, and when the Great White Hunter guy circled the green flag, those big engines fired up and down Franklin Street, fluttering the flags and banners and reverberating off the shop windows. Then the starter jerked his arms skyward and the field roared away for their three practice laps. We heard them snort and grumble through the hard right-hander past the Atlantic station and thunder up Old Corning Hill, fading off into the countryside. And then it got all hollow quiet, even with thousands of spectators lining the street eight- and ten-deep along both sides. Why, you could even hear the rustle of a slight breeze through the early-fall leaves and the gentle flap of the red, white, and blue cloth pennants they had strung up between the telephone poles and even the birds chattering to one another up in the trees.

It seemed to take forever for the three Cunninghams to reappear at the far end of Franklin Street, all tied together and accelerating brutally out of the last corner. Briggs was on the point, and you got the notion that neither Phil Walters or Johnny Fitch was about to take a dive inside and try to outbrake the boss. At least not during practice, anyway. A little ways back was Tommy in our Allard, working hard on finding an empty bit of pavement so he could try out the new engine on his own rather than mixing it up with other cars. Creighton was right behind him, probing to find out what the Allard had and where it was weak, and you could see Phil Hill was doing exactly the same as Tommy, working on an open piece of track where he could come to terms with what the C-type could do for him at a place like Watkins Glen. The really good drivers are always thinking and plotting and planning ahead about what they're going to do after the flag drops. The other guys just *go!*

Like Big Ed, for example, who was still way back at the tail end but obviously giving it everything he had. He was winding that poor engine right up to 6500—maybe even more!—and shifting like he was trying to rip the damn lever out by the roots. So it was no huge surprise when he didn't come around at the end of the second practice lap. I just hoped the damage wasn't too serious, seeing as how Big Ed's Jag was *supposed* to be my ticket home when the racing was over.

"You think he blew it up?" I asked Cal.

"Well, if he didn't," Cal allowed, "it wasn't for lack of trying."

The field formed up down the middle of Franklin Street at the end of the third and final practice lap, and I ran out real quick to see if everything was OK with Tommy's car and find out if he knew what happened to Big Ed.

"She's running like a bloody rocket," Tommy grinned. "But I didn't want to show my hand to the three blokes in those white cars up ahead."

"You think you can actually *take* 'em?" I asked incredulously.

"I don't rightly know," Tommy said with a wink. "Let's just say we'll have a little something on tap for them when the bloody green drops. You'll see. . . ."

"Did'ja see Big Ed?"

"Oh, he's all right." Tommy paused to check his gauges. "Although I don't know if I can say the same for his car. . . ."

"Oh?"

"He's got it parked on the downhill to the stone bridge. Looked like an awful lot of smoke and oil. Think he might've dropped it into first instead of third there for a moment. That's all it takes, you know."

"Yeah. I know."

Shit.

Then one of the armband people rushed up to shoo me away, so I grabbed Cal and we started bulling ourselves a path toward corner one. We really could've used Big Ed right then, and I had to think he would've been better off there with us, too, instead of out on the circuit with a busted Jaguar. We only got about halfway before the green dropped, and you couldn't really see much through the crowd as the pack thundered past in a tumult of splattering exhaust and swirling rubber dust and cars streaking by one after the other like a rocket-powered freight train. Brake lights flashed as they slowed hard for corner one, feinting and darting for position, and then the noise wailed up Old Corning Hill—louder and more desperately than before—and faded into the distance until it was deathly quiet all over again. I remember a large gray cloud inched stubbornly in front of the sun just then, and the temperature seemed to drop eight or ten degrees in an instant. There was nothing you could do but look back and forth at the people packed along the snow fencing and wait. . . .

It was the three Cunninghams of course, roaring out of the last turn one-two-three and rocketing down Franklin Street. But Tommy's Allard was on them like a shadow, and there was no mistaking the move when he pulled out and passed one—right in front of us!—and made it stick all the way through the first turn. *"He's GOT 'em!"* I whooped, clutching Cal's arm.

"He sure does!" Cal shouted right back. *"And I bet he's not done yet!"*

"Not hardly!" I hollered, jumping up and down. *"Not hardly at all!"*

It was a good hundred yards before the next cars came by, and sure enough it was Phil Hill in the silver C-type with Creighton Pendleton's Ferrari glued to his decklid. You could see the Ferrari was faster in a straight line and trying to pass, but Phil kind of clogged up the middle so there really wasn't room for a decent move on either side, so Creighton had no choice but to think better of it. By the next time around, Phil had enough distance that it wasn't much of an issue anymore. After those two came a bunch of other Allards and XK120s and right away Cal and me looked at each other with the same question in our heads: Where was The Skipper and his green C-type? But no sooner had we thought of it than Skippy's Jag appeared, stuttering and banging up the start/finish straightaway at barely a walking pace until the engine cut completely and he coasted to a silent halt right in front of us.

Oh, Lordy, I thought. *What's he* done *to that poor car?*

The C-type had come to rest in a pretty bad position—right on the line Tommy'd taken to pass that third-place Cunningham—and of course Skippy was grinding the starter like he was ringing the doorbell to an empty house, trying to fire it up again. It obviously hadn't occurred to him that there might be a *reason* why the fire had gone out. Milton Fitting was nowhere to be seen so Cal and me hopped over the fence to see if we could help out. Or at least get him out of the way before the cars came around again. We had a little less than four minutes before the cars came around again, so we flipped the latches and lifted the one-piece alloy hood—The Skipper still grinding away relentlessly on the starter—and it didn't take a mechanical genius to figure that Skippy's new C-type Jaguar was out of gas! We were just a few yards up the road from that Atlantic station where I'd gotten Big Ed's tires handled, so I vaulted the fence, ran to the pumps, and the kid who'd helped me that morning was already out there with a jerry can, filling it for us. I figured we had a couple minutes at best, so as soon as he had a few gallons in, I grabbed the can, crashed my way through the snow fencing, and did a high-speed jerry can waddle back to the green C-type. Skippy was still hard at it with the starter button, and you could hear it was already groaning and making that occasional, disheartening *click-click-click-click* noise that starters make when the battery has had quite enough of them, thank you.

We fueled her up and slammed down the hood, and by then there was no way that poor old car could start itself, so Cal and me and the armband people who'd been screaming at us to *"GET OUT OF THE GODDAM WAY!"* gave the Jag a hefty push (putting, I might add, several nice-sized palm dents in the alloy rear deck) and the C-type caught after about fifteen feet and stuttered away, gasping for the float bowls to fill up and feed the suction. Me and Cal gave each other a quick appreciation nod, and then the armband types were shoving us back behind the fencing because the leaders were due any moment.

And this time Tommy was up to second! And bearing down on the lead Cunningham, too! But I couldn't help noticing that Briggs himself was in the lead car, and I wondered if the other two Cunningham drivers were maybe holding back a bit to see if Briggs could stay

ahead of Tommy's Allard. Surely if he got passed, the other two would
be within their rights to run a little harder and pass Briggs so a Cunningham could still win the race.

Phil Hill was about halfway between those guys and Creighton's
Ferrari, running all alone, and you got the idea that he might be a
factor before this thing was over. The C-type may not have had the
legs on sheer power, but you could see how smooth and nicely balanced
it was running by itself, and Phil Hill was getting the most out of it
and yet still saving plenty of car for the last half of the contest. A
hundred miles is a long, *long* way around a track like Watkins Glen,
and the really gifted drivers have the knack and patience to see all the
way to the checker flag from the instant the green goes down.

We strained our eyes up Franklin Street again, and this time the
first car to appear was—Omigod, it was Skippy Welcher in the green
C-type!—sailing out of the last turn in an unkempt broadslide and
blaring that sweet Jag six right past the redline in every gear as he
charged towards us. But not a thirty yards behind was Tommy's roaring
black Allard—*in the lead!*—with the three Cunninghams in a vicious
clot right behind him. You could see that Tommy was going to pass
The Skipper just as they approached the braking point for turn one,
and I could feel the hairs rise to attention on the back of my neck. The
corner workers were waving the blue overtaking flag furiously, and
Skippy obviously saw them, because he looked down at the mirror on
the dash and nodded like the situation was well in hand. Tommy swept
out to pass on the inside, and that's when The Skipper did the one
thing a slower driver should never, *ever* do when being overtaken. He
pointed his finger towards the *out*side and pulled right across the Allard's nose to leave room for Tommy on the proper inside line. He was
just trying to be courteous, actually. Only Tommy was already committed, and he had no choice but to yank Hard Left to avoid The
Skipper while the Allard was already up on tiptoes under heavy braking. The car slewed left, tail swinging wide, then caught traction for an
instant and swung back the other way—for a heart-stopping moment
teetering up on two wheels!—and then made that final, uncontrollable
snap back the other way. It would have spun all the way around . . . if
only there'd been *room!* Instead it sideswiped the snow fencing, sending
fence slats and cardboard boxes and race programs and half-eaten hot
dogs flying like an explosion. Then the outside wheels bit *hard* and the
Allard went into a tumbling, flailing barrel roll, shedding wheels and
fender panels and headlight buckets and even Tommy Edwards himself.
The car skated across the pavement and smashed into a light pole—
upside down—while Tommy's body skidded and bounced up the racetrack, coming to rest in a tightly curled lump right in the middle of the

road. *With the whole damn field bearing down at a hundred-plus miles an hour!* Corner workers grabbed every flag they could find and brandished them wildly, and I saw Tommy's form curl even tighter as race cars came thundering around him on all sides, some missing him by inches—even fractions of inches!—time and time again. It seemed to take a lifetime before the last car passed....

Somehow—incredibly—none of them hit him, and as soon as the final car cleared, I was over the snow fencing and running full speed toward where Tommy's body was curled up on the asphalt, twitching. I got there before anybody, but didn't know what to do. I was afraid to touch him—like I might make things worse—and a wretched feeling of helplessness came over me. Then Cal got there with a few armband people, and it was Cal who finally reached down and tapped him gently on the shoulder. "You OK down there, Tommy? Can you hear me? Are you OK?"

"Believe it or not," Tommy's voice came from what sounded like very far away, "I think I am." He eased his helmet up between his shoulder blades and gingerly eased it left to right and up and down. "Bloody hell," he said in an amazed whisper. "I do believe I am...."

"You *sure?*" one of the workers asked.

"Don't move!" Charlie Priddle commanded.

"Oh, piss off," Tommy groaned, and pulled unsteadily to his feet. You could see he had a bad cut on his forearm and an absolutely huge pavement raspberry down his thigh, but as he gently shook himself here and there and here and there again, nothing else seemed terribly amiss. "No broken bones apparently," he said with a halfhearted smile, "but I reckon I'll be pretty bloody sore tomorrow."

"Thank God!" I told him, totally amazed that *anybody* could be that lucky.

"But I suppose I've about used up my bloody car." He turned to take a look, and that's when he saw all the anguish and confusion going on where he'd sideswiped the fence. Spectators were scattered like fallen bowling pins with corner workers and armband types crouched over them and the first medics on the scene dashing madly from victim to victim, trying to assess the damage and take care of those who needed it most. And there, right in the middle of everything—crumpled against the curbing like a heap of soiled laundry—was the crushed, battered, and lifeless body of a seven-year-old boy. *"Oh my bloody God."* Tommy gasped, sagging to his knees, *"Oh my bloody God in heaven...."*

18

DEATH IS NEWS

IT TOOK forever to get things sorted out that afternoon at Watkins Glen. A bunch of ambulances came to take care of the people who were hurt, and most of the injuries were just cuts and bruises and broken arms and shinbones from when Tommy's Allard hit the fence and sent people flying. Except for that poor little dead boy, who was pressed right up against the slats and probably froze solid when he saw that car careening toward him instead of diving for cover like your average grown-up. Tommy's left-rear fender caught him dead center at about 70 or so, and that's all there was to it.

I have to admit the S.C.M.A. armband types and local volunteers did a pretty good job cleaning everything up—especially given the circumstances—and then there was even a brief discussion about whether the race should be restarted. A few of the S.C.M.A. clubbies who'd driven in from all over the country wanted to do it, and the truth is there was a certain heartless merit to their argument. I mean, nothing on God's green earth was going to mend those broken bones or close those open wounds or bring that seven-year-old boy back to life, and the idea of *quitting* because people got hurt just didn't sit right with many of the racers. And the fans, too. But the State Police had other ideas, and the discussion was finished in a hurry once those guys put their collective feet down. The party was over, and it was time for everybody to pack up and go home. *There's nothing more to see here, folks. . . .*

Tommy Edwards was in pretty rough shape. He tried walking back to the paddock with us, but he didn't make it more than a few choking, unsteady steps before the exhilarating *I got away with it* rush bled off and he realized that he was hurt worse than he thought. Turned out he had a broken wrist, five cracked ribs, and a dislocated shoulder in addition to the cut and the pavement rash you could see at first glance, and he finally had to sit down kind of sideways on the asphalt and wait for an ambulance to take him to the hospital. Cal and me tried talking to him, but he was off in a different world, just staring straight ahead without seeing anything and shaking a little every now and then like he was cold. "Do look after the car now," he said blankly as they loaded him into the ambulance.

Big Ed's car needed looking after, too. The ivory Jag came down the hill on a hook about an hour later, and things didn't look too promising when I popped the hood and saw oil all over the place and a jagged hole about the size of a league ball in the side of the engine block. Obviously, he'd wound it so tight a damn rod broke, and no question this was going to be one of those "devastatingly expensive repair bills" the other XK120 owner warned Cal about earlier in the day. "I was right next to this guy, see," Big Ed explained ruefully, shaking his head, "and I couldn't hear my own motor because his was makin' so much racket." He looked down at the oily mess in the engine compartment. "I dunno, maybe I just forgot to shift. . . ."

At least you had to hand it to him for not coming up with a bunch of lame excuses. Anyhow, we had a hell of a time making arrangements to get Big Ed's broken Jaguar and Tommy's wrecked-and-rolled Allard back home. There weren't any spare trailers around to get the job done, and it would've cost an arm and a leg to have one of the local tow truck operators haul the Jag all the way to Jersey. And Tommy's Allard was well past towing in any case. Big Ed finally managed to get hold of one of the truckers who hauled scrap steel for him, and they dispatched a flatbed semi with a bunch of rope and tie-downs from someplace in northern Pennsylvania to pick the cars up. Without even thinking about it, I told him to have them both hauled back to Old Man Finzio's gas station in Passaic.

Naturally there was also a big official flap going on with Charlie Priddle and his armband posse. This was a major opportunity for them to flex their muscles and actually *do* something, and by God, they were not about to miss out on anything as irresistible as that—regardless of the seriousness of the occasion. They huddled in a private banquet room in the Jefferson Hotel for hours, listening to eyewitness reports and jabbering back and forth and interviewing anybody they could lay their hands on like the damn House Un-American Activities Committee. They were still hard at it long after we got the remains of Tommy's Allard dragged back to the Atlantic station where the Jag was stashed. Big Ed had slipped the kid there a fiver, so the weekend was really a step into a brand-new tax bracket for him.

Nobody heard the official results of the Jefferson Hotel meetings until a week later in New York. They pulled Tommy's racing license for a year—can you *believe* it?—and hit Skippy Welcher with a dinky little one-race suspension. I mean, he *pointed*, right? Far as I was concerned, it was the most flagrant miscarriage of justice since the Sacco-Vanzetti trial. But it sure got everybody's attention, and, when you get right down to it, that was really the whole idea.

Big Ed and me wound up riding home in the back of Barry Spline's parts truck, sitting on cases of 40-weight Castrol and kind of wedged in sideways between the spare wheels and tires. Truth is, I don't remember anything about that ride except it was uncomfortable as hell and seemed to take forever. Oh, and Barry charged both of us halves on the gas (but I guess that went without saying, you know?). Anyhow, it was well past one by the time we hit Big Ed's house, and he lent me the black Caddy to follow Barry down to Westbridge so's I could pick up my stuff and a bunch of Butch's tools that I'd weasled over there. I wanted to be sure and have everything ready over at the Sinclair come Monday morning. It was amazing how right and natural that seemed. It was like from the very beginning I'd known my job at Westbridge was only temporary, and that I somehow *belonged* back in Jersey, working at the Old Man's gas station and sleeping in my own bed every night and, most especially, being closer to Julie.

For sure I'd miss Sylvester, but then I knew I'd see him all the time when I came over to pick up parts for Big Ed's Jag and any other British cars I could line up as customers at the Sinclair. And somehow I knew there'd be quite a few. So I didn't feel anything particularly sad or momentous as I loaded Butch's tool chest into the trunk of Big Ed's black Sixty Special. Except maybe it was much heavier than I remembered it, what with all the British Standard sockets and wrenches I'd added to his collection. It was a pretty damn complete set of English sports car tools now, and that's exactly what I intended to need over at the Old Man's gas station.

I arrived back at my aunt's house on Buchanan Street just as the first purplish-black silhouettes of the trees started standing out against the sky, and I made sure to lock up Big Ed's Caddy before heading up the creaky stairway to the apartment over her garage. And did I ever have a surprise in store when I opened the door and gave the light cord a tug. Somebody'd been *in* there while I was gone and cleaned it up for me! Jeez, the floor was swept and there were no orphan socks scattered everywhere and all the dishes were squeaky clean and neatly stacked under the sink and all my clothes were washed and ironed and folded away in the little broken-down chest of drawers I had over by the window. Why, the damn bed was even made! And with fresh sheets and pillowcases, too.

At first I thought maybe my mom did it, but that didn't make any sense. I mean, she had enough to do cleaning up after my dad. And it sure wouldn't be like Aunt Rosamarina to go snooping around somebody else's apartment, even if she did own the building. And no way would any of my sisters make my bed unless it was to short-sheet it for me. No, it had to be Julie. Sure enough, under the pillow was one of those sappy Hallmark cards with hearts and flowers all over it. "Welcome home, Buddy," it said inside in Julie's perfectly rounded script, "Love, Julie." And then, down at the bottom: "P.S. I threw away those horrible magazines you had hidden under your mattress. They're disgusting!" And I knew right away she'd looked through every one.

I felt my ears starting to burn, but at least it made me smile. That was the first smile I could remember in what seemed like ages. But there was no way I could relax and go to sleep. Every time I closed my eyes, I kept seeing my own personal newsreel footage of Tommy's wreck over and over on the inside of my eyelids. I had this crazy feeling like it was just some kind of nightmare, and if I could just manage to stay awake, the day somehow wouldn't be over and there was some impossible chance that things might turn out differently. But if I allowed myself to drift off, that day would be sealed forever and turn into history that could never, ever change.

That's when I opened my eyes to brilliant sunlight streaming in through the window and heard some of my mom's birds chirping back and forth in the trees. My alarm clock said it was past 12:30, and I'd already jumped halfway out of bed before I realized it was Sunday and all I had to do all day was unload Butch's tools over at the Sinclair and get Big Ed's Cadillac back to him. It felt strange and unnatural not to have some desperate emergency to attend to and I even felt a little *guilty* while I made myself a cup of coffee and laid down in bed again. But I couldn't go back to sleep. And as I laid there, staring a hole through the cramped little tin shower stall my dad and I put up at the far end of the room, everything that happened over the weekend started seeping back like a slow water leak, and I knew I had to get up and get out if I ever wanted to be able to sleep there again.

Outside was a gorgeous late-September day, with a late-summer sun beaming down and the trees all turning and the smell of burning leaves rising from smoky piles along the curbsides. I saw families walking home from twelve o'clock Mass and it reminded me how far I'd drifted from that kind of life. Why, I used to go to Mass with my mom and sisters every Sunday. My dad'd crack me one if I didn't. Sometimes he'd even come with. Truth is, I couldn't remember exactly when or why I stopped going, except I knew it was about when my dad and me stopped getting along. I think I did it as much to piss him off as anything else. Not that I liked going to church all that much (I mean, who does?) but I could take it for an hour a week just to keep the peace.

I got in Big Ed's Caddy and decided to tool over by the Doggie Shake and see if maybe Julie was on duty. And sure enough she was. But the place was pretty busy with the after-church crowd, and so Julie had no choice but to give me the brush-off when I waltzed up, planted a sweet little peck on her cheek, and thanked her for cleaning my apartment. "Hey, no problem, slobbo," she said, ruefully eyeballing a family of nine—everything from a craggy old grandmother with her hair in a bun right down to a bawling baby in a fuzzy pink blanket—who had just sat themselves down at the last available table in her section. All the parking stalls outside were full, too, so she had to go to work. I guess that fat little drip Marvin was really keeping an eye on everybody. There was nothing to do but sit myself down on one of those rotating stools and order an oliveburger, some french fries, and a root beer float (which I can't really recommend for breakfast, but it's sort of the Specialty of the House over at the Doggie Shake). While I waited for my food to come up (which it usually does at the Doggie Shake, later if not sooner), I kept trying to get Julie to come over and sit with me. But she was real busy with all the people and more or less ignored me. Even when I gave her my absolute best imitation Clark Gable "c'mon over here, baby" wink-and-nod combination.

So there was nothing to do but just sort of hang around and wait for the crowd to thin out. Somebody'd left a *New York Times* on one of the chairs, so naturally I started thumbing through it to see if there was anything about Watkins Glen. Sure enough, there was a sedate little one-column blurb back on page 54, right next to an ad for a new recording of Giuseppe Verdi's opera *Don Carlo*. Why, a story like that would've made the damn front page of the *Daily News!*

Especially if they had some really gruesome pictures.

Anyhow, the *Times* story read like this:

SPORTS CAR RAMS CROWD, KILLS BOY

Watkins Glen, N.Y., Sept. 20—A seven-year-old boy was killed and at least twelve other persons were injured today as a sports car participating in the fifth annual running of the Grand Prix race veered into spectators on Franklin Street, the main street of the village.

The accident occurred shortly after 5:35 P.M., as forty cars of foreign make swung into . . .

"Foreign make?" I muttered out loud. "Haven't those idiots at the *Times* ever heard about the Cunninghams?"

"You talking to yourself now?" It was Julie, of course, standing over me with her eyes all bright and cheery and that fabulous movie-magazine smile.

"Nah," I said, folding the paper so she maybe wouldn't see the story. "I just saw something dumb in the *Times* is all."

"I saw it, too," she said, a slow, dark cloud passing over her face. "Did you see it?" she asked quietly. "I mean, did you see it happen?"

"No, I didn't," I lied. "I was way over on the other side of the track." I really didn't feel like talking about it. Especially with somebody on the outside of the sport. Fact is, it made me feel all dirty and guilty and ashamed inside, like maybe *I'd* had something to do with it, just because I'd been there and not incidentally helped put together the damn car that killed that poor kid and injured all those people and almost did in my friend Tommy Edwards as well.

"It must've been awful . . . ," Julie said softly, her voice trailing off.

"Yeah," I told her. "It was." And then we just kind of sat there for awhile, looking around at everything but each other's eyes. "Hey," I finally said, trying to make a little conversation, "thanks again for cleaning my place up."

"Somebody had to do it."

"No, really. That was an awful nice surprise."

"No big deal," she shrugged. "I just didn't want to pick up some terrible fungus or disease off you from living in that dump."

"Yeah, I suppose I could use a few lessons about housekeeping."

"Men are pigs," Julie snorted. "They never know *anything* about keeping a nice place to live. . . ."

I had to agree. I mean, she was right.

". . . They want you to cook for them and clean for them and wash dishes for them and pick up after them. . . ."

It sounded like a pretty good deal to me.

". . . and then they expect you to be around all pert and pretty and ready to go whenever the heck they feel like it. . . ."

I could hear her mom's voice coming through loud and clear, and I was starting to wonder what exactly had gotten into Julie, you know? But she was really rolling now, and there was nothing to do but sit back and shut up and wait for her to run out of gas. If you just sat there and kept your mouth shut and nodded every ten seconds or so, it generally took about two and a half minutes.

You could time it on a watch.

Sure enough, Julie ran out of steam right on schedule, and then I thanked her again for cleaning my place.

"Like I said," she shrugged again, "no problem."

"Well, it was an awful nice surprise when I got home last night. Or actually, more like this morning."

"So," she said, kind of letting the word hang there, "you think you're finally about through with those races?"

"Oh, I don't know. It's hard to say. See, I'm goin' back to work at your uncle's gas station tomorrow morning—"

"I know." You couldn't miss the happy little spark flickering in her eyes, and I must admit it made me feel all warm and safe and cozy inside. Then again, I knew in my heart I was hooked on racing and the excitement of hanging around with all those fabulous cars and crazy characters. I mean, Real Life was just too damn dull and predictable and, well, *unimportant* by comparison. But there was no way you could explain it to somebody on the outside. Especially when the body of that poor little seven-year-old kid wasn't even in the ground yet.

"I dunno, Julie," I said, giving it my very best Detached Professional voice, "I been working on an awful lot of those cars lately, you know?"

"I sure as hell do!" she said with an unfunny laugh. "That's why we never see each other anymore. You're always down at that damn dealership in Manhattan at all hours—*supposedly* working on cars—and we don't even go out for a damn Coke or a movie on the weekends 'cause you're always off to hell-and-gone for the races." She wasn't really *mad* at me, but it wouldn't be like Julie to pass up a free opportunity to give me some shit. It's one of those involuntary reaction things like farting and sneezing they teach you about in science class.

"Well, I wouldn't worry about it too much," I told her, circling around the subject. "Racing season's over until next spring, and I'm planning to plant myself smack-dab in the middle of your uncle's service bay and go to *work*. Hell, it'd be nice to have some real damn folding money for a change."

"It sure *would*," Julie agreed, visions of sit-down restaurants and tuxedoed maître d's dancing in her eyes. "We could do a *lot* of stuff on two incomes."

That one flew right by me. But that's because I was picking my spot to zoom in for the kill. "That's why I think I should keep working on sports cars when I move back to the Sinclair. We could make a pisspot fulla money off of them. Butch thinks so, too." Not that I had actually *asked* him about it (or even spoken to him in quite a long while) but I was pretty damn sure that's what he would've said if I'd bothered to call him up and ask.

"But no more racing?"

"Well, that depends," I said, kind of backpedaling. And then I told her about the fat wad of tens, twenties, and fifties Barry Spline stuffed into his pockets every race weekend. You could see Julie seemed pretty interested in the money, but she was still real suspicious about racing. Like it was another woman or something, you know?

"That means you'll be *away* all the time," she said in a perfect New Jersey whine. "What's the point of making money if you're not around to *spend* it?"

I had to admit, there was a certain obtuse logic to her argument. But that was my opening. "Well, seeing as how you work there part-time yourself, I was thinking maybe you could go to the races *with* me sometimes. As my sort of, you know, *assistant*."

"Oh, *sure!*" Julie snorted. "My mom'd really go for *that*. . . ."

"But it's *business*. . . . "

"Look, Buddy, both you and me and my mom and uncle know *exactly* what kind of business that is. Monkey business. Do I look stupid to you or something?"

"Well, no . . . ," I told her. "A'course not, Julie. It's just—"

"Listen to me, Buddy Palumbo. And listen real good." She leaned forward and stared me right square in the eyes. "I like you, Buddy. I like you a lot. And I'm really looking forward to having you around the station again and maybe goin' out on dates and stuff on the weekends." She inhaled a long, slow breath. "But I'll be damned if I'm gonna wind up five or ten years down the road in a stinking little apartment in Greenwich Village like your sister Mary Frances, with some damn beautician or dental assistant for a roommate and nobody to go out with but a bunch of leftover creeps while my friends have nice church weddings and move into decent houses and start raising families. You understand me, Buddy?"

Obviously, Julie had done herself a lot of thinking on the subject while I'd been busy with racing. "Gee whiz, Julie," I told her, "we're just talking about a couple lousy race weekends here, you know. . . ."

"Forget about it, Buddy. Just *forget* about it. I like you an awful lot, but I'll be damned if I'm gonna let myself turn into one of those tramps who go around passing out free samples. Not Julie Finzio. Not in *this* lifetime. I wanna be able to look Father Dominico right in the eye when I come out of confession. . . ."

"But that's supposed to be, you know, *confidential,* isn't it?"

"They recognize your voice. Everybody knows that."

"And anyway, you hardly ever go to church except on Christmas and Easter. At least not that I've seen."

"Yeah? Well, maybe I oughta start. In fact, I'll be there next month for my friend Serafina Massucci's wedding"—all of a sudden everything made sense!—"and it wouldn't hurt you one bit to be there with me!"

"Oh, s-sure," I stammered. "I'd, uh, *love* to go."

"In a pig's eye."

"No, honest, Julie. *Really* I would. . . ."

And that's how I wound up at a big Italian church wedding in Passaic, New Jersey, on Sunday, October 26th, instead of down in Albany, Georgia, with my racing buddies at the S.C.M.A.'s first-ever SOWEGA event at Turner Air Force Base.

Truth is, the S.C.M.A. was lucky to be able to hold *any* kind of races after the well-publicized disaster at Watkins Glen. Naturally the press made a big deal out of it—including a grisly two-page spread in *Life* magazine—and, seeing as how it was an election year, everybody

with a hat in the ring and a soapbox to stand on was coming out against
road racing in a big way. After all, it was an easy target. The state of
Wisconsin decided to enforce a law they already had on the books
banning contests of speed on public highways, and that was pretty much
the end as far as the races around Elkhart Lake were concerned, while
the enormous media outcry about the tragedy at Watkins Glen threatened to shut down that event as well. The only way they could keep
running at the Glen was to set up a new circuit way out in the countryside where they could maybe control things a little better. In fact,
there probably wouldn't have been much sports car racing at all in this
country if it hadn't been for a tough, cigar-chomping Air Force general
named Curtis LeMay. General LeMay was head of the Strategic Air
Command, hated Commies, owned an Allard, and traveled in high-
powered social and political circles where he rubbed elbows with the
kind of rich, and, influential bigwigs you generally found cluttering up
the paddocks at S.C.M.A. race events.

General Curtis LeMay turned out to be the savior of sports car road
racing here in the States. And the way he pulled it off was nothing
short of amazing. See, the Strategic Air Command had these bomber
bases scattered all over the countryside—mostly out in the boondocks
where they were safe from prying Commie eyes—and he convinced his
buddies at the Pentagon that it would be a swell idea to hold road races
on the runways of those Strategic Air Command bases as motivation
and entertainment for the men in the field. And believe it or not, they
went for it!

Now running on airfields was nothing new. Most of the tracks over
in England were actually leftover airfields where B17 Flying Fortresses
and Arvo Lancasters and such used to take off for raids on Germany.
Here in the States, they'd run airport races on the runways and taxiways
of the Convair Airfield in Allentown, Pennsylvania, and another in a
driving rainstorm up in Janesville, Wisconsin, plus a couple more out
on the West Coast. Not to mention that big twelve-hour contest down
in Sebring, Florida. But it was difficult to do, what with having to shut
down the entire airport for a day or two and rerouting air traffic to
make it happen. At least, it was difficult for anybody except a guy like
General Curtis LeMay, who could get it handled with a couple quick
phone calls once he had the rest of the brass hats in the Pentagon on
the bandwagon.

And that's exactly what he did.

In fact, General LeMay worked out a deal where "his" airmen did
all the work setting things up and manning the corners and keeping
an eye on the crowds as part of their normal duty, and that naturally
raised a few eyebrows on Capitol Hill. Letters started pouring in from

Concerned Citizens wanting to know why Their Tax Dollars were being used to put on sports car races for a bunch of spoiled rich kids and
wealthy bums instead of keeping their eyes peeled for the advancing
Commie Menace. But General LeMay wasn't the kind of guy to run
from a fight or back off once he had his mind made up, and he coun-
tered all the flack by charging spectator admissions and funneling the
money into "hobby rooms," which were shops where his off-duty serv-
icemen could pursue a little R 'n' R wrenching on fast, powerful automobiles so his ace pilots could show those lah-de-dah sportycar guys
a thing or two next time they rolled into town.

At any rate, the SOWEGA event (which stood for Southwestern
Georgia, and was not a hog call) was the first of the S.A.C. races, and
they pretty much became the meat and potatoes of the S.C.M.A. racing
schedule for the next few years. Some of the drivers—and especially
the really *good* drivers—complained that the flat, featureless airport
tracks were Mickey Mouse compared to the daunting hills and swoops
and beautiful (if occasionally too close to the roadside) scenery at places
like Bridgehampton and Elkhart and Watkins Glen. But the airport
tracks were *safe,* and that was a huge improvement from the open road
circuits. If you went off, about the worst that happened was you plowed
through a bunch of pylons or hit a stack of hay bales. Or just kept
going, since the runways were generally five or even six lanes wide
instead of the scant two lanes you had on country roads.

By far the most important difference was that you could control the
spectators at a S.A.C. race and keep them a meaningful distance from
the cars. Sure, they couldn't get down close anymore, where they could
feel the howl of a twelve-cylinder Ferrari or the thunder of a V-8 Allard
as they hurtled by with the throttles wide open. And, though you could
see most everything at an airport circuit (at least if there were grand-
stands or something so you could get up high enough), spectators had
a hard time appreciating the speed and cornering action on those wide,
flat, empty-looking runways.

But at least it was safe.

Even if it took all the poetry out of it.

THE TWO-PARTY
SYSTEM

AS PROMISED, I showed up at the Old Man's Sinclair bright and early Monday morning, wearing a nice clean pair of coveralls (thanks to Julie, natch) and a pretty good attitude, too. That didn't last long, since Old Man Finzio was mean as ever and wanted me to start on a nasty-looking muffler job on some out-of-work meat cutter's '49 Nash. He was about the third or fourth owner, and you could tell that neither he nor any of the previous owners owned a garden hose or scrub bucket in decent operating condition. Or at least they never used them on that Nash. One look at the interior was enough to make you want to stop buying meat.

It made me realize how much I'd taken for granted all the hidden benefits of working on sports cars, and especially ones that were raced regularly. Except for the odd shitbox like Cal's raggedy TC, they were almost invariably neat and clean and free from rusted-up bolts and thick, smelly layers of sludge on the undercarriage. Racing cars were usually kept in the kind of condition that Big Ed insisted on for all his cars, and working on them made you forget about all the greasy, corroded, ill-maintained, broken-down crud wagons that John Q. Public drove to work every day. At least until you had to pick up a ratchet wrench and a cutting torch and tried to put a muffler on one, anyway. It didn't help matters any when that flatbed semi showed up with Tommy's wrecked Allard and Big Ed's blown-up Jaguar lashed on top. I wanted to drop what I was doing under that shitty Nash and start tearing into Big Ed's Jaguar right away. But Old Man Finzio wouldn't hear of it. "Yew jes' finish that job yew got already," he rasped, tugging out yet another bent-up Camel. "Them damn furrin' contraptions of yers kin damn well wait."

I wasn't about to start arguing with him. At least not on my first day back. And especially seeing as how I wanted to talk to him later about how I saw things and my plans for the station's future. Still, it didn't make much sense to me. I mean, we could charge good money—and I mean *real* good money—for an engine overhaul on Big Ed's car, and you had to wonder if the out-of-work meat cutter with the broken-down Nash could even pay his bill. He was one of those down-and-out types who always want you to do a Basic Butcher patch job (even if you *know* it won't hold up) and, if you absolutely insist they pay the price of a brand-new muffler, they inevitably want you to hook it up to the rusty old pipes that are already there, just so they can put off paying you the other five or ten bucks that they're going to wind up paying you anyway—and then some!—just a few short paychecks down the road. I used to sympathize with people like that, but that's a weakness you just have to outgrow if you're ever going to make anything of yourself in the world of automobile mechanics. "I'm afraid poor people make poor customers," was the way Colin St. John phrased it.

I came to realize that he was right, because people like that never want to pay for anything except the cheapest spit-and-baling-wire repair that will get their wheezing old heaps clattering down the road again—engines sputtering and egg-shaped wheels wobbling in four different directions—under some semblance of their own power. Not to mention they often brought their own parts (so you couldn't make a reasonable markup on the discount you got from the parts store) and lots of times they were wrong or no good or cut from some junkyard wreck that was maybe not the same exact year or model. And then it was *your* fault when the damn things didn't fit. The sad truth was, if you allowed yourself—out of decent human charity—to do business with poverty cases, you inevitably wound up trying to figure and fight your way through the scummy, illogical residue of Band-Aid repairs made one on top of the other by the cheapest, dirtiest, worst damn butcher mechanics in town. And none of them more than once. So you always lost money. And sometimes you even got threatened with a baseball bat.

None of that bothered Old Man Finzio. He *loved* doing business with folks who were down on their luck, because it just about guaranteed him a chance to be mean and belligerent above and beyond the call of duty. It would always come to a head when the car was done and the poor sap came to pick it up. That's when the Old Man presented the bill, and it was *always* more than the original estimate. That went without saying on most every job, but it was a lock when you worked on one of those raggedy heaps because it always took longer and got you dirtier and more frustrated than any car a Solid Citizen might own. And of course the poor sap would wail and moan and argue like hell on account of he really didn't have the extra five or ten bucks floating around in his pocket to cover the difference. And that's when Old Man Finzio would come out from behind the service counter and stick his grizzled, bony chin with its four-day growth of stubble right up in their faces—usually with the glowing tip of his latest Camel leading the way as a sort of Advance Guard—and inform the poor bastard that he was holding the car hostage until the ransom was paid. It was the same damn thing he pulled on Cal when we brought his wrecked TC in after the mess at Bridgehampton back in May. And, just like Cal, those people'd fume and fuss and threaten to sue and even cuss the Old Man out until they were blue in the face. But Old Man Finzio would just stand there serenely and enjoy it, basking in their anger like he was sunbathing on the beach. I swear, he'd even roll ever so slightly from side to side now and then to make sure he got a nice even tan.

But eventually, after all the screaming and yelling and cussing and pleading, the deadbeats who owned those poor old cars would have to go break their kid's piggy bank or put the touch on the relatives— again—or maybe go in for an eight-hour shift of cheap day labor or sell a couple pints of blood, but whatever happened, they inevitably came back to the station with a furious, humiliated look in their eyes and their tails dragging between their legs and paid the damn bill. And that's when Old Man Finzio would give them the keys and throw them off the property. *"And don't come back!"* he'd yell after them, his eyes dancing.

"You don't hafta worry about *that,* asshole!" they'd yell back as they drove away with their middle fingers extended like Fourth of July flag-poles. "You don't hafta worry about that at *all!"*

Then Old Man Finzio would smile a thin, bright smile, light himself up another bent-up Camel, and just kind of stand there by the cash register for awhile, swaying ever so gently from side to side, savoring the moment.

But regardless of the pleasure he took from it, doing mechanical work for people like that wasn't good for business. It was one of the things I wanted to talk to him about changing. Especially after I saw he wasn't taking his usual measure of joy out of Presenting The Bill or throwing that poor out-of-work meat cutter off the property when he came back a few hours later to pick up his stinking lousy piece-of-shit Nash.

Fact is, the Old Man wasn't looking his old self much anymore. He could still get mad as hell at the drop of a hat and screech until the turkey-neck skin over his collar turned damn near purple. But he couldn't *sustain* it anymore. At least not more than a few minutes, any-way. And he wasn't moving right either, kind of shuffling around the office and out to the pumps like a windup toy with the spring running down. But the biggest change was that he really didn't seem to care much anymore. Not about anything. So when I went up to him later that afternoon and told him about my ideas for the station, he just sort of nodded and shrugged and looked out the front window like he was staring at the ocean. Then he sighed and said, "Sure. Why not. You do it any damn way you want. Any way at all," and got up, went out the

overhead door, climbed into his tow truck, and drove off down Pine
Street. Just like that.

He was gone all afternoon. And I was in business!

My first big sports car job at the Sinclair was Big Ed's blown-up
Jag, and I had to grab a few passers-by to help me push it into the
service bay for a postmortem diagnosis. But then the phone rang and
it was some tax accountant about the starter motor on his Hudson. So
I set him up a service appointment and made a note that somebody had
to pick up his car when the tow truck came back. Then I went back
to work on the Jag, but right away a lady in a DeSoto pulled in for a
fill up, and I noticed one of her tires was almost flat on account of it'd
picked up a nail, so I had to fix that before I did anything else. Except
run the pumps and clean the windshields and do an oil check on two
more cars that rolled in off the street and answer the phone a couple
more times.

One of the calls was Carson Flegley, about maybe doing a little
hush-hush speed tuning on his MG. He'd read some article in *Road &
Track* magazine about hopping up MGs, and he was all excited about
doing it to his car so he could go down to that SOWEGA race in
Georgia and maybe finish all the way up in midpack for a change.
Personally, I thought he was crazy for even thinking about it. I mean,
the biggest problem with that car —as Cal had proved beyond any
doubt—was the loose nut behind the steering wheel, and it didn't make
sense to start hot-rodding the engine and getting it too high strung for
normal street duty when he couldn't get near all the potential out of it
bone stock. But Carson had fallen victim to "The Bumper Syndrome,"
which happens when a would-be racing driver sees another car's
bumper out in front of him during a race—like a carrot dangling off
the end of a stick—and he can't do a damn thing except follow it
around. Nine times out of ten, that driver will daydream all day and
lay awake nights trying to figure out how to turn that rear bumper
ahead of him into a front bumper in his rearview mirror. And he will
go to some pretty ridiculous lengths to make it happen. He will also
spend a *lot* of money, and that's why I told Carson I thought it was a
swell idea and I'd be happy to help him out. Only he'd have to give
me a deposit for parts and leave the car for a couple weeks. "How
much do you want?" he asked without skipping a beat. Like it was
nothing, you know?

"Oh, I dunno," I told him, trying to figure out some kind of plau-
sible number, "maybe seventy dollars or so...."

"How about a hundred? I'll drop it off tomorrow."

"Uh, sure. That'll be fine."

So now I had two major racing projects lined up and some guy in a pickup out by the pumps waiting for gas and that DeSoto lady's tire to finish (not to mention a speedo cable job on a Mercury that had to be ready by five o'clock) and somebody in an Oldsmobile with Ohio plates pulling in to ask directions. And then who should swoop in but Big Ed Baumstein. And you should've seen what he was driving! He'd made a deal with the local Cadillac agency to get the very first '53 Eldorado convertible in New Jersey—creamy white with a red leather interior, natch—complete with chrome wire wheels and that new panoramic windshield that was exclusive to Eldorados that year. Why, it was about the most beautiful hunk of homegrown Detroit machinery I'd ever seen. "Hey, how'ya doin'?" Big Ed grinned around his cigar. "Good t'have ya back in Jersey."

"Hey, thanks," I told him, running my eyeballs down his new Caddy. "Nice car. When d'ja pick it up?"

"Just this morning. It's still in the wrapper."

"Yeah, I can smell it." There's always that special smell to new cars.

"Yep, she's cherry all right. But I'll fix that soon enough. Get a few miles on 'er. Let her hump the road a little and develop herself some personality."

I knew exactly what he was talking about. Cars get their guts and bodies on the assembly line, but they get their souls from the roads they travel. "So," I asked him, "how does she drive?"

"Aw, nothin' like my Jaguar. That's my *baby*. But y'cant beat a Caddy convert when it comes to cruisin' around town or oozin' down the highway."

"Especially a brand-spanking-new one," I agreed.

"Yeah. And a special edition, too. They ain't gonna make many of these babies."

I could see the DeSoto lady was starting to pace up and down like people do when they're politely trying to tell you that you're ruining their entire day. "Look," I told Big Ed, "I'd love to chew the fat some more, but I got a lotta stuff to take care of and I'm here all by myself."

"Where's that rat-bastard Finzio?"

"Dunno. He took off in the tow truck a couple hours ago."

"Well, you tell the sonofabitch I said hello."

"He won't care."

"I know he won't care. That's not the point. I'm tryin' t'be *nice*, see?" Big Ed pulled the cigar out of his face and flashed me a fake grin. "It's *important* t'be nice in this life. It gets you places."

"I wouldn't know," I told him, and we had a good laugh off it.

"Say," he said as he got ready to pull away, "what's the late word on my Jag, anyway?"

"I just started on it a couple minutes ago, and I won't know what all's involved till I get it torn down. But I do know this." I looked him square in the eye.

"What?"

"It's gonna be pretty expensive. You got a connecting rod right through the block."

"Hey," he said with a helpless laugh, "anything worth doing is worth doing all the way, right?"

"Yeah, I guess so. By the way, what'd you rev that poor thing to?"

"I dunno," Big Ed shrugged. "I wasn't exactly watching the tach, you know?"

"I'd say that's pretty obvious—judging from the hole in the crankcase, anyway. . . ."

"Say, you need any money for parts or anything?"

"Oh, I probably will when I get some idea what we're up against."

"Nah," Big Ed told me. "You take something now. That way you can get started right away and get the damn thing fixed."

"Don't you want an estimate first?"

Big Ed looked at me like I'd hurt his feelings. "I don't need an estimate. Not from *you,* Buddy. You just take a little down payment here"—he reached into his pocket and pulled out a fat wad of bills—"and let me know if and when y'need any more." And just like that he peeled off two hundred dollars in twenties and fifties— *two hundred dollars!*—and handed it over. Like it was *nothing!*

"S-Say," I gulped, "you need a receipt or anything?"

"Take that receipt and wipe yer ass with it," Big Ed laughed as he slipped his brand-new Eldorado into drive and wheeled away from the pumps with its virgin whitewalls squealing. And that's when I noticed the phone was ringing again and that the DeSoto lady with the flat tire wasn't looking nearly so polite and quietly desperate anymore. In fact, she was starting to look very genuinely pissed off.

So I answered the phone and made an appointment for a tune-up on some guy's Ford and got the lady with the tire squared away and took another quick look under the hood of Big Ed's Jag and filled up a Buick wagon at the pumps and realized I'd better get busy on that Mercury speedometer cable before the owner showed up and found it sitting right exactly where he'd left it. People *hate* that.

The Old Man finally rolled in around 4:30 wearing an even more far-off look than when he left. I told him about the Hudson with the bad starter motor that needed to be brought in and explained as how I really couldn't get much done with all the damn interruptions. "Where'dja go, anyway?" I asked him.

"Hadda go see my stupid quack doctor," he snorted, spitting on the ground. "Gotta go see the sonofabitch again next Monday." That sounded like trouble, on account of Julie was only coming in on Tuesdays and Thursdays, and there was just no way I could get anything done in the service bay if I had to shag phone calls and tend the pumps and take care of every rube asshole who dropped in off the street.

"Look," I told him, "I'm gonna need me some help in here if I'm gonna make us any money on the repair side."

Old Man Finzio looked at me like I was threatening him with a straight razor. "Look here, sonnyboy," he started in (and I always knew it meant trouble when he started in with that "sonnyboy" stuff), "I can't hardly earn enough off the damn pumps to make ends meet as it is, and now you wanna go out and *hire* somebody?" He shook his head like I was some kind of prizewinning idiot.

"Listen," I tried to explain, "the *real* money is in fixing those English sports cars, see. We can raise up our rates a dollar an hour on those things. Easy. Maybe even a dollar-fifty. The guys who own 'em will be happy to pay it, just so long as I do good work and get the damn cars finished on time. . . ."

"Finished on time?" he sneered, as if I had uttered the unspeakable. After all, failing to meet delivery promises was something of a sacred canon in the car repair business. Not just down at Westbridge, but everywhere else, too. Although you had to admit Barry and Colin St. John had raised it to an art form.

But then I showed the Old Man Big Ed's two hundred dollars—cash money!—and all of a sudden his face softened like wax melting down off a candle. "Aw, what the hell," he grumbled. "Y'run the damn place any way you see fit. I just don't much care anymore." And without another word, he headed out the door and down the street toward the liquor store on the corner.

He didn't even take the two hundred bucks.

After that I started spreading the word that I was officially in the foreign car repair business at the Sinclair, and it didn't take long before I had more damn work than I could handle from all the S.C.M.A. racer types and their lah-de-dah sports car friends (many who'd sworn they'd never go back to Westbridge again, not even on a bet). They'd learned it took a little talent and experience to do things properly on those cars, and it was not the sort of thing you found at your average street-corner filling station or back-alley repair shop. But I couldn't count on the Old Man much because he was always running off to see his damn doctor (and even when he was there, he wasn't much good except for pumping gas and pissing off customers) so I asked Julie if maybe she could come in a little more often to take care of the phones and the office stuff. But she was making pretty good money over at the Doggie Shake, what with tips and everything, and there was just no way I could offer her that sort of deal at the Sinclair.

And that's when I had a brilliant idea. I called up old Butch Bohunk to see if he'd like to get his ass into the gas station business again. *"Me?"* he damn near gasped. "You want *me* to come back to the station?"

You could tell he was pretty interested. To say the least.

So I explained to him how weird the Old Man was acting and how I couldn't get the damn cars fixed—and I had 'em lined up, for God's sake!—on account of all the damn interruptions and other piddly bullshit I had to take care of. "Hell *yes!*" he shouted into the receiver. "I've about gone buggy just sittin' around this friggin' house with my dick in my hand."

"Can you get yourself over here tomorrow morning?"

"Sure as hell can, Buddy. I'll have Marlene drop me off."

"That'd be great," I told him. Then something else occurred to me. "Uh, Butch?"

"Yeah?"

"We, uh, see, the fact is, we can't afford to, um, to *pay* you very much. At least not right away."

"Aw, that's okay," he said, not the least bit upset. "I ain't worth very much these days, anyway...."

And that was the beginning of my stint as Chief Operating Officer and occasional Parts Washer and Floor Sweeper at the Old Man's Sinclair. Hiring Butch turned out to be a real stroke of genius, because he knew how to order the right parts over the phone and he could even get around good enough to handle the pumps now and then once I made a little wood ramp to get his wheelchair down the little concrete step outside the office. He'd pretty much given up on those crutches once he realized his legs were just not about to get any better. But he'd made some real improvement in what he could do with his decent left hand and that fingerless lump on the other side. Why, he could do bench work like carb rebuilds and distributors right there in the office, and he'd gotten to where he could wield a welding torch left-handed and still lay down about the prettiest damn bead you ever saw.

So life was good. I had help so I could concentrate on fixing the cars we had lined up behind the shop and along the edge of the lot. I'd show up at seven ayem to write up the new repair business coming in, then walk across the street to the sandwich shop when Butch rolled in at eight and have myself a jelly doughnut and a couple cups of coffee while I leafed through the morning paper. There was a lot of interesting stuff in it, too. Stuff about a great big world out there that I'd forgotten about all summer while I was working my ass off for Colin St. John.

Rocky Marciano'd won the heavyweight championship off thirty-eight-year-old Jersey Joe Walcott, and even though Walcott was from Jersey, I had to go with Marciano because he was white. Not to mention Italian. I mean, that went without saying.

It was rough going trying to run my own show for the very first time, and I learned you can't help biting off more than you can chew because the natural surge of human greed makes you take in work you should probably turn away on account of you can't resist the lure of the old Long Green. In fact, I was starting to work the same kind of crazy hours I did at Westbridge, staying until nine or ten at night—sometimes even later!—and yet always being there bright and early every morning so's I wouldn't miss any new prospects. But at least I was making decent money, since I'd force-fed Old Man Finzio a deal where I was getting a percentage off the hourly shop rate on top of my regular pittance grease monkey wages, not to mention a chunk of the markup on parts. Plus I wasn't wasting my time on that two-hour train-and-bus ride into Manhattan twice each day. Truth is, it felt pretty wonderful having fat stacks of currency piled up in the Old Man's ancient cash register every night at closing time, and it was especially nice to have a wad of green in my own pocket come Friday evening.

It was plenty enough to take Julie out for a real sit-down dinner and a picture show, and I always had my pick of the customer cars for transportation, since it was understood that a skilled mechanic needed to personally test-drive the cars that passed through his hands in order to alert their owners about impending service needs, developing problems, and timely maintenance requirements. Especially when those cars included sleek, sexy Jaguars and jaunty little MGs. One night I picked Julie up in Carson's black TD and whisked her off for an evening of highbrow entertainment that included antipasto, minestrone, and spaghetti with meatballs up at Bachigalupo's in the suit-and-tie part of town, followed by a trip across the bridge into Manhattan to see that new wraparound Cinerama movie on Broadway. Geez, it was like you were really *on* that roller coaster, you know? Other nights we'd maybe take in a regular movie on the Jersey side or roll a few lines at the bowling alley or skate around to the organ music at the roller rink. Afterward we'd drive along the Jersey shore and maybe park over by the Coast Guard station to watch the submarine races. Truth is, it was starting to get a little cold for that sort of activity—especially in an English sports car that didn't have much in the way of what a person raised on Fords and Chevys would call a heater. Those cars were never exactly cut out for that kind of duty anyway, since you had to be a bona fide contortionist to share even a little body heat in something as cramped and awkward as an MG. And it was even worse in cold weather with the top and side curtains in place. Besides, all that was starting to change between Julie and me. Oh, I still wanted to get into her pants bad as ever, but all of a sudden I wasn't in such a mad, desperate *rush* about it. Sure, we still made out in parked cars, and one night Julie even asked if we could borrow one of Big Ed's Caddies on account of she wanted to go to the drive-in to see Betty Hutton and Cornel Wilde in *The Greatest Show on Earth*. Turns out it was the anniversary or something of the first time we went out to the drive-in and kissed in the front seat of Big Ed's black Sixty Special. I never would've known, of course, but women have a sort of sixth sense when it comes to stuff like that. In fact, they can tell you to the month, week, day, hour, and minute when you first asked them out or kissed them good night or made them cry or tried to cop a feel.

Speaking of Big Ed, I had the engine out of his Jag and scattered all over the shop in crates and boxes, and, if you want to know the truth of it, I was feeling pretty nervous about getting it back together again. I mean, for all the wrenching I'd done down at Westbridge, I'd never had one of those twin-cam Jag sixes stripped to the bare block before, and, as I looked around at all the boxes of bolts and castings and miscellaneous hardware, I started to have doubts about whether I could turn it back into a living, breathing, internal combustion engine. Luckily, I had Butch around to give me encouragement, which generally amounted to disgusted head shaking and uplifting comments such as: "Ya *call* yerself a goddam automobile mechanic, but far's I can see yer nothin' but a crybaby sissygirl with a damn toolbox," and, "Jesus Christ, asshole, didn't I teach you *anything*?" In spite of his many years in the Marines, Butch didn't know a whole hell of a lot about morale. But that was just his way, and once you understood and accepted that, he could be enormous help on a serious car project. And no matter how upset he got with my rank stupidity or lack of confidence, he'd always wind up leaning his head in and showing me what I was missing so I didn't have to put things together and then take them apart umpty-kazillion times before I got them right.

Roman Szymanski turned out to be a big help, too. Sure, it was a long haul to get to him on the other side of Manhattan, but he could run his eyeballs over stuff (like the engine block from Big Ed's XK120, for example) and rub his chin and move in a little closer with the magnifying lenses flipped down over his eyes and then tell me he could fix it every bit as good as a new one. And believe me, Jaguar engine blocks were not exactly easy to come by in 1952. Or cheap, either. Roman welded up the block, pressed in a new cylinder liner where the rod had blown out, and refinished the crankshaft. But he insisted we put in all new connecting rods instead of just replacing the busted one.

"All same. All bad," he told me. He re-balanced all the pistons to match them up with the new one, and did a balance job on the clutch-and-flywheel assembly as well. "Zo tell me," he asked in a thick middle-European accent, "how does thiz perzon drive?"

"Like an animal."

"Might az well put in new clutch az long az is apart." As you can see, I had a lot of good people I could go to for advice and secondhand wisdom in my new sports car business in Passaic. But even so it was a little nerve-wracking to have engines torn all the way down like I did on Big Ed's car. I bet surgeons feel that same spastic sort of panic dancing in their guts when they look down and realize they've got somebody split wide open and it's their damn responsibility to put everything back together and close them up again.

Which is exactly what was bothering Old Man Finzio. Turns out his doctors wanted him to go into the hospital the second week in October so they could open him up and take a look inside. I couldn't imagine what you might find inside a guy like him except for maybe lizards and scorpions and cornered rats, but I guess the doctors figured they might find something even worse. And Old Man Finzio thought so, too. He didn't say much about it, of course. Fact is, he didn't even tell me he was going in until two or three days beforehand, when I was already trying to figure some way I could finesse myself out of taking Julie to Serafina Massucci's wedding so I could sneak off to Georgia for the SOWEGA races. I guess the horror of the accident at Watkins Glen faded after awhile and I was starting to itch for the desperate, swaggering, devil-may-care *fun* of racing again.

Like I explained before, it's a disease.

Besides, I had cars down there. Well, one car, anyway. I'd finished going through Carson Flegley's engine according to that *Road & Track* article, milling damn near an eighth of an inch off the cylinder head and fitting bigger valves and stronger valve springs and having Roman open up the ports with a die grinder and polish the combustion chambers to a perfect mirror finish. Then I put in richer carb needles and Champion LA-11 sparkplugs and a high-output Lucas ignition coil, and when it was done, I took it for a spin over by Carson's family's funeral parlor so he could take it for a little test-drive. I left the air cleaners off, too, and although I couldn't tell how much was actually added power and how much was just the mighty rush of air sucking through the carburetors, the car certainly *felt* faster. Carson thought so, too, although he had to kind of shoo me around the side of the building and sneak off for a quick ride—somber black suit and all—on account of they had a funeral going on for some bigwig local politician and he had to drive the hearse once the chapel service was over. It simply wouldn't do for one of the funeral directors to come sprinting up in an MG TD with an unusually crisp exhaust note just as they were carrying the casket out. Not even a black one.

Big Ed wanted to go to the SOWEGA races, too. But there was just no way I was going to have his car done in time. I had pieces over at Roman's machine shop and parts coming in from England and I could see from two weeks away that it simply wasn't going to happen. But Big Ed was not about to give up, especially since this was the last S.C.M.A. race of the year (east of the Rockies, anyway) and he really felt he had to make up for his dismal performance at Watkins Glen. Like actually starting a damn race, perhaps? And when I told him his engine wouldn't be ready, he started asking if maybe there was someplace we could find another whole engine—like out of a wreck or something—but I called Westbridge and even out to the Jaguar distributor in California, and there was simply nothing around that we could pick up on a moment's notice. "That's okay," Big Ed told me, "I got an idea. . . ."

I didn't much like the way his stogie started rolling around in his mouth.

Sure enough, he drove up the very next day in—you guessed it!—Skippy Welcher's ex-everything XK120M. What with his new C-type and all, The Skipper didn't much need his old 120, and Big Ed was able to cut himself a pretty slick deal on it, too, especially considering it was a last-minute thing and Big Ed was in a mighty big hurry to own that car. But Big Ed could be pretty shrewd when it came to buying automobiles (Lord knows he'd had enough practice!) and he was fortunate to catch The Skipper in an unusually good mood following a regular visit by his nineteen-year-old Oriental masseuse.

Personally, I was a little gun-shy about getting close to an automobile that Skippy Welcher had anything to do with—like I might catch some kind of creeping mental disorder off it, you know?—plus I wasn't real big on trusting Milton Fitting's wrench work without checking it over first. So I spent three long nights in the garage going over every damn nut and bolt on that car until I'd convinced myself that everything was in solid working order and nothing looked real likely to fall off or self-destruct. At least nothing I could find, anyway. And I didn't charge Big Ed a penny for it, either. "Nah," I told him as he hopped aboard for the long, hard drive down to Georgia, "this one's on the house."

"Aw, I can't let'cha do *that,* Buddy."

"No, really. This one's on me."

"Well, geez, *thanks.* I'll really try t'bring it back in one piece fer you this time."

"You do that."

Just then Cal and Carson Flegley came wheeling up to the pumps in Carson's black TD, waving like idiots and tootling the horn. "Well, s'long," I said to Big Ed.

"Yeah. S'long. Sure wish you was goin' with us."

"Yeah. So do I. But what with the Old Man in the hospital and everything, there's just no way I can go. Besides, if I miss that damn wedding next Sunday, Julie'll *kill* me. And it'll be a slow, painful death, too. She promised."

"I bet she did," Big Ed laughed as he pulled away. I felt part of me go with them as those two cars rumbled off down Pine Street, heading south, the MG all jaunty and upright and the Jag as smooth and sleek and silky as a wet circus seal.

I have to admit I had a pretty good time with Julie at her friend Sarafina Massucci's wedding. And if you've ever been to a real Italian wedding, that should be easy to understand. Sure, the church service was all gushy and flowery and weepy like they always are—that part's for the women anyway—plus it was a little edgy in there since Serafina's family came from Tuscany in the north of Italy and the groom's people were pure-blooded Sicilian, so the friends and relatives split like the Red Sea when they came into church. All I could think about was how much I'd rather have been down at the races in Georgia. Even so, it was kind of nice when the bride and groom came up the aisle together and Julie snaked her fingers into mine and gave them a gentle squeeze. Afterward there was the mandatory big reception party in a rented hall, and that actually turned out to be a lot of fun. After about my third or fourth free drink, anyway. Like all the weddings in our neighborhood, it started out with the wives and girlfriends twittering around the tables like chickadees about how lovely everything was and how radiant the bride looked (even if she was a couple months gone already) and weren't the little nieces that played flower girls just *precious?* It was enough to make you puke if you were stupid enough to listen to it. But of course the guys never did. They bellied up ten-deep around the bar and swapped dirty jokes and ruinous stories about the hatcheck girl at the Pompeii Club over on Columbian Avenue. I guess that's one of the big differences between males and females, and you can really see it at weddings. Women like to get all teary and emotional—even when there's no rea-son—while male types always do their best to avoid acting sappy, even when maybe they should.

But of course the best part was the food. North or south, Italians just love to eat, and everybody's got their own, highly vocal opinion about the basil and oil in the tomato sauce or what kind of seasoning belongs in the sausage or how hot the peppers and *giardinaire* should be. And that's what ends up breaking the ice. That and the booze, anyway. Speaking of which, I ran into a short, beer-gutted older guy at the bar named Vinny Grimaldi, who worked for the Teamsters Union and knew my old man from the V.F.W. or the Knights of Columbus or the Order of the Slippery Salamanders or something. "Hey, you Frankie Palumbo's boy?" he asked through a beery grin.

I allowed as how I was.

"Hey, he's one hell of a guy."

I agreed as how he certainly was one hell of a guy.

"And what a *fan!* Hell, ol' Frankie knows more about the damn New York Yankees than Casey Stengel himself. You should be really proud of that."

"I suppose I should," I told him, wondering just what made the dumb, third-person act of *spectating* anything to be proud of. In fact, right there was one of the big differences between these people and the racers. That and the idea that this was a strictly *Italian* (or Italian-American, anyway) type gathering, while the racing crowd, in spite of its snooty Protestant roots, was pretty damn cosmopolitan. In a racing paddock, we were all just road gypsies, no matter if we were English or Scottish or German or French or Irish or Italian (or even Jewish like Big Ed, assuming you could get in) and most of the culture and aristocracy came out of the cars instead of down the old family bloodlines.

"How'dja like this here wedding?" Vinny asked, just making conversation.

"Aw, it was all right." I told him.

"You with the bride's or the groom's side?"

"I came with Julie Finzio. She's one of Serafina's best friends."

"I know her. She's the gas station guy's niece."

"Yeah. That's how I met her. I work there."

"Well, she's one hell of a hot-looking piece."

I wasn't so sure I liked the tone of Vinny Grimaldi's voice or the way he was looking at Julie. So I decided to let him know how things were. "Hey, watch it, OK? She's, um, she's sorta my girl, see."

"Oh? You *serious* about her?"

"Yeah," I said without thinking about it. "I think maybe I am."

"Humph," he snorted. "How old are you, anyway?"

"Well," I told him, kind of straightening up to make myself maybe look a little taller, "I'll be twenty pretty soon."

"Oh yeah? And exactly how soon would that be?"

"Uh, well," I could feel the air leaking out of my spine, "next year, actually."

"Listen, kid," my dad's union buddy leaned over and whispered in my ear. "Your dad ever tell you why God put hair down there between a woman's legs?"

I shook my head.

"To hide the hook!" he bellowed, and all the married guys at the bar burst out laughing. Personally, I didn't think it was all that funny. In fact, I could feel my ears burning a little, just in case Julie or one of the other girls heard him.

I had a couple more drinks and maybe a wine or two while Julie and the other girls oohed and aahed over the bridesmaids' outfits and the china and the silver patterns and all the fat white envelopes inside the little satin bag Serafina kept clutched tightly to her side. We met up again for dessert after the usual garter business and the throwing of the bouquet (Julie caught it, but I have a feeling it was rigged) and watched Serafina cut about a two-pound slice of cake and shove it in her new husband's mouth while everybody applauded and the poor sonofabitch damn near choked to death. But he was smiling. So was everybody, in fact. Except for maybe the two ushers having a fistfight out in the parking lot. But they were back around the bar not long afterward with their collars and shirttails out, laughing like hell about the shiner on one and the split lip on the other, buying each other drinks. Or pretending to buy each other drinks, anyway, since it was an open bar. Later on Julie and me danced a few rounds—mostly slow stuff, not those polka-style tarantella things where all the drunks, old people, and little kids go make fools of themselves—and I was surprised to find we were the two last people out on the floor, just kind of drifting along to a dreamy violin and accordion version of "Blue Skies." We werer still there when the lights came up and the drummer started packing his stuff away.

I can't say as I remember going home, and I wouldn't be surprised at all if Julie drove us. All I know is that she was there the next morning in my apartment—still in her pink satin bridesmaid's dress—handing me a couple aspirin and a glass of Bromo-Seltzer almost as soon as I started moaning. I could see getting used to service like that. "I gotta run," she said, and gave me a peck on the forehead.

"Jeez, isn't your mom gonna be sore?"

"Nah. I called her and told her I was staying at one of my girl-friend's house."

"So you were here all night?"

Julie nodded, a secret sort of smile spreading across her face.

"What did we, I mean, um, what did you *do?*"

"Not much," she answered with a helpless little laugh. "Mostly, I just watched you sleep."

"Watched me sleep?"

"Yeah. It was nice." She gave me another peck on the forehead, only slower and softer this time. "Not as nice as T.V., or a show, but nice anyway." She straightened up and brushed haphazardly at the wrinkles on her dress. "Listen, I gotta run. I'm supposed to be over at work by nine."

I looked at her standing there in her bridesmaid's dress. She looked pretty damn great for somebody who'd been up all night. "Say, you want me to drive you or something?"

"Nah. You sleep it off. I'll take the car and bring it by later on."

"The car?"

"Yeah. We stopped by the station and swapped the tow truck for some guy's Jaguar convertible so's we could go for a little spin after the wedding last night."

"We did? I don't remember that."

"Well, you probably wouldn't. You were pretty out of it."

"Oh. Where'd we go, anyway?"

"Just down along the Jersey shore. It was nice. We had the top down and you even talked a couple times, I think."

"And *you* drove?"

"Why not? That passenger-side seat gets pretty dull after awhile."

That Julie Finzio was one hell of a girl, no two ways about it.

I guess all the racers had themselves a pretty good time down in Georgia. Big Ed actually got to run a few practice laps and even started the race before he got a little overexcited and clouted the hay bales with his ex–Skippy Welcher, ex–everything XK120M. Fortunately, it wasn't much of a dent, and, seeing as how that poor Jag had been crunched just about everywhere at one time or another, it wasn't like he was breaking its cherry or anything. But it pushed the fender down into the tire and so Big Ed had to drop out. On the very first corner of the very first lap of the race, in fact. Oh well, at least it was an improvement.

My buddy Cal got to drive that Ford-powered TC again, and from what I heard, the beast was very much improved from Elkhart. Like this time the brakes held up for a whole six laps before the pedal started going mushy and he sank back through the field to finish just outside the top ten. But he ran right up near the front for those first six laps, even harassing Creighton Pendleton's Ferrari for third overall and holding off the best of the standard-issue XK120s until the car wouldn't slow down anymore. Johnny Fitch won again in the C4R Cunningham—nobody could stay with him—and both he and Creighton's Ferrari were clocked at over 170 down the long main runway at the Turner bomber base. Skippy Welcher went down in spite of the stupid one-race suspension he got for causing the accident at Watkins Glen (they should have banned him for life!) and after all attempts at getting his suspension lifted fell on deaf ears, he handed the green C-type over to another longtime S.C.M.A. racer named George Huntoon of West Palm Beach, Florida, for the 4-liter and under contest. Which he won going away, proving beyond any doubt that the C-type was a car to be reckoned with anywhere.

But the big news was how well the event was run and how incredibly *safe* it was. General LeMay drove all the way down from his headquarters in Omaha in his Cad-Allard (along with his wife, who must've been one tough, durable sort of lady) to keep an eye on things, and his Strategic Air Command boys did a job that made the regular, all-volunteer S.C.M.A. armband crew look pretty lame by comparison. All the races started exactly on time (except for one that ran some thirty seconds late, and you can bet the poor enlisted man responsible heard plenty about it afterward) and everybody except the drivers and crews was kept far enough away from the action that a guy named Ned Dearborn from the National Safety Council said: "I have never seen anything comparable to the safety measures taken by this meet to ensure safe crowd control and I want to compliment everyone who had a part in it."

That was pretty darn impressive, no question about it.

Of course, the bad part was that none of the estimated 60,000 people who turned out could see much of anything, since it was like watching a bunch of loud, brightly colored toys running up and down some flat concrete runways way off in the distance. But I guess smaller thrills and less red-blooded excitement will always be the price of guaranteed security, in racing and everywhere else in life.

By far the highlight of the entire weekend (at least for those of us on the Jersey side of the George Washington Bridge) was the surprising performance of Carson Flegley and his newly hotted-up MG TD, which, thanks to the undeniable engine-tuning genius of one Buddy Palumbo, Esq., finished way up near the middle of the MG herd duking it out tooth and nail about halfway between Jim Simpson's winning OSCA and the last-place Crosley Hotshot. Better yet, Carson finished at least seven or eight sets of bumpers ahead of where he'd run at the Glen. As you can well imagine, he was *ecstatic*. In fact, Carson decided to host a big season-ending race party at his place of business just as soon as he got back to Jersey. And that was a really perfect fit (considering Carson Flegley's line of work, anyway) since the very next available Friday night after the races in Georgia was ... *Halloween!*

It was decided by general consensus that the Friday-night gathering at the Flegley Memorial Chapels in East Orange should properly be a costume party (what else?) so I put a cheesy beard on my face with greasepaint and blacked out a tooth to go along with the rest of my halfhearted pirate outfit (a bandanna around my head, a black eye patch, and a six-inch plastic cutlass from Woolworth's five-and-dime) before I went to pick Julie up in the Old Man's tow truck. There just weren't any decent cars running over by the Sinclair that night. Julie was all done up as a gypsy, what with her hair all frizzed out and these big gold hoop earrings and a lot of bright crimson lipstick. She was wearing a white men's shirt with the sleeves cut off and about three buttons undone (which quickly turned into four once we were safely out of eyeshot from her mother) and a flared red skirt with a wide black patent-leather belt and matching shoes. She actually looked more like a hot streetwalker than a gypsy (if you want my personal opinion, any-way) and no question it was hard to keep my eyes off of her. Or my hands for that matter.

"*Hey!*" she squealed. "Knock it off, Palumbo. You'll mess up my costume."

"It's destined to happen sooner or later, wench," I told her in my best pirate voice. "So why not sooner?"

"Just keep yer frickin' hands to yourself, Palumbo," she laughed, her eyes dancing. "Don't let the look fool you. I'm not one a'those girls who goes around handing out free samples. . . ." And she wasn't, either.

We got to Carson's funeral parlor about nine, and you could tell the party was already going on account of all the MGs and Jags and such parked out in the lot. Naturally, the building looked all somber and dreary the way mortuaries always do, what with thick velvet drapes drawn over all the windows and just a weary, golden-yellow glow com-ing from the small brass coach lights on either side of the front entrance. All things considered, it was the kind of place that made you feel like talking in whispers before you ever even knocked on the door.

At least until that door swung open with Carson Flegley behind it, all done up as Count Dracula with a satin-lined cape, plastic fangs, and a pint of fake blood running down his chin. "Gooot eeeveningggg," he said in a truly decent Bela Lugosi imitation, "and vellcommm to my castle. . . ." This was a side of Carson Flegley I'd never seen before. Then again, he had all the working credentials for the part, didn't he?

We came in and Carson quickly closed the door behind us. I guess he didn't want any past, current, or potential future customers to get a whiff of what was going on inside Flegley Memorial Chapels this par-ticular Halloween night. After all, it wasn't very dignified, and families trying to find a properly delicate way to dispose of their deceased loved ones are always real big on dignity. Although I personally don't think it matters much one way or the other. Anyhow, Carson had all the racing people jammed into a long, sad-looking chapel room at the far end of the hall, and you should've seen the getups some of them were wearing. Of course, a lot of them were rich—in fact, some of them were *very* rich—and rich people just love to show off by taking frivolous things like Halloween costume parties to ridiculous extremes. It's part of the basic responsibility package that goes along with being wealthy. Charlie Priddle had on this incredible Dead Aristocrat outfit from the French Revolution, complete with a satin vest, a powdered wig, and this nifty fake guillotine blade embedded in the back of his neck. If they'd been giving out a prize for best costume, no question Charlie would've won it. In fact, I'll bet that's exactly what he had in mind.

Big Ed came as a gorilla—another perfect fit!—but the head part was real hot and he couldn't smoke his cigar, so he spent most of the evening walking around without it, and it was amazing how natural he looked with his real head sitting on top of that huge, hairy gorilla suit. He was with some girl in a German milkmaid outfit complete with waist-length blond braids, and she kept one of those little Lone Ranger masks over her eyes all night long. Fact is, I don't believe she was the current Mrs. Big Ed (if you catch my drift). Barry Spline just turned his white shop coat around backward so it looked sort of like a strait-jacket and wore a pair of those goofy eyeballs-out-on-springs glasses you can pick up at any trick store (or even at Woolworth's around Hallow-een) and topped it off with some goofy plastic teeth. "Say, you supposed t'be an escaped lunatic or something?" Big Ed asked.

"Certainly bloody not," Barry told him, trying his best to talk around those stupid teeth, "I'm supposed ter be Milton Fitting!" But he had to whisper it, on account of Milton and Skippy (or was it Skippy and Milton?) were standing right behind him in a rented horse outfit. As you can imagine, there was a lot of conjecture all evening about the fight they must've had over who got the back end.

Tommy showed up wearing his old R.A.F. uniform, and you could see he was working hard at keeping a stiff upper lip and putting to-gether a major hangover. Truth is, things were going pretty lousy for Tommy at the time. He still hadn't recovered from the accident at Watkins Glen, and even though he knew in his head it wasn't his fault, he was having a hard time getting his guts to agree. Plus he was having what looked like the end of his troubles with the wife, and the rumors circulating around the room hinted that she'd already seen a top divorce lawyer. Not to mention that the S.C.M.A. wasn't looking real likely to reverse itself about his suspension, even though everybody you talked to privately (including that tight-ass Charlie Priddle) thought it was a crock of shit. It seems the problem had nothing to do with making the proper decision in the case, but rather with reversing a decision that had already been made by the stewards of the meet and admitting that there had been a screwup in the first place. That was a hard thing for a group like the S.C.M.A. armband squad to face up to.

So Tommy had sort of changed, turning from a quick, sly, devil-may-care ex–fighter pilot who could drink all night long and never show a drop of it into a melancholy loner who could drink all night and get stinking, fall-down drunk. I saw him standing over in a corner by himself, sucking up entirely too much of Carson's lethal Halloween punch (served in brown glass embalming fluid bottles that I hope had been properly cleaned for the occasion!) and I decided to bring Julie over and see if I could maybe snap him out of it. "This is Julie," I said, and Julie gave him a little curtsy. "She's kinda, um, my girl...."

"Bloody pleased to meet you," he nodded, raising his fingers over his eyebrow and clumsily flopping his heels together. "I say, Buddy," he grinned, "she's a bit of all right, isn't she?"

"Yeah," I told him, snaking my arm around Julie's waist, "she sure as heck is."

"You're a bloody lucky man," he allowed, raising his glass. "A bloody lucky man indeed. If she's faithful and knows how to cook and is any bloody good in the sack at all, you ought to marry that girl."

I felt the color coming up on my face, and right away Tommy knew he was out of line and started to get all fumbly apologetic about it. "I say," he told Julie, eyeballing the floor, "I'm awfully sorry. Awfully sorry indeed." He stifled a belch. "I'm afraid I've had a bit too much to drink."

I looked over at Julie and saw that everything was OK, so I decided to change the subject. "Hey, don't worry about it, Tommy," I told him, "we've all of us been hittin' the old Halloween punch pretty hard. Haven't we, Julie?"

"Yeah. Sure we have," she said, and there was a nice, soft, understanding quality to her voice.

"So, I heard you went down to that race in Georgia."

"So I did." Tommy took another slug of punch. "But not to race. Can't bloody race for another year, according to those twits on the competition committee. Funny part is, they don't appreciate all the marvelous little ironies, the most basic of which is that you can have another chap's bloody accident *for* him. Happens all the time." He slowly shook his head and took another snort. "If any of those bastards had any seat time, they'd bloody well understand. But oh, no. *My* bloody car hit the fence so *I'm* the one who's bloody responsible!" You could see Tommy was getting pretty worked up about it. "Those idiots on the competition committee need to look up their bloody assholes to see if their hats are on straight." Then he remembered Julie was right next to us. "Oh, um, pardon me, Julie," he said quietly, looking at the carpet. "What I meant to say is that I question their judgment. In fact," he added, starting to seethe again, "I question their bloody ancestry as well."

"So it's no soap with those guys, huh?"

Tommy shook his head. "But I'm thinking of going back to England anyway. Things have fallen apart a bit for me here, and at least I can still race over in England. Besides"—he polished off the last of Carson's embalming fluid—"who the hell wants to hang around here and race on a bunch of bloody airfields?"

"You don't like the airport races?"

"Bloody hell *no!*"

"But why? Everybody says how safe they are...."

"Well, just *look* at them! They're just one bloody drag strip after another." He shook his head disgustedly. "And then it's hard on the brakes for another flat, fiddly little second-gear corner, and then another bloody drag strip after that. I mean, where's the bloody *penalty?* If you go off the bloody road at Elkhart or Watkins Glen, you're in some deep, *deep* trouble. And believe me, that's as it *should* be!" Then Tommy Edwards excused himself to get another refill that he hardly needed from around Carson's seemingly bottomless punch bowl.

It was sad to see Tommy like that, and it made me think about how racing could break your spirit just as surely as it could batter your body. But then, that's exactly what Tommy was talking about when he mentioned "the penalty" just seconds before. And I came to realize it was that very penalty—which could rise up at any moment with sudden, ugly finality—that was at the heart of what made racing so consuming and addictive. The good part was it didn't happen very often (if it did, then everybody involved would have to be an idiot) and the odds were that you could most likely race your whole damn life and walk away without a scratch. And many did. But the fact that the danger was *out there,* lurking in the shadows of the fast curves and high-speed esses, made everything that happened at a racetrack seem more Real and Noble and Urgent and Important than the rest of everyday life. No question Tommy understood it, too. He probably knew deep inside that this was simply his turn to play the victim. And, if he kept at it, most likely not his last.

Creighton Pendleton and Sally Enderle were the very last to appear—fashionably late, of course—and Creighton was just wearing his powder blue driving suit with CREIGHTON PENDLETON III embroidered over the pocket and his racing helmet dangling oh-so-casually by his side. He took pains to explain as how "a costume party is where you get to dress up as what you'd really *like* to be, and I guess there's frankly just no one I'd rather be than who I am." Far as I was concerned, it was amazing he could get that head of his into the damn helmet. Naturally, Sally went the whole nine yards and then some, arriving in a dazzling harem girl outfit with shimmering silk pants you could pretty much see through, plenty of smooth, tan midriff showing, and about six pounds of glistening gold necklaces, waist chains, and earrings. I got kind of embarrassed about being in the same room with both her and Julie at the same time, and I could feel my ears starting to burn when she headed over in our direction. But she swept right past us like we were a couple uncomfortable folding chairs on her way to the punch bowl, so it came out all right after all.

Julie and me had another round of embalming fluid ourselves, and then Carson Flegley came around to take anyone who wanted on a Halloween tour of his mortuary. Truth is, I felt a little nervous about it. I mean, this wasn't exactly the spook train ride at Palisades Park. No, this was the real McCoy, and Julie didn't look real thrilled about the idea, either. But it would've been worse to just stay by the punch bowl and listen to all the catcalls and *bok-ba-bok-bok* chicken cackles when everybody else filed out of the room. So we got in line and followed Carson Flegley down the hall and up a flight of stairs to the second floor. I'd never thought about it before, but every funeral parlor I'd ever seen had either a second floor on it or a wing with no chapels in it, and up those stairs and behind those closed doors was where the actual business part of the funeral parlor business went on. Not the bodies or anything (those are kept down in the Cool Room in the basement), but rather where the dollars-and-cents money transactions take place that pay for things like new hearses and marble headstones and hopped-up MG TDs. There were a couple quiet offices with heavy wooden conference tables off to one side and thick, sound-deadening wallpaper on the walls (so you could handle more than one set of sobbing, red-eyed relatives at a time when business was good) and just across the hall . . . the *showroom!*

"The *what?*" somebody asked.

"The showroom," Carson said menacingly, rubbing his hands together and rolling his *r*'s like Bela Lugosi. But everybody was looking at him like they didn't understand, so he switched back to his everyday pip-squeak voice and explained. "You know," he said simply, "for the *caskets. . . .*" And with that, he opened up the heavy, leather-covered door so we could follow the back of his cape into this low, dimly lit room where a dozen or so caskets of various size, material, color, trim, hardware, and most of all price range were arranged on raised, carpet-covered stands. It looked like Count Dracula's New Car Showroom. "This place gives me the creeps," Julie whispered in my ear.

"Yeah," I whispered right back. "Me, too."

But lots of Carson's other guests seemed to be enjoying the hell out of it, laughing and sniggering and making sick jokes and even lying down in some of the merchandise to try them on for size. "Hey, be careful now," Carson Flegley warned them in his normal, highly excited voice, "those things are *expensive!*"

"Hey, what's this one over here?" somebody asked.

We wandered over and there on one of the stands was the biggest damn coffin you ever saw. Why, it was as wide across as a damn grand piano, and painted a smooth, creamy ivory with gold gilt trim and handles. Jeez, was it ever huge. "Oh," Carson said sheepishly, "that's what we call our, um, er, well, our Lard-Ass Model. Every big funeral parlor carries one. After all, you gotta have something on hand if a really, ahh, *large* loved one passes on...."

I looked all around and the only guy anywheres near big enough for it was Big Ed Baumstein. And even he would've had room to spare. Even in his gorilla suit. "Jeez," Big Ed whistled, eyeballing the workmanship, "it looks pretty damn fancy, don't it?"

"Well, uh, it's sort of like this, see," Carson mumbled, even more sheepish than before. "When somebody that large passes away, the family doesn't really have very much to choose from, you know? So we sort of, um, only put the very top-of-the-line model on display."

"What a splendid idea!" Colin St. John toasted from the back of the room. He was dressed up as a damn pilgrim, can you believe it?

"Boy, that thing looks big enough for two!" guillotined French nobleman Charlie Priddle observed.

"It bloody well does, doesn't it?" R.A.F. pilot Tommy Edwards agreed, leaning unsteadily against a nice polished mahogany model. "I say, Buddy, why don't you and your young lady try it on for size?"

"Geez, no, Tommy. I *couldn't....* "

And of course that was all I had to say to get the catcalls and chicken cackles started up around us, and they kept on growing louder and more insistent until there was nothing left for me and Julie to do but either slink out and never see any of those people ever again or lie down together in that creamy white casket and let them lower the lid on us. Just for a second, you know?

And so there we were, lying side by side in the pitch-black darkness while all the racing people milled around that huge white coffin, laughing and drinking and carrying on. But they might as well have been in another room, since all we could hear was a faint shuffle of feet and a few muffled, indistinguishable voices. It was darker in there than anyplace I'd ever been, but it wasn't scary at all because I could feel Julie all warm and cozy next to me and smell the heavy scent of her gypsy perfume working its way up my nostrils. Without thinking, I let my hand sneak over where it wanted to go. *"Hey!"* she whispered, not sounding mad at all. "Whaddaya think you're doing, Palumbo?"

"Nothing," I whispered back, leaving my hand exactly where it was. And she let me, too. And that's when I heard myself propose marriage to Miss Julie Finzio, there inside that wide, white casket big enough for two laid out in the showroom of Carson Flegley's funeral home on Halloween night with all my costumed racing friends gathered around us but somehow a million miles away.

I guess there are things in this life that you worry and reason and agonize over and try your best to evaluate in advance, and then there are the things you just *do*. And even when they turn out wrong, those are always the ones that feel best when you do them. It's like what Tommy once said about driving: "You can't bloody *think* about what you're going to do. You've got to *know*. By the time you try to think over a situation and decide what to do, it's generally over." And that's what it was like asking Julie to marry me. No matter what happened afterward or how much it made my guts go hollow at the time, I *knew*.

When they finally opened the lid, everybody saw that Julie was crying just a little, and I suppose they all thought it was because she was scared or something. Which just goes to show how little any of them knew about my Julie and what kind of a tough, gutsy girl she was. But they'd find out soon enough. No question about it.

Later Carson led all the real die-hard sickos downstairs for a peek in the Cool Room where they kept the stiffs that were waiting to get dressed and planted, but that sounded way too grim for Julie and me. So we just hung back and let all the mainline ghouls file down ahead of us, then headed back into the main parlor, grabbed ourselves another couple bottles of embalming fluid, and went out into the parking lot. It was dark and cold and peaceful out there, with a chilly fall wind rattling through the naked tree branches and a few withered-up leaves scraping across Sherman Boulevard like fiddler crabs scuttling for their holes. You could feel winter coming, and so Julie and I climbed into Old Man Finzio's tow truck and started it up to get the heater going. But we didn't drive off just yet. We just sat there in the cab with the engine running, not turning on the lights or the radio or even saying much of anything. And then Julie leaned over and gave me the best damn kiss she'd ever given me in her life. Not the hottest, maybe, but without question the absolute *best*.

Then we just kind of sat there, leaning the tops of our heads together against the seat cushion, watching all the costumed party-goers coming out one by one between the pale, yellowish-gold carriage lights flanking the main entrance of Carson Flegley's funeral home. And as I watched them climb into their Jags and MGs and what have yous and heard them pull out on the choke cables and grind the starters and stumble off into the night, I knew deep down inside that I'd be seeing a lot of them again. Especially if they insisted on trying to drive those things through the winter. I knew I'd be going to the races with some of them, too. Oh, maybe not all the races. But at least some of them. I just hoped that would be enough, seeing as how I'd been bitten pretty hard by the racing bug myself, and, no matter what else happens, that's a disease you never really get rid of.

Not hardly.